CJ Skuse is the author of the YA novels *The Deviants*, *Monster*, *Pretty Bad Things*, *Rockoholic* and *Dead Romantic*. She was born in 1980 in Weston-super-Mare, England. She has First Class degrees in Creative Writing and Writing for Children and, aside from writing novels, lectures in Writing for Children at Bath Spa University, where she is planning to do her PhD. *Sweetpea* is her first novel for adults.

SWEET PEA

C J SKUSE

ONE PLACE. MANY STORIES

This novel is entirely a work of fiction. The names, characters
and incidents portrayed in it are the work of the author's
imagination. Any resemblance to actual persons, living or
dead, events or localities is entirely coincidental.

HQ
An imprint of HarperCollinsPublishers Ltd.
1 London Bridge Street
London SE1 9GF

This edition 2017

1
First published in Great Britain by
HQ, an imprint of HarperCollinsPublishers Ltd. 2017

ISBN:
HB: 978-0-00-821667-2
TPB:978-0-00-821668-9

Printed and bound by
CPI Group (UK) Ltd, Croydon, CR0 4YY

Our policy is to use papers that are natural, renewable and
recyclable products and made from wood grown in sustainable
forests. The logging and manufacturing processes conform to
the legal environmental regulations of the country of origin.

Find out more about HarperCollins and the environment at
www.harpercollins.co.uk/green
TM

For my cousin, Emily Metcalf.
For the years I spent at your mansion while mine was being decorated.

Sunday, 31 December

1. *Mrs Whittaker – neighbour, elderly, kleptomaniac*
2. *'Dillon' on the checkout in Lidl – acne, wallet chain, who bangs my apples and is NEVER happy to help*
3. *The suited man in the blue Qashqai who roars out of Sowerberry Road every morning – grey suit, aviator shades, Donald Trump tan*
4. *Everyone I work with at the* Gazette *apart from Jeff*
5. *Craig*

Well, my New Year has certainly gone off with a bang, I don't know about yours. I was in a foul mood to begin with, partly due to the usual Christmas-Is-Over-Shit-It's-Almost-Back-To-Work-Soon malaise and partly due to the discovery of a text on Craig's phone while he was in the shower that morning. The text said:

Hope you're thinking of me when ur soaping your cock – L.

Kiss. Kiss. Smiley face tongue emoji.

Oh, I thought. It's a fact then. He really *is* shagging her.

L. was Lana Rowntree – a kittenish 24-year-old sales rep in my office who wore tight skirts and chunky platforms and swished her hair like she was in a 24-hour L'Oréal advert. He'd met her at my works Christmas piss-up on 19 December – twelve days ago. The text confirmed the suspicions I'd had when I'd seen them together at the buffet: chatting, laughing, her fingering the serviette stack, him spooning out stuffing balls onto their plates, a hair swish here, a stubble scratch there. She was looking at him all night and he was just bathing in it.

Then came the increase in 'little jobs' he had to do in town: a paint job here, a hardwood floor there, a partition wall that 'proved trickier' than he'd estimated. Who has any of that done the week before Christmas? Then there were the out-of-character extended trips to the bathroom and two Christmas shopping trips (without me) that were just so damn productive he spent all afternoon maxing out his credit card. I've seen his statement – all my presents were purchased online.

So I'd been stewing about that all day and the last thing I needed that New Year's night was enforced fun with a bunch of gussied-up pissheads. Unfortunately, that's what I got.

My 'friends' or, more accurately, the 'PICSOs' – People I Can't Shake Off – had arranged to meet at the Cote de Sirène restaurant on the harbour-side, dressed in Next Sale finery. Our New Years' meal-slash-club-crawl had been planned for months – initially to include husbands and partners, but, one by one, they had all mysteriously dropped out as it became a New Years' meal-slash-*baby-shower*-slash-club crawl for Anni. Despite its snooty atmosphere, the restaurant is in the centre of town, so there's always yellow streaks up the outside walls and a sick puddle on the doormat come Sunday morning. The theme inside is black and silver with an added soupçon of French – strings of garlic, frescos of Parisian walkways and waiters who glare at you like you've murdered their mothers.

The problem is, I need them. I need friends. I don't want them; it's not like they're the Wilson to my skinny, toothless, homeward-bound Tom Hanks. But to keep up my façade of normality, they're just necessary. To function properly in society, you *have* to have people around you. It's annoying, like periods, but there is a point to it. Without friends, people start labelling you a 'Loner'. They check your Internet history or start smelling bomb-making chemicals in your garage.

But the PICSOs and I have little in common, this is true. I'm an editorial assistant at a local snooze paper, Imelda's an estate agent, Anaïs is a nurse (currently on maternity leave), Lucille works in a bank, her sister Cleo is a university-PE-teacher-cum-personal-trainer and Pidge is a secondary-school teacher. We don't even have the same interests. Well, me and Anni will message each other about the most recent episode of *Peaky Blinders* but I'd hardly call us bezzies.

And it may look like I'm the quiet cuckoo in a nest of rowdy crows but I do perform some function within the group. Originally, when I first met them all in Sixth Form, I was a bit of a commodity. I'd been a bit famous as a child so I'd done the whole celebrity thing: met Richard and Judy; Jeremy Kyle gave me a Wendy house; been interviewed on one of those *Countdown to Murder* programmes. Nowadays, I'm just the Thoughtful Friend or the Designated Driver. Lately, I'm Chief Listener – I know all their secrets. People will tell you anything if you listen to them for long enough and *pretend* you're interested.

Anni, our resident Preggo, is due to drop sometime in March. The Witches Four – Lucille, Cleo, Imelda and Pidge – had spared no expense on the nappy cake, cards, streamers, balloons and booties to decorate the table. I'd brought a fruit basket, filled with exotic fruits like lychees and mangoes, starfruit and ambarella, as a nod to Anni's Mauritian heritage. It had gone down like a whore on a Home Secretary. At least I wasn't driving, so I could quaff as much Prosecco as my liver could cope with and snuggle my brain into believing I was having a good time while they were all clucking on about the usual.

The PICSOs themselves like talking about five things above all others:

1. *Their partners (usually to slag them off)*
2. *Their kids (conversations I can't really join in with 'cos I don't have any, so, unless, it's cooing over school Nativity photos or laughing at Vines of them wiping poo up the walls, my contribution just isn't called for)*
3. *IKEA (usually because they've just been or are just going)*
4. *Dieting – what works/what doesn't, what's filling/what isn't, how many pounds they've lost/put on*
5. *Imelda's wedding – she only announced it in September but I can't actually remember a time when it wasn't on our conversation rota.*

In my head I'm usually thinking about five things above all others...

1. *Sylvanian Families*
2. *My as-yet-unpublished novel, The Alibi Clock*
3. *My little dog, Tink*
4. *When I can go to the toilet and check my social-media feeds*
5. *Ways I can kill people I don't like... without getting caught*

Before too long a tray of drinks came over: Prosecco and a selection of slightly smudged glasses.

'What's this?' Imelda asked.

'Compliments of the gentlemen at the bar,' said the waiter, and we looked over to see two types leaning against the counter, evidently looking to score with the nearest friendly vagina. The one wearing gold-hoop earrings and too much gel raised his pint in our direction – his other arm was in a sling. His friend in the Wales rugby shirt, and sporting tattooed forearms, a cut on his left eyebrow and a protruding beer gut, was unashamedly salivating over Lucille's ridiculous breasts. She says she 'doesn't do it on purpose'. Yeah, and I don't bleed from my crease every month.

'How marvellous.' She smiled, swooping into the bread basket. We each took a glass and 'cheersed' the men, before continuing our conversational merry-go-round – babies, boyfs, IKEA, and how draining it was just generally having tits.

Anni opened her presents, all of which she thought were either 'amazing' or 'so cute'. Of all of them, I found Anni the least annoying of the PICSOs. She always had an anecdote to share about someone brought into A&E, with a Barbie doll shoved up their arse or a motorcyclist with his head hanging off. This was at least mildly entertaining. Of course her baby would come soon and then there would be nothing left for us to talk about other than Babies and What Fun They Are and How I Wish I Had One. That's how these things usually went.

We all ordered steaks, in various sizes with various sauces, despite the rainbow of diets we are all on. Mel's on the Dukan, or GI, I forget which one. Lucille's on the 5:2, but today was a five day so she had three rolls and twenty breadsticks before her meal hit the tablecloth. Cleo 'eats clean', but she's had Christmas and New Year off. I'm on the Eat Everything in Sight Until 1 January Then Starve Self to Death diet, so I ordered a 10oz sirloin in a béarnaise sauce with triple-cooked French fries – I asked for the meat to be so raw you didn't know whether to eat it or feed it a carrot. The taste was unreal. I didn't even care if the cow had suffered – his ass was delish.

'I thought you were going veggie?' said Lucille, tearing off another hunk of complimentary bread.

'No,' I said, 'not any more.' I couldn't believe she remembered me saying that about eighty-five years ago. It was actually my

GP who told me to give up red meat to help with my mood swings. But the supplements were doing their job so I didn't see the point of going full McCartney for the sake of a few bitch fits. Besides, I always find earwigs in broccoli and sprouts are the Devil's haemorrhoids.

'Did you get anything nice for Christmas?' Cleo asked me as the waiters brought out a selection of lethal-looking steak knives.

'Thank you,' I said to the guy. I always made a point to thank waiting staff – you never knew what they were stirring your sauce with. 'Some books, perfume, Netflix voucher, Waterstones voucher, Beyoncé tickets for Birmingham...' I left out Sylvanian stuff – the only people who understand how I feel about Sylvanians are Imelda's five-year-old twins.

'Ooh, we're seeing Beyoncé in London in April,' said Pidge. 'Oh, I know what it was I wanted to tell you guys...'

Pidge started this inexorably long speech about how she'd gone to six different pet stores before she found the right something for her house rabbits – Beyoncé and Solange. Pidge's conversation starters were always somewhere between Tedious and Prepare the Noose; almost as dull as Anni's midwife appointments or Lucille's Tales of the Killer Mortgage. I zoned out, mentally redesigning the furniture in my Sylvanians' dining room. I think they need more space to entertain.

Despite the ongoing gnawing fury in the centre of my chest, courtesy of Le Boyf, the meal was nice and I managed to keep it down. I noticed there were fake flowers in the vases on all the tables – which won't please the Tripadvisor fairy – but as restaurants go, I'm glad I went. It was almost worth the two hours I'd spent crowbarring myself out of the pyjamas I'd lived in since Christmas Eve and dolling myself up. Well, it was until the subject of Imelda's wedding came up. Lucille was the culprit.

'So, you got your hair sorted out yet for the Big Day?'

Now this was the rare occasion when Imelda *did* hear what Lucille said – because she had asked about Imelda or weddings or Imelda's actual wedding.

'No,' she whined. 'I want something up at the crown but not spiky. French plaits for the bridesmaids, keep it simple. Did I tell you about our photographers? We're having two. Jack found this guy from London and him and his partner – his work partner that is (cue chorus of unexplained laughs) – are coming down to see the church in May. He's going to be at the back so that he can take pictures of everyone's faces as I come down the aisle, and his mate's going to be at the altar.'

'No chance of anything being missed then?' I added.

'Exactly.' Imelda smiled, seemingly ecstatic that I was taking an interest.

'What you wearing for your night do? Did you decide?' asked Anni, returning from a third toilet break.

'Oh, the dress again, definitely.'

'You're going to have it on all day?' said Cleo.

'Yeah. It's got to be something striking. It *is* my day and everyone will be coming to check me out so... and that way, the people who didn't get invited to the day do will be able to see it then.'

'Yeah, wouldn't want *them* missing out on anything,' I mumbled, checking my phone. And again she smiled, like I was right on her wavelength.

Anni nodded, biting her lower lip. 'You'll be stunning, Mel. It's gonna be such a good bash. And I'll be able to drink again by then, too!'

I cleaned off my steak knife with my napkin. There was an abundance of veins in my left wrist. I could have ended it all right then if I'd had the balls.

'I won't be stunning,' said Imelda. 'I'll probably break both camera lenses!'

Lucille's turn: 'Babes, you're gorgeous. You'll be all princess-like and there'll be flowers everywhere and with that amazing church... it'll be like a proper fairy tale.'

'Yeah,' she scoffed. 'If I can't shift this bloody muffin top in the next six months it *will* be a fairy tale – *Shrek*!'

Cue the shrieks.

'And June's always sunny, so you're bound to have the best weather for it,' said Pidge, rubbing Imelda's arm. 'Don't worry, it'll be wonderful.'

Enough?

'Yeah, I suppose you're right.'

(Note: I have cribbed this endless ego massage here but please understand, Dear Diary, that Imelda's wedding takes up at least 90 per cent of every social occasion.)

Then she brought up the very thing I've been dreading since it was first mooted last September – the Weekend That Must Not Be Named.

'You're all coming to my hen weekend, aren't you? No buts. You've got six months' notice after all.'

Fuck it. In a fairly large bucket.

'Oh, yeah, what are we doing again?' asked Anni, swigging her orange juice.

'Not sure yet – possibly Bath for a spa day or Lego Windsor. But it's deffo Friday to Sunday.'

'Rawther!' Lucille giggled. She was matron of honour.

Then it was onto Man Bash Central – Woman Bash Central in Cleo's case – how Rashan/Alex/Jack/Tom/Amy had stayed out all night on a job/booze run to France/coach trip to Belgium/job/pub crawl/austerity protest. How Rashan/ Alex/Jack/Tom/Amy had got so unadventurous in bed these days. How big Rashan/Alex/ Jack's dicks were (Cleo and Pidge always carefully avoided this subject) and finally how Rashan/Alex/Jack/Tom/Amy had given them a Rolex/flowers/Hotel Chocolat salted-caramel puddles/a

holiday/a hug just to say sorry after a row that Anni/Lucille/
Imelda/Pidge/Cleo had instigated.

The only thing Craig ever gave me that meant anything was
bacterial vaginosis, but I kept that to myself.

'What's Craig up to these days, Rhiannon?' asked Anni. She
always brought me into the conversation. Imelda sometimes did
this when vying for the gold medal at the Passive Aggressive
Olympics. She'd ask, *'Any news on your junior-reporter thing
yet, Rhee?'* or *'Any sign of Baby Wilkins in that womb of yours
yet, Rhee?'*, when she knew full well I'd have mentioned it if I
had news of huge job change (please, God) and/or womb invader
(please, God, no).

'Uh, the same,' I said, sipping my fifth glass of Prosecco.
'He's fitting out that shop in the High Street that used to be a
hairdresser's. It's going to be a charity shop.'

'Thought there might be something sparkly waiting under
the Christmas tree this year,' said Imelda, loudly to the entire
restaurant. 'What's it been now, three years?'

'Four,' I said, 'and, no, he's not *that* thoughtful.'

'Would you say yes if he *did* propose, Rhiannon?' said Pidge,
her face full of wonder, like she was thinking about Hogwarts.
(She and Tom were planning to get married at the Harry Potter
Experience in Orlando soon – I shit you not.)

I hesitated, the gnawing in my chest biting down harder.
Then I lied: 'Yeah, of course–' I was about to qualify that with
an *If he could stop taking Lana Rowntree up her aisle for five
minutes long enough to walk me down one*, but Lucille cut me
off before I had chance:

'Talking of charity shops, I bought this great vase in the one
opposite Debenhams; such a bargain…' she began, launching
into a new topic of conversation and leaving me behind on my
Island of Unfinished Sentences.

Not that I *wanted* to talk about Craig or Craig's dull job.

Neither were interesting subjects to talk about. He built things, ate pasties, smoked the odd spliff, liked football, played video games and couldn't pass a pub without eating enough pork scratchings to fill Trafalgar Square. That was Craig – *Gordon Ramsay clap* – done.

So they were all wanging on about The Weekend That Must Not Be Named when a random bloke with bad neck zits appeared at our table, clutching a glass of lager.

'All right, girls?' said Random Bloke with Neck Zits. He produced a couple of red-wine bottles, emboldened by a six-strong gaggle of blokes with neck *and* chin zits at the bar. Surprisingly, the corks were still in the bottles so there was no danger of us being Rohipped and dragged to the nearest Premier Inn for a semi-conscious rape-fest. Yeah, I think of these things, another reason I'm a useful friend.

These weren't the same guys who'd bought us Prosecco, this was a different lot. Younger. Louder. Zittier.

'Mind if we join you?' Winks and knowing looks all round.

Cue giggles and shrieks.

I had intended to order the double chocolate brownie with clotted cream for pudding but we were at the part of the evening where we all had to hold our stomachs in so I resisted, wondering if I could get home for some leftover Christmas tiramisu ice cream before the bongs signalled the death knell of fun-eating habits.

Imelda, Lucille and Cleo made the usual ribald comments, clearly turned on by the attention. Pidge started joining in too, once a sufficient amount of wine had been imbibed. She was always too Christian to participate in either tittage or bants before alcohol allowed her to. I wasn't nearly pissed enough for either.

So the evening dragged on like a corpse tied to a donkey cart as the Seven Dorks squeezed onto our table and allowed their eggy breaths and chubby fingers to fog our air and tweak our knicker elastic. We had Grunty, Zitty, Shorty, Sleazy, Fatso, Gropey and Mute.

Guess which one I got stuck talking to. Or rather, at.

And, one by one, the PICSOs all left me. They each did the 'you're only young once' speech and hooked up with the Dorks to go on to a club for a New Year's foam party – can't remember which one as I had no intention of following them.

'You coming, Rhee?' asked Anni, weighed down with gifted baby detritus. 'Me and Pidge are just gonna shove this lot in the car and meet them there.'

I don't know why she was so excited to be tagging along to a nightclub. She was the size of a barge and was on orange juice and bi-hourly toilet breaks. Nightclubs weren't known for facilitating either.

'Yeah, I just need the loo,' I said, sinking my wine.

I was testing them now. Testing to see who would actually wait for me. Who was the true friend? But, as I expected, nobody waited. I paid my part of the bill, stood on the doormat of Cote de Sirène and watched them all waddling and cackling up the street with the Dorks circling them like sharks around chum. Not a second thought did I get.

So there I was, alone, in the centre of town, preparing to hike the two miles back to my flat, on New Year's Eve.

But this is where my fun began.

As it turned out, walking across town went without incident. I'm not counting the tramp with a tinsel halo, pissing in streams down both legs, using NatWest as a walking aide. Or the couple shagging behind the wheely bins at the back of Boots' car park. And I'm not counting the fight that broke out inside Pizza Express then spilled onto the pavement, during which a bald man in a striped shirt yelled, 'I'M GONNA RAPE YOUR FUCKING SKULL, MATE!'

None of that was particularly noteworthy.

Whereas, what happened down by the canal, was.

It must have been about 11.30 p.m. by the time I reached the playing fields and took the short cut along the cycle path and down to the canal towpath, a mere five hundred feet from our flat. It was here that I heard footsteps behind me. And my breath shortened. And my heart began to thump.

I shoved my hands into my duffle-coat pockets and turned around to see a guy I recognised. He was the one in the Wales rugby shirt with the tattooed forearms who'd bought us the first lot of Prosecco at the restaurant.

'Where you going then, baby?'

'Home.'

'Aww, can I come?'

'No.'

'Please? We can make each other happy tonight. Still got a bit of time before the bongs, ain't we? You look sad.'

He sidestepped in front of me. I stepped away. He stepped back. He laughed.

'You followed me, didn't you?' I said.

He leered, eyeing me from head to toe with a lingering look at my crotch area, which I'll admit did look inviting in my too-tight skirt. 'Just seeing where you were going, that's all. Don't be like that. I bought you a drink.'

'I said thank you at the time.' Like, of course *that* would be enough.

He put his hands on me.

'Could you take your hands off me, please?'

'Come on. You were giving me the eye.'

'Don't think I was. Get off.' I wasn't raising my voice. I didn't need to. His molestation attempts were pathetic. A hand on my boob. A motion to his belt buckle.

'How about you get your laughing gear round my old boy then? Just for 'Auld Lang Syne', eh?'

He was strong; a prop four or something. As well as the cut on his left eyebrow, he had the beginnings of a cauliflower ear. He slathered all over my face and I let him. Nobody else was around. Even if I screamed, the nearest people over in the Manette Court complex would take five minutes to get to me. And that's if they even bothered. He'd have come in me and gone by then and I'd be another statistic, getting vaginal swabs and drinking tepid tea in some police waiting room.

No. That might be my sister but that would not be me.

'Come in here,' he gasped in my ear, taking my freezing hand inside his hot clammy one and pulling me towards the bush. An upended Lidl shopping trolley lay on its back.

I stayed rooted. 'There's no room in there.'

'Yeah, there is.' He tugged harder on my hand.

'Pull your jeans down,' I said.

He smirked like his ship had just come in – a ship with a massive hard-on. 'Oh, yes, baby girl. I knew I could thaw you out.'

Unsteady on his feet, he fumbled at his belt. Then his zip. His over-washed jeans collapsed in a heap at his ankles. So did his boxers. There were little Homer Simpsons all over them. His cock sprung out like a small Samurai, ready to do battle.

Ba-doing!

It had a bend in it. I wasn't sure whether he was pleased to see me or giving me directions to the bus station.

He stroked it upwards. Well, upwards and towards the bus station. 'All yours,' he said.

'Mmm,' I said, 'lucky old me.'

The temptation to laugh was so strong but I choked it down and made it look as though I was starting to wriggle out of my knickers under my skirt. All keen.

'Can you get on all fours?' he panted.

'Like a dog?'

'Yeah.'

'Why?'

''Cos I wanna fuck you like a dog.'

I grew breathless. 'But the ground's hard.'

'So's my dick. Get down. Go on, don't tease.'

'I'll suck you off but no more,' I said.

'That's a start,' he said, eyes lighting up. I crouched down and took his little warm Samurai in my grip.

'Shall I finger myself as I'm sucking it?' I asked, heart in my throat.

'Fuck, yeah! Dirty bitch!' he chuckled, growing harder and more veiny.

He waited for it – for my lips on his bell-end. I pulled on his dick as though about to milk it.

'Knew you were a dirty bitch.'

I saw Craig's face on his as I held the cock steady and, reaching into my pocket, I closed my fingers around the handle of the steak knife. Bringing it out slowly while stroking him into full submission, I waited until his eyes had closed and his chin tilted to the sky in ecstasy before I hacked down hard on it and started carving through the gristly meat. He screamed and swore and beat at my head with his fists but my grip was tight and I sawed at it through slipping, bloody fingers until I had yanked his penis from its roots and pushed him backwards into the murky green water. His forlorn manhood dropped to the cold canal towpath with a bloody slap.

The splash was loud and he was still screaming but, despite all the hullaballoo, no one was coming to either of our rescues.

'Aaaaaaarrrgghhh! Aaaaarrrrrrgghh!' he went, splashing around like a child at its first swimming class.

A little curl of steam rose up from the penis, lying dejectedly on the towpath. I found a spare dog poo bag in my coat and picked the severed member up, then ran towards the footbridge, my heart still banging like a bastard on a jail-cell wall. I lost my breath completely as I reached the top and looked down over the water.

'Fucking... sick... bitch!' he gargled, flopping about.

He kept splashing, sinking under the murky water, then bobbing up again and spluttering. The last thing he must have seen in this world was my face, on the bridge, smiling in the moonlight.

Thanks to my cruel improvisation, I was feeling something I hadn't felt for a long time. That same feeling you get when you're a kid and you spy an adventure playground. Or when you poke your foot out of the bed on Christmas morning and feel your full stocking hanging there. It radiates out from a deeply exciting inner squiggle until your whole body feels electric all over. The best feeling in the world. It's an exquisite privilege to watch someone die, knowing you caused it. Almost worth getting dolled up for.

Monday, 1 January

1. *Teen boy and girl in the park who kicked their black Labrador that time*
2. *Derek Scudd*
3. *Wesley Parsons*
4. *The guy with Tourette's who sits in the Paddy Power doorway, shouting about spacecrafts and the time he got fisted by a priest*
5. *Craig and Lana. To save on bullets, I'm putting them both together here – one shot, right through both skulls*
6. *The man in the blue Qashqai who pulled out of Marsh Road and beeped when I didn't walk fast enough. 'Stupid slow bitch,' that's what he'd said. All the way round the block I was picturing his suited body hanging by its neck – wriggling and twitching and me standing beneath him, just watching*

Did a BuzzFeed quiz this morning – How Psychopathic Are You? Turns out – very. I scored 82 per cent. They even accompanied my results with a picture of Ralph Fiennes in *Schindler's List*. Don't know how I feel about that.

The quiz had been right about one thing, though.

Do you try to evade responsibility?

Well, yes, yes, I do. Remorse-wise, the canal incident has left little impression. I haven't killed anyone for three years and I thought that when it happened again I'd feel bad, like an alcoholic taking a sip of whiskey. But, no, nothing. I had a blissful night's sleep. Didn't wake up at all and, for once, no bad dream either. This morning I feel balanced. Almost sane, for once.

*

Craig and I spent the first day of the New Year in front of the TV, eating pizza, the blue Quality Streets and watching '80s movies – *Pretty in Pink*, *The Outsiders* and that one where Demi Moore has a pink apartment and goes nuts at the end. He is an exceptional liar, I'll give him that. I know he saw Lana today, under the pretence of 'meeting Gary and Nigel down Wetherspoon's'. He was vay convincing, to the untrained eye.

Sadly, *my* eye is hyper-trained – like an Olympic sprinter when it comes to rooting out bullshit.

We'd planned to do so much this week – stuff we never got round to do when we're both at work: power-spraying the bird shit on the balcony, sorting out boxes for the mythical car-boot-sale-we're-never-going-to-do, and Craig was going to clear out the mountain of rubbish and offcuts of wood from the back of his van and then paint the bathroom. We had one day left before we both went back to work and we'd done precious little. Craig had made a start on the wall above the toilet on Christmas Eve – a little surprise for me for when I got home from work, to keep me sweet before he mentioned he'd invited the boys around again to watch Boxing Day football on Sky. But when I'd seen the colour, I did not like the colour.

'Mineral Mist, I said!'

'I got Mineral Mist, see?' He held up the tin. It said Morning Mist.

I took Tink for a walk at lunch as Craig was playing *Streetfighter* and making bacon sandwiches and the smell was making me dribble (I'm trying not to have bread because ass). I like looking in people's gardens on our walks. I miss having a garden. There were all sorts of Christmas debris strewn about the pavements. Smashed baubles. Strings of tinsel. Half-chewed sweets. A carrier bag blew across the road out of somebody's bin and Tink had a conniption, probably waking up half the country. Of all the things in this world my dog hated the most, sneezes, spaniels and rogue carrier bags flying at her as if from nowhere were definitely the Top Three.

Tried teaching her Shake a Paw again, the one trick she won't do under any circumstances – still nothing.

Craig sorted out all his unwanted Blu-rays for the car-boot-sale-we're-never- going-to-do and pressure-washed the balcony with our new pressure washer, a Christmas gift from his mum and dad. I waxed my legs and drove over to my mum and dad's house late afternoon. All quiet on the Western Front. Still can't get the stains out of the bedroom carpet. Craig is still buying all my lies about 'going to Cleo's aerobics class' and 'working late; so I can go over there. It's almost too easy.

Gave Tink a bath in the kitchen sink. She doesn't like it but puts up with it because she always gets chicken bits afterwards. As I was trying to towel her off, she legged it round the flat like she had rabies. Craig laughed too, which broke the ice. Then he said he was 'going over Homebase' to get me the other paint. He said he needed some new wallpaper scissors for work as well.

I said, 'Why don't you just have my dad's old wallpaper scissors from his toolkit? I was going over there tomorrow to sort out Mum's filing cabinet. I can get them then.'

He said that meant a lot to him, like Dad was giving him his blessing from beyond the grave. The hallowed Tommy Lewis toolkit that Dad carried with him like an extra limb and Craig was never allowed to touch. I thought he was going to cry.

'They're just wallpaper scissors, Craig,' I said. 'It's not an engagement ring.'

He nodded and left the room with a distinct clear of throat. I'm terrible with crying people. How do you make them stop? I deliberately caught the wrong bus once because a woman was blubbing in the bus shelter. Didn't know what else to do.

Do I love him? I haven't known what love is in a long time. He says he loves me but isn't that just something that gets said? He told me on Christmas Eve that, coupled with the hand jobs and my excellent trifle, I'm *almost* the perfect girlfriend. I don't nag him as much as his mates' wives nag them either. I asked him what would make me perfect.

'Anal,' he said, no hesitation. 'What would make *me* perfect?' he asked.

Well, it'd be a start if you stopped shagging Lana Rowntree behind my back, I thought. Instead, I opted for the safer:

'You can't improve on perfection itself, can you, darling?'

He laughed and I flicked him a V sign behind the *Radio Times*.

Wednesday, 3 January

Hi ho, hi ho, it's back to my shitty job I go. Actually, there is a dwarf where I work – he's upstairs in the Accounts department. He's the reason we had all our light switches moved to three feet above the ground. Madness.

Today went as all days at the *Gazette* go – long, coffee-stained and dull. The first half was me telling anyone who asked what a good Christmas I had and some dull-as-ditch tasks of inputting local schools' thank-you letters to Santa, updating the website and making coffee in the new £5,000 (yes, that's £5,000!) coffee machine. There were four new mugs in the staffroom – Christmas presents no one wanted at home but which everyone wants at work because they're clean. I nabbed one with dinosaurs on and the words TEA-REX. Hardy har.

The usual New Year signs have gone up everywhere, unstained and laminated. Signs telling professional adults helpful things like IF YOU'RE LAST OUT OF AN EVENING, PLEASE TURN OFF ALL THE LIGHTS and PLEASE WASH YOUR OWN CROCKERY. The toilets are full of them: PLEASE ONLY FLUSH TOILET TISSUE DOWN THE TOILET. PLEASE REPLACE TOILET PAPER IF YOU USE THE LAST PIECE. PLEASE TURN OFF THE TAPS AFTER USE. There's even one

as you leave, saying, PLEASE LEAVE THESE FACILITIES AS YOU
FIND THEM – THANK YOU.

I'd like to suggest some new signs for the office, specifically
for my benefit and/or amusement:

PLEASE REMEMBER TO WIPE YOUR ASS AFTERWARDS FOR THE
GOOD OF YOUR GUSSET.

PLEASE CLOSE ALL DOORS QUIETLY, STAY HOME IF YOU ARE
SICK, OR AT LEAST TRY TO DIMINISH YOUR SNEEZES – NOISE-
SENSITIVE PSYCHOPATH IN THE BUILDING.

PLEASE DO NOT WEAR CROCS TO WORK – THEY ARE AN INSULT
TO FOOTWEAR (MIKE HEATH –T HIS MEANS YOU).

DON'T DRINK SO MUCH OF THE OFFICE MILK – MIKE HEATH
THE MILK THIEF THIS MEANS YOU TOO, WHAT WITH YOUR DAILY
OVERFLOWING BOWLS OF CEREAL AND SIX CAPPUCCINOS.

PLEASE DON'T EAT CHEESY NACHOS OR FRIED BREAKFASTS AT
YOUR DESK – THE SMELL MAKES US ALL WANT TO VOM.

PLEASE DON'T TELL RHIANNON LEWIS WHAT YOU DID AT THE
WEEKEND – SHE WAS ONLY BEING POLITE.

The Gulp Monster – aka, Claudia Gulper, our desk editor – is
responsible for the signs. She puts pass ag labels on her food in the
staff-room fridge with the same marker. I stayed late tonight to
help her with her article on the mismanagement of power-station
funds, which she hopes is going to win her some big journalism
prize (it won't). I asked her to look at my unsolicited article about
the rise of drug-related crime and we talked about my theory
that the ladies' dress shop Paint the Town Red was the hub of
distribution. I thought it could earn me some extra Brownie points.

More fool I.

I'd liked Claudia for about five minutes when I'd first started
at the *Gazette* as a receptionist but, nowadays, she treats me like
some kind of home help. She insisted on giving me endless boring
'News in Brief' snippets to type up or deaf Golden Wedding
couples to interview, and once shouted at me in front of everyone

for missing three semi-colons in the Fun Run results – not to mention a billion other reasons for me to want to jump through the fucking window. I long ago decided she was just a pubic louse on the vaginal wall of the cunt witch from Hell. I'm glad her third round of IVF failed and her husband left her. No spawn deserves *that* for a mother.

Craig was cooking when I got home (guilt food, obvs). Pasta from scratch with home-made pesto. Since I only had an apple and a black coffee for breakfast and just a salad for lunch, I allowed myself a troughing.

It's safer to have than to have not, isn't it? Even if the Have is crap. And if you're not with someone, you get questions about it, All. The. Time. When you're hooked up, that all stops. You feel embraced in the safety of having someone. And other people are contented because they don't have to worry about setting you up on blind dates or going out in couples with a walking gooseberry bush.

What I *should* do is leave him. I *should* make him a dog-shit sandwich or cut all the crotches out of his Levis and hit the road. But it's complicated. Craig worked for my dad and took over his building firm when he died. I like having that link. And it's his flat and he pays most of the bills. And he puts up with all my kinks – my need to not have sudden, repetitive or loud noises, my need for quiet periods of time alone and for no one to touch my doll's house. What other guy would put up with me?

Regarding the sex, there were 'mixed reviews'.

When it's good, it's OK. No intense orgasms but nothing to complain about. And when it's bad it's brief. He comes, he goes to sleep. We've tried kinky stuff (he's worn my knickers, gone down on me on a night bus, and I keep nakes of him in my phone) and sometimes if we're at his mum and dad's and they're asleep in front of *Antiques Roadshow,* we'll creep upstairs and do it on their bed. Then it's not bad at all because there's an element of risk, I suppose. But his general repertoire in the sack had become as predictable as *EastEnders*. I know where his tongue's going next, when he wants me on top, how many thrusts it's going to take. It's all become a bit yadda yadda. I've tried introducing different positions to the event but, you try turning tricks like Simone Biles when you've only got an average of four minutes thirty-seven seconds to do it in.

I once mooted dogging as a possibility. He thought I was joking.

'What are you, a pervert or something?'

Why's everything so complex? Half the time, I admit, I crave normality, domesticity: a family, other heartbeats around, a comfy sofa of an evening and little pots of floral happiness growing silently on the balcony. The other half of the time, I want nothing more than to kill. To watch.

This sort of tallied with my BuzzFeed results.

Do you rarely connect on an emotional level with other people?

No, of course I don't. I never *meet* anyone on my emotional level. A part of me wants to know what love feels like again. I know I must have felt it once. I wonder if it's the same feeling I get when I take a life; when all your nerve endings feel like they're reanimating. The thinking about it all the time at work. The craving to do it again and barely managing not to. I keep replaying the night of Canal Man in my head – the parting of the skin as the knife sliced through his penis. Him struggling beneath my hands. The trickling blood. Him beating at my head with his fists. Cutting through the layers – skin to flesh to muscle. Standing on the bridge, waiting for the water to calm and for his body to upend and float. The anxious gnawing in my chest has diminished.

Was that what love was? Did I 'love' to kill? I don't know. All I do know is that I want to do it again. And, next time, I want it to last longer.

Our kleptomaniac neighbour Mrs Whittaker knocked on our door at 9.30 p.m., back from visiting her sister in Maidstone. She asked if we needed her to look after Tink tomorrow. Craig told her that he was only working a half-day so he could take her with him. I stayed on the sofa, pretending to be asleep but I saw her through a crack in the cushion, scanning the living room from the doorway, probably eager to get further inside and nick more of our decorative pebbles or an unguarded stapler. She's in the first flush of Alzheimer's so it's not as though we can complain.

Drove over to Mum and Dad's house around 8 p.m., under the guise of 'seeing the PICSOs for a drink'. Julia wasn't happy to see me. I only left two of the three chocolate treats I'd intended to leave from my selection box – a Drifter and a Crunchie. The state the room was in, she definitely didn't deserve the Revels.

I'm so looking forward to killing her.

Ventured a look at the scales before bed – I've put on five pounds over Christmas and today's starvation has done nothing. I am *so* having a bagel for breakfast.

Friday, 5 January

1. *Derek Scudd*
2. *Wesley Parsons*
3. *People who eat with their mouth open – e.g. Craig*
4. *The first Kardashian – maybe if I figure out how to go back in time I can kill him then we can stop all the rest*
5. *Septuagenarians who chat in clusters inside shop door-ways*
6. *Celebrities who bang on and on about loving your body and being comfortable in your own skin, then lose a boatload of weight and release a fitness DVD. Just. Fuck. Off. You. Cunting. Hypocrites.*

Had another Dad dream, the third since Bonfire Night. Woke up in a bath of sweat, even though the temperature was, like, -2 degrees. It's always the same dream: that last day in hospital, his dry little face staring up at me from the pillow, eyes pleading with words his brain couldn't send to his mouth.

Still, this week's front page was more enjoyable:

LOCAL FAMILY MAN'S BODY FOUND IN GRISLY CANAL DREDGE

A MAN whose body was discovered in a local stretch of canal on New Year's Day has been named.

A passer-by made the grim find at around 8.30 a.m. on New Year's morning and police were called to the waterside at the roving bridge near the library. The body has been named as that of 32-year-old Daniel John Wells, an electrician who had been out socialising the night before.

Mr Wells worked as an electrician for Wells & Son Electricals and has two daughters from previous relationships, Tyffannee-Miley, 3 [I shit you not!] and Izabella-Mai, 18 months [similarly, the fuck?].

Police have yet to rule whether or not there are suspicious circumstances surrounding Mr Wells's death and are appealing for witnesses.

Nothing was mentioned about his jeans being around his ankles. Or his drunken state. Or his tendencies to opportunistic rape. Or his missing appendage. I guess 'socialising' is the umbrella term to cover all that.

Work was dull. I swear that Chinese kid who was locked in a cage for twenty years wouldn't swap for my life at the moment. We have a new kid in, called AJ – Claudia's nephew from Australia. I say 'kid' but he's actually eighteen and on a gap year and working as a 'Part-time Hourly Paid' assistant for the next six months. His top half dresses like he's going to the beach; his bottom half has just come back from Glastonbury. I don't know what the A or the J stand for but, as far as I'm concerned, anyone who goes about calling themselves by their initials is just begging for a slap.

He's actually very good-looking, tall and tanned, covered in friendship bracelets, and he smiles all the time. I don't normally get drawn towards cheerful people – the urge to hurt them becomes too strong – but I think he does allow for modest gusset dribble. Bit eager to impress Claudia. He's staying with her. Maybe I can besmirch him somehow; that would get right up her bunghole. You know when people say a smile 'can light up a room'? I know what they're talking about now. AJ has a smile that does that.

Not my room, though, obviously.

I nodded off typing up seventeen letters pertaining to dredging on the Somerset Levels and the steep rise in recycling fees for garden waste. The miserable Home and Properties sub, ironically called Joy, commented on how much weight I'd put on over the holidays. Joy is censorious by her nature to all of us but today it pissed me off more than usual. She thinks she's being helpful, pointing out our insecurities – my weight, Lana's breakdown, Claudia's moles, Jeff's limp and, worst of all, Mike Heath's impotence (she'd noticed a bag he brought back from the chemist one lunchtime). I think Joy once weighed about fifty stone but lost it all and had the NHS cut off the slack. Now she considers it her duty to verbally maim everyone.

The irritating thing is, we can't say ANYTHING back to Joy because she has a ton of disabilities. She's one of those rotund, deeply ugly Cromwellian-faced women you see around who've dyed their hair bright pink or blue in an attempt to make themselves more appealing, but all they've done is accentuate their ugliness. So I can't comment about her big left leg or her stutter or the Bell's palsy that has caused her mouth to start sliding off her face because then I'd get done for disablism. Crazy. Wouldn't you rather have someone like me working with you? Someone who did the decent thing and bitched about you behind your back, rather than right to your face?

I don't particularly want to go to the effort of killing Joy but I do sometimes like to imagine her, stuffed and glazed, prostrate on a silver platter, surrounded by tufts of parsley with a big green apple wedged between her jaws.

The mayor came in at lunch to see Ron. She's pleasant enough and she's got a foster-care past, a disabled kid, and her husband keeps having heart attacks, so she's clearly had to swallow several shitty spoonfuls from the Bowl of Life. I try not to get too close to her, though – she smells like a Glade PlugIn on full-whack. She is also gluten intolerant, which makes buying lunch intolerable. I have to go to that smelly deli on the corner, where the guy with black fingernails and dreadlocks shuffles around in a hummus-covered apron, twiddling his nose ring.

Lana smiled as she sashayed past my desk at lunchtime, robin's-egg-blue blouse straining against the pressure of her sizeable assets. I'm pretty sure half the time she doesn't need to walk past my desk – she could go the other way round – but she does it to look at me. Like a killer going back to the site where she dumped a body, just to marvel at the rate of decomposition or to fuck the remains. I smiled back anyway, for the sake of The Act, and we had a short chat. I smiled again when we were done. Cue the hair swish. Cue the giggle. Cue me imagining her pinned to a snooker table and stabbing her in each hole. I can see why all the men fancy her. She's bubbly, easy-going, has tits like water balloons. Her last two boyfriends dumped her – I heard it on the staffroom grapevine. She had a breakdown after the first one. And, apparently, after the second one left, she tried to take her own life. I don't know the severity of the attempt – whether it was a proper go or just a token pills-and-finger-straight-down-the-throat job – but it did explain Craig's predilection for her. He likes them broken.

A lesbian couple whose kid had choked on a grape in Pizza Hut came in to chat to Mike Heath in the conference room, along with the waitress who'd done kiddy Heimlich and saved his life. I wrote up a press release on a student's Kilimanjaro climb for moon bears and helped Jeff input the match report from the finals of the County Bowls Championships. There was a Kinder Egg on my desk when I got back from lunch.

Jeff Thresher is the newspaper's chief sports editor. I think he'd been put in with the foundations. He sits at his desk in the corner all day; holey red cardigan, fingerless gloves, three back supports on his chair. I like Jeff. He holds the door open for me and laughs at my jokes. He's an expert gardener too and enters all the country shows with his massive courgettes. He's taught me some of the Latin names of my favourite flowers – *Bellis perennis* (daisy), *Centaurea cyanus* (cornflower) and *Amaranthus caudatus* (Love Lies Bleeding). If the office were flooded with shit, I'd definitely throw Jeff the other life raft.

Drove over to the house in my lunch break. Julia is not a happy camper. She's broken a window at the back. It's only a small hole but it made me mad. So, of course, she had to be taught another lesson. Back into the cupboard with you, Little Chip.

Met Craig for a Nando's after work and he brought the car-insurance documents along so we could Compare the Meerkat 'cos the renewal price was too high. My chicken was tough. I didn't complain though. Didn't have it in me tonight.

Thank God for porn. The moment Craig mooted the possibility of sex that evening, I took myself off to the bedroom under the guise of 'working on my novel' and chowed down on every old favourite I could find to lubricate the old pink matter. When I think back to being a kid and sneaking off to read the dirty bits in my mum's Jackie Collins or rewinding Dad's *Basic Instinct* tape about six bloody times, I wonder how I survived. Now, it's everywhere and not so titillating.

Chat rooms can be another source of titillation. I know modesty forbids me to say I'm brilliant at dirty talk but I am *brilliant* at dirty talk. How it works is you snare them in the chat rooms, get them begging for a private text chat in WhatsApp or Kik and then haul them in. Once they're in the app, they're in my trap.

Hee hee hee.

Admittedly, sexting gets a little annoying when predictive text spoils the fun – I've lost count of the number of times I've said I wanted to 'duck his vock' or asked a guy to 'cum in my wasp' or 'lick my Pudsey'. One guy offered to 'suck my bipolars'. Some of them get quite demanding. Skyping works better but it involves shaving and losing weight and I just can't be bothered at the moment. Chatting to three or four at once, it's like working in Argos during the Christmas rush. One wants an ass shot, another wants a tit shot, some guy in Australia's going to bed soon and needs to watch me cum on camera and one guy in Toronto wants to chat about suicidal thoughts he's had since his brother's death. Oh, yeah. I get all sorts.

Last time, me and one of my regulars were on about meeting up at a London hotel – he wanted to tie me up. Another said he'd meet me in a dark alleyway and do exactly what I said: grab me and tear at my clothes, grasp my neck like a nettle and bite my ear as he whispered nasty things into it – just like I wanted him to.

I stop short at asking if I can kill them after; if I can lie underneath them, dressed in their blood, while they emit their dying breaths on top of me.

Baby steps and all that.

But the best – the absolute best thrill of all – is going fishing. And I don't mean for carp or tench. I mean big fish. Big, horny fish who only come out at night to prowl the streets, looking for female office workers walking home alone or pissed-up damsels in distress stumbling back from the clubs. I like to play said damsel from time to time. I like to play the victim. It's so damn easy when you've got an eight-inch chef's knife in your coat pocket.

Sunday, 7 January

1. *Derek Scudd*
2. *Derek Scudd's lawyer*
3. *Wesley Parsons*
4. *Our local whack job, Creepy Ed Sheeran, who hangs around Lidl car park, tearing the leaves off the bushes, sniffing them and chuckling*
5. *Anyone who buys, sells or creates* Star Wars *merchandise. I can't even buy a Snickers without seeing a token for a sodding light sabre*

Dreamed about Dad again last night. I asked him who his favourite child was, and he smiled and told me, 'You, of course.'

I could talk to my dad about anything. There's no one now. Craig's pathetic – he's always got one eye on the TV and, even if it's turned off, I figure he's mentally rerunning an old episode of *Game of Thrones*. I can't talk to Seren, of course. She hasn't been back to England since Dad's funeral and, every time we talk on the phone, I get the impression she can't wait to hang up.

And as for the PICSOs, when I want derogatory comments about my lack of kids or non-selling novel or my low-grade job, maybe their opinions will matter.

I don't know what Mum or Dad would tell me to do if they were still around.

I didn't grieve for them like an ordinary person would. Seren said it was 'very unsettling' seeing the way I grieved about Dad. She said it was like 'looking through a window when it's raining' – the rain trickling down it and cold as ice. I didn't know how to feel. I was just numb. I googled it once – WebMD said 'bereavement numbness for the first few days is very common as your brain tries to process what has happened'. I couldn't find anything about numbness that went on for years. Apparently, that wasn't a thing.

The two seniors, Claudia and Linus, came back from court at lunch, to say that the paedophile Derek Scudd, sixty-eight, had got off with a three-year suspended sentence, a two-month rehab order and a place on the Sex Offenders' Register. We've all been following the case for over a year. Un-fucking-believable! The man needs to be skinned alive and fried while he was still screaming.

Thursday, 11 January

1. *Mrs Whittaker – neighbour, elderly, kleptomaniac*
2. *'Dillon' on the checkout in Lidl – he overcharged me for Craig's paper*
3. *The suited man in the blue Qashqai who roars out of Sowerberry Road every morning – grey suit, aviator shades, Donald Trump tan*
4. *Derek Scudd*
5. *Wesley Parsons*

The camellias are flowing in the front garden at Mum and Dad's house. They look gorgeous. My mum planted them. I saw them when I took some more stuff round before work. Julia did some more begging. She'd made another attempt to smash the window.

'DON'T YOU DARE SMASH A WINDOW!' I yelled at her, yanking her head back hard until she crumpled to the carpet. 'You carry on like that I'll cut your other thumb off.'

I reminded her about 'my friend who is watching her kids'. She shut up after that. I wanted to kill her today – it's getting terribly tedious driving over there and feeding her and having to repeat the same threats over and over. It's like looking after a very annoying horse. And I still can't get the stains out of the carpet.

But it's not the right time. Once it's done, it's done and I want to make sure it's done right.

The police have released more information about Daniel Wells, the electrician whose life (and schlong) was brutally cut short by yours truly – he was indeed found with no attachment. The office was full of jokes about Dickless Dan all day. They've somehow ruled out terrorism. Apparently, he was involved in a bar fight on New Year's Eve, so they're following up that blind alley. That would explain the cut on his eyebrow, now I think of it.

Another salad for lunch. God damn you, Cucumber.

AJ has started flirting with Lana. He's all 'Hey, L, how you going?' when he first gets in, and offers to make her peanut butter and banana on toast like he has in the morning. I've noticed, too, that he brings her chai latte *before* he brings over my cappuccino, *and* he chats to her longer. They both like swimming, both their dads ran out on their mums when they were kids and they both had cockatoos. Claudia's clocked it and I do believe she is trying to keep him busy. She had him on filing duties upstairs for the best part of the afternoon.

I wonder how Lana screams. I wonder if her death scream will be the same as her sex scream.

Jeff and I had one of our debates over our 3 p.m. tea break. Today, it involved turning the historic almshouses in the town centre into a bail hostel. I said it was a good idea, owing to the amount of homeless in the town; Jeff said what about history? We didn't reach an agreement but we clinked cups when we'd finished so I think we're still friends.

Tonight, a planned protest in the town centre about Council Tax rises turned into a full-blown riot that spilled over into the retail park at the end of our road. There was looting, home-made missiles and unleaded Molotovs causing spontaneous fires. I've just got back. Took some great pictures – one of them, I think, is going to knock their socks off tomorrow and, I don't mind telling you, I think it has a good chance of being next week's front page. Maybe I can impress Claudia and Linus with them tomorrow and *finally* get where I'm meant to be in life – on the front page. A front page with my name on it would make it all worthwhile.

I didn't run into any opportunistic rapists down any side streets on the way home. It's always the same when you're prepared for it. Like bloody buses.

Did some writing in bed. It's not going well. My stomach was rumbling throughout, owing to no tea (Craig had made full-fat lasagne and garlic bread), and once you've likened a hot guy's teeth to 'a graveyard of white surfboards in his mouth' you know you're in the shit. Had another rejection letter today, this time from one of the big guns: The Garside Agency. They said my work 'lacked emotional depth'. Just like me, I suppose. Thirty-seven agents I've sent it too now. They can't all be wrong. Think it's time to dismantle *The Alibi Clock*. Who wants fiction anyway when you've got good old fact to have fun with?

Friday, 12 January

1. *Woman with the two brown spaniels who always attack Tink and are never on leads – today, she was wearing Crocs*
2. *Derek Scudd*
3. *Wesley Parsons*
4. *Jonah Hill*
5. *People who cast Jonah Hill in films*

Some moron on Twitter is trying to galvanise the local community into a 'Bring Your Own Broom' party to clear up after the riot. Bloody millennials.

My car wouldn't start this morning so I had to bus it and run it to work. Two of the usual routes in were cordoned off while the police cleared away burnt-out cars and broken glass from last night. I don't know why they're calling it a riot. It had all been done and dusted by 10 o'clock. People are so lazy when it comes to public protest. It's like, 'Yeah, let's throw a few bottles, scrawl on a few bits of old cardboard, swear at some police, then be home in time for *Game of Thrones*.' Amateurs.

The office was bustling when I walked in, sweating like a priest at a pre-school pool party. Printers whirred. Steaming cups of coffee were being handed out. The subeditors were tapping away, ensconced behind their tessellated desks. Claudia was marching around, putting important A4 sheets of paper on in-trays and generally looking harassed. The new boy, AJ, was stapling papers beside her desk, on the floor, like the office puppy (who could also do stapling). Ron was in his office on a headset phone call. Linus Sixgill was at his desk, ending a call. There were three espresso cups around his monitor and on his screen in all his technicolour glory was a picture of Daniel Wells – aka Dan Dan, the Dickless Man.

'Hi,' I said, making my mealy-mouthed presence known. Neither of them looked up. 'So I took a great picture last night in the riot.'

Linus turned round. 'Did you, Reepicheep? And what were you doing out in a riot, pray tell?'

He never called me by my actual name – just versions of it. Lovely Rita, Meter Maid was an early favourite. Reepicheep was a regular, as was Rita Ora. Reet Petite, normally on a Friday afternoon. All I could do was stand there and giggle politely like the work-suck I was.

'Ron said at the last Triple M [Monday Morning Meeting] that we should always be prepared for any eventuality. You know, if we see a story unfolding...'

'Yeah, he meant the subs and the editors, darling, not the receptionist.'

'I'm not the receptionist any more, I'm the editorial assistant,' I mewed, wiping my brow on my jacket cuff. 'Ron said...'

'That's Mr Pondicherry to you, Rhiannon,' said Claudia, barely looking up from her screen.

'Mr Pondicherry,' I corrected, 'said that becoming a Junior means researching more of my own stories. So I thought I'd take some initiative. You never know when something will go down, he said – a fight, a car crash, a child being kidnapped.'

AJ looked up from his pile of stapled pages and smiled at me, surfboard graveyard a gogo.

'That's not your job though, is it?' Claudia returned with a vicious eye-bat. 'Leave it to the professionals, hmm, sweetpea?'

That 'hmm' was supremely irritating. I'd like to rip out every hmmm in her throat. But I just smiled sweetly, like a sweetpea would.

'Mr Pondicherry said that if I showed enough willing, he might put me forward for NCTJ funding. So I can get my diploma.'

'Ahh, that'd be way cool,' said AJ, mid-*clickety clack*. I acknowledged his support and turned to Linus, as though the endorsement of a cross-legged Australian boy was all I needed.

Linus opened his desk drawer and pulled out a small box of toothpicks. 'Probably won't ever come to anything, Reet Petite. He usually takes trainees straight from journalism school. Never sent a receptionist for training before.'

'I'm one up from a receptionist though, aren't I? Could you just take a look at the pictures? Please?'

'Is he picking on you, Rhee?' chipped in Lana Rowntree, mincing through on her way into Reception. She always called me Rhee, even though there had never been a conversation where I'd said she could. She stank of cheap scent and lack of ambition and spent her work days selling advertising space, shrieking fake laughter down the phone and rubbing buttockly past desks in pencil skirts as tight as fish skins. Linus had clearly smelled her coming as he'd popped in an Airwave.

'Nah, it's just a bit of fun, isn't it?' he said, leaning back in his chair and giving Lana the full legs-open-trouser-throb pose.

'You wanna watch him,' said Lana, nudging me like we were besties, despite the fact she didn't *actually* care, she just wanted to trade sex air with Sixgill. Her nudge still stung my arm, even as the door closed behind her.

Linus watched her leave and sighed dreamily. 'She might be batshit but she's got one hell of a set of alloys on her, that girl.'

'Don't be disgusting, Linus,' sneered Claudia over her telephone.

'What do you mean?' I said. But Linus and Claudia just threw each other a look and ignored me as usual.

I'd run through various scenarios in my mind about how I would eventually kill Linus Sixgill. I could anally violate him with his Mont Blanc, then there was the strapping-him-to-his-swivel-chair-and-deep-throating-his-cock-until-I-bit-it-off-at-the-hilt method. I could smash the glass on the Emergency Fire Axe and chop his head off, kicking it across the carpet into the recycling bin. Or I could just stick up my middle finger and yell, 'TWAT!' and run out of the room. None of these were ideal, I grant you, seeing as I, a) didn't want to go to prison, b) *did* want promotion and c) Linus's wife Kira is the editor-in-chief's daughter.

And then there was the third and most sensible option – proving myself. Getting a stunning picture or writing a brilliantly insightful story, making front page news and being recommended for NCTJ funding and rising to the position of junior reporter. The title of 'junior' as opposed to 'chief' or 'senior' did still smack of nursery school – like I should be sitting in the middle of the office floor in my playpen, sucking on Linus's moob – but it would open a doorway for me.

Claudia looked up. 'What photos did you get then, Rhiannon? Anything we could use in the Friday round-ups?' She said it with a sigh, like a mother asking her kid what drawings they had done, despite the fact they'd be going in the bin.

'Oh,' I said. 'I thought maybe you could use one of them for next week's front page? You know, kind of like a "Riot Night Special"-type thing?'

Claudia looked at me with such utter contempt it was like her pupils were glued to her eyelids. 'Derek Scudd's our lead story for next week.'

They had a good picture for it too. We'd been shown it at the last Triple M. One of the photographers had caught him lighting a cigarette as he'd come out of court – a grizzly stare straight down the lense. The heading was to be EVIL BACK ON OUR STREETS. Derek Scudd's evilness was the one thing Claudia and I actually agreed on, though I still wanted to ram the bitch's head through the cross-shredder.

I handed her the disk from my camera and she shoved it into her hard drive – an action about as close to penetrative sex as she got now her husband had left her. Claudia didn't like me and that was fine. The day I needed validation from a veiny-footed shrew with permanent coffee breath and a Napoleon complex was the day I watched *Geordie Shore* without breaking out in hives. But I still had to stay on her good side. I had to think of the end game – promotion. A diploma. A career. She could give me all that if she wanted to.

My slides flashed up – all one hundred and eight of them. A lot were dark with flashes in the middle. Fireworks. Shadows of police. A police dog snarling. A wash of mild interest cleaned her face.

AJ got up off the floor with his pile of pages and studied the screen too. 'Wow, you're a really good photographer, Rhiannon.' He beamed. 'Are you trained?'

'No, not at all,' I said, before remembering to add 'Thank you though.'

The phone rang on Claudia's desk.

'Good evening, Newsdesk, Claudia Gulper speaking... Ooh, yes, one moment please.' She put her hand over the mouthpiece. 'Rhiannon, I need to take this, it's about that warehouse fire. Show Linus, all right?' *There's a good girl*, she might as well added. *Oh, you unutterable swampy bitch dog tramp licker from Hades.*

She sent AJ on a new errand, then carried on with her phone call, laughing and hair-twizzling while the guy on the other end poured his heart out about the loss of his family's sixty-year-old business. I ripped the disk from her hard drive.

'Come on then, Rheepunzel, I'll look at your happy snaps for you,' said Linus, beckoning me over with his manicure. I gave him the disk and he put it in his machine instead. 'Ooh. Nice one of the doggy. That's... interesting,' at my shot of a brick wall that had fallen down outside a playground. 'Quality's a bit muddy. What were you using for these, a Box Brownie?'

Outwardly, I shy-giggled like a twat. Inwardly, I was calling him a chinless fucktard and picturing him waking up in bed, screaming to the sight of his severed bollocks in a jar.

He scrolled past fireworks, shattered windows, a boy kicking at a front door.

Then he stopped talking. He was scrolling through more slowly now, checking each one. 'Mmm, yes, some of these are quite picturesque, aren't they? Violent delights. That's a Shakespeare reference, by the way...'

'I know,' I said. '"These violent delights have violent ends, and in their triumph die, like fire and powder, which, as they kiss, consume." *Romeo and Juliet.*'

Linus said nothing. And then he stopped scrolling. He'd found the money shot – I'd taken several of the scene but only this one was in focus. The backdrop was of snarling dogs, pink smoke fireworks in mid-air bounce. Three police with riot shields tussling with bellicose protestors and behind them the flaming tree. In front of it all, lying on the ground in the middle of the melee, two teenagers: a boy and a girl, their hands on each other's faces, as still and as perfect as a prayer.

'Wow,' he said, then eased back into his chair, just looking at the screen.

The riot lovers. They'd been there for seconds but I'd imprisoned them for ever with one click. 'You like it?'

'Yeah, I do. I do like it,' said Linus, leaning back in his chair again. 'Jeff? Come over a second, would you?'

Jeff limped over (old rugby injury) and pushed his half-moon glasses up his nose to stare at Linus's screen.

'Bloody hell. Is that from last night? Is that in town? Who took that?'

'I did,' I said, seeing as Linus wasn't going to say anything. 'I was lucky actually, they were only there for a few seconds. I saw the flames in the tree and then he grabbed her and pulled her away and then they were just lying there…'

'That's brilliant that is. I wonder who they are. Good framing, Rhiannon. Bit of a David Bailey we got on our hands, eh? Well, *Davina* Bailey.'

I didn't know who David or Davina Bailey were but I guessed it was a compliment. It had to be. Me and Jeff were pals. Everyone else thought he was a bit out of touch. He spluttered like an old engine, constantly scratched and petted his ball sac like it was a golden retriever and never updated his software. I once heard him call Linus a wanker, then apologise because 'Ladies were present.'

'Is Ron still on his call with *The Times*?' said Jeff.

We all looked across to his office. Through the window he looked to be deep in conference with a man's face on his computer screen. 'Photo like that's too good to sit on for a week, that is. Too good to sit on. I'd get it on the website now.'

Linus erupted from his chair and marched across to Ron Pondicherry's door and knocked loudly seven times. Then he just barged on in.

'Well done, you,' said Jeff as we both looked down at Linus's computer screen as proud as if we were staring at a scan of our baby. 'That's smashing, Rhee.'

'Thanks, Jeff,' I said, blushing the colour of his cardigan, sans gravy stains.

'Bet His Nibs was annoyed he didn't take it himself, wasn't he?' he said, nodding in Linus's direction.

I shrugged. 'I guess.'

'Anything that sticks it up Lord Muck's arse gets my vote.' Jeff laughed and slapped me so hard on the back my ribs quaked. 'Don't let him take credit for that photo though.'

'He wouldn't, would he? I mean I know he will write the article but it's my photo.'

Jeff sipped his coffee and did a non-committing shake of head.

'He won't pass it off as his photo, will he?' I said, my heart turning blacker by the second.

He coughed. 'I wouldn't hold your breath, love. Wouldn't hold your breath.'

Tuesday, 16 January

1. *Man in blue Qashqai, who today I learned has a huge Dalmatian. No abuse this morning but I still hate him*
2. *Mrs Whittaker, who has definitely taken a book from my shelf. And/or a green Biro, we think*
3. *Derek Scudd*
4. *Wesley Parsons*
5. *People who say 'advocado', 'marshmellow' or pronounce 'h' as 'haitch'*

Do you feel superior to your friends?

Yes, I do. And I don't know much about people but I think most of us do. And why shouldn't I? I have a degree, I do a full-time job and don't sponge off the state like they do with their nursery vouchers and working family tax relief credit shenanigans. And yeah, I do get bored easily in their company. And in Craig's company. And at work. But you'd never guess that. I am brilliant at The Act. The late great Leonard Cohen once said, 'Act the way you'd like to be and soon you'll be the way you act.' I've been doing this since my therapy sessions ended. They thought I was cured, when really I was just lying. One day perhaps it'll become second nature.

Caring is hard though. I've picked up some tips to keep people onside:

1. **Listen** – *People like being the centre of attention. Keeping your mouth shut is a lost art and people cherish it.*
2. **Ask them how they are** – *even if you've already asked, people don't seem to notice.*
3. **Compliment them** *on their haircut/weight loss.*
4. **Gifts** – *'I saw this and thought of you' often works wonders*
5. **Make gluten-free cakes** – *covers all bases but chuck in a shitload of sugar to take away the taste.*

Some people would call it bribery. I call it survival.

Even when I'm at home, I'm acting a part. I never know which bits of me are real. I wonder what it's like to truly feel, to truly 'be.' Exhausting, I'd imagine. It's easier to comfort someone online, like when Lucille's mother died and she wanted to chat on IM. It was just my fingers typing well-timed condolences – the rest of me was glued to *The Apprentice* and chowing down Aero Bubbles like they were going out of fashion.

If anything, I prefer hanging out with their kids. If I go round to one of their houses and they're putting the kettle on, I'll sit in their Wendy houses and they'll bring me plastic plates with little roast chickens on or we'll do colouring in. Imelda's twins, Hope and Molly, have some Sylvanian stuff that I don't have so we tend to play with that or look through the brochure to see what we want next.

BuzzFeed had that wrong about me. I *could* allow myself to feel for some members of the human race. Children, for instance. I don't like cruelty or unfairness to kids because, of anyone, they don't deserve it. None of us deserved what happened to us at Priory Gardens.

It was one of my rules when it came to murder…

1. *Be prepared – assess thoroughly and only go in if you know you can win*
2. *Cover your tracks – leave no fluids*
3. *Maintain The Act on all fronts*
4. *No Velcro – it's a forensic scientist's best friend*
5. *Defend the defenceless – children, animals, women in danger*

And now there's the injustice of Derek Scudd and the two little girls. Once upon a time, 'a high risk repeat offender' called Derek Scudd took two ten-year-olds back to his flat to meet his cat's kittens. But the kittens didn't exist. And the girls were forced to do things that destroyed every happy thought in their heads. The End.

The thought of Derek Scudd walking about a free man eats at my last nerve. I need to see that man die. I need to be on top of him when he does. The judge at his trial should be fucking lynched too.

One of his victims' mothers came into the office today to talk to Claudia and Linus in Ron's office – Mary Tolmarsh. I took them in some lattes and custard creams and caught the briefest glimpse of her. Blonde bob. Joules jumper. Navy jeans. Flats. Nice enough clothes but her face ran a different headline – a rag doll left out in the rain.

I heard a brief snatch of conversation – she mentioned Windwhistle Court, a block of flats on the other side of the park, and she'd sounded angry when she said it, like that was where Scudd lived now. I also heard he'd been using a false name. Windwhistle Court was about twenty minutes from the office, and a ten-minute walk from our flats. I drove over after work and waited in the car. Watching. Poised. There was no sign of him though.

Took Tink out for her evening constitutional around 11 p.m.

Craig was snoring and I couldn't lose myself in sleep at all. I was all nervy and gnawed on the inside and my legs were jumpy. I needed to get out. I took the wallpaper scissors, just in case, but all the usual alleys and canal towpaths were quiet. Probably just as well. The way I was feeling, I'd have eviscerated the bastard.

Right, I'm starving so I'm going to go have some Quavers and the rest of the jaffa cakes. I read online that calories don't count past midnight. Or is that just with Gremlins?

Sunday, 21 January

No sign of Scudd the Stud at Windwhistle Court again. I waited nearly an hour today. I'm beginning to think I misheard the address. Might try Winnipeg Court tomorrow. Or Winchester Road. Or there's Williamson Terrace, too. It definitely begins with a 'W'. He's here somewhere, in this town, walking these streets, breathing my air.

Did our weekly shop. I prefer it now we've switched our day to Sunday with just a few top-up shops in between. Fewer people around to piss me off. Craig was about as useful as a trap door on a lifeboat. And, Jesus Christ, the over-seventies are annoying. Give me screaming kids running up the aisles face first into my trolley any day over the octogenarian statue who stands in front of the tinned fish, weighing up his options between no-drain tuna and potted crab for *ten fucking minutes* with no shred of awareness of people trying to get to the anchovies.

And while I'm on the subject of food shopping, how expensive are free-range chickens? Just gimme a hen that's clucked, fucked and been plucked in woodland, and I'm happy. You don't have to feed it diamonds or anything.

Also, the diet's over. I inhaled two croissants when I got back, just to spite my fat ass. I'll walk Tink a few miles after tea to work one of them off.

Friday, 26 January

1. *I love everyone today*
2. *Just kidding – The World*

Something rather exciting has happened in the life of *Moi*, Rhiannon Lewis. Breakfast-TV show *Up at the Crack*, they of the screamingly pink sofas, rictus grins and perma-tans, have included me on their shortlist of Women of the Century.

ME!

They want to do an interview on live TV at the end of the month. I met Imelda and Pidge at Costa as our lunch breaks coincided and regaled them with my marvellous news. Imelda was steaming.

'WHAT? WHY?' said Mel, more than a little put out that I was going to have a five-minute slot on national TV and talk about something *other* than her wedding.

Pidge threw her cousin a look.

'Sorry. Priory Gardens, yeah?'

Everyone calls it Priory Gardens or The Priory Gardens Thing when they refer to what happened. It's become that handy short cut people use – like Dunblane or Columbine. You don't have to say any more – people just know.

'I'm one of ten women they're profiling over the next few weeks. I won't win.' I added that last statement for the modesty, though I knew it would take a damn icon to beat me.

'What do you mean you won't win?' said Pidge. 'Come on, be positive!'

'Who else is on the shortlist?'

I could see it in Mel's eyes: the desperate hope that the shortlist was so strong, I didn't stand a kitten in a pizza oven's chance of winning.

'Well, there's that housebound woman who lost sixty-four stone and became a PE teacher. And a human-rights lawyer who saved a load of Syrians...'

Her smile began to twitch.

'...some politician with no arms or legs who walked across Canada. That diabetic transgender librarian who's fostered over a thousand kids. And those two women who were locked in a basement for ten years. I think that's it.'

Imelda laughed. Actually *laughed*. 'Ooh dear. Stiff competition then. Maybe the judges will take pity on you cos you were a kid when it happened.'

'Malala was a kid when she was shot though,' said Pidge with a long slurp of her flat white. 'Anyway, what you went through was still incredible, Rhee. You're bound to get something. Is it a gold, silver, bronze thing?'

'I don't think so. Look, I was a national treasure for a few years, let's not forget,' I said, a little perturbed to find them hell-bent on believing I'd lose. We sweetpeas need our sunlight, lest we wither.

Pidge sucked the end of her French braid and threw Imelda look that landed on her face like a splat.

Imelda sighed, spooning another two sugars into her latte.

No, I thought, bugger it. I *did* have a brilliant chance of winning. That newsreel they used to play on interviews of my limp little body being carried out of 12 Priory Gardens always had people in tears. And mute little me sitting next to Dad on the *This Morning* sofa and the documentary the BBC made to celebrate my coming out of hospital. I was a bloody HERO, once upon a time. All right so it was twenty-odd years ago, but still. I was younger than Malala when it happened and I'd come through my trauma just as bloody well, if not better.

But before I could argue my case any further, our conversational ship set sail.

'Listen, back to the wedding, my cake woman's royally let me down – got a bad hygiene certificate. They found mice droppings in her proving drawer. Major drams. So could have the number of that woman who did Craig's lemon drizzle, Rhee?'

Wednesday, 31 January

1. *People who riot and make* MasterChef *get cancelled*

Even the subeditors annoyed me today. They're all so damn predictable, so happy. Bollocky Bill – who reminds us daily he's a testicular-cancer survivor, even when the subject isn't actually *about* cancer or bollocks – ALWAYS brings in a cheese roll and a packet of Quavers for lunch and says things like 'all the best' and 'champion' on the phone. Carol sings in a choir, doesn't own a mobile and has the same two dresses on heavy rotation: one pink with a purple turtleneck; the other green with a red turtleneck. Then there's Edmund, the office 'hottie', who is a bit exotic (born in Switzerland, private-schooled, painfully posh) and has the same haircut as my six-year-old nephew. He never swears – he uses exclamations like 'zoinks' and 'golly' and every day he opens a Diet Lilt at 11.32 a.m. On. The. Dot.

I spent the morning updating the website and our social-media pages – Claudia wants 'more contact with our community'. The post-riot Bring a Broom Party was a rousing success and she wants to 'sex up our Instagram page a bit for the readers'. How the hell do you 'sex up' tidying? Slut drop on a broomstick? Wide leg squats on a mop? How do you 'sex up' Morris dancing on the village green? Or a Women's Institute talk about buttons? Our Instagram is all flower arrangements, Food Fair snapshots of fat blokes eating pulled pork and one of Eric the handyman lugging boxes. I'm not allowed to put anything vaguely interesting on there, like the dead junkie in the park or the woman who drove her mobility scooter into the river. My God, that was hilarious. First time I've ever nearly pissed myself in a public place, including my twenty-first birthday party.

Ron wasn't in today. Pretty soon I have to ask for a pay rise or at least some idea of when they're going to announce funding for the NCTJ Diploma. They appoint one new trainee every year in January and that person does their stint before they're made up to a senior role. Linus began as a junior, so did Claudia and Mike Heath. Surely after all the stories I've done for them they'll see it's worth sending me to get properly qualified. There's nobody else in the running. It *has* to be me.

Here's just a soupçon of the extra – i.e. not in my job description – work I've done for them in the past three years...

1. *Feature article on closing the old cinema*
2. *Feature article on Rillington Manor, wedding venue extraordinaire*
3. *Feature article on the closing of the town swimming pool plus an exclusive interview with the protestor who threw a used condom at the police chief*
4. *Test-driving new Audi, plus full report*
5. *Countless film reviews – if I have to sit through another Bond, Marvel or Keira Knightley movie I'm going to put a bomb under the photocopier*
6. *Interviewing a zillion Golden Wedding couples with unnervingly floccose faces in their piss-stinking lounges, sipping greasy tea from chipped cups and listening to interminable stories about Morris Minors*

I could go on. And it is my diary so I will go on...

1. *Pimping out Tink as the guinea pig for the new grooming parlour on Milford Street, even though she was traumatised and got a rash on her ear*
2. *Photos for the power-station feature*
3. *Photos for the riot feature*
4. *Photos for the Country Life section (toffs at the cricket club)*
5. *Food critiques for twelve restaurants under the pseudonym Gaston Enfoiré*
6. *Going to the courts every week to listen to dope heads get fined for insurance fraud, Burger King rage or for trying to fuck the pigeons*
7. *Learning shorthand*
8. *Learning legalese*
9. *Not reporting Linus for copious sexist and inappropriate comments, Mike Heath for stinking of cats or Claudia for just generally being a bitch*

And that's not even the half of it!

Some doughnuts did the rounds mid-afternoon and I ate one. Fuck you, waistline.

Passed by Windwhistle Court again on my way home. Still no sign of Our Mutual Fiend. Around the corner was a block of sheltered accommodation called Winchester Place. I parked up and watched people coming out. People going in. I scanned the entire road for some telling 'peedo' graffiti or old blokes in green duffle coats. Nothing. I don't think it's good for me, going round there. It just makes the hunger to kill grow even more. But not going round there is worse because it means there is nothing at all. Just life. And Craig.

MasterChef was cancelled tonight for a *Panorama Special*

on the austerity cuts. Our riot was featured briefly – Ron was being interviewed about it with the mayor. I threw peanuts at the screen like I did when he was on *The Chase*. He got knocked out early anyway, thanks to Olly Murs.

Neither me nor Craig could be bothered to cook so we went out for a Nando's. Sue me, Cellulite.

Thursday, 1 February

1. *Linus Sixgill*
2. *Linus Sixgill's family*
3. *Linus Sixgill's friends*
4. *Linus Sixgill's neighbours*
5. *Linus Sixgill's dentist*
6. *Linus Sixgill's neighbours' dentists*
7. *Linus Sixgill's neighbours' dentist's receptionists*

This morning I saw the colour run-outs of tomorrow's front page – and guess what? MY PHOTO IS ON THE FRONT PAGE!

Excited? *Moi?*

No, of course not, and you know why? Because that TWAT, that bovaristic PRICKSTICK of GARGANTUAN proportions Linus 'The Vaginus' Sixgill has spunked his filthy name all over it. He's claiming ALL credit. *He* wrote the article, *he* took the photo, so it's fuck you Rhiannon, goodnight. I'm amazed he didn't claim to be one of the people in it. Jeff didn't even speak up for me. He just said, 'Well, I saw it coming.'

Yeah thanks, Jeff. If I had more middle fingers they'd all belong to you.

So he's next. Lying-Ass Sixgill is next on the list, trumping all others. Just break the safety glass and pass me the fucking axe.

I don't want to talk any more about today. I just want to over-eat and shit myself and die. Or shit myself *after* I die. Apparently that happens. And when you give birth too. Ugh. What a world.

Friday, 2 February

So I asked for my new contract, it being the three-year anniversary of my joining the company – and the two-year anniversary of my last pay rise. And do you know what? Do you want to have a wild guess what Ron and Claudia said?

They. Said. No.

I did get my contract – I'm editorial assistant for another year, guaranteed – and apparently I'm 'a reliable, helpful and cherished member of the company' – just not cherished enough for a £1 pay rise. They've had to 'tighten their belts lately'.

'There's just no extra money in the pot right now I'm afraid,' Ron said. And I, like the underpaid dumbass I am, took it on the chin like a ball sac.

So despite the £500 potted palm tree they've just bought for Reception and the £5,000 coffee machine and the massive clip-frame Van Gogh on the first-floor landing, despite the new carpets and blinds, new filing cabinets, Ron's and Claudia's new computers, the five-star bonding weekend in Lytham St Anne's *and* megabucks Christmas party at the golf club – champagne included – there's no more money. In. The. Pot.

I imagined Ron and Claudia in a pot – one of those giant cauldron jobs of boiling hot oil, like in medieval times. Tied back to back, dangling over the bubbling mixture, screaming; toes touching the surface. Lowering them inch by excruciating inch into the burning liquid as their naked skin grew redder and redder and started peeling away from its flesh – Claudia's face a picture of anguish; Ron sweating, crying, begging before his sweet release into death.

Yeah, that'd do it. God I am BURNING to kill again. Burning. I can almost feel it beneath my skin.

But at least I finally know what I mean to the team at the *Gazette*. Less than a coffee machine. Less than a clip frame. Less than a cock-sucking palm tree. The unfairness gnaws at me like a blade to a tin of corned beef.

And here's the cherry on it – there's absolutely no chance of funding for the NCTJ either. Apparently, they 'have had someone in mind for this for a while now'. Claudia said I 'shouldn't have got my hopes up'. After all, I am just the 'editorial assistant'.

So, yeah, I'm still just the Smegitorial Assface. And ever thus shall be.

W.A.N.K.E.R.S

It's all wrong. It should be *me* with my own office, not Ron. It should be *me* treating other people like shit, not Claudia. I do most of the work. It should be *my* castle and each one of their fat heads should be on long spikes outside the front gates, so every morning I can look up at their slack-jawed faces and fucking laugh.

AJ played it cool with me today. I think Claudia's given him some lecture about focusing on work not women if he wants a good reference – he does spend a lot of time lingering by desks, shooting the breeze with people, talking about life in Australia and how 'Christmas is always hot' and how he goes 'surfing a lot with his mates Podz and Dobbo'.

I know how to play him. I know what'll get him on my desk. I'm gonna play him like a didgeridoo.

Went round to Mum and Dad's to check on Madam after work. She's been better, put it that way. I took out my bad day on her, which I probably shouldn't have done because she played no part in it, but still. I left her in a heap on the floor. The place still stinks so I shoved in another round of PlugIns.

I fancy some corned beef now I've mentioned it. Might nip over to Lidl.

Saturday, 3 February

1. *Celebrities who have one baby then release a book about having babies, as though they're suddenly an expert*
2. *Every agent in the UK who has rejected my novel* The Alibi Clock
3. *All my friends*

Went over Mum and Dad's again to make sure Julia was set up for two days – water, food, toilet access etc. She was giving me the silent treatment *again* but her body language was screaming guilt. Then I found it – a hole in the carpet. She'd started a tunnel under the bed. It was so sad it was almost funny – a tunnel to the second floor bathroom, which I kept locked on the outside. I said, again, that escape wasn't an option and that I had someone watching her kids if she tried to leave or summon help. All she had to do was sit tight.

It's a nice area where we used to live, when I had such a thing as a family. A THANKFUL VILLAGE, the road sign says. Neighbours are few, every note of birdsong can be heard, front gardens are mown on a Sunday and Harvest Home posters go up on telegraph poles mid-June. I like it. Well, I like the silence. Especially the garden. Mum was obsessed with it – she used to say gardening kept her sane. I've always associated the sights and smells of a healthy garden with happiness. When I was a kid it was packed with colour and smell. The aroma of a different herb greeted you with every new gust of wind. Rosemary and oregano. Mint and curry plant. Lemon thyme and sage. Pale yellow daffodils as blonde as my sister popping up in the beds in spring. Then cornflowers, as blue as Joe's eyes. The lavender in late summer was the same I'd put in the little pomander that Mum kept in her handbag. The trees were like Dad – strong and tall. The beds are all empty now but the trees remain.

An odd anomaly was that even though the house was (ostensibly) uninhabited, the grass in both the front and back gardens was always neatly trimmed. This was courtesy of a neighbour, Henry Cripps, who had a ride-on mower and had come up to me at Dad's funeral and said it was the 'least he could do'.

Henry's old-fashioned. He was still passing through the Stone Age when Emily Davison was throwing herself under that horse. His late wife Dorothy had been the quintessential 1950s housewife. Cooking, cleaning, child-bearing. The arranger of flowers. The beater of rugs. Henry used to time Dorothy when she went shopping. Fairly sure she only had a stroke to get away from him.

He could be nice. When I was a kid, he would let me climb over his fence to feed dandelions to his ancient tortoise, Timothy. And he'd keep newspapers back for mine and Seren's rabbit and guinea pig 'but not if they're going to thump in their hutch all night'.

I made myself a black coffee and sat out on a deckchair in the garden playing ball up the lawn with Tink.

'I say,' came a voice. A grey head appeared over the fence. Tink went ballistic up the trellis.

'Hi, Henry, how are you?' I asked him, quickly remembering the rules of engagement and struggling out of the deckchair. I picked up Tink but she continued to growl and snarl, full on toothily, just as she did with rogue pigeons on the balcony.

'Hello, there, Rhee-ann-non [he always accentuates every syllable], lovely to see you again!'

'You too, Henry.'

Thankfully, Henry was the only neighbour around, but he was all the neighbour you needed. He'd lend you anything, knew all the local gossip and would water your plants or mow your lawn diligently when you were away. He also had the neatest garage ever. All the paint pots were labels out and alphabetically shelved, his tools hanging on the back wall with pencil lines drawn around them. His three classic cars were shone to perfection – one was kept in our garage as prearranged with Dad.

I also noticed every one of his daffodils faced the same way. I think that's what happens to people who have nothing else to think about – their mind has time to dwell on shit it doesn't need to, like paint pots and daffodils.

'I hope you don't mind, Rhee-ann-non, but I had some geraniums left over so I've put a couple of beds in over there, just to start them off...'

'No, that's fine,' I said, looking back to where he pointed.

'... and some runner beans as well, up the end there. Did you want the car moving out of the garage yet? Only last time you were here you mentioned an estate agent coming to look round.'

'No, I've taken it off the market, just for the time being.'

'Oh, right,' he said. 'Why's that?'

Tink was pushing on my boob for attention like she had a right answer on *Catchphrase* so I put her on the ground where she chased after a woodlouse. 'Just not the right agent. Thought we could get a better deal with someone else.'

Then I had to hear about his latest piano investment – he had four of them now, which took up two reception rooms in the ground floor of his house. He used to invite me and Seren round to listen to them. The pianos played themselves. It was unusual and interesting for about the first minutes. After a while, we were both looking round for the nearest gallows.

Still, I have to keep Henry sweet. Very sweet.

'You came back last week, didn't you? Thought I saw your car on the drive.'

'Yeah, got to keep an eye on the you-know-what,' I said, tapping my nose. He nodded. 'And I'm just starting to clear a few things away for when it goes up for sale again.' I chanced a desultory peep to the top of the house. It's annoying when your body does that, isn't it? Gives off little hints to the atrocities you've committed.

'Ah, I thought I heard someone in there the other day.'

'My assistant. Someone's got to keep an eye on them when I can't be here.'

'Well as long as you're all right. Just give me a shout if you need anything. I told your dad I'd keep an eye on you.'

'Yep, I'm all right for everything, Henry, you don't need to worry about me.'

He smiled, showing a line of neat yellow baby teeth, but was still standing there, as though waiting for something. Then I realised he *was*.

'Oh, sorry, Henry, I completely forgot.' I scurried over to my tote on the back of the deckchair and fished out the baggy of pot. I handed it to him over the fence.

'Golly. This lot will keep me going for a few months!' he chuckled, tucking it away inside his V-neck. 'Much thanks.'

'No problem, just let me know when you need more.'

'Are you sure you don't want paying for all this, Rhee-ann-non? It seems like an awful lot. Terribly generous of you.'

'No way. You were a good friend to my dad, Henry. It's the least I can do. Got tonnes of the stuff growing up there. Mum's the word though, OK?'

He tapped his nose and we left it at that. He practically skipped back down his symmetrical path, despite the rheumatoid arthritis in his joints.

Julia, on the other hand, didn't seem quite so keen for me to leave this time.

'But what if something happens to you in London and nobody knows I'm here? I could die of starvation.'

'There are worse ways to lose weight, Julia. Try Davina's *Super Body Workout*.'

'I'm scared.'

'Just ration your food and drink and you'll be fine. I've brought you some more magazines and a *Puzzler*. No need to thank me.'

She did the banshee impression again so I tied her back up and shut the door on her.

'Jeez, chill out, woman I'll bring the *Sudoku* next time.'

I decided against cutting off another finger to punish her for the tunnel attempt. I didn't feel the need and I didn't have any of Tink's poo bags on me anyway.

Julia was only at my secondary school for a year, but in that year she'd done her level best to ruin what Priory Gardens had left of me. The morning I saw her in the precinct before Christmas, taking her kids to school as I walked towards work, I froze. I got that same feeling I had as an eleven-year-old every morning, when she'd walk into assembly and make a beeline for the chair next to me – the chair I HAD to save. I followed her home. I saw her junkyard of a front garden. Smelled her cigarette smoke wafting over her fence. Heard her shouting down the phone to someone.

One morning, I followed her again, this time prepared. I did the old 'Hey, is that you, Julia? It's me, Rhiannon!' routine. I drove her out to the house and we'd had a nice chat over some tea and a Lyons Victoria Sponge. She worked as a hairdresser; her partner, Terry, was a removals man.

Then I beat her unconscious and tied her up using climbing ropes from Mountain Warehouse and some strong steel eyes from Dad's toolbox, screwed and bolted into the back bedroom wall.

I only saw Dad do it once, get rid of a body. I hope it's not too difficult when the time comes. I'd be lying if I said I wasn't worried. Maybe it's because she's a woman. Or because she has kids – fairly ugly kids as kids go, but still kids and, therefore, innocents. They all have their mother's genes though – her freckles, her twisted teeth. They're better off without her. She's holding them back. Like she once held me back. Julia the Puppet Master.

Julia the Sly who'd pinch me when the teacher wasn't looking because I hadn't answered her question 'Am I your best friend?'

Julia the Scribbler who'd written 'Rhiannon Fatty Fat Face' in the front of my Bible and scrawled 'Mary Sucks Cocks' over eight pages of my New Testament.

Julia the Beater who'd failed her English test and taken out her frustration on me – a selective mute with brain damage.

Julia the Firestarter who'd burnt a hole in my tunic with the Bunsen burner.

Julia the Killer who'd stamped on the frog I'd befriended beside the pond because I hadn't said, 'You're my best friend.'

Julia the Demanding who would stare at me with her evil eyes and stab my hand with her fountain pen in French if I didn't help her with her verbs.

Julia the Cutter who would sneak scissors from the Art cupboard and cut off pieces of my hair.

Julia the Rapist who'd pinned me down behind the school science lab and tried to rape me with a stick because I hadn't said, 'You're my best friend.'

I prayed for her death every night. But every morning, my heart would sink as the big fat-footed girl with the ginger hair, wonky parting and the trash-can breath appeared in the doorway of the assembly hall.

I used to dream about life without Julia – a full night's sleep, no more racing heartbeat, sitting beside whoever I wanted in class, playing with who I wanted at break-time. Getting better grades and delivering more than just a piss-poor performance as Wing Attack to impress the teachers. No more bruises. When she left, it got better. My grades went up, my voice came back stronger. I even made some friends for a while. But the hate inside me had already started to multiply. Priory Gardens had turned on the tap but Julia kept it running.

No one ever helped me. To the other kids, Rhiannon and Julia were BFFs and no one was going to come between them, as much as I would silently scream for them to do so. I was a prisoner in Julia's fist and it was reducing me to dust.

So yeah, BuzzFeed, *I was always in trouble at school* and *I was a bully* do not apply to *this* psychopath. In fact, I was a model pupil – silent, studious, obliging. Allowing any bitch to slap me or spit in my face cos she thought it was funny.

But now that bitch was my prisoner. My dust.

Sunday, 4 February

1. *Woman sitting next to me on the train who has no concept of personal space (cue elbow digs), coughs without putting her hand over her mouth and has just eaten an egg-and-mayonnaise sandwich. If I'd had a gun, I'd have shot that fucking sandwich right out of her hands*
2. *Plug hogs on trains. Woman next to me is also one of these*
3. *Pass ag ticket inspector who huffed when I showed him my seat reservation instead of my ticket, then lingered, making small talk with the nineteen-year-old blonde student nurse behind me*
4. *Man in Lycra shorts who barged past me to the last seat on the Tube*
5. *Everyone who lives or works in London*

Had my usual Dad dream. Woke up with the shakes. I told Craig I was just cold. Am on the train now, travelling to London for tomorrow's *Up At the Crack* interview. The *OK!* magazine I bought at the station is a veritable cavalcade of fake-titted reality stars and women too fat or too thin, according to what's in fashion, so I've given up. I'm now enjoying watching the people who get on board whenever the train stops at a station. I like how they look around when they alight, sizing up the competition.

Hmm, who is the least threatening person to sit next to, they think.

Will it be the group of young men sitting around the table covered with empty beer bottles at 9.29 a.m.? No, definitely not.

How about the oily old gent with the carrier bag on his lap who looks like Robin Williams in *One Hour Photo*? Not, not him either.

How about the four ginger kids whose tablets are all on full volume? Or the two old women incessantly nattering – one who looks like Helen Mirren, the other like Helen Mirren's less successful brunette sister who works in Aldi?

No. They all make a beeline for me, of course. Because I'm the woman alone. Sweet and unthreatening. Friendly faced. Quiet.

Craig had suggested a B&B for me a couple of streets away from the TV studios, one he'd stayed in when him and Stuart went up to watch QPR play Middlesbrough and his train home was cancelled. He said the fry-up was 'beyond the beyond'.

A man rubbed up against me on the Tube out of Paddington. He must have been thirty-something. Bit of a quiff going on, highly polished shoes, iPhone clutched in one hand, latte in the other, cock against my arse. The train wasn't that packed. He could have moved away but he chose not to. I don't mean just brushed against me either – this isn't me getting all hoity-toity-Calm-Down-Dear about it. He was dry-humping me. I was in a good mood so I handled it as calmly as I could. I turned to him, so we were cock to front on and I said veeeery quietly in a voice only he could hear

'You carry on doing that, I *will* slit your fucking throat.'

And I gave him a flash of my knife. And it stopped. Instantly. And the next time the train reached a station, he got off.

I got off and pootled around Covent Garden for a bit to waste some time before I could check in. I got some more money out of Julia's bank account and bought some warm cookies in a little French bakery just off the main square. Found a kitchen shop which had the most astonishing array of Sabatier knives in the window, the display created to look like a starburst of weapons. I stared at them for ages, imagining which handle would look best with my fingers around it. They were all better than my crappy little steak knife. Might go back there tomorrow. We need a new tin opener as well. Mrs Whittaker has nicked ours.

I couldn't live in London but I like to inject myself with it every now and then. It's quite nice when it's not raining or being bombed.

*

Just logged back in to report that the B&B is a shithole and my mattress is covered in piss patches. I'm sleeping on my bath towel tonight.

In other news, I'm getting bored of the chat rooms. Took me ages to cum tonight, though I do generally find it hard to climax when I'm on a mattress that was around during the Renaissance.

Monday, 5 February

1. People who design hotels – why in God's name can't you put the mother-loving plug sockets by the bed?

The fry-up at the B&B was beyond disgusting, but I kind of knew it would be because a) Craig recommended it and b) I never have luck with hotels. There's always a pube, always a stain, and always a shag-a-thon or a troupe of horses doing dressage in the next room at 3 a.m.

Up at the Crack's runner Jemimah Double-Barrelled met me at the back entrance of TV Central. She was wearing trainers with neon laces, which irked me beyond socially acceptable levels, and her hands appeared glued to the edges of an iPad. In the lift upstairs, she told me I was to be on air between a segment about a botched hysterectomy and a recipe for a three-cheese quiche.

'So we'll take you in to make-up and get you all sorted and do your hair and then you can have a quick meet with the presenters.' Her fingertips went back to the mole cluster on her neck and picked at it like she was selecting the thickest Malteser.

'Who, John and Carolyn?' I said, sending a tiny bubble of hope into the universe that the Biggest Wanger in Town, Tony Tompkinson, was ill or on holiday or something, so I wouldn't have to spend the whole interview staring down at the massive bulge in his trousers.

'No, it's *Tony* and Carolyn on today. John does it with Carolyn every other day and then it's Melinda and Tristan on Fridays.'

Tristan was the black presenter they chucked in on a Friday with the gay weather girl to even things up a bit, diversity-wise. The weekend sister show *Chatterday* they gave to the blonde in the wheelchair.

The hair and make-up women went to town on my face, and by town I mean Slutsville. Whilst doing me, I overheard them bitching about Carolyn's demands for a dressing room of her own, some boy-bander's request for no-carb toast and Tony Tompkinson's latest bust-up with his agent.

Apparently, he was shagging her.

Apparently, Tony is shagging everyone.

Well, when you've got that much hot dog it's silly to put it in just the one roll.

The woman in the make-up chair to my right was an actress in some crime thing. To my left was a bloke whose pug had just got through to the semi-finals of *Pets Who Can Sing and Dance*. I didn't feel like conversating with either to be honest but I tried my best. Well, my head was nodding and my mouth was all 'How interesting' but really I was thinking about bleeding Julia out over the bathtub at Mum and Dad's.

Then Tony and Carolyn swept in for a pre-show 'touch up' before they went live. It looked to me like they'd been touched up quite a bit already.

'Tony, Carolyn, this is Rhiannon Lewis, today's Woman of the Century shortlister.' Jemimah had reappeared behind me, sans iPad, *avec* protein ball.

'Well, no need to introduce you, Rhiannon, your reputation goes before you,' Tony chuckled. 'How you doing?' Cue unauthorised body contact #1 – shoulder rub.

'Yeah, I'm fine, thanks.'

'It's *so* lovely to meet you, Rhiannon,' said Carolyn, smiling like a grand piano. Her face was caked in foundation but there were bumps all over it. 'What do you prefer to be called?'

'Rhiannon's fine,' I said. Rhiannon was what I always wanted to be called but most people insisted on saying Rhee to save time. Linus once called me Rheetard and I nearly yanked his head back and spat in his mouth.

'We'll be gentle with you, we promise!' Tony heh-heh-hehed. My eyes were fixed so concretely on his face so as not to look down to What Lies Beneath, they were almost watering. I think they took it as nervousness, causing Tony to commit unauthorised body contact #2 – supportive forearm grab and accidental boob stroke. Ugh.

'So our womb lady's stuck on the bridge in Cardiff, which means her item's been shifted to tomorrow. You're on after the quiche but before the boy band, OK?'

They ran through the in-depth questions they would ask me in the three-and-a-half-minute slot – there's no time for tragedy when there's a three-cheese quiche in the oven, after all – and I was parked in the Green Room, to sign release forms, have my microphone clipped on and await my fate. After a fidgety age, Jemimah Double-Barrelled came and got me and we walked down a purgatory of white corridors to the studio.

The set looked more of a headachy pink and yellow colour in real life than it did in HD, like someone had puked Rainbow Skittles over it. The edges of the floor were covered with long snaking black wires and large portable cameras wheeled around back in the shadows and forth in a strange robotic dance. Carolyn and Tony were in situ and I was ushered to sit down opposite on the famous fuchsia-pink banquette. All I could smell was burnt cheese.

'OK, Rhiannon,' said Tony, 'so we'll run the competition

trailer and then come to you, all right? Try not to fidget, stammer or sneeze and if you feel a cough coming on, there's a carafe of water there and yours will be poured out. All right? And don't swear or else we get shot by them upstairs.' Heh heh heh.

'Don't say "fuck" or "bugger",' I mimicked.

They looked at me like I'd doused them both with petrol and was about to strike a match.

'Sorry. It's OK, I won't swear.'

Before I knew what was happening, the lights were brighter, a chubby brunette with drawn-on eyebrows had run on to sweep my forehead with a fuzzy brush, the end of the competition whinnied away and a camera wheeled forward.

'Welcome back,' said Carolyn. 'This month we've been meeting our contenders for Woman of the Century and, in the last instalment, we are profiling Rhiannon Lewis, the young survivor of the Priory Gardens attack. This year marks the twenty-first anniversary of the tragedy when a man entered childminder Allison Kingwell's house in a small Bristol suburb and brutally murdered her, along with five of the children she was looking after.'

Tony took over. 'When police arrived at the house in Bradley Stoke, what they found was a scene of absolute horror. Not only did they find Ms Kingwell's body, but also the tiny lifeless bodies of one-year-old Kimmy Lloyd, two-year-old Jack Mitchell, three-year-old twins George and David Archer and five-year-old Ashlea Riley-House. Also dead was the perpetrator, 37-year-old Antony Blackstone, the estranged husband of Ms Kingwell, who had taken his own life.'

The baton went back to Carolyn. 'Amazingly, one child, Rhiannon Lewis, survived against all odds, having been struck with a hammer. She lay silently beneath Ms Kingwell's decapitated body for hours. Today, the house at Priory Gardens no longer stands as it did, replaced instead by a playground, and Rhiannon herself is now twenty-seven years old and fully recovered from her ordeal. And we're delighted to welcome her into the studio today. Rhiannon, thanks so much for coming in.'

'Thank you for having me.'

I could see my face on the monitor on the edge of the floor. Jeez they'd put a lot of blusher on. I looked like I had red light bulbs stuffed in my cheeks.

'Rhiannon, take us back to that day if you can. Do you remember anything about it?'

'No, nothing before the attack,' I said. 'Only what people have told me and what the witnesses said.'

They were both nodding, like they should be on a shelf in the back of a car. Tony's legs opened like the gates to Jurassic Park. The T. rex bulged at the seam. It was All. I. Could. Look. At. I'd need a chainsaw to chop down *that* trunk.

'So you don't remember the moment Blackstone got into the house?'

'No. Apparently, he knocked at the front door and Allison told him to get lost, and then a neighbour saw him go round the back and jump over the garden wall and try the lock on the patio doors. That's when he smashed the glass.'

'With hammers?' said Tony.

'Yeah, I guess.'

Carolyn took over with a heavy sigh. 'Let's take a little look at this VT which might help shed some more light on that traumatic day.'

They cut to the same old montage of people laying posies and teddies outside number 12 Priory Gardens, old women crying and holding tissues to their noses. The vox pop of two old men saying how it was such a close community, how 'nothing like this has ever happened round here before'. The glistening red doormat. Wailing fathers. Sobbing mums. Three little stretchers. The policeman talking about the 'unprecedented situation'. My limp body, wrapped in Peter Rabbit blankets.

I was sweating through my Bare Minerals.

Just before the VT finished, someone in the darkness beyond the psychedelic sofas called out: 'And we're back in three, two, one...'

Carolyn and Tony's faces were painted with a new expression of anguish.

'Rhiannon, I can't imagine how this must have affected you. Can you give us a flavour of what life's been like for you since that tragic day?'

Flavour? I thought. *What? Like some days I'm smoky bacon, others a little more ready salted, that kind of thing?* No, no time for facetiousness, this was important and sad and important.

'Well, my parents did interviews with all the tabloids and I went on some talk shows. They flew me over for this American one and they gave us an all-expenses paid holiday to Disney World. You can still see the clip on YouTube. The whole audience is crying. I just sound like I'm broken.'

'How long did it take for you to learn to walk and talk again?'

'Um, I don't think I was fully restored until my early teens. I virtually had to relearn everything. How to talk to people, how to move. How to be. I found it very hard. For the things I didn't know, I developed a kind of act for them.'

'In what sort of way?'

'Well, my mum used to worry that I never cried when I fell over and I stopped hugging her. She'd say to me, "Why aren't you more upset? Why aren't you crying?" and then I'd try and remember that was what I was supposed to do for next time.'

Carolyn reached forward to the coffee table and grabbed the tissue box, plucking one out to dab at her eye. 'Rhiannon, I'm sorry, this story always gets to me.'

Try starring in it, love.

Tony leaned in to the rescue. 'It was the front of your brain which was affected by the hammer blow, wasn't it?'

'Mmm, yeah, the ventromedial prefrontal cortex. Frontal lobe. I had a lot of surgery to repair my skull. I have this large zig-zaggy scar behind my hairline.'

'Like Harry Potter?'

'Not as neat as that.'

Tony checked his script. 'The police said the whole attack only lasted a few minutes. Does anything bring memories or images back to you?'

He reeeeeeally wanted some dirt; some bit of gore to share exclusively with the world that the nation could chew over with their soggy Shreddies – how a child's skull makes a noise like a vase smashing when it's hit with a hammer; how the sound of a glass smashing even now can cause me to break out in a cold sweat; how Blackstone's hanging body was the last thing I saw before I lost consciousness.

'No,' I lied. 'Mercifully, I don't remember any of it.'

They were speechless. I ventured a look downwards – Tony's trouser seam was bursting with the pressure. Surely no material could hold back that penal tide.

'You won Child of Courage and Pride of Britain Awards, didn't you?'

'Yeah. That was nice.'

The Pride of Britain one had snapped in half in the back of the taxi after the ceremony. I couldn't remember what had happened with the Children of Courage one. Last time I'd seen it, it was in a box in Mum and Dad's garage.

'It must have been such a traumatic time for your family. In fact, your life's been quite peppered with tragedy ever since, hasn't it?' said Carolyn.

'Yes,' I said, not venturing further information.

'You lost a young friend in a car accident when you were still in recovery from Priory Gardens, didn't you? Little Joe Leech, when you lived in Bristol?'

I nodded. 'Yeah, he got run over. He'd been coming to visit me.'

'And your mother died of breast cancer when you were in your teens? And your father from brain cancer just two years ago?'

It was a bit of a non sequitur. I guess they were building up the public sympathy a bit more and waiting for the waterworks. Carolyn pushed the box of tissues along the banquette towards me, just in case.

Good luck with that.

Tony readjusted his position – he was sitting on at least half of his dick, I surmised. That can't have been comfortable for three hours on a daily basis. I could almost feel sorry for him, if he hadn't had reached out to pat my knee – unauthorised body contact #3.

'Yeah, death seems to have a thing for my family,' I said. 'Everyone just seems to leave me. I mean, I had a few years of warning with Mum. But with Dad it was weeks. Out of the blue.'

Tony nodded. 'That must have been a massive shock for you.'

'Yes, it was a massive cock,' I said, without even realising what I'd said until they both looked at me in abject terror. 'Shock, shock, yeah,' I said, like I'd just stuttered and was trying to claw back the blush blooming in both my cheeks. I attempted some firefighting: 'I was totally in shock about it for weeks. We had photographers camped in our front garden like I was a celebrity, which didn't make things easier. Funny sort of celebrity.'

Tony's bald patch burnt a greasy red. I could see the cogs going in his head – *Don't laugh, don't laugh, career suicide, career suicide, dead kids, dead kids!*

Carolyn had to do the rest of the segment alone with the camera focused squarely on her rock-hard expression. 'But things are going well for you now, aren't they?' She was clearly desperate for a whiff of a happy ending amidst all the doom and cock shrapnel in the cheesy air. Less skull-crushing, more yay. 'You've got your lovely boyfriend and a brilliant job in journalism?'

'Yes, that's right. Everything is... awesome.'

Journalism? Is that what we're calling it now? Yeah, everything's really awesome now, Carolyn: my journalistic career begins and ends with making coffee and typing up skittles scores, my novel has been rejected by every agent and publisher in the country, my boyfriend's having an affair with a cum bucket called Lana, I think about killing someone every twenty-five minutes, I hate all my friends and I've just made a twat of myself on national TV. Yeah, everything's gravy, baby.

When I didn't offer up any more information, she glared at me like I was the Goth girl with the pierced clit who'd announced she was marrying her son. I think she was beginning to wish that hammer had struck my frontal lobe a bit harder.

'And how do you feel about being up for Woman of the Century?'

I smiled. 'Oh, yeah, I'm thrilled. It's an amazing honour. I'm so excited about the ceremony tonight and all the people I'll meet.' I saw my face in the monitor. I really needed to work on my smile. It was as wooden as my grandmother's sideboard.

Tony had composed himself, though he was pretty red in the face still. 'Is your boyfriend proud of you?' Cue lecherous glint. Even though it wasn't bodily contact, I felt like he'd wiped his bell-end all over my face.

'Yeah, he's delighted.'

'What's his name? Give him a shout-out.'

'Craig.' I looked to the camera. 'Hi, Craig.' I imagined him and Lana waving to the TV at the end of our bed, lying in post-coital stickiness, smoking endless joints.

'Aww, that's lovely,' said Carolyn. 'Well, the best of luck for tonight, Rhiannon. We'll be cheering you on, have no fear.' It was clear that they'd cut my interview very short. They'd have to stick on a few more sofa adverts in the break.

'Yes, thanks, Rhiannon,' said Tony, and did his old man wink, and I risked one final glance down at the peen seam. The anaconda had a baby while I wasn't looking.

'Thanks for having me.' I smiled confidently.

Carolyn and Tony turned to the camera. 'We'll see you after the break, when we'll be talking about the rise in the number of nursery-school children downloading Internet porn, Michelin-star chef Scottie Callender will be in the kitchen with his three-cheese quiche and we might find time to have a chat to these young fellas…'

Four pre-pubic teen boys bounced onto the sofa from behind, scaring the crap out of me and knocking over the bowl of croissants on the coffee table.

Carolyn giggled like a drain as the lead singer and official fittest one, Joey, apologised and gave her a kiss on the cheek.

'Yes, Boytox, the YouTube-born boy band taking the world by storm at the moment, are here to chat about their sell-out world tour. We'll see you in three,' she said to camera, fanning herself theatrically. The saxophone music signalled we were clear and it felt like the whole studio breathed a sweet sigh of relief.

The youngest Boytox member, who wore glasses, stank of Emporio Armani and would certainly be the first one to announce he was gay, sat next to me. He put his heavily tattooed arm around me. 'I loved the interview. So cool that you, like, didn't die and stuff.'

I could have killed them all, one by one, right there on the fuchsia banquette.

Tuesday, 6 February

So I didn't win. Malala beat me into a cocked hat. Oh, and there *was* a second and third place and I didn't get either of them. One of the cancer women came second. The foster mum got bronze. Taliban trumps cancer. Cancer trumps hammer-wielding maniac. So, as it turns out, I'm not the big kahuna when it comes to heroism. And though my photo will appear in *Take a Break* magazine alongside all the other nominees, it turns out being the only kid at the crèche not to die from a hammer blow to the skull isn't *that* big a big deal.

The ceremony was at this massive opulent hotel in Soho. I'm terrible at schmoozing at the best of times so for the most part I stayed in a corner staring at my phone, filling my mouth with green olives so I wouldn't have to make conversation.

When I got into work this morning, it was a different story. I lied my little ass off. How I'd got a selfie with Gary Barlow and some tart from *Loose Women* (it was on *her* phone, which was why I couldn't show them). How I'd heard one of the footballers finger-banging one of the *TOWIE* lot in the lavs. How two celeb hairdressers snorted coke at the bar. How the presenters of the wildlife programme had a tiff over peanuts. How this actor tripped over some woman's Gucci dress, how that actress stumbled into a taxi and everyone saw her stench trench.

Oh, yah, I was all OVER the gossip, *dah*-ling.

The unvarnished truth was that I made a sharp exit the moment they read out the results to catch the rape o'clock train home. No man made a move though, much to my chagrin. Always the same when you're all knifed up and ready to go.

By 9:14 a.m., they'd all moved on anyway. And the empty space on the shelf above my desk, which I'd dusted clear to make room for my award, was filled with complaints about litter, press releases and some local farmer's self-published memoirs for me to do a feature on. I really needed that fucking award. The only praise I ever get is when Hotmail tells me I've got a very clean inbox.

It sucks major BALLS.

AJ was asking me about it on and off all day, bless him. I'm starting to like him again. He holds the door open for me, makes me peanut butter and banana on toast and hates Linus almost as much as I do. Linus gives him nicknames as well – Apache Junction, Angelina Jolie, Aussie Jim. Unfortunately, though, he has Claudia's boring gene and I had to hear all about his life back in 'Straya' with his teacher mum and mechanic stepdad. How his dad left him when he was five and how long it took him to learn to surf, how he doesn't like Vegemite despite the stereotype, how his high school had a terrorist attack once and how wondrous the sunsets are where he lives. He also calls charity shops 'op shops'. His breath smells good too – no aftertang. Minty. I watch his neck pulse sometimes when he's talking to me.

As of 8.31 p.m. this evening, #UpAttheCock is *still* trending on Twitter. So is #WomanOfTheCentury. I'm not mentioned in any of those tweets though. It's mostly about Ant and Dec's radical new facial hair. Typical.

Wednesday, 7 February

1. *The entire human race. Even the ones not born yet who are just poised in the birth canal, ready to come out and piss me off*

I woke up in a chronic mood, which wasn't unusual given the dreams I have, but what *was* unusual was that *every* single itty-bitty thing was annoying me. Even Tink, and she was usually the one thing that didn't. I tripped over her twice getting dressed so I shouted at her. Then I felt bad and she crawled up my lower leg, begging for a pick-up so she could lick my face.

There was an uncertain feeling in my chest at work all day long, clenching like sharp teeth. I wanted to kill again.

Carol the sub was in the staffroom when I went to make the coffees.

'That AJ's got himself a bit of a crush on you,' she told me, with a conspiratorial stir of her camomile.

'On me?' I said. 'Why?'

She laughed. 'You'll have to ask him, won't you?'

I shrugged. 'How do you know?'

'He was asking me if you had a better half.'

'What did you tell him?'

'I said he should ask you himself. Do you like him?'

'Maybe,' I said. 'He could come in useful somewhere.'

She shrieked at that, only it took me a while to realise she thought I meant that as a pun. I truly didn't. 'Watch out for Claudia though. She'll be on the warpath if you're found defiling her nephew. She keeps a pretty close eye on him.'

'I know,' I said. 'I'm surprised she doesn't make him work in a little cat basket under her desk.'

Cue another deafening shriek.

Talking of the Gulp Monster, Claudia wants me to do my own write up on the *Up At the Crack* interview – The Editorial Assistant's Eye View – as opposed to the Editor's Comment next week.

'There's a little moment in the sun for you, sweetpea,' she said with a smile so patronising it could strip paint.

Whoopee Shit. It'll be squeezed between a half-page advert for sixty years of Darlington Caravans and a story about a dead World War Two carrier pigeon someone found up their chimney. She can suck my mammaries till Michaelmas if she thinks I'm going to be grateful for that, gigantic bag of crabs that she is.

Joyless Joy slurped her tea all morning. The comment about my personal appearance today was 'What's the matter with your legs in those leggings? You couldn't stop a pig in a passage.' I still very hate her too.

There's been a robbery at the One Stop, so the reporters were all over that this afternoon. Other than that, nothing else is making headlines. Same old, same old. There's the upcoming fifty-year anniversary of the wildlife sanctuary and a hit-and-run on the retail park and they're trying to get hold of the family of a teen who live-streamed her suicide on Periscope because she used to live in the area so, technically, she's ours. No luck yet though.

Canal Bloke's death isn't worrying anyone much. I asked

Linus about it, more as a decoy – AJ was replacing his lip gloss with a joke one. We have a little wager between us – who can prank him the best.

I made it through about a third of my emails when I noticed one from Curly Sue herself – Laila at Tanner & Walker, the estate agent who had once tried to sell Mum and Dad's house and failed like a whale trying to shag a snail.

Tried to reach you on your landline but no answer. Could you give me a call first thing? Thanks.

I called straight away.

'Rhiannon! Oh, great to finally reach you!' she shrilled, so much fake she could bake a fake cake. 'I was trying to get hold of you all day yesterday.'

'I had my mobile on,' I said.

'Yeah, I tried it. There was still no answer.'

'Oh.' I frowned. So she was a bullshitter as well as a crap estate agent. Hmmm.

'Anyway, we've had a new offer on your mum and dad's place. Full asking price and no chain. How's about that? It's almost unheard of at this time of year.'

'Uh, I took it off the market months ago,' I said, heart quietly thumping away.

'Yes, I know, but the couple who looked at it last August – the Pembrokes – have found nothing else they liked and they went back to have another look…'

'When did they go back for another look?'

'They were in the area last week and drove past.'

'They had no right to.' I flicked a couple of Vs down the phone. Childish? Yes, but I was panicking.

'They didn't go in or anything, just looked at the drive and the frontage.'

'So they were sniffing around the property without permission, is that even legal?'

'No, it wasn't like that at all. They just happened to be in the area and swung by the place. They liked the idea of the woods at the back as they have four quite big dogs. They'd like another look inside if you're still looking to sell?'

'Well, I'm not. I'm not ready. Nowhere near ready.'

'They're pretty keen, Rhiannon. You'd be hard-pressed to find—'

'No, it's not happening. I took it off the market for the foreseeable future and I haven't changed my mind about that.' I grabbed my bottle of Gaviscon from my desk drawer. I swigged down two glugs and winced at the chalkiness.

'But your sister—'

'I don't care about my sister,' I shouted, garnering a couple of glances from the subs on the other side of the room. 'She's a billion miles away.'

'Okaaay,' said Laila. 'But you'll find that she has half…'

'You've no right to even contact me any more.'

'Rhiannon, I can assure you—'

I put the phone down without saying goodbye. Brutal.

I swigged again at the Gaviscon. Sodding, sodding, sodding ARSE. I mean, yes, half of £825,000 would come in handy. And yes, I knew it would 'make a great family home or a wonderful rural retirement opportunity' for two old codgers with a sit-on mower and nothing else to do but moan about the migrants.

But of course I had to deal with Julia.

After that, yeah sure, bring it on. I'll bake an apple tart and we can have an open house. Let's get the whole neighbourhood round for a coffee and a stroke of my curtains. Only just let me get rid of the woman tied up in the back bedroom first.

I swigged the Gaviscon again but it was empty.

Normally, I put up with stuff. Keep my mouth shut and moan inwardly or write it down. But today, something had shifted. I don't know if it had been due to talking about Priory Gardens again or what but my anger was off the charts. I needed to go fishing again. I needed to get out. I needed to find Derek Scudd.

This town isn't that big – he has to be somewhere, the maggot.

*

Lana went on lunch at 1.05. Today, I followed her.

I heard them as I snuck my way in through the front door and across the lounge. The bedroom door was ajar and I could see they were both naked. She was on all fours. He was at the end of the bed, thrusting against her. She was making a noise like a dying seal being repeatedly, well, fucked up the arse. He never put as much effort into it when *we* were doing it. He put more oomph into Artexing the kitchen.

I heard Tink then; an intermittent squeak coming from the bathroom. He'd locked her in so he could screw that bitch on my bed. OK, so Tink had a habit of getting in the way when me and Craig were having sex – I think she thought he was hurting me – but locking her in the bathroom? That's just evil.

I couldn't kill them both – that would be too quick and easy. And I couldn't let Tink out of the bathroom either cos then they would know I'd been home.

So I went back to the office via the small chemist where my Pill prescription was and I loaded up on more Gaviscon. Next door was Granny Smiths the grocer's – where I impulse-bought a bag of apples and some Conference pears. I needed something hard to crunch on while I thought about them doing it on my Tempur Sensation Deluxe mattress.

Lana reappeared in the office at 2.03 p.m., flushed of cheek, sex-hair brushed back – my boyfriend's cum puddle cooling in the crotch of her knickers. I wondered if she'd been the one to lock my dog in my bathroom before presenting her slick behind to my boyfriend. I wonder if Craig had remembered to let Tink out before he went back to work, stinking of Avon perfume and Marlboro Lights.

I bumped into her in the staffroom around 3 p.m. when I went up to make the drinks for AJ, who was taking meeting minutes. She smiled at me, I smiled back and then we had a little staring competition. I won.

Linus finished the day with blue lips and had to go into the office for a meeting with Ron about the murders, which can't have looked very professional. AJ and I laughed ourselves out of the building.

Tink scampered across the floor to greet me when I got in at 6 p.m. She seemed unscathed but desperate to lick my face and dog-tell me what Daddy had been up to in my absence. When I went in there, I noticed there was a small pile of treats that Craig had obviously left in an attempt to keep her quiet. Chihuahuas are loyal to their owners – she never eats until I'm home. He was making my favourite dinner – steak and peppercorn sauce, presumably so he could sizzle the smell of Lana's ass out of the flat. Red meat? You think it's a good idea to give me red meat tonight, boy?

'Post for you,' he said, looking up from the breakfast bar as he chopped green peppers. I could smell pot too – there were two joint dog-ends in the coffee table ashtray. One has the faintest tinge of hot pink at the end.

I checked my three letters – bank statement, circular, another agent rejection, this time from Thickett & Wump. *Dear Madam, Thank you for allowing us to consider your novel,* The Alibi Clock. *Unfortunately…*

Tink was still licking the epidermis from my cheek as I watched Craig tossing the salad and opening the Pinot Noir. He held it up for me to see the label.

'Nice.'

'Bit more expensive but it's a good cut of meat so it deserves it. Good day?'

'Yes, thanks,' I said, picturing the perfect spot in the woods behind Mum and Dad's house where I could bury him.

'What you looking at me like that for?' He smiled.

'Oh, just thinking how much I love you, that's all.'

And how I'd finally worked out what to do with Dan Wells's severed cock.

Monday, 12 February

1. *Creepy Ed Sheeran in Lidl's car park, who today jumped out of the bushes in front of my car wearing a Bazinga T-shirt*
2. *People who wear Bazinga T-shirts*
3. *Woman with the two brown spaniels who always attack Tink and are never on leads – though today she said good morning for the first time when I accidentally made eye contact*

Nothing more's been said about Canal Man. There's not been any teary-eyed relatives in the office, having tea and sympathy with Ron and Linus or even a public appeal to find his penis. It's most odd. I asked around.

'Have the police found out anything about that guy in the canal, Claudia?'

'No,' she sighed. 'Most grisly. They still haven't found it.' She looked up. 'Why, did you know him? I know your other half is some sort of electrician, isn't he?'

'He's a builder. Actually, by trade he's a—'

'Oh, Johnny, great, have you got those run-outs for me?' she interjected.

Johnny, one of the photographers, had appeared behind me, camera as big as my head around his neck. They chatted and it took me a minute to realise that my part in this conversation, if I'd ever had one, was over.

I didn't like any of the photographers at the *Gazette* – Stuart, Brian and Johnny. They were all arrogant tit flannels, swanning around the place like rock stars, fat in the knowledge that the party don't start till they walk in.

I asked Bogdan the receptionist if he'd received an obituary from Daniel Wells' parents. All the reporters were now calling him 'Dan', like they knew him. Like they *liked* him. Like they'd had barbecues in his garden or he'd installed Sky TV for them at a knock-down price. I even heard Edmund say, 'Golly, poor chap.' No obituary yet though. Bogdan doesn't flirt with me any more I've noticed. Obviously his asylum application came through and he's allowed to stay.

Dan Dan, the Dickless Man, as henceforth, he shall be known.

Left work early so I could take Tink to the park to play ball. I felt I'd been neglecting her of late and she's such a good dog, she deserves more attention. Tried to teach her Shake a Paw for the millionth time, to no avail. Then we snuggled on the sofa and to watch *The Simpsons* on Sky.

Craig invited round the usual suspects tonight – Eddie, Gary and Nigel – for a gourmet evening of *Call of Duty*, lager and live football. Fridays used to be my Pilates nights but I gave that up a few months back when I realised spending an hour in a room full impossibly thin women stretching and farting along to Enya wasn't a good use of my time. On football nights, I'd sit at the dining table, eating Revels and 'working on my novel'. More often than not, I was on Facebook or in the chat rooms.

The chat rooms are where weirdos congregate like frog spawn and feminism died with a boot in its neck. I call myself Sweetpea and play the part of the confident slut. There's never a shortage of takers for my filthy bravado and I've been known to bring men to climax with just a few choice words. Of course, the men were all the lowest specimens of the gene pool – sad, hunched-over beardy types who would ask for photos when their wives were out of the room and send me short video clips of the moment they tugged themselves to ecstasy over my pics. It's a cheap thrill. I get them where I can.

Tonight I tried something I'd never done – I pretended to be a guy. I sent them some of Craig's nakes off my phone. They couldn't get enough of me. It was a whole new experience and, I have to say, I had fun. Almost wish I had a penis. One of my own, I mean.

Meanwhile, four other penises congregated on my sofa. Eddie O'Connell was a failed professional footballer, now a trainee solicitor, and is distantly related to Raheem Sterling (he says). He can speak five languages. Including English, unlike Gary.

Gary fancies me, which is unfortunate because he has a face like a smashed egg. He'll drop hints like, 'I love your dress, Rhiannon,' and [when watching *Saw 3*], 'You're so brave – I don't know how you can watch this without wincing.' Yes, I am curiously sangfroid when it comes to others experiencing pain. Well, it's not happening to me, is it? Why would I wince? Thanks for noticing anyway, you patronising, mouse-dicked mother-humper from Sodom. He also says I'm funny, 'which is so unusual for a girl'. I say Gary's a twat, 'which is not so unusual for a boy'. He has a window sticker in his motorhome that says NO JAFFA CAKES KEPT IN THIS VEHICLE OVERNIGHT. I'm just going to leave that one hanging, like Gary should be.

Nigel Yardley looks like a large ball of Play-Doh with a smaller ball of Play-Doh stuck on top. Just looking at his beach-ball stomach had me taping down my Revels for another night. He has a decorating business and his own van – NYPD

EMERGENCY it says on the side. Who needs something decorated in an emergency? 'Help! Someone! Please! My wallpaper's come unstuck and my dado's crooked!' And don't get me started on the apostrophe in 'Fascias'.

'Rooooooaaaaaaaarrrrrrrrrggggggghhhhhh!!!!!!!!!!!!!!' came the cheers from Sofa Land as some winger landed a diving header, sending Tink flying off my lap, barking her little apple head off. They all squawked with laughter.

I checked the news pages for updates on Daniel Wells' watery end. No witnesses yet, the missing tallywhacker hasn't turned up and a third man they brought in for questioning has been released without charge. The police don't seem to have a clue. Dear dear dear.

'Rooooooaaaaaaaarrrrrrrrrggggggghhhhhh!!!!!!!!!!!!!!'

'Caw bloody hell, he left it wide open!'

'Plays like a bloody girl.'

'Referee needs a chuffing guide dog, that was *well* offside, that!'

Now I may have mentioned before that I don't like loud noises. Not loud noises, not raucous football enthusiasm, not fireworks. Or when someone drops a plate. My nerves just start frying beneath my skin. When I couldn't take any more of their armchair punditry, I adorned Craig's DMs and announced I was taking Tink for a long walk. By this point they were all pretty drunk and I don't think Craig even heard me.

It was quiet out. I passed Mrs Whittaker in the bin shed, throwing various black bin bags into their correct holes. We traded 'Evening's' and 'Isn't it warm outs?'s and for once she didn't try to nick anything from me.

I checked my phone at 9.43 p.m., as I reached the traffic lights by the supermarket. All seemed oh-so quiet. Half an hour passed and nothing, nobody about.

But soon I sensed a tug on the end of my line – someone was

following me. I got out a poo bag and bent down to pick up Tink's offering in the grass, lingering as I did, watching him. Definitely a Him. He stopped by the bus stop, lit up a cigarette. He was about average height but stocky – at least sixteen stone. Could be a tricky one. I pushed the poo bag in a litter bin, and carried on walking, breathless.

He started walking too, lit cigarette in hand. He wore a black beanie and his coat collar was pulled up around his neck, like it was cold out, which it wasn't. I only had a hoody and tracky bottoms on but I was boiling. It crossed my mind that he might not be following me – that my sense of self-preservation was too strong – but my suspicions were confirmed as I crossed the road towards the park. There was a shady bit with trees. A cycle path. No kids out, smoking in the bandstand or on skateboards. I was all alone and breathless with anticipation.

I could feel it about to happen. My body tingled and my lungs heaved with the expectation of it. I dropped Tink's lead and she wandered off to sniff a lamppost.

And then it *did* happen – he pounced on me from behind, grabbing my chin with one strong hand and my waist with the other. Tink barked right on cue.

'Don't scream or I'll kill your dog.'

'OK,' I said. 'Don't hurt me. Don't hurt me.'

He dragged me backwards towards the bushes. Tink yapped and growled her loudest but he wasn't paying her any attention. My heart was racing and that was pushing the adrenalin around, getting me going. My knickers were already soaking.

He had an accent. 'Stop wriggling. Let it 'appen and you won't get 'urt.'

Tink growled and gnashed her tiny teeth at his ankle hems. That was helping me too. I was so alive with the sensation of what he wanted to do to me – the feeling of his huge rough hands on my breasts – my knees almost gave out, but I had to stay standing. Tink snarled and yapped and I knew what he was going to do next and it wasn't until he did it that I reacted.

He kicked her. He kicked my dog.

More a *Get off, you're annoying me kick* than one truly intended to hurt her. But she yelped and rolled squeaking into the long grass. And that was what it took to wake up the monster within me.

I pulled the wallpaper scissors from my hoody and thrust the blades deep into his neck – one, two, three times, right up to the hilt. The kinetic energy of my sexual thrill ignited into pure focused wrath. Blood spurted and sprayed across my face in hot dabs. He gulped and he gulped and stepped back from me, eyes bulging out and hands loosening their grip on me. I pulled the scissors out and the blood ran down his neck, down into the blackness of his coat. My hand was covered in it. The scissors were covered too. I stepped back and allowed him to stagger, falling to the footpath. I wanted to mount him. I wanted to strad-dle him as he lay dying, put his dying hands on my breasts and have him hold me there but I knew I couldn't go near him now. There couldn't be anything on him that would lead back to me.

Tink was trying to climb up my leg for a pick-up, so I took her in my arms and she began frantically licking my face, shivering so violently I nearly dropped her. Still breathless, still watching him, I held out my bloody hand for her to lick. We stood over the man, watching his gargles and spits of bloody pain into the night air. I watched the last of his breaths cloud above him, his dick still erect in undone jeans.

Jesus Christ was I turned on.

I didn't cut off the penis this time. It's not a trophy thing with me. That would be stupid, like the burglars who always leave the taps on in *Home Alone*. Besides, where would I put them all? We've only got a two-bed flat. It was hard enough deciding where to put the dehumidifier.

I don't even remember walking back to the flats because I was on such a high, nothing else mattered. I don't remember getting in the car, or the entire drive to Mum and Dad's house.

Julia called out to me. I unlocked the door to the back bedroom and flicked on the light, standing in the doorway and allowing the full horror of how I looked to dawn on her face. First she winced with the brightness. Then she screamed when she saw the blood.

'I need a shower,' I announced. 'If you don't stop fucking screaming, I will do the same to you. And feed you to my chihuahua.'

*

I'm at home now. Balanced. Restored. Clean. Craig and the lads had done their usual thing of going down Wetherspoon's for last orders and a 'cheeky kebab on the way home' so undoubtedly the flat will stink of his lamby farts tomorrow morning. I don't even care tonight. Seriously, the power trip you get when you take a life – you just feel better. All the other shit washes away. Tink's sitting on the end of my bed now, looking at me with her ears down. She's still damp from our shower at Mum and Dad's. She just keeps looking at me. I wish I knew what she was thinking.

Tuesday, 13 February

1. *Man with hipster beard and pierced eyebrow, who pushed in front of me in Starbucks and asked for a gingerbread latte and a babyccino*
2. *Woman who bumped into me in Lidl and told me to say sorry*
3. *Dillon on the checkout in Lidl, who today said, 'Cheer up, might never happen.' I could have shanked his ribs*

No nightmare tonight. A dreamless sleep and a refreshing cup of coffee by my head when I woke up. Craig even made me a smoked salmon bagel without being asked and, when I was in the shower, screaming along to Beyoncé, he came in and we had stand-up sex against the tiles which was uncharacteristically hot for us. I was still buzzing from the park attack so I could easily close my eyes and imagine I was still there, being grabbed. I came quickly, for once, still panting along to 'Beautiful Liar'.

Then came work and it sucked major cheesy balls. My usual car park was full up so I had to park a mile away and, when I finally got in, I found the entire office gathered around in a semicircle, welcoming the new girl.

The new junior reporter.

Even Jeff was applauding her.

They'd given the job to a wet – fresh out of journalism school – who'd applied for the job before Christmas. Daisy Chan – quite the thinnest woman I've ever seen. She's neat, recherché, speaks six languages, got twelve GCSEs and has already won a junior reporting award at *Valley News*. I was too busy seething to listen to Ron's welcome speech or her thank you speech. It was all the same platitudes anyway. All 'so grateful' and 'amazing' and 'overwhelmed to be part of the family' blah blah blah de fapping blah.

Of course I had to say something and, when they'd all finished giving her a clit-licking, I knocked on Ron's door and didn't wait for the Come In.

'Ah, Rhianna, I was going to call you in, my dear.'

No, that's not a typo. Three years I've been here and he *still* calls me Rhianna. I shut the door and sat down, my rage bubbling close to the edge of my human cauldron but I was in no mood to turn down the burner.

'I understand this might be difficult for you but I feel firmly that Daisy is the best person for the job. She has her qualification now and she's had two years' experience on the big stories at *Valley News*.'

'*Valley News!*' I spat. 'It's hardly the *Telegraph*.'

'When you're more experienced and you've done your diploma then you can think about more regular features. I know you were a bit sore about the Riot Lovers piece...'

'Yeah, because Linus stole my byline.'

Ron closed his eyes and sat back in his chair, only opening them again when his mouth had cracked into a smile. 'It was *his* byline. He wrote the piece.'

'Yes, using *my* photo.'

'Even so...'

'EVEN SO NOTHING,' I shouted. Ron looked around his windows to see if anyone outside had heard. Nobody was even looking up from their computers. I tried deep breathing but all I could think was grabbing his silver letter opener and leaping across his desk to manically stab him all over. 'That was *my* scoop, Ron... Mr Ron... Mr Pondicherry. I took that photo. *I'm* the one who sits in on all the court hearings, *I* type up all the golden weddings, *I'm* the one who had to run alongside Will.I.Am when he turned up to do the half-marathon for the hospital scanner. Me, not Linus or Claudia or Daisy. *Me.*'

'I understand,' he said again.

'No you don't,' I interrupted, hand steadying myself on the door for fear of falling over with all the rage bubbling up like violently shaken lemonade.

'The riot story is a hot potato at the moment,' Ron explained. 'It needs solid, unbiased coverage. With all respect, I can't just give it to the editorial assistant. It's too much responsibility. I'd be letting you down, wouldn't I?'

I felt like a toddler who'd had her lolly taken away because it would spoil her appetite. I folded my arms.

'Let's make a deal,' said Ron. 'I'll give you your own column on the entertainment page where we have the cinema listings and the gig guide. You can have your own name on it. And in that column you can talk about whatever it is you want, aimed directly at teenagers. We'll call it... "Teen Talk". Or "The Buzz". How about "The Buzz on the Street"?'

'Children's film reviews? You're giving me children's film reviews?'

'What do you want from me, Rhianna? Do you want me to make you a senior reporter because you've typed up a few cricket scores and reviewed a vegan restaurant? You're going to have to learn your craft, dear. Climb the ladder. Pay your dues. You can't jump straight in with the big guns like Linus and Claudia. They've put in the time, the years, risen through the ranks and so will you.'

'What about next year? Might you sponsor me next year instead?'

Ron sighed. If he'd been a dragon, I'd have been a burn mark on the carpet. 'If you want to cultivate a career here, you're going to have to do things *our* way. That means Linus and Claudia and the seniors tell you to jump, you ask how high. They ask you to get their sandwiches, you ask what fillings. They tell you to watch every Kate Hudson movie ever made and review it for your film page, you do that.'

'Now you're pushing it.'

He smiled. 'Are we singing from the same hymn sheet here?'

I nodded, breathing out long and slow. It was time for The Act to begin. I'd harnessed my rage and stroked its neck and given it a raw parsnip to gnaw on. 'I'm sorry. It's just I care so much.'

'That's good,' he said, getting up, fists raised. 'Passion. Fight. That's what I like to see. You'll make a great reporter someday. But for now...'

'Pay my dues.'

He nodded and held the door open for me. 'And coffee two sugars when you're ready, thanks, Rhianna.'

Slam! He was never ever going to fund my diploma, was he? Never going to make me a junior reporter. I knew then that it didn't matter how assiduous my work ethic, how often I stayed late, what I did to impress them. My face just didn't fit. My sartorial choices would always be Primark in the shadow of their Armani. I would forever be 'just the receptionist'.

So, basically, work and everyone there can go fuck themselves into a coma. At lunchtime, I spent twenty minutes in the toilets gouging a hole in the wall behind the cistern because

I fucking fucking fucking HATE THEM.

Daisy Chan is off doing stories about murders and drugs busts while I'm stuck with the WI meetings, pothole protests and flashers while chugging Gaviscon like wedding champagne. Oh, sorry, I forgot, I'm now doing the children's film reviews too, aren't I? First up: some dystopian nightmare featuring a girl in too-tight clothes who saves the world from a man in too-tight clothes so she can shag a boy in too-tight clothes. I want to put bombs under all their desks.

Daisy brought in doughnuts after lunch and smiled just as sweetly as she passed them around. I declined, politely. It took all my willpower not to spit on the tray and tell her to go outside and fuck a bollard.

A bit later on there was a flurry of excitement over the body found in Victory Park. The police have cordoned off the area and are looking for a murder weapon. That would be the murder weapon Craig's taken to work today to cut wallpaper.

Wednesday, 14 February

Craig doesn't do flowers on Valentine's Day. He says we were 'above all that shit'. I gave him a card and some of his Valentino Intense aftershave, just for appearances sake. He annoyed me this morning. I was in the kitchen making pancakes and I was just hitting the high note of Tina Turner's 'We Don't Need Another Hero' and he came in and pinched my ass and asked me where his brown belt was. I was so cross I could have set him alight *and* ripped his card up.

All day, AJ was flitting about the office with bunches of roses that someone's beloved had delivered to the *Gazette* front desk. Lynette Plunket from the Accounts department, whom I affectionately call Inept from the Cunts department because she is always getting our wages wrong, came in with an enormous armful of pinks 'from her beloved'. She usually only came downstairs to hand out our payslips but today was an unexpected non-pleasure as she paraded them around so we could all marvel. She probably forced the poor sod to send them at gunpoint.

When she wasn't bragging, Inept would sit on the ends of desks, slurping tea (which is right up there with pen-tapping as a killable offence in my eyes) and moaning how she never had enough time to do anything, yet plenty of time to talk about her dull life on her canal boat with her husband and their two schnauzers, Pedro and Susie. Middle age hit that woman's body like a truck. She's in her fifties but she looks seventy. She also has the boomiest voice so you can hear her even if she's on the other side of the office. If I hear that story about her dog's hip operation and the vet bill once more, I shall visit that barge in the dead of night and drag her feet first into that fucking canal.

The Community events write-up this week comprised a Beaks and Squeaks weekend at the animal sanctuary, an evening of clairvoyance and An Audience with Some Tosspot Who'd Spent His Entire Life Growing Radishes. I now know more about radishes than I ever wanted to, thanks to that plague sore. Did you know that dreaming about radishes denotes someone close will betray you and that the Ancient Egyptians were paid in radishes to build the great pyramid of Giza? Well now you do.

I wanted to put the copy about the Parkinson's Support Group and a new Zumba class on one page and call it 'Movers and Shakers' but Jeff intercepted the copy and advised against it. Said Claudia's dad or granddad or some other family member had Parkinson's and it 'wasn't looking too good'.

Lightweights.

Thursday, 15 February

1. *Everyone at work, including Jeff – he brought Daisy a Kinder egg today*
2. *People who leave doors slightly ajar so they bang incessantly*
3. *Eric the handyman who wouldn't let me park in the staff car park because there are 'only six spaces and they're all reserved for the seniors'*
4. *Derek Scudd – international Man of Mystery*

Caught a bit of *Up At the Crack* this morning. It could be the HD but I think old Donkey Dick Tompkinson's had a penis enlargement. It practically filled the screen. Carolyn looked even more orange too. They were chatting to the resident doctor about Tinnitus Awareness Week and joining Scottie Callender in the kitchen for National Haggis Day. #UpAtTheCock is all but forgotten. And so am I.

It was Jeff's birthday at work – I made him a Bundt cake, his favourite and he gave me a kiss on the cheek. We're friends again, despite the fact he talks to Daisy now much more than me. Their desks are closer, that's all it is.

Me and AJ had lunch in the park – full-fat lattes and cheese toasties. I mentioned that I normally went for skinny lattes and he looked aghast.

'You're not fat,' he said. 'God, why do women always do this to themselves? You're gorgeous as you are.'

'Really?' I said and he blushed deep purple. 'That's a nice thing to say, AJ.'

'Well, it's true.'

'Do you want to come to the Odeon with me later to see this shit dystopia I have to review for my column? I have a spare ticket.'

'Are you asking me on a date?'

'No, I'm asking you if you want a free ticket to the Odeon to see this shit dystopia I have to review for my column.'

'Sure,' he chuckled. 'I'd love to.'

So we did. And it was shit. But we did enjoy seeing how many popcorn puffs we could wedge into this woman's perm in front of us until she noticed.

Imelda texted me to see if I wanted to come veil shopping with her – nobody else could make it. I text back 'so sorry, Craig in hospital with appendicitis – nightmare!' Cue teary-eyed emoji.

Craig said I've used that lie on them before but that time it had been a kidney transplant. They still believed it.

'Oh, God so sorry!' she texted back. I expected her to ask if he'd still be able to come to the wedding or could she cancel one of the melon boats, but she didn't.

Also, I'm officially a serial killer now, according to Google: 'a person who murders three or more people with the murders taking place over a period of time with an extended cooling off period'. I fit the bill almost perfectly.

Finally, I've accomplished something. Finally, I have a reason to go to school reunions.

'Yah, I work in the City now, turning over multi-multi-multi-million-pound deals on a daily basis, yah. Five kids. My husband

is a multi-multi-multi-billionaire oil tycoon. Got the president on speed dial. What do you do?'

'Oh, I'm an Internet billionaire. I have eight husbands, twenty kids and I drive a Ferrari. Two Ferraris actually, simultaneously. How about you?'

'Oh, I live with Calvin Harris on his yacht in the south of France most of the year, and shag my way around the Polo sets. Married twice. Divorced thrice. Twelve kids. Prince Harry? Oh, yah, all the time. Just last week in fact. Did it on the throne and everything. How about you, Rhiannon? What are you doing now?'

'Me?' Pause for hair flick. 'I'm a serial killer. Yah, I take human heads to work in my lunchbox. I keep my mother's skull as a bedpost and use my father's nipples as light pulls. Oh, yah, that is a human thigh bone I have propping up the trellis in my garden, you're so sweet to notice!'

'Yes, but are you married yet, Rhiannon? And have you got any children?'

'No. I haven't.'

And one by one they all turn away.

God, I can't even brag in my own fantasies, what hope is there for me in real life?!

I'd planned to go fishing again tonight but I can't really be bothered. There's an awful lot of planning involved in going out and killing someone. You have to really think things through, plan your routes, wear the right clothes. Think I'm going to rearrange my Sylvanians' fridge instead and watch a bit of *Grand Designs*.

Tink still won't do Shake a Paw. And she's forgotten Roll Over now as well. I'm wondering if she's got chihuahua Alzheimer's.

Friday, 16 February

Got on the scales first thing – still not lost the Christmas pound-age. Googled 'West Country Liposuction'. Can't afford it. Had an eclair.

Prepared my truly excoriating review for last night's film – it's a belter.

Big news – man in the blue Qashqai has a new car! A silver Honda. He's not such a knob behind the wheel now, strangely. He even allowed me and Tink to cross the road this morning. He revved his engine a bit, but apart from the pass-ag smile, I think we have made progress. Maybe the human race is worth saving after all?

Linus attended the police press conference about my freshest cut – Park Man – and all the details were served back to the others in the editorial meeting which, of course, I wasn't invited to attend. I found out all the main points though as I was pretending to look for news cuttings in the files when he relayed it back to Jeff.

The 'victim's' name was Gavin 'Chalky' White, a 46-year-old father of four and long-distance lorry driver from Chapeltown, Leeds. Loving, loved, missed dreadfully. Another apparent paragon of virtue. Good Old Chalk. Chalky Boy. Everybody's mate.

Top bloke. No one with a bad word to say about him. Linus left after the meeting to catch a train to Leeds – he was attempting to interview the hopelessly devoted wife. Isn't it funny how people have to die before anyone lets them know what they mean to them? Well, not funny. Just stupid. I mean, they can't hear you now, can they?

Oh, and they've ruled out terrorism, again. How do they do that, I wonder. I mean, I *could* be a terrorist for all they know, couldn't I? I'm not affiliated to anyone but I could be a lone wolf, quite easily. They could do with me, ISIS. I'm pretty gifted at this.

I saw Terry, Julia's husband, on my way into town at lunch. He was coming out of Greggs with a bag of heart disease. His van was parked illegally on the kerb so he was in a rush.

'Oh, hi… Mr Kidner?'

He looked back at me and squinted non-committally, before he recognised me as the nice little editorial assistant who'd written up his article a few weeks before. 'Oh, all right?'

'Any news about your wife? I wondered if my article had done anything?'

He shook his head. 'No, nothing yet.'

'The kids still at your mother's?'

'Yeah. I see them every day but they don't want to be at home without their mum there.'

'Understandable.'

'The longer it goes on, the more I think she won't be coming back. Police won't help. They say it's a domestic matter, not a job for them sort of thing.'

'Well, maybe she'll come to her senses soon.'

'Yeah, hope so. Anyway, got to…'

'Yeah, sorry. Hope everything turns out for the best,' I called across the road.

He put his hand up to me and smiled; a smile of genuine gratitude and warmth. He was giving up on her. They all were.

Perfect.

A new kitchen shop has just opened down by the riverside, in lieu of the overpriced women's shoe shop. Top of the range kitchenware: Le Creuset, Cornish Blue, Sabatier. Didn't have time to look in today but I've got my eye on a five-piece set of knives in the window. It's pricey but I'm worth it.

Another story which piqued my interest today was that of two reported assaults in as many weeks on women driving home alone on country roads in the area. The women – one A-level student and one 25-year-old trainee solicitor – have told police that a 'glossy black Transit van' had followed them for miles before flashing its lights. One of the men had an accent and a bald head; the other was black and wore a wedding ring. The DNA they got from the victims can't be traced on the police's database so they're not known criminals. They could be any two guys in the street. It's a massive story. Claudia is working on it with Daisy Chan – it's going to be her baptism of fire. I've been thinking about the two men all day. Two at once. That's the stuff of fantasy. They're going on my 'Ones to Watch' list.

Took some Chinese round to Julia after work... crispy won-tons, spare ribs and rice, but she refused to write another letter to her husband. Such a bitch. Says if I'm going to kill her, I should just get on with it. I suppose it's fair enough. She's given up a lot sooner than I thought she would.

'Come along, eat your din-dins.'

'Fuck you.' She threw her spring roll at my head. It missed, luckily.

'I saw Terry today,' I told her as I ate my chow mein.

She looked across at me, injecting hate into every second of eye contact.

'I wrote an article a few weeks ago, about how much he misses you. Kids miss you too.'

She started to cry, weakly, so softly so I couldn't hear it. She banged her head against the wall.

'He thinks you're in London. Living it up. Reinventing yourself. Thinks you don't want to come home.'

She closed her eyes. 'You took money out of my account while you were in London, didn't you?'

'Several times,' I said. 'Posted your last letter from there too.'

She shook her head. 'Why don't you just do it? Just fucking DO IT! Put me out of my misery!'

'Why should I?' I said to her, slurping up my noodles. 'You didn't put me out of mine.'

Monday, 19 February

Dad was on my mind all morning. I was starting to forget the sound of his voice. I had to close my eyes and remind myself of its timbre, the sweet way he spoke only to me because I was his favourite and he could trust me with anything. My default memory of him was always in the hospital during that final week. Fading and drying out like an old leaf.

Life is so beautiful, Rhiannon. I think it's only when you're dying that you really get to see that.

Promise me when it gets worse, you'll be there. You'll do it for me.

You're the only one I can trust, Rhiannon.

Good news! The police officially have 'no concrete leads in the murder of Dan, Dan the Dickless Man and are continuing to appeal for witnesses, meaning I'm all but in the clear! There's talk of a public appeal by his mum but I don't know when that will happen. He's become a bit of a local joke. They 'brought in two men for questioning' one of whom was the guy that punched him outside The Reef nightclub on New Year's Eve but both were later 'released on police bail, pending further inquiries'. They've got nothing.

There haven't been any arrests yet in the Gavin White – aka Park Man – murder either but I'm not out of the park yet and I daren't go fishing again until it leaves the front page. A witness has come forward to say they 'heard a dog barking in the vicinity' on the night it happened. Police are appealing for 'anyone who was in the area that night to come forward'.

Ummm...no.

Ooh, yeah, this morning around 11 a.m., two coppers came in and went straight into Ron's office with Linus. The blind was down so I couldn't lip-read, but they were in there for about twenty minutes. When they came out, one of them looked directly at me – I was typing up my film review – but then he nodded and I nodded back, and they both left.

I knocked on Ron's door to see if he or Linus wanted a coffee or a punch in the face but they both said no. I thought one of them might offer up an explanation for the police visit but no luck. Ron told me to ask Claudia and Mike Heath to come in, so I had to act like the Go-Between and once they were in, the door closed and I couldn't hear what was being said.

After work, I drove round to Windwhistle Court. I've lost count now how many times I'd been round there now. Still no luck. Chances are, not many people know where he lives. Chances are, the police have given him another identity or he's changed his appearance. The public all knew him as that scary-eyed, hobbling old man on a stick, with a permanently miserable expression and a bulbous nose – a bit like Robert in the old-style *Guess Who*. Maybe he'd dyed his hair. Maybe he'd gone grey. I'd know his face though. It's the kind you can't disguise.

I know exactly how I'll do it this time. I won't need the scissors or a knife. And if I can find out where he lives then I can take my time with him. I can take my time with him. I want him so badly I ache for it. My skin seems to tingle with it. I throb with it. I wish there was some short cut to finding him but maybe the long wait will make the pudding all that sweeter. I need to find him soon or else I need to find someone.

Thursday, 22 February

1. *People who don't indicate at roundabouts*
2. *People who Instagram photos of their Valentine's meal, lovingly prepared in heart-shaped bowls and star-shaped dishes*
3. *People who brag endlessly on Facebook about their fantastic lives – e.g. Imelda today: 'I have the best kiddiewinks, the extension's almost finished, and the best man in the world. Fifteen years this June! Can't wait to be married to you, baby.' [Cue hella-filtered Insta-photo where she's cropped out their double chins.] #FeelingBlessed*
4. *People who publically declare their 'utter heartbreak' at some tragic news story and how their 'thoughts are with the families' yet, one minute later, re-post an ICYMI tweet about their forthcoming wedding (again, Imelda)*
5. *People who kick trees*

They've put the *Gazette*'s two hot-shot reporters – Linus and Paul Spurdog (just back from three-months' mountain-climbing in Malaysia) – on the Park Man murder. Paul's grown another eighteen biceps since he left. To look at him, you'd think he was Idris Elba's understudy – some macho stuntman type. Then you see him hunched over his keyboard typing with two fingers and the illusion is shattered. Paul wants me to help him write up his 'life-changing' adventure in Kuala Lumpur where he got to live with tribespeople. Can't wait to hear all about *that* for hours on end.

A little laugh for me today. We have this work-experience girl in for a week called Rosie – she's stuffing envelopes and fielding calls – and she attempted a home dye job on her hair. It's distinctly more violet than Soft Rosewood and Lynette sang 'Purple Rain' at her, causing her to run out in tears.

'Bit of a Special Snowflake is our Rosie,' said Bollocky Bill, 'you might want to take it easy on the lass.' Which we all took as code for *Don't say anything in the least bit offensive against her or we'll never see her again.*

We've had them like Rosie in before and they've never lasted long. One was called Debz. She was always bemoaning her 'lack of value as a member of the team' and 'not feeling empowered by our social structure'. Couldn't handle conflict of any kind. Claudia asked her to tidy her desk one day, and the next she went on sick leave for 'a stress-related problem'. We didn't see her for four months. Cost the company a fortune before she finally did decide to leave to breed turtles or something.

And then there was Dresden, the teenage receptionist who took on the role briefly when I was newly promoted. She described herself in her Facebook profile as a 'trans-ethnic polyamorous demi-romantic genderless asexual' with 'changeable pronouns' and refused to use the staff toilets. Linus said 'she' when referring to Dresden once in a meeting and Dresden walked out, never to be seen again.

AJ hobbled in on crutches at lunchtime – he's had a skateboarding accident. And even though normally I don't mind when the kid passes my desk due to the aforementioned peachy behind and our frequent bitching about Linus and Claudia, today he annoyed me. The crutches make the place look untidy, and he was clanking all over the place like a baby giraffe. He hobbled over, *clang clang clang*, with a Gay Porn Star bumper sticker he'd bought from the joke shop.

'It was either this or one that said, *I Really Love Barnyard Animals.*'

'No, this is perfect, he'll hate it.'

We've stuck it on the back of Linus's Audi.

Christ, I'm bored. I know all this is just killing time. Killing time before I can kill again. I'm on the treadmill now. I can't see a way to get off it.

Tuesday, 27 February

1. *People who text you, and you text back, then you get NOTHING back for days (Craig, my ex-sister Seren, Lucille)*
2. *People who email straight back when you're trying to clear your inbox*
3. *People at the* Gazette *who insist on bringing smelly food back to their desks and eat it of a lunchtime. Today's example: Edmund's cheesy nachos*

Daisy Chan tried to have a conversation with me today. I wasn't having any of it. First, she cornered me at in the staffroom and tried asking me if I'd been to the new coffee bar in town.

'No, I haven't,' I said, even though I had and their cappuccinos were LUSH.

Then she tried the old 'Isn't it warm today?' line of questioning, but I roadblocked her with 'Dunno, I'm pretty cold.'

And lastly, as I was leaving the room, she called out 'I might need some copy later on the new traffic calming measures in Maddox Street, if that's all right?'

'Yeah, fine,' I called back. I don't know why she's being so friendly to me. She must be after something.

Today's court cases were all pretty sap-sucking. Three drink-drivers, one drug driver, one crop of cannabis, a drunk and disorderly and two assaults. All my bloody little offerings would go to Crown Court when someone was eventually charged. There hasn't been anything juicy at the magistrates' since last summer when that one-legged prostitute got drugged round the back of Boots. That was brilliant.

Went down to the new kitchen shop on my break. Treated myself to a new tin opener, some cork coasters for the coffee table and the block set of Sabatier knives I'd seen in the window – it's absolutely stunning. The set comprises a seven-inch Oriental meat knife with air pockets, a ten-inch carving knife, a four-inch paring knife, a five-inch boning knife, and a cleaver. It's nearly £100's worth of steel but I ADORE it. The thrill in my arms as I carried it back to the office, oh, it was like carrying a bomb! I'd imagine that's the same sort of feeling, anyway. Invincibility. Power. A feeling of winning at something for once.

Daisy saw the box under my desk. 'Nice knives. You into cooking, are you?'

'Yeah, big time,' I lied. 'I'm doing a course in French cookery in a few weeks so I thought I'd get properly prepared.' Sometimes it amazes me how quickly these lies trickle out of my mouth without any preparation.

Lana Rowntree sidled up to me at the photocopier, waiting for me to finish so she could use it. She wasn't wearing a bra today. Wanton snake-face.

'How are you, Rhee?'

'Yeah, fine, thanks.' I nudged myself to ask: 'And you?'

'Yeah, good. It's gone crazy today, hasn't it? So busy. Which can only be a good thing, I suppose.' Cue fake laugh, throat clear and hair swish.

I could smell the perfume on her – the same perfume on

our bed sheets that Craig said was 'new washing powder or summing'.

'Town was busy today, wasn't it?' I said.

'Yeah. I popped in to look at Dysons. Wish I'd got one in the January sale now.'

'Which one are you after?'

'That one they advertise on telly. You know, the cordless one.'

'Oh, yeah,' I said. She had two old scars on one of her wrists. Quite deep ones. Old suicide attempts? Particularly vicious cat? No, she didn't have cats. Allergic. 'How are things with your Richard's job now? Did his unfair dismissal claim go through?'

God, I'm brilliant at small talk when I have to be. Richard is her boyfriend. I'd overheard their shouted phone arguments as much as anyone else in the office so it's hardly eavesdropping.

'We finished,' she said, stepping up to the now vacant copier. 'Just before Christmas. I think I was putting too much pressure on him to name a date for our wedding and he freaked out. So it's just me and the cats now. Still, onwards and upwards. Plenty more fish.'

'Aww, I'm sorry to hear that,' I said, holding my pile of warm pages in front of me like a shield. 'Are you seeing anyone else at the moment then?'

'No,' she said, without a flicker. 'I think I'm done with men for the time being. Waste of bloody space the lot of them, aren't they?' Cue fake laugh with nose scratch and another hair swish.

'Couldn't agree more,' I said, eyeballing her. She just about met my stare, but only for a second, before she became very interested in the rogue paperclip on the photocopier tray. 'Well, you take care now.' I rubbed the side of her arm, taking another quick swipe at her scarred wrist.

'I will, cheers, Rhee.' She even managed one of her sparkly full-teeth smiles. I'd like her to christen my knives. I'd like to dampen every single page out of that machine with her blood.

I had to give them their due – she and Craig were expert liars. They could give lessons. Not to me though, obviously. I am the queen when it comes to rooting out pies of the porky variety.

It annoys me because I waited an entire Wimbledon fortnight to get a shag out of Craig (he said he wanted to 'make sure I was ready', the wuss) but one whiff of Lana Rowntree's undercarriage at the finger buffet and he's off like a cannon at Trafalgar.

I knew why they were doing it. It was the same reason I flirted with random men in Internet chat rooms. The same reason I walked down dark alleys in the middle of the night with half the knife drawer folded inside my coat. Because it was a thrill. It tasted good. It was the crunchy fat on the bacon. The skin on the chicken. You know it's so bad but the reward feels so good, even if it's only for a short while. What's that meme I saw on Twitter the other day? 'One crowded hour of glorious life is worth an age without a name.' Yeah, that's it. Well you have your crowded hour, Lana. And I'll have mine.

Friday, 1 March

1. *Derek Scudd*
2. *Wesley Parsons*
3. *Dillon on the checkout in Lidl, who didn't ask if I was all right for bags today and, again, squeezed my loaf as he scanned it*

MAN STABBED IN PARK WAS REGISTERED SEX OFFENDER

Gavin John White, aged 46, a long-distance lorry driver from Leeds, was stabbed to death on the evening of Saturday, January 19th in what's thought to have been a random attack. The *Gazette* has learned that White has been on the Sexual Offenders Register for the last four years. He was convicted of two rapes and one indecent assault on women in Hull and Newcastle. Avon and Somerset Police has launched a murder investigation and are appealing for witnesses.

And so shines a good deed in a weary world. My heart felt better. I should have got that Woman of the Century award just for getting that shit worm off the streets. Such is life.

So *that* was what the police were talking to Ron about, I surmised. They'll be lucky to get any witnesses to help out that pervert. Jeff was walking past my desk to go to fill up his cafetière.

'Jeff? Any idea what this is about?' I showed him the front page.

He hobbled over. 'Random stabbing they reckon. No money taken. Police say his belt was undone so it could have been a sex attack, knowing his previous form.'

'So it could have been a woman who did it?'

'Ooh, no, doubtful.'

'Why doubtful?'

'Well, it was pretty savage by all accounts. They reckon he was stabbed with a thick bar or a bit of railing or something.'

I did my baby deer eyes. 'Can't women be savage though?'

'Nah, more likely one of them gay cruisers or what have you. That happened in that park, do you remember last year?'

'Oh, yeah.'

'Why do you ask?'

'It's just scary, that's all. It happened quite near our flat.'

'Well, you look after yourself, my girl. Don't get walking around there at night. You never know what's lurking in them shadows. Smack heads, crack heads. All sorts. All sorts.'

No, I thought as he walked away. You never know what you're gonna find in them shadows. Chihuahuas, savage 27-year-old women carrying wallpaper scissors. All sorts. All sorts.

Saturday, 2 March

Got on the scales again this morning – that eclair I had last month is still punishing me. Two pounds heavier than Christmas. The consequences? Well, nothing at all really. I can grab myself in both hands around where my waist used to be. Definitely need to go to more of Lucille's aerobics classes. I wish our Nando's would just shut down. And Krispy Kreme. And Starbucks. And Greggs.

About lunchtime, I harnessed up Tink and we drove over to Mum and Dad's. The smell's even worse, like old milk, so I had to get on my Marigolds and give the carpet a good scrub once Madam was back under lock and key. Julia has a new tactic to get me onside – talking about my parents. It's to soften me up, get me emotionally weakened so we'll bond and then I'll eventually let her go.

'You have to have feelings to cry, Julia,' I told her. 'Get back in the wardrobe.'

I'm pretty lucky, being a woman and having these urges, granted. If I was a man, they would have caught me by now for sure. I'd have left clues. DNA. But I am careful when I do what I do. I wouldn't do it otherwise. No hair, no fluids, no footprints. No trace I was ever there at all, unless I want there to be.

I'll let them tie themselves in knots, the police and the mob at the *Gazette*. One day, no doubt, they'll come back to the simplest conclusion as Occam's razor dictates. It was just one very fucked-up woman out for revenge, for cheap thrills, for blood.

I am the music maker. And I am the dreamer of dreams.

And even if I am fingered by a witness, society's latent, and sometimes blatant, sexism will work to my advantage. You have to play the system. They think you're weak and girly? *Act* weak and girly. Use their own prejudices against them. Then when they're not looking, cut their fucking throats.

As the great Bart Simpson himself once said, Nobody ever suspects the butterfly.

Sunday, 3 March

1. *My sister, Seren 'Let's all fuck off to the good ole US of A while everyone back in the UK dies and rots, Gibson*
2. *Aled Jones – who died and made him king of Sunday TV?*
3. *Lewis Hamilton*
4. *Pippa Middleton*
5. *Basically anyone who covers* OK! *magazine*

Well, what a nice way to spend a Sunday – a run out in the park with my dog, a roast lamb dinner cooked by my guilt-ridden boyfriend and a phone ear-bashing from my older sister. Laila the estate agent had taken the liberty of calling Seattle and informing her, like the becankled little pig face she was, that I'd taken the house off the market. So there I was, dressing-gowned to the max, stinking of night sweat, taking a call at 2 a.m. It was around six in the afternoon there. There was a long delay.

'Rhee? It's Seren.'

'Oh. Hello, there, Sissy-woo,' I yawned.

Long pause. 'Why have you taken Mum and Dad's off the market?'

She sounded like she was inside a metal drum at one end of a factory. 'Yeah, I've taken Mum and Dad's house off the market.'

Longer pause. 'Why did you do that?' She was shouting, but I could barely hear her.

'It's a terrible line, Seren. Did you just ask how I was? I'm fine, thanks. My back's playing up again but that's to be expected with a desk job, I suppose. Otherwise, I'm pretty hunky-dory...'

'Rhiannon, why did you *mumble mumble clang clang* off the market? You had no *muffle scritch scratch* to do that.'

'The estate agent was messing me around. I didn't like her.'

Long pause. 'That house belongs to both of us and as joint executors we both have a say in what happens to it. You should have consulted me.' Her Seattle drawl had got a lot more pronounced since the last time we'd spoken. More whiny. Or it could be that she was just whining.

The next long pause allowed me just enough time to grow another lie in the window box of whoppers I was already cultivating. 'Look, don't worry, I'm going to place it with another agency – one with a much better track record.'

Longer pause. 'Why didn't you talk to me about this before *clang clang mumble*? We have to make these kinds of decisions together.'

I could tell it hurt her to say that. 'Together' was not something she and I had been for such a long time now and the words had stuck in her throat like bones.

'It would have taken too long. Seriously, the woman was such a shrew and the kinds of people she was showing round were just... ugh. One of them had needle tracks in his arm. And another I'm sure I've seen on *Crimewatch*.'

'Seriously?'

'Yes.'

'What, so you were there when *muffle muffle* showed them round?'

'Yes. That all right?'

'Oh. Yes. We don't want it going to just anyone, do we?'

'Precisely. I'm going to place it with Charles Burridge and Sons. Their offices in town are so nice. Brand-new carpets. Jo Malone handwash in the bathroom. It's fine, honest. I'm sorting it. '

'Oh,' she said. Was that a convinced 'Oh' or a passive aggressive backing down 'Oh'? I didn't know. Then she said 'Do you need me to do anything at my end?'

'No thanks. I'll send you the details when it's been placed. Shouldn't take more than a couple of days to appear on their website and email you the link. All right?'

Long pause. 'Yeah, OK. Thanks.'

She was so easy to get round. If she was that worried, she'd have got on the next plane over here and sorted me out but she couldn't, you see. Because she was afraid. My own sister, three years older, three years wiser and over four thousand miles away, was terrified of coming anywhere near me.

'What about a house clearance firm?'

'I'm sorting that too,' I lied. 'So how are you then? How's my little niece and nephew? Did Ash like his dumper truck?'

Long pause. 'Yeah, they're both fine.' Long pause. 'OK, well let me know when the estate agent's sorted out then, yeah?'

'Yep, I surely will, byeeeeeee!' I hung up. I went back to my life, she went back to her kids and her double fronted house and her pool and strings of popcorn and Twinkies and her group of Yankee Doodle mates clinking beer cans watching the Superbowl. Sisters were ten a penny to Seren, especially 'mentally deranged' ones.

I spent all afternoon Photoshopping a screen cap of a brand-new estate agent to show her. She emailed back just before I came to bed.

'Thanks for sorting it. Hopefully we'll be able to get it off both our backs sooner rather than later. Take care Sx'

That x meant little. What she was saying with that x was that 'once the house is sold, we can cease all contact, once and for all'. That x was for the sister I once was to her, before I went 'psycho'. That x was a sticking plaster on all the comments I'd heard her make to our mother, our grandmother, our father.

'I hate her. I hate her. I hate her.'

'Why can't you send her away again?'

'The only cancer in this family is Rhiannon.'

'Rhiannon was with him when he died. What if she killed him?'

Tuesday, 5 March

1. *Craig*
2. *Man in front of me in the coffee shop who was ordering about eighteen differently flavoured lattes – also, your ass is way too big for those shorts*
3. *Chemist bitch in Boots who asked if my supplements were 'doctor recommended'. Who died and made you a medical practitioner? Just let me buy my sodding Clit Vits, you cheese-breeding tripe hound*
4. *The man who whistles across the car park on his way to work at 6 a.m.*
5. *Thieves – the batteries from our remote, a half-packet of frozen peppers and a roll of Sellotape have definitely migrated to the land of Whittaker*

So a bit of a dramatic morning so far – Ron and Claudia met with the mayor and Ron said AJ should sit in on the meeting (after he'd made the coffees, of course) so he could learn more about mayoral procedure and local politics. A while later, Ron's office door opens and AJ practically runs out.

So I follow him out to the staffroom. The door is shut, the

kettle boiling to a *pheeeeeee* on the stove and he's sitting in the armchair with his head in his hands.

'Hey, you all right?' I asked. I turn off the stove and sit down on the sofa next to him, taking care to avoid the glob of taramasalata that's been there for weeks and for which no one is claiming responsibility.

'No,' he sobbed.

'What happened?'

'Ah, nuthin. Just made a complete tit of myself in front of Ron and the mayor and everyone.'

'Tell me.' It felt like a back-rubby moment so I got stuck in.

'The mayor was talking about her daughter and I made this joke about taking her out on the town and getting her legless.'

'Oh.'

'I didn't know she *was* legless, did I?'

I wince on his behalf. 'Yeah. Drunk-driver.'

'I know, Linus just told me. He was just in here. He said the mayor could have me on emotional abuse charges.'

'He's joking, AJ. He's just trying to get you going.'

'I'd *never* have said that if I'd known. Never in a million years.' He blubbed again. 'And then I was laughing at one of her jokes, probably a bit too hard to make amends for the legless thing, and I said I was going to have a heart attack.'

'Oh, gawd.'

'I didn't know her husband was in hospital, did I?'

'Everyone knows that!' I laugh.

'I didn't!' he says, evidently in no laughing mood. 'I can't go back in there, I just can't. What if he fires me? I need the money for travelling, Rhee.'

I rub his back again, all down the bumps in his spine. 'It'll be all right. Claudia knows you wouldn't say anything so insensitive on purpose. She'll speak up for you.'

'What about the mayor? I've hurt her feelings.'

'Well, she's nuts for a start.'

'Ron's face, man. He hates me now. He thinks I embarrassed him. And Auntie Claudia looked at me the way my nan looked at me when I crapped on the carpet.' I frowned at him. 'I was three.'

'Right. I guess that's excusable then.'

I move my hand from his back to his forearm and rubbed that instead, looking into his eyes. I can feel his goosebumps. 'Come on, you go and fix your mascara, I'll make the coffees for them and I'll see you back downstairs. This is no big deal, AJ. Trust me. OK?'

'All right. Cheers, mate.'

'Hey, I got some fart sweets at the joke shop at lunchtime. They're dissolvable.'

His smile goes wide though his eyes are still teary. 'And why would you be telling me that, Miss Lewis?'

'Well, Mr Sixgill will be wanting his daily cappuccino pretty soon, I imagine. They're in my desk drawer.'

There's been another serious sexual assault out on the old road between town and the quarry. Two men again, driving a shiny black or possibly blue Ford Transit van. The latest woman – this one in her fifties – has given the police some good descriptions and the police are 'as sure as they can be that the three crimes were perpetrated by the same duo' and are maintaining a 'very visible presence while the investigation continues.' I'm wondering if I should start making my presence felt too.

AJ told me later how he made it up with Ron and the mayor. Ate shit, like a pro. I wasn't surprised. He has one of those winning smiles that gets even the coldest heart onside. You can't be mad at him for long. And dat ass, my God. No one could be mad at dat ass.

*

OMG OMG OMG, I've just got back from lunch and Craig has just informed me he wants to have a baby.

WHERE HAS THIS COME FROM?!

I was so not prepared for this today. It's probably a case of him trying to build a bridge over the canyon that had opened up between us ever since he started bonking Lana. I made the fatal error of taking him a bacon roll and an Americano out of the goodness of my cold black heart. He's refitting a shop in the High Street. My new patent wedges got covered in white dust the moment I set foot in the place and the expletive-filled conversation immediately stopped because, of course, ladies were now present. His chubby chippy mate Steve, whom he affectionately calls Stevewise Gamgee, didn't make any eye contact, or affect a greeting, so in love was he with his task of planing down a bit of wood.

'I thought you had to work through lunch today?' said Craig. I think he was pleased to see me. He smiled anyway. It could have been the effects of the roll and the aroma of nicely crisp pig.

'I do. I just took fifteen to get some lunch. Then I remembered you were here.'

'Ah,' he said and kissed me on the cheek. It was unexpected. We hadn't been this intimate in weeks. The nearest we got to touching lately was when his sponge lay on top of mine on the side of the bath, like a sort of pube sandwich.

'Steve's wife brought their baby in earlier. She was just on her way back from Debenhams. Bought it the cutest outfit – black and yellow stripes, like a little bee.' And then he got out his phone and showed me a picture he had taken. Two pictures actually – he kept scrolling back and forth between them. 'Look at his little feet.'

'Why do you have a picture of some random kid on your phone? Do I need to inform Operation: Yew Tree?'

He laughed. 'Just thought it was cute, that's all.' He had this glazed look in his eyes and he was still rubbing my back from the 'thanks for the bacon roll' conversation.

'We're not having a baby, Craig.'

He laughed again. 'Might bring us a bit closer together, you never know.'

'Yeah, it *would* bring us closer together. Then it would split us right down the middle. You'd fertilise my bored little egg, then bugger off to work every day while I'm back at the flat, stinking of shit and crying my eyes out.'

'It wouldn't be like that.'

I gave him a look. Steve of the Shire, or whatever his name was, walked past with a different plank of wood.

'He was getting all broody earlier when my Mrs brought the nipper in.'

'So I hear,' I replied.

'You wanna watch out, Rhee,' said another stubbly bloke in jeans covered in white paint. 'He'll be begging for a good seeing-to tonight. It's all he's talked about all morning.'

'Oh, well, I'll look forward to that then.' I smiled and rolled my eyes as though he did this all the time.

Truth was, Craig *didn't* do this all the time. He never mentioned babies, ever, never even showed an interest in them, and I wondered where this latest flurry of interest had come from. Then I put some pieces together – Lana. He hadn't seen her for a few days. I wondered if he'd broken it off – or if she'd broken it off. The way they'd been at it previously, it was any wonder it hadn't broken off by itself.

'So can we talk about it tonight?' he said more quietly, moving me slowly back towards the entrance so the other guys – who were now entranced by pasting chintz wallpaper and painting cornices – couldn't hear. 'Just talk, that's all. See how we both feel about a little Criannon?'

'Criannon?'

'Yeah. Or Rhiannaig, if you prefer? Baby Wilkins. Can we just talk about it?'

'Well, you could talk and I could sit there and laugh at you.'

He took a great greasy fat bite out of his roll and swigged his coffee. 'Come on. We've been together nearly four years. You're not getting any younger, you know.'

'And you're not getting any better looking.'

He stopped chewing. 'Do you wanna get married first, is that it?'

'No, I mean, I haven't thought about it,' I said, sipping my latte and looking out into the street where an old lady pushing a shopping trolley had stopped to chat to a robin on the edge of a planter. 'I'd have a pretty empty side of the church, wouldn't I?'

'That doesn't matter. We could elope. Gretna Green. Nigel did that. Stayed in a great Travelodge.'

'Oh, how marvellous, look can we have this conversation another time? Like when I'm not standing on wood shavings and staring at the inside of your mouth?'

'Cheers for the food.' He sighed and went back to his ladder with the scrunched-up Greggs bag and his coffee. No kiss this time. Hmm, I thought. This could be the clincher. A baby to save to relationship, or else he's out. Maybe we had been climbing up the water slide to Splitsville for some time and now he had just lain down his mat. Down or out.

A little thought flittered across my mind – I had to keep him sweet. I had to remember the long game.

I stood there in the doorway, internally debating my options for a moment. And then I just came out with it. 'OK, we'll talk about it tonight. If that's what you want.'

His face turned away from the ladder, his mouth still full. 'Seriously?'

'Yeah. We'll get a Nando's and we'll talk about it. We'll talk about you impregnating the shit out of me. All right?'

He blushed and looked around at the other guys who'd both stopped pasting and sawing and were now looking at him in amazement.

I walked out of there feeling about three feet taller.

*

In other news, Linus took A LOT of trips to the toilet this afternoon.

Thursday, 7 March

Craig's full of romantic gestures at the moment, all guilt-driven of course, but I'm enjoying it nonetheless. Yesterday, he bought me a jar of Nutella without having to be asked. Today, he came home with a small mushroom nightlight he'd seen in a gift shop in town 'because he knows I like all that woodland shit'. How precious.

The baby talk went well. Craig feels he is ready; I feel I'm not. He wants to leave something of himself behind when he dies; I want a book deal and a cottage retreat with my own beehive. He wants a 'son and heir to play football with and teach how to ride a bike'; I want size-10 hips and a new Sylvanians' bathroom.

But I gave in. Because I'm nice like that.

'OK,' I said, all out of argument, 'let's do it. Let's make a baby together.'

'Are you sure?'

'Yeah. I'll stop taking my pill and we'll go for it.'

And that was all the encouragement he needed. We went to bed straight after we got back from Nando's and didn't see daylight again till breakfast. And even though he must have had multiple showers since he last saw Lana the Organ Grinder, all I kept thinking about was her microscopic vadge mites all over his dick. Ugh, God, her asshole germs as well. I hoped against hope that he'd scrubbed it as well as he could with that antibacterial soap I kept leaving out for him.

Boy, did I make sacrifices.

We did it again this morning. As soon as his eyes were open, he was nuzzling my neck and murmuring in my ear. Sadly, I couldn't get my vagina going at all. He was suckling it and prodding it for all he was worth but there was more life in a dead gerbil.

'Come on then,' I said. 'Put it in already.'

'It *is* in. You're not wet.'

'Well, it's not my fault. You're not turning me on enough. Pass the lube.' There wasn't enough lube in the world to get that sucker going today. 'Pass my phone.' He grabbed it from the nightstand. 'Give me five minutes. I'll find that porn vid of the district nurse and the five black guys.'

He rolled over onto his back and sighed, hands behind his head.

And then I saw something online before I'd even clicked onto PornHub that immediately got things moving in the gusset vicinity. My phone screen bore a notification from the *Gazette* group's news app:

IS THERE A SERIAL KILLER LOOSE IN THE SOUTH-WEST?

And the article talked about Gavin White, but it linked it with three murders several weeks ago in London, all of which were strikingly similar. Men in parks stabbed and left to die. And how weird is this – two of the men were called Gavin!

The other one was called Clive.

My Park Man was being linked to an actual serial killer investigation involving Scotland fucking Yard! My little Park Man had made me NATIONALLY famous (sort of). And I throbbed. My nether regions actually *throbbed*.

So, yes, BuzzFeed, you can put me down as being *Sexually*

excited by deviant acts. But I have never, ever, EVER wet the bed or tortured a small animal. Unless you count how excited Tink was at Christmas when I ate all the After Eight mints then gave her just the empty packets.

'I'm ready. Do it. Put it in.'

Craig seemed to like the dominant me. I closed my eyes and we really went for it, banging the headboard and everything, which had never happened before – it was rarely troubled. At one point I heard something snap beneath the mattress – one of the slats. Bloody IKEA.

At the last second, when he was jackhammering and repeating, 'I'm gonna cum, I'm gonna cum,' and I was yelling, 'Well, fucking cum then!' I ordered him to cum deep inside me. At once, he thrust into me hard and I clenched my legs tightly around his back and he roared out into the pillow. And you know that moment just before you know you're gonna cum? You know you get an image flash through your mind which takes you 'there'? For me at that moment, it was Gavin White. It was him inside me as he lay dying, dressed in his own blood, my hand around the scissors in his neck. It was him cumming inside me as he gasped and gargled and died. My hand on his silent, cold chest.

'Fuckin helllllll,' Craig sighed, beaded in sweat.

Our hot heads pressed together at the temple, it must have looked like such a meaningful moment. A couple in love. A couple trying for a baby. In reality, it was a couple in bed; one of them trying for a baby, the other one still on the Pill and thinking of a dying man.

I didn't often cum with Craig – normally I had to wait for him to go to the bathroom while I finished myself off with my Rampant Rabbit and a good long think about Tom Hardy in *Mad Max* – but today was different. Today was a brand-new day. When he came out of the bathroom, I went in and drained him out of me over an empty jam jar.

Friday, 8 March

1. *Linus 'Smack my face hard, preferably with a breeze block' Sixgill*
2. *Lana Rowntree – sales assistant and Spunkbucket Extraordinaire*
3. *AJ – I now know what it stands for too. Absolute Judas*

Today I reached levels of annoyance I didn't know existed within me. It got to the point where I physically had to remove myself from the office for fear of throwing my coffee mug through Ron's window. It took three events to make me almost unutterably homicidal:

1. *Everyone's phone was going off, even Eric the handyman's. Little whistles, all bloody day, all over the office floor like dead firemen*
2. *AJ has started making Daisy peanut-butter-and-banana toasties and sitting on the end of her desk for little chit-chats. And he didn't forget the sugar in her coffee (unlike my two Canderel, which he's always forgetting)*
3. *Linus has not only taken over the 'Riot Lovers' photo and article and made it his own, he has COPYRIGHTED*

the picture and it's been shared – get this – over 135,000 times on social media. But that's not all, oh, no. Today, that spineless little runt invited the ACTUAL Riot Lovers into the office and INTRODUCED them to the team!

'Everyone, this is Sam and this is Delilah. A real-life Samson and Delilah! We finally tracked them down!'

And everyone, like the great trunk of malignant tumours they are, applauded as the two biblically-named teenage sops stood there stooped and embarrassed – him with his skinny jeans and wallet chain; her with her hoody sleeves over her hands and Tippexed DMs, Linus's hands on each of their backs like he was pulling their strings.

I've never seen anything look less biblical in my life.

Linus escorted them both into Ron's office for coffee and cupcakes, courtesy of 'their friends at the *Gazette*'. Guess who had to run out and buy the cakes? Guess who had no idea who the cupcakes were for? And guess who wasn't allowed into Ron's office to partake?

I seethed at my desk, eyes fixed on Ron's door until Jeff hobbled over with the darts scores for me to type up at which point I rose from my chair and walked.

And I just kept walking.

It was a fine day, but even if it wasn't, I wouldn't have gone back for my coat. I eventually got to the park and sat down on a bench in a quiet area under some trees and just cried. I wished Tink was with me. She normally licked my face at times like these, when everything got too much, but she and Mrs Whittaker had gone out for the day. There was no one around to see or hear me. But then I'm fucking used to that. No one ever sees.

I couldn't remember the last time I'd cried properly, with tears and meaning. The noise that came out was strangled and squeaky; pure snot-driven anger. The missiles in my mind were directed at so many different things I couldn't separate them out. It was work, it was Craig, it was the PICSOs and their constant Facebook updates about how charmed their lives were. It was Sam and Delilah. It was Seren's amazing life in America. It was Mum and Dad. It was Derek Scudd.

I wanted to murder the world. Nothing real was any good. And nothing living was worth living for. Everyone just needed to die.

Maybe God or whoever it is up there on that cloud has been trying to tell me this since Priory Gardens – nothing good will ever happen to me. There's been pockets of good – summers spent at Nanny and Granddad's. School when Julia had left. When Craig and I first got together. Even the *Gazette* when I had just got the editorial assistant job and Linus Sixgill hadn't joined.

Nobody even noticed when I walked back in the office, wiping my eyes. Nobody even ASKED where I'd been. It's all very well having tantrums but what's the fucking point if nobody sees them?

AJ talked to Lana for fifteen minutes this afternoon. He sat on the end of her desk and drank his whole coffee there.

I thought about my Sabatier knife block. I visualised his taut, sinewy neck underneath that cleaver. If only he knew what I was capable of. If only they all knew what this quiet little sweetpea could do.

Saturday, 9 March

1. *People who leave pointless status updates on social media – e.g. I've just eaten some toast or Why has the Strike It Lucky theme been in my head all morning? or I feel like killing myself. You feel like killing yourself?! Try reading your updates. You make a burning monk want to top up on diesel*
2. *People who call out across the street to one other like fishwives*
3. *Creepy Ed Sheeran – he was hanging around the bus stop this morning with his jeans undone singing 'Baby You're a Firework'. Badly.*

This morning, Craig left his phone unguarded to take the bins out. There was a new picture in his photos – a selfie. Him and Lana in bed. *My* bed. Him nuzzling. Her giggling. Their cheeks pulsing with afterglow. I sent the picture to my phone. The gnawing feeling is back.

So I've made a decision and luckily, the universe seems to be in favour of it. He's away tonight watching Athletico Someone play Inter Someone Else at Wembley (I was barely listening – I just heard the words 'crashing at Nige's' and praised the Lord I didn't have to have another tedious baby-making session to look forward to after *Match of the Day*). Also, my mum and dad's neighbour, Henry Cripps, has gone down to Cornwall for the weekend with 'Anne from his bridge club' who is 'just a friend, nothing more'.

So I'm going to murder Julia tonight.

I hadn't planned on doing it yet but what with everything that's happened this week, something's gotta give and there's only so many bowls of Crunchy Nut Cornflakes I can eat. It's not fun for me any more, going over there and feeding her and threatening her to keep quiet. The 'my friend is watching your kids' bullshit has worked so far but I just want her gone now. Beside which, I am itching to christen my knives. They are vibrating with anticipation; I can feel it. Gonna drop Tink off at Klepto Whittaker's then I'll catch you on the flip side...

*

♫DING DONG, THE WITCH IS DEAD ♫

It's precisely 11.17 p.m. and I've just got back. It's been a funny day. Almost like old times. Except this time it was me doling out the threats and gratuitous violence and her sitting there taking it like a bitch.

She'd tried to gnaw through her restraints again when I first got there. That cost her another finger. Also – my new knives are the bee's, the wasp's *and* the ladybird's knees. Ruthlessly efficient. Mercilessly sharp. They hardly needed me at all.

I threw her a handful of Smarties – all the blue ones, the last of my Christmas selection box. She scrabbled round the carpet and gobbled them down without even chewing.

'I'm done with you,' I said. 'You're leaving tonight.'

'Going home? Really?' she cried. She believed me. She *thanked* me, strangely. I wouldn't thank me if I'd been locked in a back bedroom for over three months and had three of my ten fingers severed.

'Come on. It's dark enough now. I'll drop you back.'

I said we'd take Henry's car in the garage. She still had her hands and feet tied as I marched her down the stairs and through the side door into the garage. I flicked on the light.

'I really won't go to the police,' she said. 'I mean that. I'll make something up. I'll protect you. Will you call off your friend? The one who's been watching my kids?'

'There isn't anyone watching your kids. I lied.'

'What?'

'I lied to keep you compliant.'

That's when I killed her. I knew I couldn't kill her indoors because I couldn't afford to get any more blood on the carpet when I didn't know how to use the carpet steamer properly. The plastic tarp was down under Henry's Triumph Herald, and it seemed as good a place as any. So I did it there.

It was the smallest of my Sabatiers but my God did it do the job. With one clean action it cut straight through the centre of her neck, no messing. Well, there was mess but most of it went on the tarp, thankfully. Have you ever tried to get blood out of a concrete floor? Nightmare! She turned and clung on to me as I stabbed her front on, her filthy hands clinging to my forearms as I drove the paring knife into her neck, then out, then her breastbone, then out, then the middle of her chest. Then out. There was so much blood. I grabbed her hair for better purchase and pushed her to the ground so as not to get blood on my clothes. I stood over her – my eleven-year-old self clinging on to my back as we bent over, watching her dying breaths, staring her out for the last time, eyes to evil eyes.

'Still want to be my best friend?' Those were the last words she heard.

I think that's what I like about death – its utter obedience. You kill something, it dies. You ask the question with your knife and the person responds, undoubtedly, every time. No excuses, no second chances, no refunds. It does as it's fucking told. That's a very beautiful thing.

I didn't bury her in the woods at the back of Mum and Dad's house – that would have been the easy option, yes, but I had other plans. She needed to be found. All the way to the quarry Beatz FM played the best of Prince so I had a good old sing-a-long. The sunset was pied, the air was mild and the breeze on my face from the open window of Henry's Triumph Stag was sensual to the point of hysteria. My former bully growing ever colder on the back seat, eleven-year-old me sitting in the passenger's seat beside me, singing along to 'Let's Go Crazy'.

The roads were busy but moving on the way up to the quarry before the country lanes grew smaller and quieter and thicker with foliage and gnarled trees, wide enough for the one-way lorries but unwelcome for pedestrians or dog-walkers. It was a steep, winding track lit only by my headlights and, by the time I'd got to the top and drove into the main car park, Prince had belted out most of his back catalogue and the DJ had moved on to 90s classics. I turned the radio off and heaved her out of the back seat by her underarms. There was no ceremony at the top. No eulogising. I did what had to be done and then I kicked the heavy bulk of her over the ridge.

And then I listened to the susurration of her heavy body as it careered down the incline, the skittering of the loose stones as it gathered speed; the loud CRACK, the wet splat. The euphonious spring insects clicking in the grass and the rolling of the rocks. Until the last rock stilled and there was nothing. I stood at the top of the gaping pit and inhaled the night air, allowing it to fill my lungs. And I finally let it go. Stunning.

OK, BuzzFeed, you got me there. Hands in the air. I enjoyed myself tonight.

Sunday, 10 March

Me, Craig and Tink were invited down to Craig's parents, Jim and Elaine's, for Sunday lunch. It was the usual – a stroll along the sea front, then roast beef and all the trimmings, followed by tea on the lawn, admiring the new collection of garden centre plants they'd just planted. Bonus rounds this afternoon were an awkward talk with Jim about his model boats and an inane half an hour with Elaine mewing on about her latest purchase on QVC (the woman's obsessed with it) and her last WI coffee morning. I was stupid enough to ask once if she wanted me to talk to the group about my novel or my journalism career.

'I'm not sure if it's the right target audience really,' she said.

No, because they'd rather listen to some bloke called Keith drone on about his doorknob collection or watch some biddy called Jean demonstrate how to make dollies out of fucking wicker.

They're both retired now. They used to live in town but two years ago they bought this bright yellow house right on the coast. It always reminds me of a giant wedge of lemon meringue pie. Jim has a small property portfolio of houses and flats in the area which he co-manages with an old friend of his called Bernie but for the most part they're just blah people. There's nothing to dislike about them per se – Jim could bore for his country while Elaine is so neurotic she is one cracked egg away from a nervous breakdown – but all in all, Sundays with them are never greatly enjoyable. They're churchgoers too and neither of them swears which means I can't either so I've been sculpted into a version of me called Lovely Girlfriend while in their company. And Lovely Girlfriend never swears or farts or accidentally offers an opinion. Even when they are blatantly wrong, you don't argue with Jim and Elaine. It's all part of The Act.

I'll have the last laugh though, of course. When they find out their beloved son has been fucking a serial killer, they'll have two strokes apiece.

We had a large lamb roast dinner – each portion could probably have fed a family of five – then we all fell asleep in the lounge watching Roger Moore keep the British end up. Unbeknown to us, Tink was demolishing the leftover lamb joint on the counter before throwing it all up again over Jim's hostas.

I dreamed about being at school. At the swimming gala. Winning the butterfly when I was fourteen. A big fat gold medal and no Julia. I slept right through the *Antiques Roadshow*. Didn't even find out how much that Queen Anne cabinet went for.

Monday, 11 March

1. *People who tag you in Facebook posts/add you to
   groups – e.g. 'Imelda's Hen Weekend – The Toppan's
   Masseeeeeve!!!' – so now I have to join in with all their
   planning and scrapbooking ideas. Woe, thy name is me*

If I was ever in any doubt that my night work afforded me some
kind of nepenthe to cure the humdrummity of my life, that
Monday morning ended that doubt. I was in a very good mood.

No nightmares all weekend and this morning they found
Julia's body first thing – the quarry foreman tipped off the police.
Ron announced it in the meeting.

I did my best shocked and appalled faces, but inside, it was
champagne bubbles. Daisy cried for Julia's kids, then for her
own. I was amazed to learn Daisy even *had* kids. Her hips were
so narrow a kidney bean would have trouble sliding out of there,
let alone an eight-pounder.

'Poor lass,' said Bill.

'Can't imagine what she went through,' said Carol.

'I hope to God she didn't suffer,' said Paul. 'What a bastard.'

I managed a tear and Jeff rubbed my shoulder. Later on,
Claudia asked me to go down to the hospital with Johnny and

report on a charity abseil. It was all pretty pour-petrol-over-me-and-strike-the-match stuff but at least The Act was intact.

Linus was in a bad mood when he got back from the police press conference – he'd been pulled over by a policeman for the bumper sticker and he was spoiling for a fight with anyone who ass-grazed his desk. Me and AJ risked a mini high-five when he came over to ask me if he could borrow my Pritt Stick.

I wish this feeling of contentment would last. I wonder how long it lasts for other people, if anyone else feels like this all the time – happy and fulfilled. For me, it's like when you eat a Chinese meal – you feel satisfied for about twenty minutes until you start thinking about the weight you've just put on and the leftover prawn crackers in the bag. It took me six years to get back to relative normal after Priory Gardens. I got my voice back. I got my legs walking and (eventually) running again. But Happiness is the one thing that didn't really come back. Anger came back twice as hard so maybe it ate all the Happy there was.

Went round to Mum and Dad's after work to cut up the bloody tarp in the garage and wash everything down. Julia's blood had dried to sticky patches. I climbed over Henry's fence and fed it in sections into his chimenea. Once I removed the steel eyes from the wall in the back bedroom, steam cleaned the carpet, Polycelled and painted over the holes and folded up the rope into my bag, there was no visible evidence that Julia had ever been there. When I was done, I sat on a deckchair in Henry's back garden, sipping a little crystal glass of his cream sherry and watching the tarp melt away in the flames. I got out my phone and looked at Craig and Lana's sex selfie. I didn't feel so bad about it today. It was as though Julia had cleansed that feeling for me.

Tink sat beside me on the grass, head resting on her paws, just looking up at me; for all the world like she was saying, 'You're so weird.'

Thursday, 14 March

1. *Wheelchair woman who I held the door open for in Waterstones and who didn't thank me. RUDE MUCH?*
2. *Old couple who called Tink a 'little rat' when she barked at them outside Lidl. In Tink's defence, they appeared from nowhere so they were in the wrong. Ninja grandparents + recently traumatised chihuahua = carnage*
3. *The man who invented Henry vacuum cleaners – the hose is too short, the bag's always full and they're heavier than a 10-tonne truck. Thank God we only have carpet in the bedrooms*

Another novel rejection came today, this time from Salinger, Martyrs and Wady. I'd followed a couple of their agents on Twitter as it seemed like my style of writing would suit them. Not so. 'You have a unique style, but sadly it's not quite in keeping with our list. May I take this opportunity to wish you the best of blah blah…' I don't think I even care any more.

I'm not Liking any more of their stupid cat memes, that's for damn sure.

Work was a turd on a turtle's back and went twice as slow. Our resident anal twitch Linus Sixgill was preparing his copy on his follow-up piece, 'The Riot Lovers: Unmasked', Claudia was in a non-descript huff for most of the morning and had her prickles out for anyone who dared cast a shadow across her tits (i.e. Me) and I did the usual boring-assed stuff I always do. AJ's back to flirting with me properly and making me peanut butter and banana toasties and completely ignoring Lana so there's a silver lining.

The Van Rapists are still on the loose. I'm going to look for them. Not yet, but soon. I'm going to take the cleaver. Been itching to try it out. I wonder if it's brought down hard enough on a limb whether it will sever completely or just in half. Depends how much force is applied, I suppose. There are some things I remember from school science class.

Also, Dan Wells's mother, in conjunction with the police, has put up a £20,000 reward for information into the circumstances of his death (i.e. who cut his cock off). No one has come forward thus far but this is a trifle worrying. Not a full cause for concern yet but it has definitely put me back in the woods.

AJ wanted to go to The Basement for lunch, which is a student hang-out with a sticky floor, tub-thumping house music and where they serve smoothies, tuna melts and syphillis. I suggested The Roast House – an independent coffee shop in Periwinkle Lane, more befitting to my sensitive tastes. They play soft jazz, have comfy seat cushions and, if you can handle the constant gnashing of dentures on stale fruit cake, it's a nice place to just sit and watch the world. They don't have fancy barista machines so there isn't the incessant clanking or pissing steam that you get in the chains. It was a nice day so we sat and had a coffee then grabbed some sausage and caramelised onion 'sangers', and took them over to the churchyard. I told him about the tramp who lived under the tree. His foot was sticking out between the low-lying branches and we attempted to hoop-la some onion rings on his big toe.

'So how are you liking it round here?' I asked him.

'Yeah, it's good. Colder than Straya but nah, everyone's been beaut. Auntie Claudia said Ron's quite impressed with my work so far.'

'You and the mayor made friends then, have you?' I winked.

He laughed embarrassedly. 'Yeah, she was cool. I blew it out of proportion, I always do. She was telling me about her son travelling all round the States. I'd love to go there.'

'So are you still leaving in June then?'

'Yeah. I haven't seen anything of the UK yet so I just want to get some money under my belt then hit the road.'

'Where will you go?'

'Round the UK for a bit. Then Europe. I wanna see Russia too, and meet up with some mates in India, then back to Oz. I wanna go everywhere. Did you go travelling?'

'No,' I said. 'Never wanted to. Is Claudia OK with you going?'

'Yeah. She said she's never done anything like that so she wants me to go. She's been great about putting me up but she'll probably be glad to have her house back.'

'I've got no desire to travel at all,' I said. 'Me and Craig went to Cyprus a few years ago. Couldn't stand it. Too hot. Guess I'm a home bird.'

'But wouldn't you like to see more places before you die? India? Malaysia? Maybe Australia?'

'No,' I said. 'I just want some stability in my life. I want a house with four front windows and two hanging baskets and a garden where I can grow things. A bigger lawn for Tink. And a better job. And a book deal. It's not too much to ask, is it?'

A silence fell as we ate our sandwiches. I sensed he wanted to ask me something.

'Do you want to go for a drink after work? The pub over the road looks...'

'Like a shithole?' I suggested.

'Oh,' he said. 'How about the one in the High Street?'

'Weatherspoon's?' I laughed. 'Yeah, if you like having your head kicked in and your food spat in.'

'Ah forget it,' he said, with a blush. 'It was just a thought.'

'I have a boyfriend, AJ.'

'Oh, God, no, I didn't mean on a date-like-thing, I just meant as a mate. A colleague. We can just talk and stuff.'

'I'm a bit busy tonight after work. I have... Body Pump.'

'Cool, cool. No worries at all.'

It was awkward between us all afternoon after that. He only came over to my desk once, didn't smile *and* he forgot my Canderel in my coffee. What have I done?! I've said actual no to that face, that ass, those hands on my breasts. How strong am I?

You have no idea.

I Facebook-searched Wesley Parsons to pass the time between WI write-ups and darts scores. I haven't done this for a while as there are so many Wesley Parsons on Facebook it's just not funny. I know his family lived in Bristol when we did but Parsons himself could have gone anywhere when he came out of prison. Half of the avatars are non-specific sports cars, symbols or pictures of babies, few of an actual face, so I've reached a bit of a dead end there. I live in hope that one day he'll make himself obvious.

So too with Derek Scudd. It turns out that Mary Tolmarsh, the mother of one of the abused girls, is the one who lives in Windwhistle Court not him. I'd totally misread the situation, having stalked the fucking place for weeks. I saw her going into her house today when I swung by. I put a note through her letterbox.

Craig greeted me with a bunch of beautiful guilt freesias when I got home. He's out tonight – I can't remember what the excuse was, either 'a burst pipe' somewhere or 'round Eddie's playing "FIFA"'. Either way he was with her. I was in the chat rooms.

I wasn't really in the mood. I was there trying to eat my jacket potato in front of *MasterChef* and my alerts kept *bing-bong*ing away. My replies were all very half-hearted.

Mmm mmm, baby, don't stop, you're getting me so hot.

Mmmm, I'm loving it. You're such a big boy.

I love watching you strike your big fat clock.

Etcetera etcetera. I was too focused on the semi-finals and whether or not the roast venison with parsnip and vanilla purée was going to impress the food critics. I wanted Josephine to win. She had a dog that looked like Tink.

Friday, 15 March

1. *People who walk in groups along the pavement so no one else can get past, like they're fucking in Reservoir Dogs*
2. *Middle-class people who believe it's their God-given right to bring their babies into restaurants and allow them to squawk all through a meal*
3. *Interrupters – have you any idea how hard it is to get a thought train moving again when you're psychologically disturbed, LUCILLE?*
4. *Millionaire celebrities asking the general public for money – I know there's no water in Africa, Ewan McGregor, and I know little Malaika needs an eye operation or she'll go blind, Simon Pegg, and that Lucas drinks dirty water all day long while looking after his twenty-six siblings, Michael Sheen, so why don't you dip your hand in your pocket if you're so concerned?*
5. *'Dillon' on the checkout in Lidl – I know that look, boy. Don't think we're friends now just because you know what brand of tampon goes up my hoop*

My tits are sore, I woke up feeling more tired than I was when I went to bed and I have a HUUUUGE craving for sour-apple

MAOAMs. Going to run out in a minute before work and see if they have any over Lidl on my lunch break.

*

Am back from Lidl. They didn't have any sour-apple MAOAMS. Also, I feel a bit sick sick. I'm praying it's not pregnancy-related. No, it can't be. My pill's never let me down before.

But what if it is? I can just hear the PICSOs now, delighted I'm finally officially one of the Mummy Club…

'*Oh, congratulations, babe! You'll be showing on my wedding day!*'

'*Your whole life will change. Most important job a woman can do.*'

'*You'll be such an amazing mummy, Rhiannon!*'

These are all things I'd heard them say to each other at various stages of pregnancy. And I won't be an 'amazing mummy' at all. Look at the state of me. I'm selfish, unspeakably angry with every aspect of the world and I've killed a man for wanting a blow job. Throw a baby into the mix and you've got yourself a nightmare of *Daily Mail* proportions.

It'll be hanging off my tits for months. I won't get a wink of sleep. What if my nightmares return? Craig'll be no help. I'll have to take it to that horrible nursery in town, the one where the mournful howls and shrieks follow you all the way up the street. Ugh, no, I can't bear it.

And there's no way it's playing with my Sylvanians doll's house. Nobody plays with my doll's house but me.

*

I've calmed down now. Bought a preggo test at lunch and it was only one line that equalled negative. Thank fuck for that. God bless you, little pill. God bless you, Marie Stopes, whoever the hell you are.

*

I'm at work and I'm bored. Just googled Honey Cottage, my nanny and granddad's old place in Wales. I haven't done that for ages, maybe a year but, amazingly, it's still up for sale and the asking price has come down again by almost £7,000. The inside hasn't changed a bit – still the same large wooden beams and eaves, still the peeling pink wallpaper in the master bedroom, still the damp patch on the kitchen ceiling – and the gardens are just as I remember. The vegetable patches. The chicken coop. The greenhouse. The river with the mountains in the background. Everything was so simple then. So quiet. There wasn't such a cacophony of thoughts in my head all hours of the day.

In a fit of curiosity, I dialled the agent's number. I hung up just as someone answered.

AJ had plonked a copy of this week's edition before me on top of my keyboard – this week's cover star was Julia Kidner.

LOCAL WOMAN'S BODY FOUND IN QUARRY – POLICE SAY IT'S MURDER

THE BODY of 28-year-old Julia Kidner was discovered on Monday morning by staff at Chipchase Quarry in the hills.

A source has said that Ms Kidner left her marital home just before Christmas last year with no explanation. Ms Kidner's partner, Lloyd Fletcher, 36, is being questioned by police who believe he may have had some communication with her since then.

Ms Kidner's three children, Scott, 12, Ciara, 9 and Tyler, 5 are currently in the care of Social Services.

Sniffer dogs and officers combed forests and roadsides close to the quarry yesterday as well as the location where Ms Kidner's body was found, nearly 40 miles from her home address. Investigations are ongoing.

Met Lucille for a coffee at the Apple Blossom Café – she had some ideas about Imelda's scrapbook that she wanted to share with me 'because I have an Art A level and I know how to make it all neat and stuff'. She's still on the 5:2 but, handily, today was a 2 day so she stuffed her face with a triple chocolate brownie and a mocha with whipped cream. I had a hot water with lemon and a chia seed protein bomb, just to claim the high ground.

AJ brought me back a Creme Egg from lunch. 'Just for the hell of it.' His smile twinkled. He's still on crutches so he'd carried it in his pocket all the way back from town. It was still slightly warm from being next to his groin.

Craig treated me to a guilt-fuelled steak at Cote de Sirène tonight, the place I went with the PICSOs at New Year. I put the knife I'd severed Dan Wells' choad with back where it came from.

Don't look so shocked, I washed it first.

Sunday, 17 March

Me and Craig and Tink had a run out to the country to a little farm shop where I bought some herbs for the balcony – basil, mint, sage, rosemary, oregano, lemon thyme and parsley. I potted them this afternoon and they smell DIVINE. I also bought a little strawberry plant because it reminded me of the strawberries Granddad used to grow in his greenhouse. I do enjoy that feeling – dry soil beneath your toes. I spread some out over the balcony and just walked through it. Tink didn't know what to make of it and stood inside the flat giving me bug-eyes. There was dirt all over the flat. Craig thinks I'm crazy too. I think he's a twat.

Our afternoon delights lasted all of six minutes twenty-eight seconds. Then I made some lemon drizzle cake while he crashed out on the sofa in front of *Countryfile*. His phone went earlier; now he's 'popped out to grab his tool belt from the van'. I watched him through the stairwell window. Lana was waiting in the shadows.

Tuesday, 19 March

1. *People at the* Gazette *who think it's all right to bring smelly food back to their desks and eat it of a lunchtime. Today's example: Inept Plunket and her Brie-and-apricot sandwich and close-quarters conversationing*
2. *Shop assistants who chat to their colleagues on the next till about their hip operation when they're meant to be serving you*
3. *That Scottish comedian who shouts*
4. *That old chef who is always bemoaning the state of the British farming industry – yeah, we get it, you're really fucked over on milk prices. Move on.*
5. *Man in the silver Honda (formerly blue Qashqai) – waved at me this morning as I crossed the road with Tink. Must have upped his meds. Still don't trust him*

Daisy Chan is still trying to have normal conversations with me. I don't mind her as much as I do Inept or Joyless Joy – at least I can get some editorial gossip out of her – but I can't look at her for very long – she's so excruciatingly thin. We're talking clothes prop. Ladder rung. And I don't know for sure where she gets her clothes from but I'm certain I've seen the frilly top she wears in

Marks and Spencer's children's section. Today, she minced over to talk about an interesting theory she had.

'Rhiannon, could you look at something for me?'

'Yeah, one sec,' I said, finishing typing up my report on last year's Welly Wanging champion who has just become a father (yes, this counts as news around here, I shit you not). 'What is it?'

She sat down on the rickety vacant swivel chair next to mine, normally occupied by Jeff or AJ. 'I've run this by the others at the editorial meeting this morning and got laughed out of the room.'

'I'm never invited to the editorials.' I shrugged.

'You're not missing much, believe me,' she said with a roll of eye as she lay four torn-out sheets from past editions across my keyboard – the first was dated Friday, 10 October, nine years ago. A university student – Jonas Petchey from Vienna – had been stabbed to death in Wrayburn Park in the town. The second page was from Friday, 24 November, four years later – another student, Billy Ryall stabbed down by the canal. Both unsolved. The other two were front pages – Canal Man and Park Man.

'Now,' she said, shuffling closer so I could take in the full aromas her body had to offer – cheap nostril-burning perfume, coffee breath, some sort of chocolate and toothpaste, 'do you see a pattern here?'

'Er,' I said, studying the pages individually. 'Well, they're all dead.'

'Yep.'

'And they were all killed in the town. And all are unsolved cases.'

'Yep, what else?'

'Er…' I thought long and hard, still studying the pages. 'They're all men?'

'Yeah, what else?'

'Well… two of them are sex offenders…'

'Exactly!' She smiled. 'I knew you'd be able to see it too.'

'See what?'

'The pattern. Billy Ryall and Gavin White BOTH had convictions for sex offences. Maybe Jonas and Dan Wells had attacked girls as well but hadn't been caught. Maybe that's why Dan Wells' penis was severed before he went into the canal?'

'So you're saying there's a serial killer out there hunting sex offenders? A vigilante of sorts?'

'Yes!'

I frowned. 'What about Julia Kidner? She wasn't a sex offender.'

She frowned too. 'No, I know but she *was* raped. And that's where my theory comes a bit unstuck. The way they were all killed just seems so similar. I'm going to ask one of the policemen on the case if I can have a look at the case files on these earlier ones. Dig a bit deeper, see if there are DNA links to the ones from this year.'

'But it's not your job, let them get on with it. You won't get any extra credit from Ron if you're right.'

'I'm not doing this for extra credit, I'm doing it because I want to help the police. That's all.'

'Even so, it's a bit unlikely, isn't it? A serial killer who first struck nine years ago, then had four years' rest, then another two years off before doing three all within months this year?'

She visibly wilted. Then perked up. 'Perhaps there are some missing persons in the interim years? Other unsolved cases? Or maybe they never found the bodies? I could check on that too.'

I smiled at her.

'You think it's a long shot as well, don't you?'

I laughed. 'This is a county town where welly wanging is an annual event and people have competitions to grow massive sprouts. We're not cool enough for a serial killer.'

She frowned. 'You think serial killers are cool?'

'God, no, not at all. I think they're abhorrent. I just meant that generally speaking they operate in more famous areas, don't they? Larger areas – London, Ipswich, Yorkshire. Places they're not going to be found as easily.'

'Yeah. I spoke to Paul and he said the police aren't connecting our murders with the ones in London any more – completely different MO. But this… I dunno, it just seems so possible. *Probable*, even.'

'How long did you live in London for, Daisy?'

'Most of my life, until this year. You think I'm being too *CSI* about this?'

'I just think it's a bit unlikely. And look at the methods – they're all different. This Jonas guy was killed in broad daylight. Billy Ryall was stabbed on the towpath and almost decapitated. Dan Wells drowned, officially. And Park Man was stabbed in the neck. It's all so… haphazard. Serial killers usually have methods they like to stick to, like bind torture kill or night stalking. Know what I mean?'

'You sound like an expert.'

'I watch a lot of Channel 5.'

Daisy sighed. 'I just thought this might be something.'

I sighed. 'Bit tenuous. I'd say it's unlikely any of these deaths are linked.'

'No, the police agree with you.'

'Do they?'

'Yeah. And they said Julia Kidner was held somewhere, possibly tortured. She had some fingers missing and her hair had been cut off. She'd even been drawn on.'

'How awful.'

She nodded sadly and began tidying away the pages from my desk. 'Thanks for hearing me out anyway, Rhiannon. I appreciate it.'

'No problem. I like your top, by the way.'

'Oh, thanks. It's from Marks. In the sale.'

I gave her one of my sweet smiles – one with thinning eyes and wrinkled nose. It was on the tip of my tongue to ask her about the main story she was working on these days with Claudia – the Van Rapes – but I held back. I didn't want to lay any cable between me and them, not if I was going fishing for them this weekend.

I wonder if a little friendship can blossom between me and Daisy now; a friendship based on mutual advice, fashion tips and a deep-seated need to know what's being said in those damn editorial meetings.

*

Something a bit weird's just happened – I overheard two colleagues talking about me. I was in the Ladies' – having a poo if you must know. It was unscheduled and rather difficult so I was taking longer than normal because your anal muscles constrict when you're at work for fear that someone important will hear you. Anyway, I was all cleaned up when the door outside swung open and two female voices caught my ear: Inept Plunket and Claudia.

LYNETTE: That Priory Gardens thing must explain some of it. Why she's so quiet and starey all the time.

CLAUDIA: Yeah. She was in therapy for a few years after that. She couldn't walk for months.

LYNETTE: The nation's sweetheart.

CLAUDIA: That was a long time ago. She doesn't have many friends here. I think Ron only gave her the job on Reception 'cos he felt sorry for her. Can't bloody get rid of her now.

LYNETTE: Daisy seems to like her. I've never taken to her. She's very weird and the way she just stares at you.

CLAUDIA: I've never been comfortable around her. There's some people you just never click with, isn't there?

LYNETTE: Shame, isn't it?

CLAUDIA: She's very sore about not getting the Junior Reporter role. I mean, she didn't stand a chance anyway but she puts herself up for it, year on year. Absolute freak.

The conversation continued as they both pissed in stalls either side of me, flushed, then met at the sinks to touch up their hair. I noticed neither washed their hands because I didn't hear any water running. Then they both left, one after the other, and the conversation shifted onto Daisy Chan and her hideous lace blouses.

I sat on the edge of the toilet seat and marinated in what I'd just heard; the odd phrase or word jumping out like a flea from a dirty dog;

'Weird';

'Never been comfortable around her';

'Freak'.

So The Act wasn't working on them. It was working on Craig and the PICSOs and even Daisy, but not on these two. I'm just gonna have to dial up the nice and dial down the Me.

AJ seems to like me still, too. He's not asked me out again and he sat on the end of my desk today and talked about his dreams of travelling round India like some mate of his did for a good ten minutes while I typed up the Over-50s Hockey League results and pretended to be interested. He brought me back a flat white from lunch too and when I took off the lid to stir in my sweetener, I found a little chocolate heart melted into the foam. Bless him.

Thursday, 21 March

The new herbs are thriving, shockingly, considering who's Chief Gardener, but there are still no strawberries on my little plant.

Craig took Tink to work with him at the town house where he's putting a new guest bathroom in. Luckily, the lady has a big garden and two chihuahuas of her own. I'm glad she got to play with someone of her own ilk today; someone as into sniffing butts and chasing moths, as she is.

There was something of the pathetic fallacy about all the articles I had to type up today. Everything was so miserable; the outlook on the world so gloomy, so hopeless.

Letters about dirt-poor teenagers sucking balloons in the park.

A new AA support group.

The problem of dog poo on Town Centre pavements.

Another flasher on the golf course.

Two lawnmowers stolen from sheds and the ram-raiding of the laptop shop.

Drugs. Drink. Shit. Sex. And theft.

The film review for this week is of the latest Pixar offering – some crap about a lost shoe. AJ's going to come with me again and basically write the thing for me. He bought me a gonk today too which we saw in a toy store window and which I mentioned looked a bit like him. I stuck it on the top of my computer. The resemblance is uncanny.

Oh, and Pidge is up the spout. Imelda texted and said the PICSOs were going out for a celebratory curry on Saturday. Oh, joy. No fishing trips for Van Rapists for me. Instead, I have to endure a few more hours of baby talk, wedding talk (Imelda's bound to cram it in somewhere) and another fat slice of my life pretending to enjoy the company of people I'd gladly leave screaming under rubble.

I texted back, saying, 'Yep, that sounds great. See you then.'

'Meet you at the Shahryar at 7.'

'I'll look 4ward to it.' Slurpy-faced smiley. Kiss kiss kiss.

Ugh.

Lynette from Accounts came round with the payslips this afternoon – aka, the bitch who thinks I'm 'quiet and starey'. This month I have no student loan repayment and two pension deductions. The woman is a joke. And I'm the only one who doesn't find her in the least bit amusing.

About 8 p.m., I headed out under the guise of a 'PICSO barbecue' (it was the first thing that came into my head) and headed for the Old Road, looking for the black or blue Transit van. There are a few lay-bys along that road – I'd heard one of their victims was raped in the van in one of them, but I wasn't sure which. Another was dragged out of her car into a thicket just off the road down Copperton Lane. No sign of them, but I'll come back. I'll come back every night if I have to. I want them. I want them to meet my cleaver.

And I heard a great joke today on the Internet: How many men does it take to tile a bathroom? One – but only if you slice him veeeeery thinly.

Saturday, 23 March

1. *The PICSOs*
2. *People who get married*
3. *People who keep telling you they're getting married*
4. *People who use ancient bridal photos of themselves as their Facebook profile pic, just cos they were thin then (Lucille)*
5. *People who have hen parties*
6. *People who invite me to hen parties*
7. *The person who invented hen parties*

We had every intention of doing the car-boot-sale-we're-never-going-to-do today only it was raining and the draw of a warm flat, takeaway pizza and a re-watch of *The Lost Boys* were too much to resist.

Had sex again this morning – all of three-and-a-half minutes of fun. It's become so regular and organised and I'm getting through lube like Lurpak.

In/out, shake it all about then work. In/out, shake it all about, then Lidl.

In/out, shake it all about, then over to Nando's for a Churrasco Thigh Burger with chips – *Gordon Ramsay clap* – done.

'Shame we can't crack the case,' Craig said this morning. 'I thought we'd be pregnant by now.'

'Yeah, don't worry, I'm sure it'll happen soon,' I called out from the bathroom as I popped my pill and located my jam jar.

*

Curry with the PICSOs tonight was barely edible but the accompanying wine went down a treat and quelled my simmering urge to kill everyone in sight. Pidge held court with tales of previous failed impregnations and what 'hell it's been to get to this point' (failed IVF attempts, couples counselling, Tom walking out on her after an argument in Home Sense when she threw a Yankee Candle at his head) but for the most part she was as happy as an Osmond on speed. The subject all evening should have been Pidge and Tom finally becoming parents – instead, of course, it was all about Mel's wedding.

Tonight's debating subjects: Wedding Favours and How to Arrange Them, Worries About the Best Man's Speech and Which Take That Song To Walk Back Down the Aisle To.

'I want "Rule the World" but Jack's adamant he wants "Greatest Day", but I said that could be our first dance. There's me trying to be flexible about the whole thing but we had this blazing row...'

Anni threw Imelda eye daggers as our pickle carousel arrived. She's currently two weeks overdue and the spiciest vindaloo on the menu is her last resort to push the lil' sucker out. She tried, admirably, to move the discussion back round to the evening's main topic.

'So when's your due date, Pidgey?'

'November twenty-fifth.'

'Ooh,' said Lucille, 'that means he'll be a Sagittarius.'

'Is that good?'

'Yeah, it is good actually. He'll be a good friend and he'll live life to the fullest. Loyal and generous souls, Sagittarians. My Alex is Sadgy as well.'

'Aww, is he?' I said, trying to hop onto the conversation train as I could see Mel waiting for a gap so she could show something she'd found on her phone – most certainly a wedding-related Pinterest board.

'Are you into all that then? Horoscopes and stuff?'

'Oh, yeah,' she enthused. 'I always read my stars and I consult my Tarot woman for every big decision – new house, kids, when I switched jobs. She's spot on.'

'I've always wanted to have my Tarot cards read. Can you read them?'

'No,' said Lucille. 'But my woman in Glastonbury, Lolita Starflower, is fantastic. I've got her card somewhere.' She started rooting in her handbag.

I turned to Pidge as Imelda began to draw another breath. 'Do you have any names picked out yet or is it too early to say?'

But Imelda thrust her iPhone in the centre of the table so none of us could ignore it. It was a picture of a tiny jar filled with Smarties and around the neck was a tag saying 'Newly-weds' in italic writing. 'What do you think about these for wedding favours? They work out at £3.50 each and there's Smarties, Jelly Tots or Shrimps.'

'Ahh, they're nice,' said Lucille. 'Yeah, go for Jelly Tots.'

Imelda thrust the phone into my face. 'How about you, Rhee?'

'Shrimps,' I said.

'Anni?'

'You're spending £700 just on jars of sweets?'

'Maybe, I haven't decided yet. What do you think of them anyway?'

'That was *well*-quick maths, Anni.' I laughed, draining my

wine and clicking the waiter over for another. He took my empty glass.

Anni continued: 'I saw somewhere that a cancer charity's doing wedding favours for two pounds fifty pence. Badges, key rings, buttons. And something like ninety-five per cent of the money goes directly to a hospice. Jack's auntie died of cancer, didn't she?'

'I'm not doing that,' said Imelda. 'I don't want to bring everyone down remembering Jack's auntie. What do you think about "How Deep Is Your Love"?'

The waiters cleared our empty poppadum plates and pickle trays. On the opposite table, a chorus of 'Happy Birthday' was in full flow for a little boy. The waiters wheeled out a little hostess trolley and in the middle of it was a small birthday cake with a sparkling candle in the centre. Imelda looked disgusted.

We were midway through our main course, when Lucille brought up the unthinkable.

'Oooh, I know what I wanted to talk to you guys about – Hen Weekend! The Toppan's Masseeeve! I need to start booking it. No one's going to drop out on me, are they?'

Imelda looked daggers at each one of us in turn. 'They better not.'

'I can't wait,' said Pidge. 'I'll be past the worst of the morning sickness by then, with any luck, though I won't be allowed to drink. How many of us are going?'

'Ten,' said Mel, chewing on a piece of lamb shashlik that wouldn't quit. 'Me, Lucille, You, Anni, Rhiannon...'

Note that I don't get asked to these things, it's just assumed I'll turn up.

'. . . Lucille's sister Cleo, your friend Gemma, our auntie Steph, and two girls I work with, Jane and Sharon. They're a right laugh.'

'And what are we doing, exactly?' asked Anni.

Lucille lit up. 'Stags and Slags Weekend: the Over 18s Weekender at Toppan's. Didn't you get my text?'

Ugh. Toppan's Holiday Park – Where Good Taste and Refined Dining Crawled Away to Die in Pain.

'Oh, that's for definite, is it?' I said. 'I thought a spa day in Bath with cream teas at a five-star hotel was mentioned? Or Legoland?' I'd take Legoland over Toppan's at that moment. I'd take *crucifixion* over Toppan's. Save me, Legoland Windsor, you're my only hope.

'No, we decided that could be a bit boring, didn't we, Luce?' said Mel, fumbling in her bag for a crumpled-up leaflet. 'If I'm going to let my hair down, I'm letting it down all the way.' She giggled and they clinked glasses. 'I mean it's the last time I'm gonna have any fun, isn't it? It's symbolic.'

Imelda and Jack had been together fifteen years and had three kids, a fixed-rate mortgage and a joint bank account. Jack had two affairs under his belt (that we knew of) and Imelda had at least three one-night stands in the past year alone (that we were all sworn to secrecy about). So unless marriage was going to cut off his dick or her libido, I didn't see what was going to change. Jack's a miserable bastard anyway.

'They've got clubs, bars, entertainment all laid on every night,' said Lucille, 'so we won't get bored. And when you've had enough of partying all night long, you can just roll back to your chalet and sleep it off.'

'I'm going to get SO wasted,' said Mel, tucking into her vindaloo, fully back in the Land of the Not-Sulking now. 'Seriously, we are taking ALL the alcohol.'

They all shrieked, Anni included. And back I was on the outside, looking into the nest – the cuckoo without a cause. The Toppan's leaflet came round. There were photos of groups of men and women, bleary-eyed, club-sweaty, glitter cleavage and neon-painted. The men were all in superhero costumes or

Where's Wally outfits; some of the women in naughty schoolgirl uniforms and doing thumbs-up to the camera and rabbit ears above each other's heads. All kinds of zany hilarity.

Toppan's – by day a family water park; by night, a Petri dish of chlamydia. The place looked impressive in the central picture on the leaflet – three large see-through structures, a bit like a square Eden Project except there was nothing exotic growing underneath those roofs. Each building was labelled Club Land, Pub Land or Grub Land. So one minute you'd be grinding up against someone in the Club, then shagging them behind the Pub, and finally eating fried chicken with them inside Grub. Sorted.

'Do you know what we are dressing up as, yet?' I asked, thinking maybe they'd come up with something truly original. Perhaps we'd go as suffragettes, complete with 'Votes for Women' placards, or members of the Bloomsbury Group, or even nuns in full-length habits, Bible in hand, rosary beads round necks. Maybe I could use the beads to strangle myself with.

I braced as Lucille smiled. 'Our theme is – prostitutes.'

'Prostitutes?' I said. 'Cool, Mafia-type gun-slinging prostitutes? Jack the Ripper-esque long-skirted, ripped-abdomen prostitutes?'

'No,' she chuckled, showing more teeth than a dentist's waiting room. 'Just prostitutes. Modern day ones. Slaggier the better.'

'Great,' I said. 'That sounds absolutely… magnificent.'

'And the higher the heel and the lower the top, the better. When you're out shopping for your outfit just think…'

'. . . whore?' I said.

'Exactly.'

Monday, 25 March

Bollocky Bill walked in first thing and belched his poached haddock and eggs breakfast in my face when asking how my weekend was.

'Get all your ironing done, did you?' he laughed.

'What ironing?' I said. 'I don't iron.'

'Women love ironing, don't they? My wife did three loads this weekend. Kids were back from university.'

'I'm thrilled for her.'

'You one of them feminists then, are you? Hate men and make them do their own washing?'

'I don't hate men,' I said. 'I hate everyone.'

He laughed himself back to his desk, mumbling about Germaine Greer. Prick.

Saw another joke online today – *Never break someone's heart because they've only got one. They have 206 bones, break them instead.* I doubt I could *find* Bill's bones under fifty-seven years of his wife's plum crumble.

Linus told me a song came on the radio while he was having his protein granola and it made him think of me.

'It was called "Rhiannon",' he said. 'I didn't catch the artist.'

'Fleetwood Mac,' I said. 'My parents named me after it. It's about a Welsh witch. And my family are Welsh so...'

'Really?' he said, his interest clearly wrapped in plastic.

'Where did your parents get the name Linus from? The Snoopy cartoon?'

I hadn't said it as a joke but Claudia and AJ laughed like semi-automatic rifles. I have never heard of anyone being called Linus apart from the kid in the Snoopy cartoon who carries around a blue blanket and sucks his thumb. Still, Linus seemed to take offence to that and replied that his 'father was Swedish and it was his grandfather's name and probably his grandfather's name too'.

'Oh, did your grandfather like Snoopy, too?' I said, again, not in jest and Claudia and AJ continued to giggle. Linus walked away at that point as Lana was standing by his desk with a pile of papers. I think his dick would have just dropped off if he hadn't got to her and started flirting when he did.

AJ winked at me today, apropos of nothing, he was just passing my desk. He said he's got a 'pretty awesome prank' planned for Linus that is going to blow mine out of the water but he won't tell me what it is. He's teasing me, like a little dog. He's also stopped wearing his 'singlets' as he called them and has now taken to wearing Diesel aftershave and a long-sleeve black V-neck which clings to his biceps and shows off his tanned clavicle. I keep wanting to lick it.

Oh, yeah, and ULTRA big news, courtesy of Daisy Chan – the police have made an arrest in the Park Man murder; a known local junkie called Kenny Spillane, who lives in a bail hostel in the centre of town. He's been their Person of Interest for a while now apparently, though he's known to everyone else as the guy who sits in the doorway of Argos shouting abuse and throwing cider cans at pigeons. Yeah, he'll do.

There's still radio silence from the public with regard to witnesses though, gawd bless 'em. Well, I say radio silence but one person has told police he saw 'a woman in a hooded tracksuit walking a dog'. But who's going to believe a woman had something to do with such a savage crime? Criminal justice system in this country is as fucked as the weather.

They're interviewing 'a number of suspects in the murder of Julia Kidner' and are saying it was 'definitely sexually motivated'. So it looks like I could be in the clear there as well. Big yays all round today.

I literally can't think of a single other thing to write but I'm pretending to because, as I speak, Claudia is looking across at me like I'm making bad smells. She knows I'm up to something. I can see it in her eyes. Ugh. The woman is a mouldering codpiece on the diseased cock of a Shakespearean leper. La de dah de dah.

Hmmm, what can I say? Ummmm… the weather's that pleasant sort of jacket-needed-but-no-layers-type that pleases me so much.

She's still looking.

And my Sylvanian doll's house is looking pretty up together now too. Craig picked me up a brand-new telephone and bookcase set from the toy shop on his lunch break yesterday, another guilt spree just for me, so I've got that in situ now underneath my little Van Gogh—

Right, she's stopped looking at me now cos her phone is ringing. She must be aware that I've caught up on all my work so I'm just fiddle-faddling round the Internet and doing jobs that nobody ever has time for, like filing or helping Bogdan with the obituaries.

She doesn't have many friends here. I think Ron only gave her the job on Reception cos he felt sorry for her. Can't bloody get rid of her now.

Hmmm. How to get Claudia onside. That one's a poser. She doesn't like me, that much is true, but what if she has no choice *but* to like me? Like, if I saved her life or something? I wonder how I can engineer that. Maybe if she choked and I ran over and administered the Heimlich? AJ likes me, so why doesn't she? Maybe it's *because* AJ likes me. Aha, I see. Tricky.

Just had a text from Cleo – Anni had a baby boy called Samuel at 3.19 this morning. Nine pounds something and no drugs. Her vagina must look like a lasagne dropped from a department store roof.

*

Just back from seeing Anni at the hospital – she has her own room in the private building at the back of the NHS bit. Jesus, it's like another world. She's got a widescreen TV, smoked salmon lunches, the nurses aren't rude and nothing stinks of piss. The other PICSOs were there, taking it in turns to cuddle Sam who looks like a shrunken, slightly annoyed version of Rashan, who was there too, stroking Anni 's head and nipping out to get us all coffees and biscuits (all free!). Even though he'd been up all night he was still buzzing.

Anni didn't look too happy but then she had just pushed a human watermelon from her stitched-to-fuck foof so I made my excuses after an hour and left. I'd done my bit by turning up with a card and a hastily bought blue teddy bear with musical notes on his bib. The Act is intact. I am once again the Thoughtful Friend.

*

Drove along Old Road again tonight, looking for signs of the Rapemobile. There were a few big vans around – none of them black or blue – pulling in to the lay-bys, making calls, men checking clipboards by the light of their phones – so close but no goldfish. I'd have waited there all night if Craig hadn't promised me a stir-fry.

Wednesday, 27 March

1. *Every single living creature at the* Gazette. *Even the mouse in the staffroom who keeps nicking the rice cakes*
2. *Tony Tompkinson – get this he's been SACKED from Up At the Crack for shagging a fifteen-year-old school friend of his daughter! Major scandal all round. Wife's left him, career's in tatters. Knew he was the sort*
3. *The tramp at the graveyard – who has said hello to me twice this week alone. Getting far too friendly for my liking*

They've done it this time – I'm now doing the one job, besides actual toilet cleaning, that all lowly editorial assistants at small-town newspapers dread...

The farmer's market report.

Imagine a two-page spread in your average tabloid-sized local newspaper. And that entire two pages are filled with text. Just. Text. Text that some poor cow (aka Me) has had to painstakingly input on a very old, very slow computer that crashes whenever you press Shift. You might find a small stock image of an Aberdeen Angus cow or Gloucester Old Spot pig in among the wall of writing, but for the most part, that's all it is. Writing. And nobody – and I do mean nobody – other than farmers actually reads it. And now it's become one of my jobs.

Courtesy of Claudia. Just because she can.

'AJ hasn't got the attention to detail yet for this sort of task, so I'm assigning it to you, Rhiannon. Thanks, Sweetpea.'

Hmmm.

So there I was, for the best part of the day, putting in this endless copy about Holsteins and grazing cows and Charolais heifers and 'excellent entries of billy kids and fat pigs' and sows and boars and longhorns and FUCK MY LIFE.

The only enjoyable part of this whole shitty-arsed task is that some other poor bastard has to check it for typos. And the only someone with enough patience to do that is Jeff.

'You've got a couple of semi-colons in the wrong places there, Rhiannon. And that farmer's name's wrong too, look. But for the most part, it looks fine.'

Jeff doesn't talk to me as much as he used to. He didn't even joke with me that I'd accidentally called one of the farmers Mr Cunt from Howbridge, rather than Mr Hunt from Cowbridge. I think he's been nobbled by The Gulp Monster. Jesus Christ, high school never ends, does it?

'Let's not talk to her today because she's not our friend. Let's play Off Ground Tig but without Rhiannon.'

Wankers.

Ooh, and a funny thing happened mid-morning – a bumper box of adult nappies arrived addressed to Linus and he went absolutely puce in the face when Bogdan brought it in to him. He had to qualify it all day long.

'They're not bloody mine, how many more times?! It's a mistake! I didn't order them!'

And as if to ram home the point after the twelfth barbed comment about incontinence, he marched out of the office, across the road and threw them in the wheely bin at the back of the church.

Inept said it was 'a terrible waste' when so many old people were shitting themselves at the NHS's expense. Me and AJ had a sneaky fist bump when nobody was looking. He looked fine today. I think I like him in his tight blue jeans the best – they're deliciously tight around his splendid arse. Whenever he walks past I just want to ram his head between my legs.

Daisy Chan was allowed the morning off PAID because she has to wait in for a new fireplace to be installed. Like, HELLO?! If I pulled that one, they'd have me out of here quicker than Lana when Craig texts to say he's got an erection.

Oh, yeah, they're still seeing each other. Despite all the sex he's getting from me to 'make our little Criannon' (cue the vom) he's still having his vanilla cupcake and eating her out. I read a text thread on his phone the other night, when he was in the shower:

CRAIG: *I'm trying to make things work with R. We're trying for a baby.*
L: *You can't drop me like this. It's not fair. I haven't done any-thing wrong. You said you loved me.*
CRAIG: *Lana, it's just too difficult at the moment. I still have feelings for you, course I do, but you've always known how it is with me and R. I love her.*
L: *Please just come over. Let's tlk. No pressure. I just want to see you.*
CRAIG: *Babe, I want to see U2.*
L: *Come round later. Just for an hour. I'll cook. I get that you don't want to leave her but we can make it work. Please, baby. I love you.*

Craig was 'working late tonight' so, once I'd taken Tink for her early evening walkies, I was back on Old Road looking for signs of the black van. A palm-sweaty, window-steaming urgency had come over me tonight and my temper was short.

'I want you,' I said to the empty night. 'I want both of you. Come and find me.'

But for a fox sprinting across my headlights and an owl hooting somewhere in a high branch, there was only silence. I wonder if I need to make myself more obvious. I mean I'm a woman alone, sitting inside an unlocked car on a deserted country road at night with the light on. I may as well have a neon sign outside saying 'All You Can Eat'. It's so frustrating! Am I fundamentally un-rapeable? I'm not *that* fat.

My void for risky business had to be filled so when I got back, I ventured into the chat rooms. I hadn't hit them in a good long while but it was like I'd never been away. Joberg was all over me like a rash. I've learned something new about him too. He's a banker in the City. London, that is. Well, he *says* he is. I told him I'm a librarian. Tonight, after a two-hour discussion about the usual, he said he wants to meet me:

Joberg: *Hey Sweetpea, wanna do this for realz?*
Sweetpea: *Why? Wifey got a training course coming up, has she?*
Joberg: *How did you guess?!?! Actually she's going on a hen weekend to Blackpool. We could meet up and have some fun.*
Sweetpea: *Can't. I won't have a good enough excuse for the BF.*
Joberg: *I need you, baby. Nobody on here gets me as hot as you do.*
Joberg: Babe? You still there???
Joberg: *Baby, just the thought of you and me is getting me hard again.* **Joberg:** Babe???
Sweetpea: *Where do you want to meet?*
Joberg: *Hotel?*
Sweetpea: *What would you want to do to me?*

Joberg: *I wanna tie you up. And then wok you all night long. I'm gonna ruin you for all other men. You've seen how big I am.*
Sweetpea: Wok?
Joberg: Sorry, *fuck
Sweetpea: *Can't wait. But can't I tie you up as well?*
Joberg: *No. I'm the master, remember? Little bitches have to play nice or they don't get doggy treats.*
Sweetpea: *What if I wanna play master for a change?*
Joberg: *Maybe, I'll see how you behave for your daddy.*

We named the hotel – a posh one in Canary Wharf, used mostly for business meetings and stopovers by bankers and celebrities filming in the area. We named the time: 8 p.m. on Friday, 5 April, the nearest date when we were both free and his wife had a hen weekend and the kids were at his mum's house.

The BuzzFeed quiz says people like me *Need to take risks just to feel alive*. I have to admit they're right about that. This is becoming clearer to me with each passing day:

Joberg: *I'm rock hard.*
Sweetpea: *Mmm, I'm throbbing just thinking about* it.
I was giggling and shaking and my fingers had gone cold from all the typing.
Joberg: *Meet you in the bar first, yeah? I'll check in for the both of us. How will I recognise you? Can you send me another pic of your face? I've seen everything else, might as well* ☺
I sent him a picture of Craig I had taken when he was cooking the other night.
Sweetpea: *I'll be sitting at the bar. I'll be wearing a red T-shirt and jeans.*
Joberg: *Baby, you're gorgeous. Next week is gonna go so slowly without you. I can't wait to get my lips on you and my dick in your ass. I'm gonna duck you so hard, boy.*

Sweetpea: *Can't wait for all the ducking. See you soon xxx*

Hahahahahahahahahahahahahahahahahahahahahah-
ahahahahahahahahaha!

Friday, 29 March

1. *Wesley Parsons*
2. *Derek Scudd*
3. *Man in North Face coat in the newsagent's who stepped on Tink's paw and said, 'Get a bigger dog and I might see it.'*
4. *The guy with Tourette's who sits in the Paddy Power doorway, shouting – today he was trying to pull his own tongue out*
5. *Craig*

I still have the newspaper cutting from when my best friend Joseph Leech died. He'd gone to my school and lived just down the road from us in Bristol. Joe had been one of the few kids who hadn't used me as an Instabrag in the months after Priory Gardens. He'd come round and read to me and make up stories about the posters on my bedroom walls. He'd make me Nutella sandwiches and push my wheelchair down Park Street to the museum, talking me through all the exhibits like a guide. I'd point to paintings and he'd read the descriptions. We liked the 'Dead Zoo' the best – the prowling tiger in the wild grass, the enormous cloudy-eyed giraffe, the greying gorilla they called Alfred.

Wesley Parsons had smashed into Joe at 36 miles per hour. There was a rumour that Joe's brain was coming out the back of his head when the police got there. The newspaper cutting's gone all yellow now. I keep it in the back of his *George's Marvellous Medicine* that his mum gave me.

No one's claimed the Dan Wells reward money yet. No more information's come out. And still no revelations about the missing penis. Looks like I'm on my way out of this particular little arboreal labyrinth. Also, rather worryingly, they've identified the murder weapon – a serrated steak knife, lightweight, possibly stainless steel. Luckily, any restaurant in any town or city in England worth its salt will have this type of knife in stock so I've just got to hope that the police don't DNA test the ones at Cote de Sirène.

Regarding Park Man, Gavin White, there's been no more of the mysterious 'woman in a hooded tracksuit walking a dog'. Seemingly, she has just disappeared.

Was given the 'honour' of doing next week's Puzzle Corner page today, for two reasons: 1) Mike Heath is ill (nobody knows why); and 2) nobody else wanted to do it.

Baked some gluten free ginger and raisin cookies and took them to the hospital for Anni (she's still in, really milking her private healthcare for all it's worth). She asked if I wanted to hold the baby and because of The Act, I had no argument set up against it.

So I sat in the chair beside her bed and the nurse placed Sam in my arms. He wriggled into place and I watched his little breaths. And held his little fingers. And blew softly on his tiny head of soft black hairs. He's a decent enough chap.

'Lush, isn't he?' Anni smiled. 'You have to admit.'

'Yeah, he is cute.' Cue the worried smile.

'What's up?'

'Just stuff,' I said. 'My piss pot of a life, you know, the usual.'

'Anything I can help with?'

'No.' I stroked Sam's little fist. 'You've done your bit, haven't you? You've reached the summit of Peak Human. Achieved the ultimate – kids. You've earned the right never to be asked what you want to achieve in your life ever again. And what have I ever done? Fuck all.'

'Don't say that, you've achieved loads. You met Ellen DeGeneres, you've been on *Jeremy Kyle*, you held will.i.am's Olympic torch.'

'Wow,' I scoffed. 'Be still my bubbling gusset.'

'How's Craig?'

'Um, trying to impregnate me with one of these things actually.'

'Oh, my God, that's awesome, Rhee!' she said through crumbs. She was on her fourth cookie. 'You not happy about it?'

'Well, I'm afraid he'll leave me so I'm just kinda going along with it.'

'Rhiannon, you shouldn't force yourself to want a baby.'

I looked down at Sam again. 'I just don't think we're strong enough. I've…'

'What?'

'. . . found some pictures on his phone.'

'Pictures of what?' said Anni, breathless with anticipation, fifth cookie in.

'Men. Naked. Naked men.'

'Craig? Oh… my… God.'

'At first I thought they were a joke. You know, some of the blokes at work having him on. But I've looked a couple of times now and there's different pictures on there. Different angles. Different men. Different… spillages.'

'Oh, God, Rhee. He's on Grindr or something.'

'What's Grindr?'

'You don't know what Grindr is?' Anni laughed.

'No,' I lied, trying to make my eyes look as baby deer-like as they could get.

'It's a gay social network app thing.'

'Oh,' I said.

'Maybe he's bisexual? Maybe it's just a bit of harmless titil- lation with no strings attached. Just picture swapping.'

Sam sighed in my arms.

'I think he's seeing someone though... the phone will go and there's no answer. Or he'll pop out somewhere in the evening using some crap excuse. And then there's what I heard when I came home one lunchtime...'

The sixth cookie hovered over Anni's lips.

'Sex noises, coming from our bedroom.' She gasped. 'I only peered through the crack in the door for a second but he was definitely... shagging someone.'

Her face was an absolute picture. 'What...up the...?'

'Yeah. I didn't see who it was, but well, put two and two together and what do you get?'

'A cheating bastard.'

'Please don't tell anyone, will you?'

'No, of course not.'

'Imelda would have a field day with this. I just wish he'd be honest with me, you know? Four years we've been together. I'm so confused. Does he want me and a baby or does he want anal sex with random men off the Internet?'

'Sounds like he wants both. Has he ever asked *you* for a backstage pass?'

I nodded. 'All the time.'

'Rhee, you need to talk to him. He's obviously using this baby thing as some kind of palliative remedy for what is quite a serious cancer in your relationship.'

I eyebrowsed her. 'Been watching a lot of daytime TV while you've been in here, have you?'

'You know what I mean. You can't have a baby to mend a relationship. You have to be rock solid or it won't work. I think you should have it out with him. He doesn't treat you with the respect you deserve.'

And with that, Sam farted in my hand. 'No, no man ever does,' I said and handed him over to her. I managed a little cry, we hugged, and then I left with my empty cookie box. She'd eaten all twelve.

Got home to Craig making guilt dinner again. Tonight – pork ragu with parmesan and spaghetti.

'I don't think I'm gonna manage much of this,' he said. 'I had three bacon baps for lunch.' He looked as proud as Mo Farah on a podium.

'Where was that?'

'That roadside burger van in the centre. We're doing up that old bakery in the precinct, turning it into a hairdresser's.'

'Another hairdresser's?'

'Yep.' He belched in my face. I caught it and rubbed it in his hair. 'Oh, I need to pop round Nigel's a bit later. He's got some offcuts he wanted me taking to the tip.'

'Why do you have to do it?'

'I offered.' He wouldn't look at me, just kept tucking into the pasta he said he couldn't manage. 'I won't be long though.'

'OK,' I said. I quite hate him today.

Sunday, 31 March

1. *Kenny Spillane – the Person of Interest arrested in connection with Park Man. Bloody police have released him back to his Argos doorway. He couldn't possibly be out on the night in question, could he? He had to be back in his bail hostel, signed in and shooting up. Bastard*
2. *Craig*
3. *The PICSOs – seriously, how many Facebook updates do we need of the same baby's expression, the same wedding invite screenshot and the same beach holiday in Lanzarote?*

Sunday pork loin down on the coast at Jim and Elaine's. Same old, same old. A walk along the sand, a game of Dodge the Mobility Scooter on the way back, eat, chat, tea, sleep, goodbye. I took Elaine a card and a pot of hyacinths for Mothering Sunday and she cried, then showed me her latest purchase from QVC – a brand-new state-of-the-art vacuum cleaner with about fifty different attachments.

Seriously – she talked me through every single one.

Later on, Craig and I attempted sex on their bed when they were both in the garden, until Jim called upstairs to ask us to help him get the ladder out of the garage. It was fun while it lasted though and Craig spunked on their duvet and full-on panicked while I located the antibax. We laughed a lot. I still hate him though.

Two of my herbs are dead on the balcony but the water company's roadworks outside have stopped so every cloud, I suppose. Still no Wesley Parsons on Facebook. Still no Derek Scudd anywhere. I think they've both emigrated.

There was a message on the answerphone from Seren when we got back:

Rhiannon. I was just wondering if there had been any more offers on the house lately. You gave the new estate agent my number, didn't you? Or are they calling you first? Also I've sent you the link to a good house clearance firm in your area. Let me know what's happening, please – Seren.

I texted her *Hi, No, Yes, Yes, and Thanks. Happy Mother's Day. Hope your kids are spoiling you rotten. Rhee xx*

She texted back ages later:

It's not Mother's Day in the USA.

Twat.

Talking of Mother's Day, on Facebook an annoying self-aggrandising meme has cropped up. The PICSOs are all over it, predictably.

Imelda's status update was as follows:

Thank you, Jackie, for nominating me as a Special Mummy you know. I was nominated to post a pic that makes me happy and proud to be a mum, so here's Elijah, Hope and Molly on the swings at Thorpe Park last year. If I've tagged you, I think you're a brilliant mum too so copy text and paste onto your wall and tag other lovely mums you know. How blessed we are!

And what a blight on society us singletons with empty wombs and tight vadges are. I'm so blessed!

I've never seen such a self-righteous bunch of ass-wipers in all my life. It's not *my* fault I want to achieve something with my life, rather than knock out Little Me's faster than pinballs to do it instead.

Craig says I get so spiky about it because I'm not a mum myself yet. He says it's my hormones and that I'll calm down once I'm pregnant. I watched him while he was scoffing his pie and chips tonight. I watched every bite. Every slurp of gravy. Every lick of his lips. His sex selfie with Lana is still on my phone. I looked at it under the table, then I looked at him. I could kill him. I could do it. But I won't. It's too easy and he doesn't deserve easy.

Wednesday, 3 April

1. *Overachievers – you know the sort. That guy who does all the marathons. That woman who swam the Channel. All those people who do Iron Mans and go in for any sort of fitness competition*
2. *Brainy children – you should not be composing symphonies or know how to spell antidisestablishmentarianism when you're five years* fucking *old*
3. *Mrs Whittaker – our bloody big saucepan has vanished and I wanted to make a stew*

Typed up my Pixar film review in time for the Easter holidays. I loved it about as much as I loved my last smear test.

'That's wonderfully droll, sweetpea.' Claudia smiled when I caught her reading it on the printer tray.

'Thanks,' I said, flicking Vs at her departing back. I know, I'm despicable, me.

Daisy Chan is still convinced there's a serial killer on the loose in our town and she's just poised for the next one. They're letting her go with her theory on this one, owing to the fact that no one can prove or disprove it. She's even chosen a nickname for 'him'. I saw the page she had started on her computer screen

when she was away from her desk. There was also a printed out
list of names on top of her keyboard

> The Night Stalker
> Random Stabber
> Joe the Stabber
> Jack the Stabber
> Stabby Stabberson
> The Stabman
> The Knifeman
> The Predator
> West Country Ripper
> West Country Knifeman (Possibly With Scissors Too)
> The Scissorman
> Rip van Winkle
> Night Attacker
> The Devil
> The Monster
> The Beast
> The Vanisher
> The Ghost
> The Phantom
> The Reaper

I wonder which one she'll go with if 'he' does decide to strike
again. I don't personally like any of them. I wonder briefly about
sending a letter to them, dubbing myself something, like the
Zodiac killer did. Son of Samantha, perhaps? Or Jill the Ripper?
That's quite good actually.

Maybe I'll just settle on Sweetpea. That seems to have stuck.

Friday, 5 April

1. *Craig – for about a billion different tiny reasons, not least including...*
   a. *the bone-shaking fart first thing in the morning,*
   b. *the unswilled plates in the dishwasher,*
   c. *the pubes in his sponge that I have to look at when showering,*
   d. *his holey red Porsche towel hanging up in the bathroom, which I also have to look at when showering,*
   e. *all the messy gaming cables and accessories behind the TV,*
   f. *the phone-checking midway through reverse cowgirl sex,*
   g. *his Tinder app that he doesn't think I know about,*
   h. *the pocket billiards INSIDE THE POCKET while cooking,*
   i. *the not-listening thing,*
   j. *the sport-watching thing,*
   k. *the eating-anything-he-wants-without-weight-changing-AT-ALL thing,*
   l. *the smell of his roll-ups,*
   m. *his friends,*
   n. *his parents,*

o. *his penis,*

p. *the way he eats chocolate digestives – around the edge first, then the biscuit, chocolate last... FREAK,*

q. *his stupid sticky-up bit of hair at the front of his head,*

r. *the stupid sticky-out bit at the back of his head that won't grow,*

s. *and, last but not least, his double-jointed thumbs. They just remind me of all those little pricks in school who had double-jointed limbs and who showed them off regularly when I had nothing at all to offer in return. Not even tongue-rolling.*

Daisy's byline made today's front page:

QUARRY MURDER – IS THERE A SERIAL KILLER ON THE LOOSE?

Exclusive report by Daisy Chan

Police in the West Country are hunting a possible serial killer after a woman's body found in Chipchase Quarry last month is believed to be linked to two other murders in the town since Christmas.

Avon and Somerset police have confirmed they are investigating what they believe is the third murder by the same individual, committed during the past three months.

In January, the *Gazette* exclusively reported on the grisly canal death of 32-year-old father of two Daniel Wells, and again in February when 46-year-old Yorkshire lorry driver Gavin White was brutally stabbed in Victory Park. And just a month ago, the body of 28-year-old mother of three Julia Kidner was discovered at the bottom of the quarry in the Blackmoor Hills.

Detective Superintendent David Fry believes the three murders could be linked.

'We're not ruling anything out at this stage,' he told the *Gazette*. 'We have discovered evidence at three of the crime scenes which would seem to indicate an MO and a boot print belonging to the same individual so we are following all the necessary leads.

'This is a comparatively small town and we are working with police forces in the surrounding areas to ensure all developments are shared and monitored.'

Oh is that right, Detective Superintendent? I shall look forward to the knock on my door any day now then.

*

Well, who'd have thunk it? You wait ages for a tip-off about a man you want to kill and then TWO come along on the same day!

OK, so I had an email first thing from Mary Tolmarsh, the mother of one of the two girls who were molested by Derek Scudd. She said a friend of hers told her Derek Scudd 'had been skulking around the library in recent weeks'. He's also tried to get himself a membership of the bowls club but they weren't having any of it. So the library was a good lead.

And I was Facebook-searching Wesley Parsonses again at lunchtime, and, bingo, I finally found the right one.

In Birmingham, of all places. The city where yours truly is visiting for a Beyoncé concert very soon indeed.

His hair's no longer brown–it's blond now and slightly longer and he's stacked on some muscle, but it's definitely him all right. It was the same face I'd stared at for three hours in that courtroom when he wept about murdering my best friend while jacked up on pills. So I now have almost two months to get him onside before mine and Craig's little Birmingham sojourn. I sent him a Friend Request.

After lunch, two cops came into the office to talk to Ron and Claudia about yet another rape by two men driving a definitely BLUE van, on the same stretch of country road. This latest woman had broken down and was waiting for Green Flag to come out and rescue her – IN THE SAME LAY-BY I HAD WAITED JUST THE OTHER NIGHT. I'd missed them by mere days. Same lay-by, same black guy-white guy double act, same time of day – between 11 p.m. and midnight. This time they rammed her car off the road altogether and jumped her. I could have been ready for that! I'd have known exactly what to do!

I was actually allowed in on this latest meeting, but only because Ron wanted to give us all a lecture on night-time safety as lowly defenceless women on our own. Prick.

'So, ladies,' said Ron earnestly, looking directly at me, then Daisy, then Joy. 'Please be careful when you're out and about at night. Make sure someone is with you at all times. Don't take any risks. Make sure your cars are in good working order. Get your husbands to check everything, tyres, fan belts…'

'Oh, it's so horrible,' said Carol, wringing her hands. 'I grew up in the countryside around where that last one was attacked.'

'We should start a car pool,' suggested Daisy. 'Anyone female who works here, just until they're caught.'

'I'd give them what for if they tried anything with me, have no fear,' said Joy.

I know rapists aren't exactly choosy but I'm fairly sure even the most desperate pervert would have to think twice about an elephant-legged troll with a face on the wrong side of her head.

'Don't take any chances, ladies,' said Ron. 'From what the police tell us, these guys are very nasty pasties.'

Nasty pasties? Was that really the best he could up with to

describe two men who went out driving at night with the express purpose of pinning a woman down and violently attacking her? Twat.

My heart was thumping so hard when he was telling us, I was expecting someone to comment on it. Like it would give me away. Like all of a sudden I would get the uncontrollable urge to stand up in the middle of the glass boardroom table and yell, *DON'T WORRY EVERYONE, I'M GOING TO CATCH THESE BASTARDS. JUST GIVE ME TIME. I HAVE A PLAN. LET ME AT 'EM.*

See, I'm all Caps Lock now. I need to calm down. I need to breathe. I need to stop thinking like Scrappy Doo. It will soothe me no end if I can locate Scudd or those Blue Van Vagina Vandals. Scudd and Parsons are the golden pineapples but I'd happily make do with a few rotten coconuts if they fell in the meantime.

I need something to happen soon. My boredom is off the charts. The Julia effect has lifted and now I'm hungry for more.

After the meeting, Claudia Gulper sidled up to me. 'Rhiannon, could I have a quick word please? In here.'

She filtered us off into Conference Room B with the long glass table and pitcher of water in the middle which had a film of dust on the surface.

She shut the door and didn't mince her words. 'Rhiannon, is there anything going on with you and my nephew?'

'Um... he's my friend but, no, nothing more than that. Why?'

She sighed and gripped the back of the head chair. 'He's very smitten with you. He talks about you at home all the time.'

I smiled. 'That's nice.'

'I don't want him to get false hope,' she said. 'He's very young, very impressionable and it's my job to look after him while he's staying with me. I don't want him... messing up his gap year. Getting distracted.'

'I haven't done anything to lead him on if that's what you're suggesting, Claudia.'

'No, I'm not saying you have. I just... he's mooning about at home all the time. He's becoming lazy here and I think... I'd rather you and he remain just colleagues.'

I frowned. 'Where has this come from, Claudia?'

She held her tongue between her teeth, as though afraid to say it. But then she did. 'I don't normally go rooting through bins but I found a pregnancy test in the ladies' bathroom the other day, just after you'd been in there. I need to know if it was yours. And if you and him are...'

'Yes, it was mine,' I said. 'My boyfriend and I are trying for a baby but I'd rather nobody knew about that, thank you very much.'

She seemed to wilt, until the sun came out on her face again. 'Of course, of course. Good.' She smiled. 'I'm sorry to confront you with this, I just feel very protective of AJ and I need him to focus on what he's doing and prepare for the next six months rather than tie himself down to anything.'

'Well, I won't be knotting any ropes for him, Claudia, I promise. If he does have a thing for me, it's a one-way street. Now could I get back to my work, please?'

She nodded and apologised again, showing me out of the room. God, that woman is SO hung up on not being able to get pregnant she's OBSESSED with anyone who could be. It's quite sad.

Lana was in the staffroom, taking a long time folding tea towels when I went up on the afternoon coffee run. I was poised for some weak conversation starter about the weather. Instead, nothing. Not even a smile. Maybe Craig had dumped her for me. Maybe she was plotting to strangle me with a tea towel or pour the scalding coffees over me. It took me a while to notice but she was actually just crying silently. I stood in front of her. I put my hand on her forearm. I gave her forearm a rub.

'Want to talk about it?' I offered.

She shook her head.

'Need a hug?' I said.

She didn't shake her head, so I enveloped her, like a spider gathering the fly in with its long black legs. 'It's all right. Whatever it is. It'll be all right.'

She sobbed against me. I stroked her hair. She smelled of many things – Aussie Miracle Moist shampoo. Cigarettes. The ever-so-distant tang of Valentino Intense aftershave.

'Don't be nice to me, Rhee. I don't deserve it.'

I rubbed her back like they do in the soaps. 'Ssh, it's all right, it's all right.' Rub rub rub.

We had quite a nice chat. She wouldn't tell me anything about her and Craig of course but I learned some useful things. I'm going to bring her in some Rice Krispie cakes. They're her favourites.

Oh, and I found out why Mike Heath's been off work – tried to kill himself. Painkillers. We're to pretend he's 'been on holiday' and not to question him when he comes back. I want to know though. I want to know how close he got. If he saw the bright light, if Jesus took him by the hand or whatever.

I wonder if JoBerg's at the hotel now. He's going to HATE me. I want him to.

Saturday, 6 April

1. *People who measure things using stupid measurements – e.g. man in a Weetabix factory on TV this morning. 'If I stretched all the Weetabix made in this factory in one day end to end, they would stretch from here to Aberdeen and back again.' SO?????*
2. *JoBerg*
3. *Wesley Parsons*
4. *Derek 'Where Are You, You Bastard?' Scudd*
5. *The Scout who packed my shopping today in Lidl, who puts eggs at the bottom of the bag and two bottles of bleach on top a tray of meringues?*

The police have issued an appeal for the Blue Van Men again – this time with some information. Part of their number plate – BTY – and a fuller description. One of the men is gaunt-faced, was wearing a grey hoody and blue tracksuit bottoms and has a star tattoo on his right wrist. The other is black, aged between thirty and forty and answers to the name Ken or Kev. Excellent – *cue Mr Burns hands*

Googled Honey Cottage again today. Thoughts have started to

collect and I can't shake them off. What if I could buy it from my share of Mum and Dad's place? I wouldn't have enough, of course, but maybe I could get a mortgage. Be a bit daunting on my own but I'm used to daunting. I hold a knife to daunting's throat. I bleed daunting out.

Cleo has posted in the Facebook group, Imelda's Hen Weekend – The Toppan's Masseeeeeve!!!, that she has started a hashtag on Twitter: #LetsGetGaryBarlowToMel'sWedding. She is trying to get us all to 'retweet the shit out of it and get all your friends to as well'.

Uh… no.

I ventured a look inside the chat room to see if JoBerg had sent me any messages last night. And, yes, there were lots:

Friday, 20.30: *Hey Sweetpea where are you???*
Friday, 20.34: *I'm at the bar, in case you can't find me, babe.*
Friday, 20.46: *I'm giving it another ten and I'm off.*
Friday, 21.02: *Knew you'd wimp out on me, you fucker*
Friday, 21.04: *You there? Answer me. Please.*
Friday, 21.15: *You're a fucking pricktease. Why say you're gonna show up if you ain't?*
Friday, 21.37: *At least have the decency to answer my messages.*
Friday, 21.39: *So that's it is it? All the hours we've spoke the last few months and you're just gonna disappear? I'll tell everyone in the chat room not to talk to you. See how you like being the fucking fool.*
Friday, 21.55: *You know what? I'm glad I didn't fuck you. I bet you do this ALL THE TIME. And I bet you're fat. Your ass is disgusting.*
Friday, 21.57: *I didn't wank over your dick pix, I lied. Ha aha ha.*
Friday, 22:07: *I'm gonna pick up a whore and think about you when I'm ducking her. I'm gonna hurt her. I ducking hate you.*

Saturday, 08.38: *Babe, just answer please, just tell me to fuck off or something? Please?*
Saturday, 08.40: *I'm so done with you. So fucking done.*
Saturday, 8.59: *Can you delete my pix please and delete my number from your phone.*

Suffice to say, I don't think JoBerg and me gonna be skipping through any meadows together any time soon.

I messaged Biggus Dickus and MrSizzler48, to see if they were still talking to me or if JoBerg had nobbled them.

Both responded almost instantly with pictures of their erect penii.

Blossom on the trees, you know how I feel.

Monday, 8 April

1. *Derek 'Man of Mystery' Scudd*
2. *Wesley Parsons*
3. *Coupon collectors – cos they're not annoying at all at checkouts*
4. *Chuggers – you're not going to go away are you, little Amnesty International man who waits for me outside Boots. One more 'Good morning, madam' and I'm going to slice your head clean off with that clipboard*
5. *Anyone on* Geordie Shore, TOWIE *or* Made in Chelsea. *STOP ELEVATING ILLITERATES!*

Mike Heath is back, one race whiter and twice as silent. I asked AJ if he wanted to make a bet as to how long it would be till his next suicide attempt but he frowned at me and said, 'That's pretty sick, dude. We're all fighting our own little wars.' He's such a good person, I often wonder if I sliced him across his abdomen whether lemon curd would ooze out.

We walked into town at lunchtime on a mission to get something else to wind Linus up with from the joke shop but all we could find were fake winning scratch cards. Not too original, but we bought one anyway as Linus has been known to do the

Lottery, though he never talked about it – he likes people to believe he's loaded, but he's not – I've opened his credit card statements.

There was no sign of Our Mutual Fiend, Derek Scudd, at the library. I'll keep the faith for now but I've passed by a few times with no luck. I may have to take a day off soon and just set up camp there like a fan girl.

'So, Claudia's warned me away from you,' I said to him as he matched my stride. 'Said I shouldn't encourage you.'

'*What?*' he cried. 'She had no right to... ugh, that bloody woman! I told her to stay out of it.'

'She's just protecting you. You're living under her roof...'

'. . . so I have to play by her rules, yeah, I get it. Two more months and I am out of there, man, I'm telling you. What with this and the fucking adoption thing, she's driving me psycho.'

'What adoption thing?'

'Oh, she's trying to adopt this kid from China. She's seen it on some website, I don't know. I'm sick of hearing about it.'

'Oh. I didn't know.'

'Don't tell her I told you. She doesn't want anyone to know. But, yeah, she's tried everything else. Surrogacy thing fell through, then a woman in Russia let her down and shafted her for thousands on a phoney insemination. At home, she doesn't talk about anything else, it's chronic. Can't wait to get out of there.'

'Where will you go when you leave?'

'Up country. I've got an extended visa for a few months so I'm going to go up and see some friends in Manchester, and Liverpool, then maybe Scotland. Maybe around some of the islands.'

'Cool. So, in other news, I hear you fancy me,' I said.

He didn't answer, just sort of cleared his throat and pretended to be very interested in a sign about an interest-only mortgage in the building-society window.

'I fancy you too, you know.'

He still wouldn't look at me, scuffed his foot on the pavement and nodded.

'But your auntie Claudia says we mustn't do anything, so I guess we should abide by her rules, right?'

I smiled at him until he caught my eye. And then we both started laughing, uncontrollably, like two little kids.

Called the hospice about clearing out the furniture at Mum and Dad's. They're coming at the end of the month to clear away the last of my childhood, so that'll be fun to oversee – the bed that me and Seren were conceived in, the wardrobes the skins of all our years hung in, the fridge with all our magnets and Good Work stickers on, all pushed into a van under scratchy dust sheets and bound for strange lands.

Lana liked her Rice Krispie cakes. She cried again.

'You're such a sweet person, Rhee.'

'It's only cakes, Lana. It took five minutes.'

'No, really. It means a lot.'

'Well, we're friends aren't we?'

'Yeah, definitely.'

She made up some counterfeit story about her ex-boyfriend wanting custody of their cats and them having a furious argument about it. *That* was why she'd been crying. *That* was why she'd threatened to take sleeping pills. *That* was why she's started seeing her therapist again. Dear oh dear oh dear. The woman was unstitching at the seams. It wouldn't take much at all to tear her in two.

Wednesday, 10 April

1. *Those parents you see on TV with 20+ kids – I don't CARE if you buy 60 pints of milks a week, I don't CARE if you fry 108 sausages for dinner. I don't CARE that your back garden can't cope with any more play equipment. Keep your fertile loins out of my cornflakes you selfish breeding bastards*
2. *Man in the paper who beat his Staffordshire bull terrier to death with a baseball bat – suspended sentence. Pah! I'll suspend his sentence. Give me a rope and a nice strong bannister*
3. *Shops that don't allow tiny dogs to be carried in even if they're being good as gold and not peeing at all– aka, our town library*
4. *Derek Scudd*
5. *Wesley Parsons*

Linus won the Fake Lottery this morning – he was *briefly* ecstatic, before Paul Spurdog pointed out he'd been diddled. And with that he went on a MAJOR rant about workplace bullying and weeding out the culprit. He's started threatening lawyers and everything. AJ is panic-stricken – I had to hide behind the monkey puzzle in case my smile gave me away.

Later we were told to attend a hastily called meeting where Ron announced that Jeff Thresher has announced his decision to retire. Didn't tell me privately or anything. I always thought we were mates. Fucker.

Mrs Whittaker couldn't have Tink today – she had some old person bus trip to Scarborough to eat whelks – so I asked Claudia if I could leave early for a doctor's appointment. I mentioned the word 'cervix' and she let me, no more questions asked. She knows what it's like with womb issues – apparently, hers fell out during a game of badminton.

I don't think I'll be able to get a mortgage for Honey Cottage on my own, not without Craig's money as well and his immaculate credit score. I'd also need a job waiting for me in Wales. I *need* that place. I think it needs me. We could be happy there, me and Tink. Just us, breathing in that clean air. The scent of the yellow roses. Tending to our vegetables, growing our herbs.

It's a fucking pipe dream though, isn't it? I'm not destined for Happy so I may as well piss that idea up the wall right now.

No sign of the Scudd Missile yet again outside the library. I got bored waiting so I ventured into the chat rooms. Mr Sizzler48 needed a quick talking-to but Biggus Dickus wasn't around. Sizzler wants to meet up now in some sex dungeon in Soho. He says I'm the 'sexiest guy he's ever met in a chat room' and wants to do me in a swing. These guys just crack me up.

I'm going out tonight, I've decided. I miss the feel of a knife in my coat pocket. I'm gonna find me some Blue Van Men and I'm not coming back until I've got their blood on me.

*

I'm on Old Road in one of the three lay-bys, the one nearest

Copperton Lane. This was the scene of the first rape. I'm parked up and pretending to look at a map. It's precisely 10.23 p.m. I've been here nearly half an hour but I'm not giving up yet. They *will* come tonight, I know they will. And it will be me they come for this time. I've never been more ready. For both of them.

I don't think a single car has passed in ten minutes.

'Blurred Lines' has just come on the radio – shamefully, I know every word.

*

It's 10.47. I'm now in the lay-by nearest the Old School Hall at the junction to Long Lane. Still no sign. The windows keep steaming up and it's annoying me.

Maybe they won't do another one this soon after the last. But they might, there's still that agonising hope. Always the hope. I'm here. Look for me, look for me. Find me.

My knives are spread out on the front passenger seat. The blades are freezing. They just want to be touched.

*

11.07 p.m. – I'm at the third lay-by. No landmarks nearby. Craig's texted me to ask where the new *Radio Times* is – I've told him I'm staying at Pidge's tonight for her birthday sleepover. A pretty weak excuse but it's the kind of birthday celebration Pidge *would* have so it's not technically a lie. It's just that her birthday's in December. Cars have passed, no one's stopped or pulled in for a moment. A few vans have passed too, but none of them blue. There are puddles in the road – that's about the only interesting thing I can think to comment on. Starting to nod off. I'm going to give it another ten minutes then I'm going home. Well, to Mum and Dads' ex-house anyway.

*

It's twenty-five minutes after I wrote that. Still nothing. Think I just heard that owl again. Tried to google the hoot. Can't get any signal out here. Another five then I'm definitely off. Maybe.

*

HOLY FUCKING SHIT, IT'S ALL KICKING OFF! UPDATE LATER.

*

Well THAT didn't go according to plan. Jesus Christ! I'm back at Mum and Dads' now and my hands have stopped shaking long enough to be able to record this but holy motherhumping HELL that was stressful. You go out of your way to help the poor and unfortunate and you get nothing but GRIEF!

The Blue Van Rapists are both dead, don't worry about that; *that* at least was a piece of cake. But I've left SO many loose ends tonight and I'm SO annoyed with myself that an eventuality happened that I didn't plan for – I got seen.

So I'm heading back along Old Road, thinking any minute now I'm going to give up and drive home when I spot it – Lay-by Number 1, the original spot on the bend near Copperton Lane. I very nearly drove straight past when I caught a flash of something from the corner of my eye – a lemon-yellow flash. A scarf. A woman's scarf, around a woman's neck, as she was being bundled into the back of a van – a midnight blue Transit van. Licence plate: WD64 something something something…

BTY? Well, let's see, I thought.

Then I realised – shit. This sting was meant for me. I never *dreamed* I'd catch them in the act with *someone else*. She's stolen my thunder! So I pull in on the mud track of a field about 200 yards down from it, grab my stuff off the front seat and run back to the lay-by where the van is parked, still, no lights on, no sounds at all. Except it *is* the right van – BTY is indeed the second part of the plate.

And I know they're in there.

And I know *she's* in there.

I creep around outside the van and I have no idea what to do – I'm flying blind, which I hate doing, but I know this is my chance with them so I just have to swim with the fish I'm with. So I get my two biggest knives from my rucksack, pull up my face scarf and stand at the back of the van, waiting, preparing to knock.

Then *ding!*, a bright idea emerges in my head and I put the knives away. By this point I can hear them – banging about inside. Arguing with each other. I can't hear her though – I wonder if she's gagged.

Then the banging about stops and I hear one of them say he 'heard something'.

And my heart is racing and I'm sweating and breathing heavy and all that fucking shit and it crosses my mind that I should just run back to my car or call the cops, but the thought is fleeting and I am AMPED so I have to go with it.

I grab Julia's climbing rope out of my bag and I thread it through the door handle, wrapping it right around the outside of the van, encircling it twice like I'm dancing around a frigging maypole, tying it off at the back. It's extra tight. They're trapped inside, all three of them. The rapers and the rapee.

'The fuck's that?' I hear one of them again, the other one, louder this time. The woman screams; a Julia scream. So they haven't gagged her. It's then I spot the open driver's window and the keys in the ignition. I get in and turn the keys and pull out of the lay-by before the reasonable side of my brain can catch up with me and yell, WHAT THE FUCK ARE YOU DOING?

And the truth? I still don't know. I had no idea at that moment where I was going or how tonight was going to end. All I knew was I had three people in the back of the van and I was driving them somewhere in the dark. I didn't know where, I didn't know why, I just knew I had to do something.

And yeah, looking back now, in the early hours of the morning, I should have driven straight to the police station. I should have called the cops and been sensible about it and been the big hero. Been the *real* Woman of the Fucking Century.

But that thought didn't occur to me. Because I don't have a normal brain, did you not REALISE this by now!? I don't think like normal people. I think like me. So I drove to the only place I could think of at that moment in the dark, desperate time I was in – the quarry.

The woman screams again – she sounds older. Posh. I put my foot down, hear something bang against the side of the van. One of them must have fallen over.

The other one shouts, 'They're fucking robbing it!'

And she won't stop screaming. I speed up.

One of them threatens her. 'Shut up, bitch.' Pretty standard dialogue for rapists. I think he whacks her because I hear another bang. He has an accent – London, south of the river. Or north, I can never remember. Sounds like Ray Winstone, anyway.

The other accent I can't place – Scottish, maybe Glasgow? Sounds like the guy Craig argues with on Sky Sports.

The exhilaration is incredible. The window open, the night air chills me to my bones as I head towards the steeper back roads following signs for Chipchase Quarry. The country lanes grow narrower and steeper and I have no spatial awareness in the van because my car is so comparatively small. Whole branches are whacked off hedgerows, I splash through huge muddy puddles, gravel pinging off all four wheel arches. I'm making no secret of this journey – I'm just driving.

I drive into the same car park as I had the night I killed Julia. I drive right to the edge of the big pit and stop the van, flicking the headlights off and grabbing my bag from the passenger seat. I'm amazed they haven't ring-fenced this place by now, what with all the bodies me and Dad have thrown down it

I pull off my face scarf and cut the rope, banging on the back doors.

'Let the woman out.'

I sound so female it's excruciating. One of the few things I don't like about being a woman is my inability to do a convincing man's voice on command. I sound like a CBeebies presenter doing the giant in *Jack and the Beanstalk*.

There is banging from inside again and whispered shouts.

'I have weapons,' I say. 'Let the woman out.' I try to pack it with more threat. 'You've got five seconds. One... two...'

The doors click. One of them opens, slowly. The light is on inside, a small dim little beam in the corner. There's a mattress on the floor. The woman is scrunched up at the very back of the van, in the corner, underneath a little fire extinguisher fixed to the wall. She has curly brown hair and huge eyes. There's velvet pink cushions encircling the mattress. Magazines. Strawberry-flavoured lube. Handles dangling from the ceiling. It's a moving sex den. One of the blokes has on a balaclava. The other I can see clearly – he's black and wearing red gloves. He's the one who opened the door. He keeps one hand on it.

He sees my two knives and backs up slightly.

'Let her out,' I say.

Neither man moves. I spy a sliver of Red Gloves' skin atop his red-gloved hand, still hanging off the door. I bring the knife down hard and fast against the sliver of skin. Blood spurts out at once.

'Aaaaah fucking hell!' he yells, grabbing it with his other hand. I point the knife at him again. 'Let her out.'

Balaclava Boy laughs – ACTUALLY LAUGHS – and grabs the woman's arm and she whimpers as he pushes her forwards and out of the van. She falls to a crumpled heap on the gravel, then scampers off to the bushes, hair a bundle of brown wires, knickers on one ankle, yellow scarf trailing behind her on the ground.

I focus back on them.

'Shut the door.'

Balaclava Boy laughs again. He thinks I'm the woman's daughter – go figure – come to rescue her. He tells me he'll rape me as well. Yawn.

Red Gloves starts to protest but his wrist hurts too much. It's bleeding everywhere. The knife has cut to the bone. Balaclava Boy makes to get out but I step closer to the van and hold the knife out again. 'Shut. The. Door.'

'Fuck you, bitch,' he says and makes to leave and his disbelief that I will call my own bluff is what lets him down. I stab him, right there in his chest (he's only wearing a cheap blue polo shirt so it's relatively easy) and he falls to the ground. I would keep stabbing him but I just need him docile so I slit his throat deeply just beneath his chin, then once through his Adam's apple until he calms his tits.

'Jesus F-F-Fuck!' yells Red Gloves and jumps out of the van, making for the bushes. I manage to grab his arm and stab it through with my biggest knife. He shouts, but then he has me, grabs my shoulder with his good hand and pushes me to the gravelled ground, my knife still stuck in his arm. Then he's on top of me, beating my face with the back of his hand – his other arm's fucked. I take the fruit paring knife from my pocket and stick him in the ribs. Weakened but still stronger, he punches me hard, twice in the centre of my face and I lose myself for a few seconds. When I come round, he's lying on the ground, crawling towards Balaclava Boy, who's bleeding like a sacrificial cow, feet scuffing and gouging the ground in a vain attempt to cling to life.

'If you'd just fucking done as I asked, I wouldn't have had to do that,' I pant, regaining focus and, with my knives in both hands, I walk across to him. I tear into his body like a loaf of freshly cooked bread. I pluck my fruit knife from his forearm and check both their pulses. Peeled and cored – *Gordon Ramsay clap* – done.

Jesus H Christ. If I hadn't been two stone overweight, they could have had me. If my dad hadn't taught me how to fend off an attack it could be me raped in that van right now. Closest call EVER. And I'm dry-mouthed and shaking all over.

I listen for sounds on the air. The crickets. The buzz of flies. A whispering in the grasses. Then I realise it's not the grasses at all – it's the woman with the yellow scarf, sniffling somewhere behind me.

'Help me get them in the back,' I say.

No response.

I turned around. 'Did you hear me? I said help me get them both in the back of the van. Quickly.'

Taking her sweet time, the woman stumbles out of the bushes and follows my lead, taking the men's legs, and we bundle them like two very inept removal women, into the van. Red Gloves is much heavier than Balaclava Boy so it takes an age but eventually, when they are both inside, I close the doors.

The woman looks at me. She sees my whole face. I remember my neck scarf and pull it up.

'You're bleeding.'

'I know.'

'Did he hurt you?'

'No.'

'W-what are you doing n-now?' she sniffles.

'This,' I say, kicking the back of the van and it rolls obligingly forwards and disappears over the edge of the quarry.

The noise is unspeakably loud as it tumbles and thunders down over the incline and crashes down the quarry walls to the bottom. And, in the one piece of luck I have this evening, it then has the good grace to blow up. Some spark has hit petrol and *WHOOSH!* up it goes, illuminating the enormous pit in the darkness. It heats my face as I look down over.

Of course I realise then that my car is fucking miles away. So I start walking.

'Wait,' says the woman. 'Where are you going?'

'Home,' I say. 'Duh.'

About ten minutes down the country lanes, I realise my face is fucking stinging all over like I've been stung by wasps. She is hurrying behind me, heels clacking.

'You can't leave me out here,' she cries.

'Do you have to make so much noise when you walk?' I say, stopping briefly, causing her to collide into my back.

'Are they really dead?' she asks.

'Do you want to go back and check?'

'No.'

We carry on walking. 'This is so bad. We're so going to be seen. I've left myself wide open this time. Broke all my rules. Stupid.'

'What do you mean, this time?'

'Shut up.'

'Have you done this before?'

I say nothing.

'You saved my life,' she says.

'Yeah yeah.'

'You did. You stopped me from...'

'You shouldn't have been there.'

'What?'

I stopped walking. 'Why were you driving alone? Haven't you seen all the warnings in the paper?'

'I had to work late.' She must have been in her late forties I guessed. 'My name's Heather...'

'I don't want to know,' I say.

'But what happens now?'

'Just keep walking.'

We finally reach her car about an hour later, having crossed through fields and in and out of ditches which I vaguely remembered from childhood trips up to the quarry to pick blackberries with Seren. My nose is bleeding and I just know I'm going to have bruises all over my face by morning. Gonna take a shit load of Boing to cover *that* breakout.

'There,' I say, still annoyed with myself and with her and with them for fucking up my plans. 'G'night.'

'B-b-but what do I do?' Her voice is all wobbly. She's wringing her torn scarf and fumbling with the lock on her driver's door.

'Get in and drive home.' I find an old tissue in my jeans pocket and shove it under my nose. Both my hoody sleeves are covered in blood – at least it's black (the hoody that is, not my blood).

'I can't! I can't just go home and act like this hasn't happened. I've got a family. Look...' She holds up her hand. It's trembling like a jelly.

'You go home and you act like Meryl fucking Streep if you have to but don't talk about this again. It's the only way to keep your nose clean. I've got a headache now.'

'I don't know if I can say nothing.' I turn to walk towards my car but Heather stops me, grabs my arm. 'I can't be on my own. Please stay with me. Just till I calm down. I can't drive like this.'

She fucking HUGS me. At the scene of the crime! The Act really went to fuck tonight.

'I'll go to the police. I'll tell them what's happened,' she says, pulling away from me.

'You can't,' I say.

'I won't mention you.'

'If you *don't* mention me, you'll have to say *you* were at the quarry alone and then they'll have *you* for a double murder.'

'Oh. But…'

'And if you *do* mention me, they'll have *me* for a double murder.' I tap my head. 'Use your loaf.'

'But…'

'Say nothing. Do nothing. You were never here. You do not know me.'

'But my car's been parked here all night. What if someone's seen it? We've probably left evidence everywhere.'

'Oh, God, don't say that,' I say. 'Dammit.'

She checks her phone. 'I can't think straight. I've got six missed calls from my husband.'

'Text him back. You were driving home, you had car trouble. You went to get help but got lost. You tore your scarf. You… broke a heel, whatever. You got back to your car and the car started working again. Praise be – it's a miracle. Just don't mention the van *or* me.' My nose was still pouring with blood.

'What are you going to say about your face?' Heather asks.

'I tell lies for a living, don't worry about *me*.'

She starts sobbing against her car door. 'I don't know what to say to you. I need to thank you properly. You don't know what you've done. Did I thank you?'

'Yeah, you're fine. The best way you can thank me is by forgetting you met me. G'night.'

She nods.

I don't know if that nod meant *OK, I won't mention you* or *OK, but I'm driving to the cop shop with or without your blessing.* Either way, what a fucking night. I don't know what happened to her after she got in her car. All I know is that I need to keep my head down now for approximately twenty years.

Thursday, 11 April

1. *Cold callers – I swear a circle of Dante's Inferno is missing some inhabitants*
2. *Those self-righteous people who brag about not throwing anything away for an entire year – how do you recycle fanny rags? Seriously?*
3. *Whoever sits in my office chair when I'm not there and adjusts the height*

Everything hurts. I got back to the flat around 6 a.m. after a freezing cold shower at Mum and Dads' house. In the mirror, I looked like I'd been beaten up. Well, I *had*, technically. But I couldn't let anyone know that of course so I had to load a shit ton of make-up on. Luckily, thanks to a shitload of YouTube tutorials and some expensive concealer, I just looked 'a bit puffy' to Craig. I snuck into bed beside him. He seemed pleased enough to see me and utterly in the dark about where I'd been.

Walked Tink before work. It was a drizzly old day and I kept my hood up, just in case. It was one of those days when all around you there are scrapes of wet dog shit on the pavement and your face hurts from being beaten up by an abusive dead rapist and there are blocked drains in every gutter and your chihuahua is barking and yapping at every single other canine she passes.

Top story on the local news was the van fire in the quarry. Police are calling it suspicious because of 'signs of a struggle' at the top near the ridge. I have so much make-up on I look like I've face-planted a Clinique counter. And it's all puffed up. Eric the handyman has already asked if I'm pregnant because I'm 'all big and glowing'. Fucker.

The worst part about it all is that the yellow-scarf woman – Heather – saw my face. I have a pretty recognisable face, because of the national treasure years after Priory Gardens. She didn't *say* that she recognised me but that doesn't mean she didn't. What if she saw *Up At the Crack*? What if she happens to see an old episode of *This Morning* or *Ellen* on catch-up? And then there's my *Gazette* column – Lews Reviews – my fucking picture is on the top of it! It's a very tiny, very grainy picture, granted, but it's still there. If she lives locally, she'll see it. She could come to the *Gazette* offices and ask for me. Oh fuck, I can't think straight now cos I'm panicking. I need thinking cake.

*

Bought an iced bun on the way to lunch but it turned out to be a depressingly bad iced bun. You would think that there's no such thing – it's just bun and icing, right?

WRONG.

For a start it was stale and there was a live fruit fly stuck to one end. And if that wasn't enough, half my icing was stuck on the bun next to it in the window and the bitch with the tongs never even scraped it off and put it back on mine! So rude.

I saw a sign in the church window on the way back to the office. The sign read, WHAT MAY SEEM LIKE A DISAPPOINTMENT

COULD BE GOD SETTING YOU UP FOR A RESCUE. TRUST HIS PLAN
EVEN WHEN YOU DON'T UNDERSTAND THE PATH.

I don't think that applies to my bun cos I still ate it. Food for
thought though. Sometimes religion can be quietly meaningful
when it's not spouting homophobic insults from a lemonade
crate in the High Street. Didn't make me stop worrying about
the yellow scarf woman though. I keep coming back to the same
thought: it's just a matter of time.

Wrote up some old woman's 105th Birthday announcement
this afternoon. The accompanying picture was of this gnarled
little dear clutching her card from the monarch and two care
home nurses either side of her, basically holding her up. None
of my family have made old bones. I wonder how many more
lives I will take in the time I have left. How will I die? Et in
arcadia ego, after all.

My face aches and throbs like it's been rubbed against the
cheese grater. I'm chowing down painkillers like they're Haribo.

Friday, 12 April

1. *Picky eaters – seriously, Edmund, pick some more salad ingredients out of your sandwich, I dare you*
2. *People who can't spell, can't apostrophise and who don't know the difference between 'they're' and 'their.'* GO TO FUCKING SCHOOL
3. *Sick people at work –* GO FUCKING HOME
4. *Sick people on Twitter – I don't care about your chronic pain, arthritis and/or depression and,* Newsflash, *neither does anyone else*
5. *Women's clothing outlets that NEVER have anything in a size 14/16. Only ever size 6 or size 26*
6. *Bouncy Rowena at last night's aerobics who had to do everything at twice the speed and power of everyone else, just to show off how damn fit she is. If we'd been back at school, I'd have wiped my ass on her face towel*

I ache all over today. My bruises have come out like purple flowers in my face. Craig saw before I'd done my make-up. I had to tell I fell over in the lift and he wants to bollock the landlord about the carpet tiles and the cheap glue he's used. I couldn't even be bothered to argue.

Typed up some press releases: the local church fete, the Brownies' 'wool bombing' of the High Street and one about diabetes affecting over six thousand people in the district.

UGH UGH UGH UGH UGH UGH UGH UGH!

I'm sooooooooooo booooooooooooooored.

God, I want to kill again. It's like this terrible itch inside me all the time. The unfinished orgasm. The unsatisfied appetite. The bucket listing I have yet to tick off. The Blue Van Rapists have done little to quell it. Like a McDonald's quarter-pounder – you slather for it, then when it's swallowed you think, *God, I really wish I'd got some chips with that.*

Or some McNuggets at the very least.

It just wasn't enough. And I didn't have long enough to get my knickers wet because I was too angsty and totally out of my comfort zone. The plan went out of the window. I was panicking too much about getting it done and putting as much distance between me and the quarry and the yellow scarf woman as possible. I spent half the night dodging cowpats and fucking mud. It's made me *more* ragey, if anything. And the pain in my face isn't helping.

I can't be the only one who feels this way about taking life. Everyone has their madwoman in the attic, don't they?

Daisy was positively buzzing when she came back from the quarry after lunch.

'Why did you go up there?' I asked, floating past her to put some black pieces of paper in the file behind her desk. 'I thought Claudia and Paul were covering it?'

'Oh, my god, Rhee, I had to. It's him again! It's The Reaper. He killed those men in the quarry. It's the same place where they found Julia Kidner!'

I have to admit I was a little disappointed she'd gone with The Reaper as a moniker. 'Is that what you're calling him? The Reaper?'

'Yeah. I talked it through with Linus and Claudia and they said it fits the area quite well. You know, with all the farms around here. A reaper harvests... '

'Yeah, I know what a reaper is,' I said, slamming the filing cabinet drawer. 'Have the police confirmed it was him then?'

'They don't have to, I *know* it was! It's a midnight-blue Ford Transit, part-registration BTY. There were two guys in it – they're going to need dental records to identify them but I KNOW it's them!'

'The same ones doing all those rapes you mean?'

'YES!'

'Oh, my goodness, Daisy, that's AWESOME! You totally called this, girl!'

'I know! God, it's so exciting, isn't it? I mean, he's targeting sex offenders. It's sort of... I don't know, like, reassuring in a way. Still horrible and ghastly how he's doing it – the quarry foreman reckons at least one of them bled right out before he was put in the van – but wow. What a guy, eh?'

'Totally. What a guy.'

She had the same look on her face Michelle Pfeiffer has at the end of *Grease 2* when she's looking up at the ghost of her mystical motorcyclist.

'You fancy him a bit, don't you?'

'The Reaper? Don't be daft! No, of course not.'

'Yes, you do,' I sing-songed. 'You've got the hots for this fly-by-night do-good pest controller.'

Her face changed. 'Well, it remains to be seen if he raped that poor Julia Kidner woman, doesn't it? But if he hasn't and he really is doing what I think he's doing and cleaning up the streets of rapists and kiddy fiddlers, well, then, yes, I think you can put me down as being a little bit in awe of the guy.'

We sniggered and giggled like two Beliebers and I made her

a 'celebratory coffee' for being such a gosh-darnit mega-good journalist.

Small boo-boo though. We were just talking and Daisy was getting excited about potential journalism prizes and promotions and I was sitting there listening to her dribble on when suddenly she reached out and hugged me in thanks for listening to all her theories on the subject. Why do people feel the need to hug me so much lately? Who am I? Huggy Bear? Anyway, she hugged and I winced. Loudly.

'Oh, my God, what?' she said, recoiling in horror.

'Sorry. I... played netball the other night and fell arse over tit. Got a really tender face.'

She looked me up and down.

'Yeah, that's why I've got so much make-up on today.'

'I didn't know you played netball?'

'Yeah, most weeks.'

'Which team?'

I raced my mind through the last few months of copy I'd had to type up for Jeff. 'Just a local ladies' side. We meet on a Wednesday night.'

'Oh, right. What position are you?'

'Wing Attack.'

Her face said it all. She was putting things together, working things out, weighing things up. And what it amounted to was that, though my lie was comparatively little, she did not believe it.

Clever girl, I thought in a Bob-Peck-seeing-the-velociraptors-kinda-way as I sipped my latte. Clever, clever girl.

At the library, all the staff were either out the back seeing to a late delivery or milling about in the stacks. There was a fairly cute guy I'd seen with a lanyard on saying TRAINEE and it crossed my mind to inveigle him into my affections so I could snag the address.

'*Oh, hi, my granddad dropped his library card in here, has it been handed in at all? Yeah, his name's Derek Scudd. Can I just check you've got the right address on your system because he moved recently...* ' Pauses to bat lashes.

But again, too risky. If I ever *did* find out where Scudd lived, I did not want any kind of trail back to me and that included Hot Library Guy, who could tell the police I'd been asking for his address. No trail – that was the rule.

I finally know how those fan girls feel when they're waiting for their fictional beloveds to come through Arrivals at Heathrow, screaming and holding placards and Sharpies out for some kind of contact. Any kind of contact. Even if the guys just spit in their faces. At that age, you just want to frame the spit.

Or do you? I am brain-damaged. It's possible that I'm just talking shite.

Saturday, 13 April

1. *Women who wear bodycon dresses*
2. *The old woman who stood in front of the chickpeas in Asda today and hadn't moved by the time I'd come back from Sweets and Biscuits. And she didn't even buy any arsing beans!*
3. *People who cough incessantly without leaving the room/restaurant/cinema/planet*
4. *People over twenty-one who say 'amazeballs', 'totes' and 'totes amazeballs'*
5. *People over ten who do cosplay – did you bump your head when you fell into your nursery school dressing-up box or something?*
6. *Mrs Whittaker – our new jar of Nutella has gone walkies*

Me and Craig had quite a nice day today. I took Tink out in the morning over to Victory Park – no blood on the path any more – then did some shopping in town. Bought some bath bombs in Lush, some proper coffee (Craig had bought the cheap shit again) and I almost bought a clown fish in the pet shop – a black-and-white version of Nemo. I was going to call him Jeremy. In the end, Craig talked me out of it. 'Tropical fish tanks are well expensive and they need special food and blah blah blah blah.' Plus, the guy behind the till had coke nails and his hair stank of cheese.

The local daily is all over the van in the quarry story. They're calling it a double homicide and appealing for witnesses. A mugshot has flashed up of a man – definitely a man – wearing all black with a face scarf over his jaw. I don't know where they got that idea from. There was no one about, no one. A few cows in the corner of one of the fields we ran through. Maybe one of them is the rat? A cow-rat.

There's some big comics event on over at the convention centre so town is full to the rafters with grown human beings dressed as Iron Man and The Joker and gliding along wearing capes and waving wands. Craig joked about digging out his prized Stormtrooper outfit and going over there – I said if he did, he'd be on his own. He begged me to dig out the Harley Quinn outfit from last Halloween and I said that if he made me, I would amputate both his ears. He thought that was funny for some reason. Luckily, AJ has got the baton to cover the convention for next week's *Gazette*. We flipped a coin – the joke one I keep in my desk that only lands on Heads.

I looked out for Scudd in town but it's like looking for a rat in a sea of mice.

And then this evening I cooked us some pasta thing from scratch and we cuddled up watching the *Royal Variety Performance*. Bedtime sex was thankfully brief because I'd eaten too much and almost vommed up my puttanesca. He fell straight to sleep meaning me and Tink could watch *Ramsay's Hotel Hell* in peace without all his usual comments. Connecticut's oldest inn is saved – Gordon Ramsay clap – done.

Tink *still* won't do Shake a Paw.

Sunday, 14 April

I really needed to not be around people today – it was one of *those* days. I slipped in the shower, banged my toe on the sodding Henry vacuum *and* burnt my bagel. By lunchtime even my own fingernails were annoying me.

Craig was out all day – 'starting early on a job fitting out a new bathroom showroom on Abner Street' (seeing to Lana's plumbing) so I took Tink out early then decided to tidy up some of my Sylvanian rooms – I've been thinking about redecorating the children's bedroom with itty-bitty Beyoncé posters – when my fucking heart stood still – I noticed some things were missing:

1. *The little yellow block of soap from the bathtub*
2. *The hamster baby – Peaches – in the yellow bib*
3. *The grandfather clock from the dining room*
4. *The miniature copy of Great Expectations from the lounge bookcase*
5. *The older sister's red shoe*
6. *Three croissants*
7. *And the pig dad, Richard E. Grunt*

'The actual fuck!?' I shouted, making Tink jump and start

barking because she thought we had visitors. I've spent YEARS collecting all that stuff and Klepto Whittaker's been coming in here and meddling with it. There was a little tray of chocolate eclairs I always kept on the coffee table that the pig dad is reaching for and that had gone too, but I found it had been moved to the fridge.

And that wasn't the only thing that had been moved around – the one remaining baby was in the bath, instead of his cot, the mum was doing the ironing instead of having a lie-down and the boy rabbit was doing his homework at the dining table, instead of skateboarding along the landing.

'I'm going to kill her,' I blurted out, trying to concentrate on my breathing but my chest was too tight to co-operate. 'Think, think,' I said. 'Maybe she's just moved things. Maybe nothing's actually been taken.'

And so I looked. And, sure enough, I found things. The soap was in the fridge. The hamster baby in the yellow bib was in the conservatory on the slide. The grandfather clock, for reasons best known to someone else, was in the bathroom. The little Dickens had been tucked into the boy rabbit's school satchel. The sister's red shoe was in the mum and dad's wardrobe and the three croissants were in the toilet, bizarrely – who shits croissants? I was almost sane again.

But the pig dad, Richard E. Grunt, was nowhere to be found.

'She's had him!' I seethed and, with that, I stormed out of the flat, and down the stairwell to number thirty-nine. I knocked sharply on the door four times. She didn't open until the seventeenth knock.

'Hello, Rhiannon.' She beamed, false-toothily, 'I was just boiling the kettle…'

'Where's Richard E. Grunt?' I said, keeping a lid on my voice as best I could.

'Where's who, love?'

'Don't give me that. What have you done with it?'

She smiled, like it was a joke. 'I don't know what you're talking about, Rhiannon. Who's Richard…'

'He's the dad in my doll's house. And you've taken him. Where. Is. He?'

She frowned, bloody Oscar-winning. 'I'm sure I haven't seen it, Rhiannon. Are you sure Tink hasn't…'

'Don't blame Tink. She knows not to touch my doll's house. And so does Craig. The only other person who goes into that flat is you because you've got a key. And I know you take things from there, don't deny it. And normally I don't mind but when it comes to my doll's house I mind, so WHERE IS HE?'

Her eyeballs were wide now, because I was shouting. 'Love, I haven't taken your doll, I haven't touched…'

'Haven't touched?'

'Well, I have a little look at it, now and again. It's such a pretty house, I didn't think you would mind.'

'I don't mind people looking at it, as long as they keep their mitts off.' I had my hands on my hips. I meant business and I wanted her to know it.

'I just had a little play in there the other day, when I was looking after Tink.'

'We pay you to look after Tink, we don't pay you to play with my Sylvanians. I'll give you one more chance – where's Richard E. Grunt?'

She swallowed and opened the door a little wider, so I could look inside her flat. I barged past her. Nothing too untoward at first glance. Same beige and brown furnishings, still the soft aroma of old woman perfume and ammonia. Still the tidy rack of old woman slip-ons in the corridor.

And then I saw it – or rather him – Richard E. Grunt, sitting on her mantelpiece, next to a carriage clock and some birthday cards. I marched over and grabbed him.

'Oh, you found him, good,' she said, back with the smile. 'I don't know what he was doing in there, I'm sure.'

'He was "in there" because you put him "in there", you thief, and don't play the old card. You were a klepto long before Old-Timers Disease crept in. Don't. Take. My. Things.'

I almost left it at that but she had to go and put her big fat Dr Scholl in it. 'Do you want me to have Twink again tomorrow?'

I marched back down and faced her in the doorway. I held out my hand. 'Key.'

'Pardon?' And yet again, with the smile. I wanted to tear her whiskery lips right off her face.

'I want my key back.'

She reached behind her and took our door key off the hook by her coats, handing it to me.

'I don't want you to look after Tink any more. I can't take the risk.'

'I won't touch it again, Rhiannon, there's no need to be silly.'

I got right up in her old, creased, hair-tufted face. 'Damn right you won't touch it again, you old cunt. Because, if you do, I will gut you like a fucking pig and wear your entrails as a belt.'

And then I went. And it wasn't until I got back inside my flat that I realised I shouldn't have said that. 'Guts' would have been a much better word than 'entrails'. More punch to it. But at least I had Richard E. Grunt back. I put him back on his armchair and wedged the two sides of his *Telegraph* back in his trotters.

Sylvan peace restored.

Monday, 15 April

1. *Derek Scudd*
2. *Wesley Parsons*
3. *That window company who keep phoning my mobile and asking if I'm 'ready for us to quote you on your mum and dad's patio doors'*
4. *People who have body odour (aka Paul in our office) but who have absolutely no idea. What are you nose blind as well as filthy?*
5. *People who look anywhere but at you when talking (aka Mike Heath). Also, get away from me with those home-made cakes, Mike. There's no way you wash your hands after you've used the bathroom – I've timed you*

Craig took Tink to work with him today, now we don't have old Whittaker to rely on (I told him she'd been the one stealing his pot so we clearly couldn't trust her any more).

Everyone in the office is acting like they've all been administered with electric shocks – I've never seen them all so alive, so animated. Not only have the Blue Van Men been stopped in their rapey tracks in the most grisly of ways, but it looks as though we have a serial killer on our patch. Everyone's SO happy. AJ's flirting has gone off the charts – winks, smiles, compliments, risqué gestures using poster tubes, you name it. It's wonderful. And everyone else is being courteous and enthusiastic and giving me not-so-shit jobs to do like interviewing wrongful arrest victims and local Olympians. It's almost an enjoyable place to work again.

I did that.

But I couldn't enjoy the new atmosphere for long today as I was sent to do a report on the local arts festival at the community hall – or the community fuck-all as I call it.

'It'll be a great scoop for your column, won't it, Sweetpea?' said Claudia as she marched out to the editorial meeting. At least she smiled as she said it. One day, I'd like to see that smile face up in a frying pan.

The rooms in our community hall still stink of the same biscuits and farts it did when I did my ballet exams there in Year 6 and everyone who attends one of these community events is so old they need an oxygen tank to move around. I felt like an extra in the Thriller video. In the first room were the art installations where local 'artists' had installed their, well, art. 'Art' these days seems to be lumps of chicken wire wrapped in bandages and a pile of copper pipes arranged interestingly on the floor.

In the next room was a music and movement class where the children's dance group were pratting about in leotards. Imelda's twins waved when they saw me. I pulled some faces to put them off, earning me some giggly adoration from the troupe and a death glare from their bunned-up, big-arsed teacher.

In the room beyond that was a live watercolour class, so people could stand about literally watching paint dry. Upstairs, things got slightly more stimulating – the chocolate master class was underway. A man on the door was holding out a tray of samples.

'They're free, my dear,' he said in a 'don't be shy' tone of voice. 'Have as many as you like. We made them with our own fair hands.'

I spotted a couple of members of the White Ankle Sock Brigade in the class and decided against it. 'I'm actually allergic,' I told him.

Yeah, to snot and dingle berries.

Now I have to put together a 'light-hearted and enthusiastic report' to accompany my experience. Oh Lord, will all this pleasure never end?

*

I'VE SEEN HIM. I'VE SEEN SCUDD! HE WAS GOING INTO THE ARTS FESTIVAL AS I WAS COMING OUT! I'm SURE it was him! Will report back later.

*

UPDATE: I lost him. In the crowds. He's like a fucking ghost. But at least he's a ghost who I know is still alive. It's made me all the more determined to kill him.

Maundy Thursday, 18 April

1. *In jokes – keep them in then*
2. *People who say 'a million per cent' and overuse the word 'awesome'. Time was people used that word only for moon landings or cancer cures. Now it's used if there's a well-risen soufflé on* Bake Off
3. *Overusers of the word 'amazing' – normally the same type of people who say 'a million per cent'*
4. *Judgy dieters – aka Joy in our office. I've learned this week that corned beef, mayonnaise and chocolate 'will put you into an early grave' and that cooking with olive oil will 'definitely give you cancer'. 'Bring it on,' I said. Turns out, her aunt had just died from cancer. 'Was it olive oil related?' I asked. 'Or did Popeye do it?' She pretended she hadn't heard*
5. *People who act like a football team losing is the end of the world (Craig, Nigel, Eddie, Gary)*

BIG SCUDD news. So just one day after seeing him for myself, this happens…

I'm ensconced behind my desk, thinking about my forthcoming long weekend, Simnel cake overdose, chocolate overdose,

Craig overdose and typing up some shit about loose paving stones in the High Street when in walks the postman – this nondescript guy with ginger hair who always delivers the post but who I've never taken much notice of before.

Anyway, he's become quite thick with AJ and I'm eavesdropping on their conversation as he's handing AJ the post.

'I just saw that paedo going into the post office.'

'What paedo?' asks the Aussie.

'You know, that Scudd bloke what got done for messing with those two kids at his flat. He got let off, didn't he?'

'Where was he?'

'He was just going into the post office with a couple of parcels.'

'Guy gives me goosies.'

'Had his coat collar pulled up and a flat cap on. I knew it was him though.'

I didn't wait to hear any more. I threw my coat around my shoulders and shoved my arms through the holes.

'AJ, I've got the dentist's. I won't be long.'

There's always a queue at our post office. The weeks before Christmas, it would leak out on to the street. I scanned the line from the back, and I clocked him, four people away, clutching two parcels and leaning on a walking stick. My heart raced, like seeing an old lover, not a seventy-something half-crippled convicted rapist wearing a flat cap. He was older and a lot more stooped, but facially, he had not changed one bit since his front page trial picture. I pretended to scan the magazines.

When he left, I waited a little while before I followed him, keeping well back but never once losing sight of that flat cap or the tapping sound of that walking stick as it weaved slowly through the crowd of shoppers. Paddy Power. Getting cash out of NatWest. Up Castle Lane. Along the High Street. Boots the chemist, then Iceland. Looking in the freezers. Buying a shepherd's pie for one and a two-litre bottle of cider. Looking in the window of Clarks shoes. Through the precinct.

Across the car park.

Across the county courthouse.

Past the hospital.

And finally into a town house. Number four Hastings Row. I waited a little while across the road, before I went to look at the names on the door buzzers. They were flats. Number three – empty. Number two – empty. Number one – Derrick. I saw the TV flicker on inside, through the thick yellowy net curtains.

Derrick? His first name was his surname now? Or was that a coincidence? I wasn't sure. Either way, I've got him right where I want him.

The rat is in the trap.

Saturday, 20 April

1. *People who pay for pop-up adverts on websites – you could be reading a tragic article about some woman who lost all her kids in a bomb blast in Aleppo and then up pops an advert for a new frappuccino. Mind you, it was a bloody good deal and triple points too*
2. *Double dippers (aka Craig and Linus)*
3. *People who write unfunny things on dirty vans – there's one on Craig's at the moment that says 'Rolf Harris's Tour Bus'. I don't think he's noticed yet*
4. *People who make bad sandwiches – I asked the new woman at the Apple Blossom Café if I could have some bread with my butter this morning.*
5. *Indian call centres – I'm sorry and all that but WHAT THE FUCK ARE YOU TALKING ABOUT?*

Another bad dream. My old faithful. Hospital, the pleading eyes, the dry lips, the pillow poised. Yadda yadda yadda. After two years, it's getting tedious. Fuck knows what my brain is up to now.

I did Craig 'hands down the best sausage casserole he's ever had' for tea, plus waffles and peas. I made a chocolate brownie with squirty cream for pudding AND sliced up a strawberry for the garnish. Then the lads came round the football – Manchester Someone vs Sheffield Whoever – so he, Eddie, Gary and Nigel were ensconced on my three-piece for the rest of the evening, chugging back Stella Artois and farting into my cushions. The whole flat stank to Murgatroyd in no time.

Neither Biggus Dickus nor Mr Sizzler48 were online, so I couldn't even distract myself by talking to them so I decided to call up Anni and see if I could pay a visit. She cried on the phone, but through the tears, I heard her say, 'That would be so lovely,' and I surmised that the rest of the PICSOs had already forgotten she existed and that post-natal depression doggie was beginning to lick her neck.

I took round the leftover brownie in a Tupperware box. It was time for Operation: Golden Pineapple Part 1.

She cried when she opened the door. Sam was crying too as he wriggled on her shoulder like a little bag of beans.

'How are you doing?' I asked, though one look at the living room behind her told me all I needed to know – the place was a landfill site, with a small carpeted pathway through to the kitchen. It wasn't dirty, just cluttered. I could see where everything was *meant* to go – there were cupboards and drawers carefully labelled with things like Nappies and Teething Rings. It just hadn't quite made it to the right places yet.

'Sorry, you've caught me at a bad time. It's a bloody tip.'

Ramsay's Hotel Hell was on silently in the background, the episode where he helps this struggling lodge in Oregon where the guy's too stoned to focus. I've seen it before but it's still a good one. I nodded. 'Yeah.'

'He doesn't sleep. Ever,' she told me, starey-eyed like a banshee. 'And when he does, when I finally get him down, I go to make a start on all this but I just can't be bothered. I just want to sleep. And I've got *three* haemorrhoids now. Three!'

'Where's Rashan? Why isn't he helping?'

'Oh, he is, but he's taken on extra work so he's working week-ends now as well. He hasn't stopped going to the gym either. *I* have. *I've* made sacrifices for this baby. He hasn't sacrificed... Is that brownie?' She opened the box and inhaled it.

'Freshly made tonight. Just for you.'

She started crying again. 'His mum's been over twice this week. My mum and dad are due to fly over from Mauritius next Monday but... ugh, it's just hard.' She shoved a brownie in her mouth and replaced the lid on the box. 'Couldn't be bothered to cook anything tonight.'

Rashan reminded me of Paul in our office. The obsession with going to the gym, the pictures all over his Facebook of him kayaking in Canada and rock climbing in New Zealand, before he and Anni even met. He still hadn't changed his header or his profile picture to the baby. I have noticed, several times, Paul phoning home to wifey saying he was 'under the kosh from Ron' and had to work late because he was 'backed right up' and then I'd walk past his desk and he'd be in the middle of an online poker game. He just wanted to miss the dreaded bedtime.

'Sorry, do you want a tea or gin and tonic or anything?' Anni offered, sitting on the edge of the sofa and jiggling the grizzly bundle about on her shoulder. She picked up the remote and switched *Hotel Hell* off, just as Ramsay was getting in his stride.

'No, I'm fine, thanks. Listen, say no if you want to, but why don't you make use of me while I'm here? Go and get some sleep for a few hours. I'll mind him.'

She shook her head. 'I can't ask you to do that, Rhiannon.'

I sighed. 'Anni, to be honest, you're no company in this state and I don't want to go home cos the boys are doing their football and farting thing in my lounge. Why don't you go and rest? You'd be doing us both a favour. He's changed, isn't he?'

She looked down at Sam, who was still full of *waah*. 'His nappy? Yeah, just.'

'Fed?'

'Yeah. He should be a-bloody-sleep!'

She cried again. I marched over to her, hands out for the baby, and she plonked him in my arms.

'Are you sure? Are you OK with babies?'

'I'll have you know I babysat Lucille's two when they were this age. Remember when she walked out at their christening? Four hours she was gone and I was the only one keeping an eye on them. I didn't like the way that uncle of hers kept staring at them.'

Anni afforded me one watery smile of thanks and a brief look back before trudging up the stairs. She then stopped and looked back at the baby. He had actually stopped crying the moment she put him in my arms.

'See? We'll be fine. Go. Sleep. That's an order. We'll be here when you get up, don't worry.'

See what a brilliant friend I am?

Sam had a milky smell about him – tit milk I realised, with a stomach churn. I rocked him for a bit then placed him on his back in his basket in the corner. The childminder used to stroke our eyebrows when she wanted to get us off to sleep after lunch sometimes. It worked on Sam in no time.

'You are a good chap, aren't you?' I told him, folding his yellow blanket over his legs. 'Now, Auntie Rhee-Rhee has to go and tidy up this mess for your mum so you be a good little man and go sleepies and I'll be back in a minute, all right?'

Then I got to work. I even found the Mr Sheen and had a dust round once everything was in situ and got the place looking habitable again within the hour.

Mary Poppins – eat my ass. I even made Anni a sandwich for when she woke up. God, I could lick myself sometimes.

Then I checked to make sure Sam was OK – his little sleepsuit going up and down in the middle – and crept upstairs, remembering the last-but-one creaky step from the last time I'd visited.

'Anni?' I said, softly knocking on her bedroom door but I could hear her snoring. Her bedside light was on. I moved over to her wardrobe and eased it open, flicked through the racks of clothes until I found what I was looking for – three pristine mauve tunics, folded over hangers. I eased out the first one and stuffed the whole uniform up my jumper, replacing the empty hanger and closing the doors.

I looked at Anni asleep on the bed as I left. Dead to the world. 'Jesus world, you make this far too easy.'

Back downstairs, I folded the uniform into my bag and checked on Sam – poor little sod was snoozing soundly, probably relieved to have someone looking after him who wasn't capable of any emotion. I wouldn't dream of hurting Sam, any more than I'd hurt Tink. I *can* stop myself. I *can* be a good person around the right people.

By the time Anni came back downstairs, two and a half hours and nearly three episodes of *Hotel Hell* later, she looked disorientated but refreshed.

She was still thanking me as I was halfway up the street to my car.

'I've told you, you're welcome,' I called back. 'Just say you owe me one.' And I threw her a smile that dazzled like diamonds.

I stuffed the uniform bag in my boot, ready for next week.

Easter Sunday, 21 April

1. Marathon runners – how sanctimonious can you get?

It was the London Marathon today. Some Kenyan no one's ever heard of won – again – same guy who won last year. I didn't watch it.

Me and Craig went for a pub lunch with the in-laws. Or I should say 'pube' lunch, seeing as that's what I found in mine. The guy carving the meat on the buffet looked clean enough but you never can tell what goes on behind the scenes, can you? He could have scratched his balls just before slicing up my lamb, we'll never know.

Back at the ranch things ran to their usual form – Jim harped on about the 'foreigners taking all our jobs' (he's been retired for the past five years), while Elaine serenaded us with tales of terrible local vandalism (a spurting cock has been drawn on the village hall) and the WI coach trip to Agatha Christie's house (some woman called Marjorie fainted on the bus on the way back). I did quite enjoy it today actually. Dull, as always, but safe and familiar too. And Jim gave me one of his tiny model boats. He'd even painted my name on the side of it in wavy white script – *Rhiannon*. I've put it on top the TV.

Elaine cried when we left today and snuggled Tink for the longest time – Jim said she always cries when we leave and that it was 'just unfortunate we saw her today'. I think that woman has serious issues and I'm not just talking about her stack of *Woman's Weekly*s.

Thursday, 25 April

I haven't updated for a few days because literally nothing's happened. Life has generally plateaued to almost bridge-jumping proportions.

BUT...

The little nugget of excitement on the horizon comes in the form of Derek Scudd and Operation: Golden Pineapple, which has begun now in earnest.

So this week, my first week off of the year, I've spent each day monitoring the situation from a bench in the churchyard opposite his house on Hastings Row. Or stalking him, if you will. I've been pretending to sketch the gravestones while Tink roams about pissing on them and barking at the ducks on the river. Craig thinks I'm at work. He thinks they won't let me have a holiday at this time of year because we're 'so up against it with deadlines'. Sucker.

Here's what I've learned about old D-Scu...

He's virtually housebound. He has three carers whom he lets in at three times during the day: 8.30 a.m.; 1.30 p.m.; and 6.30 p.m. Presumably, he needs assistance getting washed and dressed and fed, ironically, like a child. The first carer of the day is blonde and middle-aged with cankles; the lunchtime one looks like David Walliams in drag; and the tea-time treat is so fat she has to walk into the house sideways.

Each carer spends no longer than half an hour inside, they all have a cigarette when they leave and they wear white plastic aprons when they come out again. Aside from the odd postman, nobody else visits. The other two flats must be empty. Scudd himself has only been out twice this week – once on Tuesday lunchtime, to the betting shop and to Iceland, and once again this morning to the paper shop.

The 6.30 p.m. slot seems to be the right time to make my move. I cannot fucking wait.

Friday, 26 April

I'm writing this with shaking hands. The deed is done…

Derek Scudd is an ex-paedophile.

'The fat cow's just been,' he growled at me when he opened the door. 'I don't need anyone else tonight.'

I was quite breathless as I faced him, boobage constricted slightly by Anni's super-tight tunic. I can only describe it as the feeling one gets when one meets a celebrity, even a crap one like an ex-member of Atomic Kitten. Or a bloke who's been in some advert. I was sick with it – with expectation, with intense longing. Is this how lovers feel, I wonder.

'Sorry to bother you, Mr Derrick, but your form wasn't filled in properly.'

He didn't want to let me in and we had quite the argument on his doorstep. Eventually, he left the door open behind him as he withdrew back into his shell like an old tortoise. Inside it stank of damp and strong tobacco. The curtains were drawn and the place was shrouded in a stygian gloom. I noticed he was wheezing.

'There's tea in the pot. It'll be stewed.' He retreated into his lounge.

'That's all right, I don't drink tea,' I lied. I *do* drink tea but only Lady Grey, and if you are anywhere and you ask for Lady Grey, you sound like a ponce.

'You go and sit down, Derek, that's right.' I just wanted to do it. To get on him and start squeezing the breath from his neck. But I knew the importance of the performance. The Act.

He sat in his armchair, surrounded by everything he could need – tartan slippers, folded newspaper, little table with his ashtray, fags and lager can on, pristine memory foam pillow behind his head.

'She's always messing up, that one,' he grumbled.

I laughed with a theatrical eye roll as he sipped his lager. 'She says she's dyslexic but I think she's just bone idle.'

He mumbled something and scrabbled around in a bag of dry roasted peanuts. I pretended to scribble down my notes and watched him, his eyes fixed on some church programme. Aled Jones was interviewing a woman bishop.

'How are you feeling today, Derek?'

'The fat one asked me all that,' he growled. 'I got to go through it again?'

'No, sorry. I didn't think,' I said, my heart pounding through Anni's mauve uniform.

'How come you don't wear green like the other ones?'

'I'm different,' I said. 'I'm special.'

He nodded and went back to the TV and his lager. I watched his lips accept the can, his throat swallow. His hand fumble with his cigarette lighter and his packet of Silk Cut. He plucked one out and lit up.

'So have you had your dinner then, Mr Derrick or did you want me to make you something?'

A soloist was belting out 'Amazing Grace' on the TV, backed by a gospel choir and a too-tall Scottish guy with a set of bagpipes.

'Shut up,' he said, 'I like this one.'

I stood up. And walked towards his chair. 'Can I just check your pulse, Derek?'

'No,' he grunted. 'I'm watching this.'

'You still having sex with children, Derek? Or have you given all that up now?'

His face tilted to look at me, devoid of all expression. I grabbed his wrist and squeezed it, fingers tight around the bones.

'I'm curious. Is it the kind of thing you can just give up on or do you sit beside that window of a morning, watching them all trot to school with your hand down your pyjamas?'

'You're hurting...'

I squeezed tighter. 'I can see why you prefer kids. Much easier than a consenting adult, aren't they? You don't have to put the time in, wine and dine them. Just stick on *The Little Mermaid* and make some threat about hurting their parents.'

The TV choir grew louder. He put down the half-finished cigarette, then reached for his stick. 'Get off me!'

'Kids are just easier, aren't they, Derek? Takes no effort at all. Lazy, just lazy.'

'Get out of my house!'

'It's not your house, the council pays for it. There's better people than you on waiting lists as well. People with children. That turn you on, does it?' I squeezed again and heard a snap.

'Ahhh, you evil cow!' he roared, and made to get up, grabbing again for his stick, but I beat him to it. I threw it across the room and grabbed the memory foam pillow from behind his head.

'Sit down, you bastard, or I'll snap your other one. I've been waiting for you.'

I straddled his lap and clamped the pillow down onto his face. The force sent his armchair backwards with a loud thump. Then I had full purchase. I could press down as hard as my body weight could manage. And he slapped at me and punched me hard and for an old-timer with crap lungs, he did connect a few times. But I was just too strong. When the fight was almost out of him, I removed the pillow and watched him struggle for air but no way able to get up with me on top of him. I put the pillow back and pressed down hard again, and he kept hitting me and his legs were shaking underneath me.

And I let it go, again.

And put it back, again.

And off.

And back. Harder.

And the more he struggled, the more it turned me on. And the more the memory of that last day at the hospital with Dad was washed away.

I allowed it to fill me up, the thrill of it. The power of what I was doing – taking life.

Promise me when it gets worse, you'll be there. You'll do it for me.

You're the only one I can trust, Rhiannon.

I did it because he asked me to. I took Dad's pain away. But the memory of that day was expunged with this one act – it was Derek Scudd's face I would see beneath that pillow in my dreams now, not Dad.

After five minutes of pushing and pressing and struggling and teasing, lying on top of him, straddling him in a hideous, sweaty embrace, the struggling stopped altogether. I removed his murderous muffler. His mouth and eyes were still open – bloodshot. Tears on his cheeks. Blood on the pillow – he had bitten right through his tongue. His arms and legs slack like a marionette's. I righted the chair, put the pillow back behind his head, so he looked like he was sleeping.

I placed the cigarette in his lap, waiting until the first crease in his jumper had caught ablaze. It was only when I was halfway back to my car that I realised the gusset of my underpants was soaked.

I burnt the uniform in a bin at the back of Boots car park. The CCTV was always being vandalised there – I'd done the story on it last December when Linus couldn't be bothered to cover it again – so I knew I was safe. And then I drove home singing at the top of my lungs through all the open windows. I don't need dollar bills to have fun tonight – I got cheap thrills.

Saturday, 27 April

1. *That Saturday-morning cookery programme – why do they never wash their hands after chopping meat?*
2. *Conversational gazumpers – people who one-up you ALL THE TIME, e.g. Imelda. If I say anything remotely impres-sive, she'll come back with 'Jack's taking us to Disneyland' or 'I've won ten grand on a scratch card'. The first time I saw the PICSOs after Mum's death, she said, 'There's no pain like losing a child. You never get over that.'*
3. *Any Kardashians who escaped the last cull*

A dreamless sleep last night, all good. But I woke up feeling incredibly down in the dumps. It was the same New Year's Day-kind of feeling, where you know it's Back to Work soon and all the trimmings have to start coming down. A Kirsty MacColl song came on the radio while Craig was out on the balcony with his joint texting Lana and I just started crying. I didn't let him see me though, I took Tink out for a walk and cried it out behind my sunglasses.

I couldn't put a finger on it, why I was so damn miserable, so I googled it. It could be part of the 'serial-killer cycle'. We can handle the inanities of our daily lives while we are killing but when the killing's over, there comes a phase of depression. This phase can kick in at any time. For some serial killers, it's instant. For some, they can go days and months on a high. Apparently, the inanities of my life – my dull friends, my insignificance at work, my errant boyf – are simply stop gaps in my 'spree.' We are living for the next one. I understand it better, but it doesn't go any way to helping me overcome it.

My dad once said something to me that I've never forgotten. We were talking about John Lennon – I think a song of his came on the radio when we were in his van. He said, *'There are three ways to make your mark on the world. Do something ordinary, do something extraordinary or kill something extraordinary. You can be an average John, a John Lennon or the man who kills John Lennon.'*

As time went on, a fourth option seemed the most interesting to me – I want to be the *woman* who kills John Lennon.

I want to kill extraordinarily.

Priory Gardens had taken away my chance of being ordinary and extraordinary always seemed so out of reach. I was destined to be a Mark David Chapman, a John Wilkes Booth, a Lee Harvey Oswald. Isn't it funny how they're all guys? All the major serial killers are guys too. And, yeah, there's loads of reasons why guys do it more, but why aren't there more Aileens? I wonder. Maybe there are and they're just hiding it like I am. We're supposed to be all equal now, but we'll never be equal while those statistics remain. I'm just evening things out a bit.

Had a text from Seren mid-afternoon:

I can't see Mum and Dad's house on the Charles Burridge website. What's happening please? – Seren

I had to let it go. I had to put the past where it belonged. So, after Craig went to work, I drove over to the house to do one last clean down with my trusty Cillit Bang and boxed up the last of Dad's stuff I wanted to keep. I told Henry it was going back on the market. He seemed disappointed. Of course, now he has to move his car, his runner beans and the rope ladder over his fence that reminded him of 'the grandchildren he never had'. I gave him a baggy of pot to halt the inevitable tears.

Tink came with me to the house. I wanted her to have a proper run in the garden and the woods at the back, one last time. She peed on the exact spot where me and Dad had buried Pete's body. I wish she had more space to run about at home.

Then we drove into town and walked into the offices of Redman & Finch – a new agency on the corner of the High Street (I didn't like the way the lady looked at me on the reception desk at Charles Burridge – it was the way Claudia looked at me). Redman–Finch were brand-new to the area, a married couple called Dean and Jamie. Their colour scheme was a relaxing mixture of jade and chrome and they offered me Lady Grey *and* Jammie Dodgers *and* they had a little long-haired chihuahua under a desk, whom they called Mary-Kate and to whom Tink took a shine straight away.

So I Facebooked my darling sister this afternoon with some good news:

Valuation underway with Redman & Finch. Should be on their website tomorrow. That's my tomorrow, not yours.

Her message back was immediate: *What happened to Charles Burridge?*

I typed back: *He 'accidentally' stroked my boob while shaking hands. I didn't feel comfortable going to the house on my own with him.*

She said: *Ugh, what a creep. Fair enough. OK. Will check Redman & Who-Is-It? tomorrow then.*

'Will check' meaning 'I still don't trust you and I still hate you'.

Craig was out 'at Eddie's playing on his new pool table' so I played with Tink and my doll's house all evening while picking up some useful tips from *Countdown to Murder*.

Bliss.

Sunday, 28 April

1. *Craig – I ask him what he wants at the supermarket (salt-and-vinegar crisps, cheapo shower gel, Irn-Bru) and instead, he eats MY Kettle Chips, uses MY organic lime body wash and drinks MY elderflower pressé. Just when I think I hate him as much as I could, I find a staircase to new heights*
2. *Men who wear man buns but are not attractive – surely it's an insult to the glory of man buns. Should be a hate crime*
3. *Jim and Elaine Wilkins – for conceiving Craig in the first place*

The car boot sale we were going to do over at the County Ground was called off, owing to a group of travellers who'd pitched up on the site, which meant we *could* go down to Jim and Elaine's for Sunday lunch after all.

Oh. Yay.

So I had to play Lovely Girlfriend yet again while we walked down the Esplanade to this little cafe called The Porthole to have hot chocolate and toasted teacakes and listen to Elaine harp on about the minutiae of every single special offer at Lidl, followed by a detailed description of the next-door-but-one-neighbour's-daughter's wedding and subsequent honeymoon in Fuengirola. I could have drowned myself in my hot chocolate. Afterwards, we took Tink for a run on the beach, had lunch, then Jim showed me round their boring new conservatory while Elaine and Craig washed up with Lidl washing-up liquid – 39p a bottle.

Then the cringe clouds descended.

'Craig informs us you're trying for a baby?'

'Oh. Yeah. Didn't realise we were telling people. Yes, we are.'

'How long has that been then?'

'Only a few weeks.'

'We were trying for seventeen months before we fell pregnant with Craig. And another five years before Kirsty. You want to get yourselves tested if you don't crack the case soon, love.'

'Yeah, we will.'

'I've got a low count, you see. Weren't Elaine's doing.'

'Oh, right. Maybe it's hereditary then.'

'No, it's not hereditary,' he said. 'Does Craig use any of that marijuana stuff?'

'Umm . . no,' I lied. 'He vapes now and again.'

'Yeah but does he vape the marijuana stuff is what I'm asking.'

'No. He doesn't.'

'Good, cos that's another thing that kills off sperms. And stress. You've got to try not to get yourselves stressed. And buy our Craig some loose underpants, so his sac can get a bit of a draught going.'

If squirming were an Olympic event, I'd be crying as my flag went up the pole right about... now.

'Craig normally buys his own underpants, Jim.' Cue shy giggle and extended cringe.

'Well, you tell him from me that should be number one on the shopping list. Looser pants. Elaine gets mine from Marks. And it's never too soon for you to start taking folic acid either.'

'Loose pants, folic acid, no stress,' I repeated. I had felt a bit sick all that morning in fact but I didn't dare tell him that. He'd have made me march down to the village pharmacy tout de suite, and piss on the stick on the walk back.

I hated who I was in their company. This simpering, opinion-less, overly feminine meat sack of giggles who feigned interest in anything from antiques to golf, just to keep The Act intact.

'And plenty of sex of course, hahaha,' he guffawed. 'Every day. Twice a day if you can manage it.'

'Golly,' I laughed, praying for the clouds above us to piss down with rain so we could go inside and be around other humans.

All afternoon he was flitting around me with tips, telling me to put a cushion under my hips during sex, how yoga helped his niece, how he and Elaine did it five times a night in Malta and *still* couldn't 'hit the bullseye'. Believe it or not, this is not the most awkward I've ever been around Jim and Elaine. I had food poisoning at their house one Christmas – I was up all night in their bathroom, Jackson Pollock-ing the ceramic and letting off excruciatingly loud farts. At one point Jim came in and asked me if I wanted a cup of tea. My mouth tried to answer but my arsehole beat him to it.

I'll spare you any further details of my impregnation inter-rogation. Suffice to say that during one sitting of *Countryfile*, I'd been lectured to about my weight, height, stress levels, sexual prowess, workload, the height of my bed and the frequency with which I pluck my chin (a sure sign of polycystic ovaries).

On the way home, I said to Craig, 'If you don't kill your parents, I will.'

He just laughed. Idiot.

Monday, 29 April

1. *People who tell you in minute detail about their dreams*
2. *People who tag you in photos on your own Facebook Wall on nights out when you thought you were looking actually pretty attractive, only to find you actually look like you a walrus having a stroke*
3. *People who email you with 'Hope you're OK' before launching into the favour they want, meaning they don't actually care if you're OK or not*
4. *The Blue Van Men*
5. *Wesley Parsons*
6. *Derek Scudd*

All the reporters were clucking about Scudd first thing – he's top of the agenda. Normally, the kind of inane chit-chat you hear buzzing around an office first thing on a Monday morning is enough to make Marie Antoinette want to erect her own guillotine. Usually it's all *Did you have a nice weekend?* and the responses are always *Yeah, it was good thanks. How about you?* Nobody ever says anything different. Nobody ever tells the truth. I want to shout it from my desktop…
HOW CAN YOU HAVE HAD A GOOD WEEKEND? YOU

TRIED TO KILL YOURSELF! YOUR WIFE HATES YOU!
YOUR HUSBAND'S LEFT YOU! YOU HAVE CHRONIC
SCIATICA! YOUR KIDS ALL HAVE ASPERGER'S! YOUR
TEST RESULTS CAME BACK POSITIVE! AND YOU'RE IN
DEBT UP TO YOUR EYEBALLS!

But today, Scudd is the man of the moment. The Blue Van Men are yesterday's news for now. No one's mentioned a serial killer for Scudd's death – as far as all the facts are pointing, it's just a house fire – but he's a local celeb so everyone wants a piece of him. Of course I'm not allowed in on the impromptu editorial meeting when it's called – Daisy told me all about it outside the conference room though.

'A neighbour called the fire brigade out Saturday night. Whole building went up. They found him in his chair. He was a heavy smoker so the first indications are that it was a cigarette. Apparently there was a round of applause when they announced it in the pub on the corner last night. No one round here will grieve for Derek Scudd, that's for sure.'

'Do you think he's a victim of The Reaper?' I asked.

She shook her head. 'Doesn't look like it. It's odd though, isn't it? Another sex offender in the parish and another death.' I could practically see the cogs whirring in her mind. 'Might look into that though, good call, Rhee.'

'You're welcome.'

Good to know that the cigarette is getting most of the blame. I'm not in the clear yet though. There's not been any mention of the secondary fire at the back of Boots. Or Scudd's missing lighter, which I stuffed inside one of Tink's poo bags early this morning. You're only out of the woods when there are no more trees.

AJ dropped a small white bag on my desk at lunchtime – inside was a packet of Hot Toothpicks from the joke shop. He replaced some of Linus's Interdens with them when all the reporters were in their meeting upstairs. I feigned a smile as best I could but, to be honest, the whole thing's getting a bit tired and I'm doing what I can to reduce my conversation time with him. I'm blaming Claudia's watchful eye but, really, I just can't summon up the enthusiasm for an affair – I've got enough on my plate right now.

In other news – my breasts are still sore all over and I am officially worried again about a mini Craig growing in my Judas of a womb.

And Jeff Thresher retired today. AJ did the petty cash raid last week to buy him a card and mug and some engraved thing which I didn't take much notice of. I didn't even stay for the presentation after work. Why should I? They've replaced his desk with a brand-spanking new one already. Ergonomic, new swivel chair, no coffee stains. Like he was never there at all.

Oh, yeah, and it's my birthday. They all forgot at work what with all the 'Goodbye, Jeff' hullabaloo and I didn't remind them. I didn't fancy all the smiling that would have to accompany the hastily bought bouquet of flowers and scrappily written card, nor did I want to waste money buying doughnuts for nearly twenty people, at least two of whom actually despise me. Craig got me a Waterstones voucher, a no!no! hair remover and a bottle of perfume that brings me out in a rash. I bought myself some flowers – a huge bunch of yellow roses that smelled exactly like the ones my granddad used to grow at Honey Cottage. Every time I inhale them, I get a hit of happiness that I don't want to let go.

There was a card in our mailbox from Mrs Whittaker. So she remembers my birthday but she doesn't remember me calling her an old cunt and threatening to gut her like a pig? She must have levelled up on the Alzheimer's. She's not having her key back, that's for damn sure.

Didn't get anything from Seren. Never do.

We got a pizza and watched *Ferris Bueller's Day Off* – my

choice. Craig's parents sent me a Sylvanian Families caravan with hedgehog family figures. Craig must have mentioned it to them. I actually like them about 20 per cent more than I did, despite the personal questions and casual racism. There's a little horse that pulls the caravan too. I've called him Albert.

Wednesday, 1 May

There are bluebells everywhere and the weather has got a lot warmer, which means the majority of my colleagues have taken to wearing loose-fitting clothes and flip-flops. I have four MAS-SIVE problems with flip-flops:

1. **We're not in Lloret De Mar** – *we're in a small town newspaper office in the West Country and most of the time the bosses won't let us have the heating on so we're freezing to death;*
2. **Laziness** – *wearing flip-flops makes a person lazy. Don't ask me how the science works, it just does. Wearing a flat, floppy shoe makes you bone idle;*
3. **The noise** – *slap slap slap goes my hand against the faces of all those who wear flip-flops;*
4. **The view** – *I don't like feet. Any feet. When a person digs out their flip-flops, what they're also digging out is a pair of human trotters which haven't seen the light of day for a year so I have to look down upon fusty, yellowing, scabby, misshapen hooves which they have seen fit to display to the world.*

My breasts still ache and I can't lie on my front, which is one of my favourite things to do in the world. I've bought another pregnancy test but I'm scared to do it in case it really is positive this time. I'm on the Pill for Christ's sake, I thought that was supposed to be 100 per cent effective?

Oh, I've just googled it. Only 99 per cent effective. Ridiculous.

If I *am* up the stick, that's basically it, isn't it? I then become a fully fledged PICSO – one of that large group of saggy-uddered knackered females trudging along with pushchairs the size of small cars, shouting at their kids and pretending they enjoy going to Jungle Gyms and Little Flippers swimming classes and wanging on about Junior's chickenpox and how many times they got up in the night. I'll have to baby-proof the flat and get rid of all the dangly blind cords and baby-proof the cupboards and put the bleach up high and *uggggggggggghhhhhhhhhhhh*…

No, no way. Baby Criannon is Not. Happening.

Hang on – I'm a fucking serial killer, aren't I? I'll just flush it out. I'll up my gin intake and take more hot baths. Or I'll go to the doctor and order an aborsh. Easy-peasy. Why the hell am I panicking? I'm not panicking, no, I'm angry. That fucking pill should have worked. Maybe it has. Maybe I'm angry over nothing.

Wouldn't be the first time.

Daisy Chan treated me to lunch. Pizza at La Vela down by the harbour side. Her blouse today was an off-the-charts atrocity – some black and diamond tight number that I imagine Jessie J wearing if she fell down a mineshaft. I learned Daisy has a husband who's recently become the store manager for Carphone Warehouse. They have two kids – can't remember either of their names – and she had several miscarriages in between each one.

Quid Pro Quo – I then had to tell her about Me. She is a journalist after all – I was never going to get away with 'Oh, I just live with Craig and we have a dog' thing. She wanted dirt. She wanted Priory Gardens, the celebrity years, the reason there's a whole file on my dad in the filing system at the *Gazette* offices, the lot.

'How's your face today?'

'Oh, fine, thanks. Arnica cream – magic.'

'Yeah, I've heard a few people say that actually. So have you always lived round here or...?'

'No, we lived in Bristol until a couple of years after Priory Gardens then we moved down. My mum died when I was in my teens but Dad lived there till the last week of his life.'

'Oh, right.'

'Me and my sister are selling it. I started looking into Inheritance Tax laws this week. Boy, is she going to be pissed when I tell her how much we've got to cough up.'

'How does a family get over something like that? Priory Gardens, I mean.'

'It doesn't,' I said. 'In our case it just slowly falls apart. My mum and dad did the celebrity thing for a while, made a shitload of money doing public appearances. TV shows. Charity events raising money for brain injured kids. I don't really remember going but I've seen the YouTube clips so I know I was there.'

'I remember you on *The Ellen DeGeneres Show*.'

'Yeah. My mum did most of the talking but I got presents and met Ryan Gosling so that was cool.'

'You said you and your sister are selling their house?'

'Yeah. Our parents are both dead now – Dad died two years ago this summer – so we have to get rid of it. She wants her cut.'

A woman on an opposite table started having a coughing fit due to 'a tickle in her throat'. It took every bit of willpower to not walk over there and strangle it out of her. I hate being interrupted.

Daisy sipped her Coke. 'I was looking through the files

yesterday, actually, for something completely unrelated, when I came across one for your dad, Tommy.'

'Oh, you must know all about him then.'

'No, I didn't read it. Not yet. I just wondered…'

I was in a good mood so I helped her out. 'He used to fight for the county, before he became a builder, so he's quite well known around these parts.'

'He was a soldier?'

'No, a boxer. Middleweight. Couldn't go into a pub or a supermarket in this town without someone calling out to him or shaking his hand.'

'Wow. Bit of a hero then?'

I nodded. 'Priory Gardens changed him. He'd pick a fight with anyone. He blamed himself, cos he was the one who'd dropped me off.'

'Poor man. What did he go to prison for?'

'You've seen his file. You must know.'

A baby started crying somewhere else in the restaurant.

She looked down at her watch – it was a nice watch, rose gold with crystals around the face. 'Maybe we should start heading back.'

'He picked me up from school one day,' I told her. 'How old was I – I dunno, I was walking again by then so I would have been maybe nine or ten, but still not talking very well. Said he had an errand to run before we went home and we could get an ice cream if I was good. We parked up in this back street and he told me to wait in the car. I watched him go through the back gate of this red-brick house.'

'An affair?'

I laughed. The crying baby was being jiggled about. 'Not an affair. He was gone ages so I went over the road to see where he was. The back door of the house was unlocked and, as soon as I walked in the kitchen, I heard it. This *thwacking* sound, like a whip. I walked into this lounge-diner and at the end there was this man strapped to a chair. These four other men, maybe five, were standing around, taking it in turns to hit him, punch him. Gouge his eyes out. Stamp on his legs – I heard one of them snap like a thick stick. One of them had pliers and was pulling at his teeth. That was the first time I'd heard the C word. And the P word.'

'Oh, God,' she gasped. 'What's the P word?' Daisy frowned.

'Paedophile,' I said. 'I didn't know they existed till then. They kept saying it – "Dirty old paedo. Take that, ya paedo." I recognised one of the men from my dad's boxing club – I used to go and spar with the younger boys sometimes. Helped me get my aggression out. I struggled with that after Priory Gardens. Anyway, Dad saw me, and I turned and ran back out to the car. I sat in the passenger's seat, waiting, terrified he was going to be mad at me. About five minutes later, he came back and sat in the driver's seat and just looked at me. I remember his top lip was sweating and his pupils had blown.

Daisy looked spellbound. 'What did he say?'

'He just wanted to know what I'd seen. Dad was the only one who could get the odd word out of me. I asked him why they were hitting the man and he said they all had kids my age and that this man had hurt kids. He asked me not to tell anyone what I'd seen, not that I could, and he said he trusted me. I valued that. I valued being in his confidence. It made me feel powerful.'

I left out the bit about asking Dad if I could go in and see the man's body as he lay dying. And the way I saw Dad in a whole new light – like he was suddenly magical in my eyes. I was just about making a bridge across the river of my weirdness in her eyes and I feared that would cause a few of the planks to fall.

'That must have affected you, seeing all that at such a young age.'

'Not really,' I said, before realising that, yes, of course it must have affected a normal child. 'Well, yeah, I wet the bed almost daily. Had nightmares, the usual.'

'Poor thing. So you were a witness for the crime he went down for?' she said.

'No, he did time for a different guy's beating, a few years later.'

'This was a regular thing then?'

'Yeah. They called it "sending the boys round". If there was someone in your neighbourhood who needed a good kicking or warning off, that's what you did, you sent the boys round. Nobody talked about it, it was just an understanding. The police tried to pin the disappearance of three other men on him, all with sex offences on their cards, but they had no evidence. No witnesses. Dad was pretty careful. He did four years but two of his mates did life.'

'Do you think he was a murderer?'

I shrugged. Flashes of Dad's sweating face as he dropped Pete McMahon head first into the hole crackled through my mind like lightning. The sight of his strong hands gripped around that guy's neck in that warehouse. Stamping on that guy's head in that back alley. 'No idea.' I smiled, slurping my banana milkshake.

On the way back to the office, I realised what she was getting at with all the questions about Dad.

'Daisy, if you think any of my dad's friends is The Reaper, I can assure you that you're barking up the wrong one.'

'It was just something that occurred to me when I saw his file. One of the victims – a sex offender called Lyle Devaney – was thrown into the quarry. Like Julia Kidner. Like the men in the blue van.'

'The guy who Dad knew at the quarry's in jail now. Actually most of them are still in jail. They only let Dad out because he was dying.'

'Your Craig worked with your dad, didn't he?'

'Yeah. But he knows nothing about all that stuff. And, yes,

before you find out from someone else, he worked at the quarry for a year before he joined my dad but I promise you, Craig's not a vigilante. He's not the type.'

'I'm sorry. My mind just goes into overdrive sometimes. It's such an interesting case, isn't it? It's keeping me awake at night.'

I had to give Daisy her due – work never kept me awake at night. Maybe she had been the right woman for the junior editor job after all.

Once that was cleared up, our conversation hit lighter notes – how things were going generally, how much she was loving the job, how much her kids were loving school, AJ's crush on me, all the pranks we'd been pulling on Linus. Apparently, Linus was a lot quieter over on that side of the office these days and Daisy had an inkling it was down to us. God, she was perceptive. I thought we'd been discreet but she'd spotted it right from the blue ChapStick.

We were passing the shoe shop when I saw her, walking in the other direction – the woman with the yellow scarf from Blue Van Men night. Except she didn't have on a yellow scarf. She had on a peach cardigan and a grey skirt and she was carrying a white handbag on her forearm. My chest tightened at the sight of her. And it was definitely her but she looked utterly changed from the last time I'd seen her when she'd been all mascara-smudged, twiggy-hair and torn clothes. She looked sharp, hair all done, a vigour in her step. She saw me, I saw her, but neither of us said a word. As she passed, I afforded a look behind me. So did she.

Neither of us said a word.

And the police still had no witnesses. Apart from the cow rat, that is.

Yay yay yay. So far, anyway.

About 3 p.m., Linus Sixgill jumped away from his desk in a fit of absolute hysterics – there was a cockroach in his sandwich. AJ winked at me and Claudia saw. Sure enough, I came out of the Ladies' around 4 p.m. and she was there waiting. I'd just done my second pregnancy test – another negative. She probably heard the choirs of angels in my ears.

'Rhiannon, could I have a quick word, please?'

And I don't know where it came from but I started crying, right there in the corridor outside the lavs with the hand dryer still whirring inside and Krystle from Sales brushing past us 'desperate for a pee pee'.

'Oh, goodness. Hang on,' said Claudia, ushering me along the corridor and up the stairs towards Conference Room B. The pitcher of water was still in the middle of the table, still with its film of dust on the surface, only this time accompanied by a plate of Fondant Fancies and chocolate fingers which someone had been fingering.

'What's happened?' she said, holding me by my forearms as I stood before her. But I didn't have to say anything. She just guessed. Or rather, *thought* she had guessed. 'Another negative? Oh, sweetpea, I am *so, so* sorry.'

And she hugged me. She fucking *hugged* me! The veiny-footed shrew with permanent coffee breath who'd called me a freak and given me that pissing market report to type up every month held me as tightly as I'd ever been held and stroked my hair and cried along with me. 'I know exactly what you're going through.'

She pulled back and gently held my head, like I was a flower and she had just inhaled my face. 'It *will* happen, you've got to believe that,' she said. 'You still have plenty of time to get pregnant.'

I nodded and sobbed again and she held me against her shoulder and rocked me. I felt her tears on the top of my head. 'I wish I could take the pain away for you. Oh, darling. Is Craig upset as well?'

I nodded.

'I know, I know. Sssh.'

She was saying all the right things, being the perfect under-standing mother a child would need. Except she didn't have a kid. Even I could see that was a shame.

Once we'd both sniffed away our tears and had an stilted chat over a mint tea in the staffroom – she cleared everyone else out – we went back to work and she actually gave me some fun things to do for the afternoon – a follow-up story on the drugs bust at *Paint the Town Red* and an interview with the owner of a new sex shop in the town – *Oh, Behave*. AND I got praise for it. I got, 'Well done, sweetpea.'

It was the most enjoyable day I'd had at work since the day Ron caught his foot in Claudia's handbag and headbutted his office door open.

Saturday, 4 May

1. *Chemists who think they are doctors but are twice as patronising. Also, I KNOW you haven't memorised every 'three for two' in the shop, I was just asking if you could check whether your offer on make-up applies to nail varnish as well, you dribbling, sour-faced cock socket*
2. *YouTubers – any discernible talent to be found here? Anyone?*
3. *People who go on social media and bitch about people posting spoilers – just watch the fucking programme already!*
4. *Grown women who wear pigtails*
5. *People who say 'May the Fourth Be With You' every year on this day*

There's a royal visit to the town pending – praise be! It's not going to be one of the biggies: some duke who once shot a lion on safari but everyone seems to have forgotten that because he ran a marathon for bowel cancer. I've never been keen on the royals. I don't like their policy on killing defenceless creatures. I know I'm one to talk but still.

Saw a woman get knocked off her bike today in town. I

laughed at first. Everyone around me acted as though it was the most shocking thing they'd ever seen.

How do people do that shock/gasp thing with their faces? How do they look so stupefied? How do they do that with their eyebrows? I tried it, because everyone else around me was doing it, but I wasn't shocked and I didn't feel like gasping. It was all so forced, like when I had to give my mum a cuddle as a kid or when I was expected to cry but it just felt like rain trickling down a window. Someone else's window.

It's like when Pidge WhatsApped us all yesterday to say she'd miscarried her baby. They ALL said they were 'so sorry'; 'Can't believe it'; 'Aww, hun, it's not fair, is it?' I wasn't shocked at all. I don't think I know what shock feels like. I sent her a 'so sorry take care' message but *was* I sorry? *Did* I want her to take care? It had nothing to do with me after all. It wasn't my baby or my loss. I never feel the sorry I'm supposed to feel. The sorry that others feel.

Had my hair cut – unfortunately I got the same stylist as last time who harps on about her crush on Benedict Cumberbatch and how she stalks him on film locations. Sometimes I google photos of real crime scenes while I'm in the chair, just to shut her up but today all I wanted to do was sleep.

I did another psychopath quiz online, just to check a few things and I made a concerted effort to answer each and every question absolutely honestly this time.

Do I often get others to pay for things for me? – Yes, namely Craig.

Are you impatient? – Yes, very.

Were you a problem child? – After Priory Gardens, yes, I suppose I was. Everyone had a problem with me not speaking and biting other kids. And the whole hurting my sister thing didn't go down too well either.

Have you committed any crimes? – Yes. Lots.

Do you believe you are exceptional? – I am exceptional so yes.

Did you have imaginary friends growing up? – Several.

Are you often bored and do you quickly lose interests in set tasks? – Have you *seen* my set tasks? Duh.

Are you basically an honest person? – Inside my head, yes.

Do you believe most people around you are stupid? – I don't believe it, they *are* stupid.

Do you enjoy manipulating the feelings of others? – Well, it's so easy, isn't it?

Are your problems mostly the fault of other people? – Of course they are.

RESULT: 92 per cent.

Fucking hell – I'm getting worse!

There was a picture of Ralph Fiennes dressed as Voldemort next to my percentage again. The advice from BuzzFeed was to 'try to be more social (without kidnapping anyone), and see how you feel, you might like it!'

They obviously don't know me at all.

Sunday, 5 May

AJ WhatsApped me with a photograph of some pile cream and a question mark alongside it.

I text back: *No, I think we should call it a day on the Sixgill pranks, don't you? It's getting a bit childish. Also, your auntie's on the warpath again.* I put a little witch emoji at the end.

He texted: *Ugh, dammit* followed by a puking emoji. *But how else are we gonna pass the time at work?*

I said: *We could murder him maybe? Cut off his head with the fire axe?*

He sent back a series of hysterical smiley emojis and: *Good one. Maybe you'll get your promotion then!*

I sent back *Fat chance* with an accompanying gif of Rebel Wilson dancing.

He returned with a gif of Melissa McCarthy twerking and another succession of maniacal emojis.

He's not that bad really, for a toddler.

Monday, 6 May

1. _People who don't acknowledge you when you flash your lights to let them pull out of a side road_
2. _People who don't indicate at roundabouts or junctions – just assume these fuckers are on every single one of my lists, OK?_
3. _Those body dysmorphic freaks who have concrete injected into their buttocks or seventy-eight operations in order to look like Barbie._
4. _Anyone who downloaded that bloody 'Gangnam' song_
5. _Miley Cyrus_

Me and Craig did bugger all today except eat crap and rip the piss out of three classic Bank Holiday movies – _The Great Escape, The Sound of Music_ and _Grease._

Grease got the brunt of it.

'How old is Rizzo? And that girl who dances with Danny at the prom is her grandmother, surely. And we're supposed to believe Danny isn't actually burning for Kenicke all along? There's only one way _his_ Greased Lightning's going...' You get the picture anyway.

Took Tink out for our constitutional, as usual. Pretty

uneventful, but for the two cats I saw having sex in the bush. I've never seen cats having sex before. They always look too prim to do that, especially in public.

I do take Tink out every day, sometimes twice a day, so just take that as read, will you? I also go to the toilet quite a bit during the day, and do my hair and make-up and stuff but I'm not cataloguing everything I do. This isn't a bloody police statement – yet.

Wired Lucille my £160 for the Weekend That Must Not Be Named. I couldn't get away with it any longer. She'd already sent me three reminder texts that I'm one of the last to cough up. Now my fate is sealed – an entire weekend with the PICSOs, pissed out of my brain, deafened by 80s disco and playing Dodge the Genital Warts.

Also, there's been a bit of progress with Wesley Parsons. He's accepted my Friend Request. I've friended him under a pseudonym and fake photo of course – I've called myself Annabel Hartley – named after a girl I went to school with who hanged herself in her parents' bedroom. His hair's different now – it's short and blond, rather than the shaggy brown it was when he ran over Joe's head. Now, I have access to his whole life.

I know he lived with his parents in Bristol before he moved to Birmingham and moved in with some woman ten years older than him who had his child – a boy called Nathan.

I know he works nights in a bar in the city centre, mends televisions as another job, plays football for some low division side when he can and helps his friend Troy in his painting and decorating business.

I know Nathan is into gaming and Manchester United. Recently had his room decorated – Wesley himself painted it red and white and gold.

I know some other woman called Sierra is pregnant with

his kid – she announced it last month and tagged him in the post – he's neither Liked nor Commented on it.

And I know he calls himself Wes now.

I had a message from him:

Do we know each other? Wink.

No, I lied. *I just saw your pic come up on my friend's page and I thought you was well good-looking.* Heart eyes emoji.

You're pretty gorgeous too, he came back. Slurpy face emoji.

Thanks, I said. *Ditto.*

Do you live in Brum?

Sadly not, I lied. *But I'm coming up soon though for the Beyoncé gig. I see you work in a bar.*

Yeah, he said. *On and off. The Glass Tree on Kemp Street. You coming up with your mates then?*

Yeah, I lied. *We'll be staying right in the centre of town.*

Ooh, he said. *You'll be near me then.*

Indeed, I said. *What nights do you work?*

He took ages to respond – twenty-two minutes. *Sorry, love, was just on a call.*

Girlfriend was it?

Is that a problem, Annie?

Not for me it isn't, Wes. Cue slurpy-faced emoji.

I work most nights. First drink is on me. See you soon. Wink emoji.

You bet you will. Cue heart-eyes emoji. Kiss. Kiss. Kiss.

Craig made a bit of an effort in bed tonight – I was treated to a baby oil massage and an extra three minutes of inny-outy, during which I fell asleep. We've just changed our pillowcases and the smell of lavender was so comforting I drifted off. He wasn't happy. I gave him a blowj to make amends. Men are so easy it's embarrassing.

Ooh, better take my pill while I remember. Nighty-night.

Tuesday, 7 May

1. *Creepy Ed Sheeran – he was hanging around outside my office at lunchtime with a full carrier bag of chocolate. He sat on the wall opposite my window, eating it*
2. *Bill the sub-editor – the man farts at his desk, is a chronic sexist and can lower a tone quicker than an England flag on the side of a building*
3. *Wesley Parsons*
4. *Dillon on the checkout in Lidl who squeezed my wholemeal today as he scanned it. Not just held – SQUEEZED. Now my every piece of toast has to be accompanied by the imprint of his thumb under my Nutella*
5. *The Geordie telephonist discussing which she preferred out of Ragu and Dolmio with her mate while sorting out my car insurance. 'I'll just put you on hold a second, pet, if that's all right.' I'll put you on hold for the rest of your life. Pet.*

AJ was riding his skateboard through the park today on the way to work. I hung back so I wouldn't have to make conversation with him and watched him doing his tricks and attempting to ride it along narrow wall edges. He fell off once and I laughed, but he seemed to really hurt himself and limped into work with a wad of tissue on his knee.

May is Hell Month for birthdays at the *Gazette*. It's Daisy's today, then on the thirteenth it's Mike Heath's, then Johnny the photographer's on the nineteenth and Paul Spurdog's on the twenty-third. Claudia and Ron share a birthday on the twenty-seventh. I'm so glad we don't do the Everyone Put a Pound in the Hat for So-and-So's Birthday thing any more. Now we just take money out of petty cash for the card and the birthday person buys the doughnuts. Much fairer.

Daisy brought in ten boxes of fresh chocolate eclairs, having grossly overestimated how many mouths she had to feed. I forewent lunch and ate two. Joy watched me, eyebrowsing me with every bite. An eclair is 50 per cent air anyway – FACT.

Bumped into Lana coming out of the toilets. She asked me how I was. I asked her how *she* was. She said 'fine' but she's not. She's like an unset jelly – uncertain and watery and the smallest movement could spill her everywhere. I am the nicest version of Lovely Girlfriend I can be when I'm talking to her. I complimented her on her strobed cheeks today. She's going to give me a lesson after work one night. I've a feeling if I bring wine into the equation she'll tell me all her secrets. We're firm friends now. Trading make-up tips and secrets and everything. I can still smell Craig on her though and this alone makes me want to cunt punch her into the sun.

Still no arrests in the Julia Kidner murder but the Blue Van Men have finally been named – Kevin David Fraser, thirty-nine, originally from Aberdeen had been the one in red gloves and

Martin Horton-Wicks, forty-eight, was Balaclava Boy (Daisy had pictures of both of them on her computer, old mugshots from burglaries they'd done a few years back). And still no witnesses. How can one girl be so lucky?

Friday, 10 May

1. Woman who short-changed me in Costa
2. Two lads I saw through the window in Costa, spitting on a homeless man
3. All the onlookers waiting at the bus stop who didn't intervene in said homeless Spit Olympics before the police arrived. Why didn't I intervene, you ask? Do you know how long we had to wait for a table in Costa?
4. The man on the bus who had to sit next to me, even though the rest of the bus was empty. Every time he breathed out, his dandruff floated onto my lap.
5. The morbidly obese – they clearly want to eat themselves to death so let them. Feed 'em up, I say. We've got to keep the population down somehow and if we really are 'beating cancer' it just seems logical to me

Met up with the PICSOs in Costa at lunchtime for their perennial pursuit – Croissants, Coffees and Completely Barricading Everyone's Path to the Toilets with Pushchairs event. There were only two babies present this time – Sam and Cleo's two-year-old (I can never remember his name – either Django or Jaxon), who was asleep throughout. The place was heaving and I queued for ten minutes to get a skinny flat white and a Danish which looked as though it had a bite taken out of it. The talk, primarily, was about Pidge's miscarriage, though Pidge wasn't there.

'She sounded awful on the phone,' said Lucille, tits akimbo even in the daytime. 'I don't know how she's gonna get over this one.'

'How many's that now?' I asked. There were babies screaming all over the place. I tried to focus on my breathing.

'This'll be her third one,' said Cleo. 'Aww, she was so excited at being pregnant for the wedding as well, wasn't she?'

'Yeah,' said Anni, 'she had her eye on this maternity frock we saw in Debenhams. I was going to hand her on some of mine too.' She was breastfeeding Sam underneath a gold speckled shawl. 'I don't know whether to go round there or not. I'd have to take Sam with me.'

'I'll go round if you like,' I said. 'I'm the only one who doesn't have kids. It'll be easier for me. I can take some flowers from us all.'

'Aww, that's kind, thanks, Rhee,' said Lucille. Anni fumbled one-handed with her handbag to root out some change, prompting the rest to do the same.

That's me, Thoughtful Friend.

I sank the dregs of my flat white and tried to think of a conversation starter that would interest me. 'Hey, did you hear about that Derek Scudd dying?'

'Yes,' said Mel, nodding. She had her trial wedding nails on and was trying not to touch anything, even the handle of her camomile teacup. 'If I ever find out who did it, I'll buy them a pint.'

'*Two* pints,' Lucille added.

'I can't say I'm sorry he's dead,' said Anni, changing Sam to her other shoulder, 'but it's a horrible way to go, burning alive.'

'Oh, I don't know,' said Cleo. 'I can't think of a better way for a man like him to go. I'd have struck a match myself if he'd hurt my kids.'

'Would you really?' I asked.

She stared at me. 'Of course I would. We all would.'

'Totally,' said Mel, flaking off some of Lucille's croissant and nibbling at it delicately with her fingertips. 'Anyone laid a finger on my three, I'd tear 'em limb from limb.'

'And me,' said Lucille. 'I'd swing for any bastard that did that.'

Anni looked down at Sam. There were new lines under her eyes and in her scrappily bunned-up hair there was half a corn-flake.

'What about you?' I asked her.

'Anyone hurt Sam I don't know what I'd do. I don't think I could actually kill anyone though.'

'I bet you could if you had to,' said Lucille. 'If you were driven to it.'

'Maybe,' she said, stroking Sam's cheek. His mouth fluttered. 'Certainly not at the moment I couldn't anyway. I'm too bloody knackered all the time.'

'What about you, Rhiannon?' asked Mel. 'Could you?'

'Could I what?'

'Kill someone if they hurt your kids?'

'I don't have any kids, do I? As we've established.'

'No, but if you did.'

'No,' I lied, 'I don't think I've got it in me either. Like Anni said, I'm not sure I could bring myself to take another life.'

'Well, you'll see one day. You'll see what we mean when you've got your own. You'll either kill for them or die for them, you've got no choice in it. No choice at all.'

I went round to Pidge's straight after work with some ger-beras, a card with puppies on the front, and a freshly made Mary Berry pavlova – her favourite. Chief Listener to the rescue. I should wear a goddam cape.

In the card, I wrote '*When Mum died, people didn't speak to me for ages because they didn't know what to say to make it better. Sometimes, silence hurts and you just need the noise, however mundane. Here if you need noise. Your friend, Rhee xxx*'

See, BuzzFeed? I *do* have a heart.

Sunday, 12 May

I went round to Pidge's again this morning to see if she wanted anything brought back from town. I took her round an apple and peach crumble I made early this morning, just as an extra sweetener. It was a hot day and I fancied getting my legs out so I wore my red and white dress. Pidge was astonished to see the bruises. I knew five of them at least were from Julia and from Scudd – the rest I couldn't remember.

'Paintballing,' I explained to her worried face. 'Me and Craig went a few weeks back with some of his friends. It's good fun but dead painful. I felt like the guy at the end of *Platoon* when the helicopter's gone off without him.'

She sucked the end of her French braid and remained silent. I don't think she believed me but I also know that I don't care.

Biggus Dickus was online when I ventured into the chat rooms after Sunday lunch. He wanted a Snap Wank but no could do. Accused me of 'pussying out on him'. How rude, I said, plus some other words to the effect that his dick looked like a mole rat and his stomach was too fat to find it half the time. He's blocked me now.

MrSizzler48's still handy. Sent him some more nakes. He wants to meet up with me, just like JoBerg. City hotel. Drink in the bar first, maybe a bag of dry-roasted. And then upstairs for handcuffs, hand jobs and a whole lotta rimming.

> **Sweetpea:** OK, see u Thurs then. Meet in the bar at 8.15. Don't be late xxx
> **MrSizzler48:** Can't fucking wait. I'll bring extra lube x

I've told him I'll book the room under my name – Andrew Davidson-Smythe – and we'd split the bill after he'd spunked on my ass cheeks. The *real* Andrew was a sixth former at my old school in Bristol. He'd jumped off the Suspension Bridge after getting bad GCSE results. Poor kid. Little did he know that his one achievement in life would be to negotiate fake dates in order to piss off closet gays.

It's a funny old world, isn't it?

Monday, 13 May

1. *Iron Man*
2. *The spotty-chinned youth at the Odeon who didn't fill my 7UP to the top of the cup, even though it cost £4.50*
3. *The two teenage girls and their chipped-tooth boyfriend who sat behind us in the cinema, rustling their sweets, crunching through a family-size box of cheesy Nachos throughout the movie AND who kicked my seat twice*
4. *The old couple on walkers who had no business being in a Marvel movie anyway, who talked INCESSANTLY throughout: 'Who's he then? Was he in that thing with her that we like to watch on Sunday nights? You know, the one with the hair. What's happened to that big green one, is he dead? How did he blow that up from all the way over there?' JUST. FUCKING. DIE.*
5. *The usherette who ushed us to the wrong seat, which we only discovered at the end – our actual seats were nowhere near ANYONE so we could have had a much more enjoyable film experience. Apart from Iron Man, of course*

It was Mike Heath's birthday today but he didn't bring in cakes. There were knowing looks flying around the office all day like winged keys. *You have to bring in the cake when it's your birthday, that's the law.* Nobody said anything though.

I had to bring Tink into work because Craig had the dentist. Claudia said it was fine – we're practically bezzies since our heart-to-heart – but Ron gave me several looks of disapproval whenever he passed by. Tink herself was as good as gold, sitting on her bed under my desk and actually proved a useful bonding tool with my colleagues, particularly Daisy who has 'wanted a chihuahua for years'. Her husband won't let her. He won't let her watch *Hollyoaks* or have a washing machine either.

But with the smooth always comes the rough and because of my pooch accessory Linus has now taken to calling me Legally Blonde. Yep, he's back with a vengeance now mine and AJ's pranking has ceased. There's no denting his confidence for long.

I think the bruises and having Tink there at work today were helping to paint me in a Battered Wife kind of light. More people spoke to me and Joyless Joy didn't make one pass-ag comment about my weight or my clothes. It was still light when I walked back to my car and happiness found me.

It's hard to find Happy, isn't it? It lands only briefly before it flies off, like a butterfly. For me it always comes in brief but powerful gasps – an orgasm that brings me to tears (twice I've had this – once from a chat room encounter and once with Craig when he lay still on me for the longest time and I thought he had dropped dead).

Getting Tink from the RSPCA when she was no bigger than a large dollop of ice cream was happiness found too. She makes me happier than most, particularly when I feel her breaths when she's sleeping next to me, or when she licks my face or trots across the lounge with Craig's sock.

But it's just so fleeting. And it was tonight too.

I didn't book the MrSizzler48 hotel in London as requested but I *did* book mine and Craig's in Birmingham for Beyoncé – it's a four-star, a bit expensive for one night, but it's right in the centre of town and directly opposite a pub called The Glass Tree. A pub where a certain Wesley Parsons works. I have a strong feeling we'll be going in there for a drink at some point during our stay.

Me and AJ saw the new Marvel movie tonight – predictable tosh, superheroes save the world, stunning visual effects, blah blah blah. See *Kill List* for how the rest of the evening went.

I got home and Craig was there watering the pots on the balcony, barefoot, with a spliff between his fingers. He had his Dirt Rally game on pause and the French doors were open and a light breeze whispered around the flat. Tink immediately rushed in to greet him and he kissed and nuzzled her and plonked her down where she ran off to find her chew stick. If every day was like this, I could be happy. I wouldn't need much more than this.

I wouldn't need to kill if he was faithful. It's *his* fault I'm not happy. He's brought this out in me again. It was dormant, left alone, dead.

Now Happy means killing. Killing Dan Wells. Killing Gavin White. Killing Julia. Killing Kevin What's-his-Face and Martin Balaclava. Expunging the memory of killing my dad by suffocating Derek Scudd in his manky old armchair. I'm absolutely sure I'm not done yet.

It's all because of him.

Wednesday, 15 May

1. *That weather woman in the mornings who can't pronounce isobars and wears bodycon dresses so tight you can see all her nipples. And patronising much? 'There's a nip in the air today so pop a pulley on if you're going out.' 'There's a drop of rain on the way so don't forget your brolly if you're heading out and about.' URGHGHGHHGHGH!*

I've made a major boo-boo.

I'm writing this on Wednesday morning as I couldn't bring myself to talk about it last night before bed. I was still too shook up. Last night, Craig was out – ostensibly round Nigel's watching 'the match' (there *was* no match – I checked) so I decided to go fishing. I was angry and alone and Craig was fucking *her* again so I wanted to take it out on someone – some opportunistic drunk down by the canal perhaps. Anyway, it gets to about quarter to eleven and I realise no one's following me and I'd been everywhere – the canal, the alleys, the park. Turns out Wednesday night's not all right for raping, so I start making towards home, via the harbour side. I'm walking along, sniffing the night air, pissing on lampposts (Tink, not me) and from nowhere, this guy jumps in front of me and shouts *Boo!* and I don't think, I just drop Tink's lead and pull out my Sabatier and I hold the blade to the guy's throat, yelling, 'Fuck you, you fucking cunt! Fuck you! I'm gonna fucking slice you in two!'

Only I realise then that I know him – it's AJ.

Oh, Mothering Sunday from Hell, I think. With sprinkles on top. Am I in big fat fuck-off trouble now.

And he's staring down at the knife, eyes as black as Pontefract cakes, hands in the air, breath held. And Tink's yapping and scrapping and biting at his jean hems.

'Rhee... it's me! I'm sorry, I'm sorry!' he stutters.

I drop my knife and it falls with a clatter to the pavement. Nobody in the near area seems to have heard the hullabaloo, or if they have they're not coming over. It takes me ages to catch my breath. I pick up the knife and re-pocket it inside my coat. 'What the hell did you think you were doing?'

He was stammering: 'I-I s-saw you as I-I was coming out the Fun Pub. I recognised Tinkerbelle.'

'Her name's Tink,' I said, picking her up. She was shivering too, of course.

He keeps looking at my coat pocket. 'What were you gonna do with that?'

'It's protection, AJ. I have to walk my dog last thing at night because I don't have a garden. We don't live in a perfect world.'

He felt around his neck and looked at his fingertips. 'You cut me.' He held up his fingers. Blood on both. I looked at his neck. It was a nick, nothing more.

'Oh, God,' I said. His face went weird and he dropped to the ground like a bag of bricks.

By the time he'd roused, two minutes later, I was sitting beside him, my balled-up hoody underneath his head, pressing a wadded-up tissue against his neck. Tink was licking his cheek. Some smokers came out of the Fun Pub across the road to see if he was OK but I batted them away with a jovial 'too much to drink' gesture.

'It's all right, don't try to move. Just gather yourself.' I didn't know what I was saying. I didn't normally stick around to apply compresses and whisper sweet nothings in their ears.

He sat up and looked at me. I took away the tissue and posted it in a nearby bin. 'You fainted.'

'You cut my neck.'

'Only a bit. It's stopped now. Here.' I handed him a fresh tissue.

He got to his feet. 'Thanks.' There was an odd look about him. He edged away. 'I'm gonna go home.'

'Are you going to be all right?'

He stopped and turned back to me. He looked very odd. ''Night then.'

'Hey, what is it? Don't go. AJ?' He turned round again, still looking at me funny. 'Why are you looking at me like that?'

'Do you always carry a knife?'

'At night, yeah.'

'To work?'

'No, of course not to work.'

'Have you used it before?'

'Yeah.'

'When?'

'Uh, I don't know.'

He shook his head. 'Not that guy in the park?'

And then I just said it: 'Yeah.'

Just then his face was one only Edvard Munch could love. 'It was you?'

'Ssh. I didn't mean to. He came up behind me when I was walking Tink. He was going to rape me, AJ.'

AJ shook his head. 'You killed a guy?'

'Don't say it like that. He wasn't just some "guy". He was

a sex offender. An opportunistic rapist who went out at night specifically to target lone women.'

'He didn't deserve to die, Rhiannon.'

'Are you seriously defending him?'

'No, but...'

'You don't know me. You don't know what I've been through. I've...' I stopped. Tears were coming – I don't know how I was doing it but they were, like two little taps had turned on. 'I was raped when I was eighteen. By my sister's boyfriend. I've carried a knife ever since, for protection. I've only ever had to use it once, in self-defence. And, yes, that was Gavin White.'

'Oh, my God.'

I bowed my head and sobbed into my hands. Tink was halfway up my leg, seeing if I was all right. I felt him enclose me, carefully at first, then warmly and completely – an all-encompassing cuddle with a little rocking motion.

'No wonder you're messed up.'

I picked up Tink and allowed her to lick up my tears. 'You shouldn't have jumped out at me,' I sobbed. 'I have very high defensive walls.' That sounded better on *Jeremy Kyle*, where I got it from. I should have left it there.

'I was just trying to give you a scare, that was all. For a laugh. We always have a laugh at work.' He went to pull away.

'Don't,' I said. 'Hold me again. Keep me safe for a bit longer.'

And he did. He held on to me and Tink for minutes on end. Tink started licking his jacket lapel – he had ice cream down it by the looks. The cool night air brushed my face. It was pretty magical. Happiness was mine again.

And then it was gone.

'I'll walk you home,' he said. 'Come on.'

I told him the rest over a mug of coffee inside the flat. Craig still wasn't back.

'My sister was dating this asshole. Pete McMahon. He was

into all sorts. Drugs. Gambling. There was a rumour he was a
pimp but my dad could never prove it. Seren wouldn't listen
anyway.'

That bit of the story was a hundred per cent true.

'He had so many convictions – GBH, drugs, you name it. And
this one night, Dad was out and Seren came home with him.'

'Pete?' said AJ, sipping his coffee.

'He repulsed me. He had zits everywhere and yellow stains
on his fingers and bad teeth and he was all arms and legs like a
mosquito. Anyway, I was in bed and I heard them both arguing.'

Again, all true.

'I could tell Seren was drunk because she always got louder
when she'd had a few. I heard them coming up the stairs. Her
bedroom door shut. She was saying no to him, *again* and *again*
and *again* [note the emphasis and saying it three times]. Then
it all went quiet. I just knew she was in trouble. I was the only
hope she had.'

All of this is, again, was what actually happened.

'So what did you do?'

'I got up out of bed and I went into her room. I saw him
lying on top of her. He had her arms pinned back and he was
undoing his fly. She was so dopey, she didn't have the strength to
do anything. I guessed she was drunk or had taken something,
either that or he'd drugged her. Anyway, he told me to go back
to bed but I couldn't – I just stood there in the doorway, frozen.
Terrified.'

And this was the point where Truth got its little hat on and
said toodle-pip.

In reality, this is the point where I ran down to get the biggest
kitchen knife I could find and went back upstairs and I stabbed
his raping back several times while my sister lay comatose
beneath him on the bed.

For AJ, though, I had to play damsel in distress.

'He threw me down onto the bed next to her. Ripped off my pyjamas. And… [pause for emotion] raped me, right there on my dead mum's bed. I struggled, for ages, trying to get free. But he was so strong. *So* strong, AJ.'

AJ's face was a picture. He put his hand on top of mine and I managed to squeeze out a tear so it landed *splash* down on his watch face. I didn't leave any fictitious detail out. Pain, I kept saying. The pain of it was searing. Cutting. Burning in my pelvis. The awful nightmares I'd had ever since. The smell of his breath. The feel of his slimy tongue all over my face. God, I was good.

'Was he ever caught?' he asked.

'Yeah. I testified, like a champ, and he went to prison. Turned out he'd done some rapes before. And he went away for at least twenty years. That helps me sleep at night. Knowing he's locked up.'

By the way, this is all still bollocks. There was no trial. Dad came home and there was the inevitable scene of bloody mess and 'OMG, what have you done, Rhiannon?' and 'We need to make him disappear.'

AJ shook his head. 'You were so brave.'

I nodded, shaking loose another tear. 'Ever since then, I've been terrified it would happen again. That some bloke would take me, do what he wanted, then chuck me in a ditch like litter. I have to walk my dog, AJ. I have to. Men don't own the streets. I have just as much right to walk around at night, don't I?'

'Of course you do.'

'I didn't go looking for Gavin White. You do understand?'

He nodded.

'I didn't mean to burden you with all this. If you want to go to the police, go ahead. I won't stop you. I just wanted you to see it from my angle.'

He shook his head. 'I feel terrible.'

'You shouldn't. I hurt you.' I touched his neck where his little wound was beginning to scab over. My touch lingered as I took in his eyes, his mouth.

'I can say it's a shaving accident.'

'Oh, yeah, right, who's gonna believe *you've* started shaving?' I chuckled.

He smiled and held me, like he had done before only side-on.

'I still can't believe all this but I won't say anything to the police. I wouldn't do that to you, Rhee. I get why you did what you did.'

'So you'll keep this to yourself?' He nodded. I reached around his neck and pressed the side of my face against his. 'Thank you. I knew I could trust you.'

I kissed him, hard, on the lips. The kiss moved into a more intense one, mouths open, tongues grazing. I went all pulsy in my private place. He tasted good.

'Shit,' he said, finally pulling back. 'Sorry, I got carried away there.'

'No, it's my fault, I shouldn't have done that. God, how embarrassing. You're a great kisser though, AJ.'

'Thanks,' he scoffed. 'I'm glad you said that, considering all the practice I haven't had.'

I eyebrowsed him. 'You fly Virgin Airlines, do you?'

'Yeah. I hate to admit it, still being nineteen, but, yeah, I am.'

'I didn't lose mine till I was twenty-three. With Craig.'

'But… what about when you were raped?'

'Oh, yeah, that was technically sex too but I don't count that. I mean, I didn't have a lot of say in it, did I?'

'No, I guess not,' he said sadly. 'Sorry, that was thoughtless.'

'It's OK,' I said, stroking his brow. 'Listen, Craig's going to be back soon…'

'Yeah, of course,' he said, standing up and adjusting his jeans. I smiled. 'What?'

'You testing a missile down there?'

Just when I thought he couldn't blush any more, he did.

I laughed, standing up too. 'You're so sweet.' I pinched his cheek and kissed his mouth. 'This isn't a brush-off, I promise. Maybe we can meet tomorrow?'

'Seriously?' He followed me to the door like Mary's Little Lamb.

'Yeah. Of course. I like you, AJ. I fancy you. I want you.'

His mouth hung open. He moved towards me and kissed me again, seemingly unable to help himself. 'Auntie Claudia will be at work all day, she never goes home at lunch. We could go back there?'

'Do it in Claudia Gulper's house?' I said, a smile forming. 'Now that would be an awfully big adventure, wouldn't it, sweetpea?'

He nodded, mouth still open, a trail of saliva roped between his and mine. 'Jesus. What a night, eh? First you try and kill me...'

'... and now I want to go to bed with you.' I giggled. 'I know. Bizarre.'

I broke the saliva strand between us and opened the door. 'See you at work.'

'Yeah.' He smiled. 'Can't wait.'

I smiled back, smacking his ass as he left.

Dammit. And there's me finally on Claudia's good side too. Now I have to have sex with her very impressionable but very nice-assed nephew. Woe is me.

And here's why I think I've made a boo-boo. I acted all sexy with AJ mere moments after telling him about being raped. That wasn't natural. The Act had slipped. Even though he made the first move, and even though the rape thing never actually happened, from AJ's point of view that could have been construed as hella quick, getting-over-it-wise. Which *could* bring him back to the thought that I *am* an opportunistic murderer and he had a lucky escape. And this *could* make him call the cops. So I've got to keep this boy sweet, hence the promise of sexy times. What I'm pinning all my hopes on is that his cock will now do his thinking for him.

God, men are exhausting. I can see why the first lesbian gave up.

Thursday, 16 May

1. *People who ride mobility scooters in supermarkets – seriously, when did this become a thing? And when did it become OK to allow three of them in one aisle so no other git can get to the Pop-Tarts?*
2. *Adults who do colouring in, non-ironically*
3. *Taylor Swift – seriously, how much cock does one woman need?*

Craig and I walked to work together with Tink this morning and stopped outside a new town brasserie called William's which boasted a small courtyard garden welcoming dogs. That Happy thing washed over me again. The manager was friendly and full of 'Course you can's' and 'No problem at all's' and it was sunny outside. It makes such a difference when people aren't assholes.

We were seated in a little corner where there were little bowls of water and Tink could roam about as she pleased sniffing the flower beds. I ordered my favourite meal – pancakes with crispy, streaky bacon and maple syrup with a small pot of whipped butter. Bliss.

And then my food arrived. And a cloud descended.

The pancakes, clearly, were not fresh and the side order of

chopped fruit was an abomination. Manky strawberries, black slices of banana and the mint sprig on top was more a cry for help. But the worst offender of all was the bacon. I'd specifically asked for crispy. What I got looked like it had just been flayed from a fat woman's forearm. So then I was back to feeling ragey for the rest of the morning.

There was a bit of Good News on the work front – AJ is still on side. He's not winking at me any more – perhaps he thinks it's inappropriate to do that to rape victims – but he *did* make me my usual peanut butter and banana toastie for breakfast and today it had a little red heart on the top, made from strawberry jam. I needed to be sure though. I needed confirmation.

'So when are we gonna get up close and personal?' I said to him as he leaned across my desk, changing the bulb in my desk lamp.

'Any time you want,' he said. 'What about Claudia?'

'Does she want to join in?' I asked, watching the tendons working in his arm as he screwed the bulb in.

He laughed. 'I mean we're gonna have to keep it on the down low.'

'Yeah, of course,' I said. 'Go back to your desk and I'll text you.' I leaned in close and bit the top of his ear. He blushed hot almost immediately.

And we did, all afternoon. We had text together. Long, hard text. I ended the chain with:

My flat's free on Saturday night from 7 p.m. Boyf is going to watch Spurs with his mate.

Yesss!! he replied. *It's gonna be amazing. I'm hard for you now!*

Kiss. Kiss. Heart eyes emoji. *If I had a dick I'd be hard too.*

He wasn't to know I *did* have a dick. Kind of.

He texted me later to ask if we could do it in the Ladies' after work but I've said no. I can't bear the thought of being ravished in there. It's not only filthy, it's also damp and there's always a warm aroma of some unwashed floozy's menstrual leakings, even when everyone's gone home.

Ugh. Saturday it'll have to be.

Joy had me writing up five features for next week's Homes for Sale and Let supplement and one of them was my mum and dad's house. It's Home of the Week.

'It's not *that* great a house though, is it?' I said.

'It's got six bedrooms,' she said, in full argumentative treble-chin wobble. 'And an extension, double garage. *And* its own woods backing onto the garden. It's unique, Rhiannon.'

Not to mention it's soundproof enough to hide a kidnapped woman in for three months. Yeah, fair play, it is a pretty unique house.

When I was done, I showed her my piece and she did nothing but pick fault. She had coconut stubble all over her chin throughout.

'You haven't mentioned the apple tree.'

'Do they need to know about the apple tree?'

She tutted. 'It's the key selling point, Rhiannon. It's over five hundred years old. The house was rebuilt around it. There's even a story that Henry VIII once sheltered underneath it during a storm. Put it in somewhere.'

She didn't even say please OR thank you, the fat stinking billy-goated eunuch in piss-soaked rags that she is. And that Henry VIII story is complete bollocks. Sure it was around during his time but he didn't shelter under it or shag Anne of Cleves up against it or anything like that. It's just an old tree; an old tree that me and Seren used to play hide and seek behind. An old tree my mum sat underneath with a book and a lemonade. An old tree I'd seen my dad crying against when she came back from the doctor.

I hate Joy. I REALLY REALLY REALLY HATE Joy. But then, I guess you've already realised that.

*

BIG fat news – police have arrested two FIFTEEN-YEAR-OLD BOYS for Derek Scudd's murder. Daisy Chan took me out for lunch and told me over tapas.

'How do you know?' I said.

'Ron got it from the chief super and told us all in the editorial last night. These kids have been harassing him for months, on and off.'

'Oh I didn't know about that.'

'Yeah, quite nasty. They began with small stuff like putting notes through his letterbox and spraying stuff on his front wall. Then it was *dog poo* through the letterbox and crank calls. Last year they put a lit firework through but it didn't go off. He was expecting it and had a bucket of water ready all through November.'

'So it's definitely them then?'

'Well, they think so. The chief fire officer said it wasn't arson beyond all reasonable doubt but they aren't looking at anyone else. Except...'

'Except?'

Daisy was chewing on a particularly gristly piece of chorizo and kept rolling her eyes as though it was really annoying and apologising with her hand. Then she choked on it and had to have a drink and I had to slap her bony back (urgh) and ask her if she was all right. Eventually, the chorizo shifted.

'OK?'

'Yeah, think it's shifted now. God, that was horrible.' Her voice was all husky. She galloped down a few more glugs of water and went back to her meal, seemingly done with the conversation.

'Sorry, you were saying they might be looking at someone else?'

'Oh, yeah, there's a private-care company that visited Scudd a few times a day. You know, making his meals, getting him washed. I don't think they're looking too hard at them – it's a well-established firm. Strange he didn't bolt the door though. The care company said he always dead-bolted after their staff left. When he was found, the door wasn't bolted.'

'So... what does that mean?'

'Well, it could mean he forgot. Or that he let someone else in after the last carer left at six o'clock. He wouldn't have let those two boys in, would he? No signs of forced entry anywhere else.'

'What about family members? Anyone else have a key?'

'No, his family haven't spoken to him in years. There's a son in Ireland but it's been decades. No, so the teenagers are the best bet. I'm a bit disappointed I have to say. I thought maybe The Reaper might have struck again, you know.'

'Oh, your sex offender/serial killer theory?'

'Yeah,' she sighed. 'But he seems to have stopped for the time being. I'd say those kids did the area a favour anyway, just between you, me and the gatepost. If anyone touched my kids I'd...'

'You'd what?'

She looked at me. Stared hard. 'I don't know what I'd do. I really don't.'

'Send the boys round maybe?' I suggested.

And we shared a smile – a small, insignificant little moment to anyone else, but to me, it was actually a chink of light in an otherwise sunless afternoon.

Lynette came round with the payslips after lunch then I spent an hour up in the Cunts Department because she'd taken two student loan repayments off. Again.

MrSizzler48 has now blocked me on Snap Wank too. He sent me a message to say he's heard from another guy that I'm 'full of shit' and that I 'won't meet up because I'm having a laugh'. He thinks I'm actually 'a woman in disguise'. That's why I 'won't send live pix'.

He's not as stupid as I first thought. Amazingly.

Friday, 17 May

1. *Cyclists*
2. *People who bang on about Steven Avery/Making a Murderer – the guy once doused a cat in gasoline. They should have fried the bastard in oil.*
3. *'Hazel' the nurse, who carried out my smear test this morning and banged on and on about the Nifty Fifties Tap and Ballroom Dance class she was in. If there's anything sadder than watching old people dance, it's being over fifty and dancing. She even handed me a leaflet when she'd finished swilling surgical instruments around in my lady chamber. Bloody cheek.*

Joy's trying to organise a bonding weekend in the Lake District – the campaign of practical jokes aimed at Linus is now her top priority and she thinks it's 'driving a fissure down the middle of the team'. She's on a mission to promote harmony and stamp out nastiness in the *Gazette* offices (she's been on a course). Yeah, good luck with that with me around, babe.

AJ and I went out for a foot-long sausage baguette at lunch-time (no, that's not a euphemism and, yeah, sod the cellulite). We were in public for the most part but he sneaked a kiss behind the tree in the graveyard while we were walking back to the office. The lilies from a recent funeral smelled magnificent. I looked over to the tree where the tramp lay. He was sitting outside his tree home, surrounded by all his mouldering carrier bags and clutter, rolling a cigarette. He waved when he saw me. I didn't wave back.

Saturday, 18 May

1. *People who chat with the cashier in the supermarket, even though there's a queue behind them – I'm all for being pleasant when you're packing your bag, but when the card's been pulled out or the change has been given, kindly fuck off. Don't linger and talk about your kid's Easter play or your operation. AND DON'T THANK ME FOR WAITING. I DIDN'T HAVE A CHOICE!*
2. *Litterbugs*
3. *AJ – for forcing me to have sex with him. Well, not forcing me in the usual sense but backing me into a corner where it's my only option. It's just annoying.*

To the sex mobile, Batman…

*

AJ has just left. I lied and said Craig had texted to say he was coming back early, having missed his train to London. He seemed genuinely upset that he couldn't stay around for a cuddle (he really likes just cuddling for some reason) but at least now me and Tink have the flat to ourselves for the night so we can watch that Denis Nilsen documentary I've circled in the *Radio Times*.

Anyway the sex, if you could call it that. He was so revved up when he arrived – tenting even as I opened the door – that we had just enough time to uncork the wine he'd brought before he was on me like pondweed. There was a lot of tongue and a lot of dry humping on the sofa, until he said...

'I'm gonna cum right here if I'm not careful.'

At which point, I moved events into the bedroom. I'd go right off that sofa if it got even one drip of his spunk on it.

And then I timed it. The time it took to get from sofa to actual spunk-off – 104 seconds. That was it. He collapsed, I lay there, sans-gasm, Tink barked and shrieked outside the bedroom door, as always, and then I pushed him off and went to clean up.

'God, that was incredible,' he said from the bed. 'Did you cum?'

'Yeah, it was lovely,' I said from the bathroom, then I crawled back over to him and nuzzled under his outstretched arm like he seemed to be beckoning me to. 'You're a lot better at it than Craig.'

'Aww don't talk about him.' He kissed me and started taking off my clothes. 'I don't wanna talk about him.'

'Why? You jealous?'

He nodded, kissing me again. 'I don't want him inside you. I want to be inside you. All the time.' He climbed on-board again and kissed all around my face and neck, one hand going south.

'God, you're so wet.'

'Well, yeah, you've just unloaded your fun pump in there, darling.'

He laughed, moving back to kiss my mouth again. 'You're gorgeous.'

I wriggled out of my knickers and wrapped my legs around him. 'Thank you.'

He pulled off his shirt. I unclicked my bra and threw it to the same heap on the carpet.

'Do you want me to eat you out?'

'No, let's just have sex again, yeah?'

'I don't know if I can get hard again yet.'

'I'll get you hard.' I wrestled him onto his back and kissed him all over, spending a decent amount of time on his cock, using every available method at my disposal – hands, mouth, tits – the full works. Normally, when I did the full works on Craig, I'd expect a lot in return – a foot massage, a shelf putting up or a mixed grill at the very least.

'God, girl, you've got some moves,' he panted, as I climbed astride him.

'I watch a lot of porn.'

'Seriously?!' he shrieked, hands behind his head. 'I don't know any girls who watch porn.'

'We *all* watch it. We just lie about it to you guys. And trust me, if you have a boyfriend like Craig, you need porn.'

'Why do you stay with him? You don't have a good word to say about him.'

'I kind of hate him, in a way, but I'm used to him now. It's complicated.' I hoped he would leave it at that, and he did.

'OK, keep talking about dirty stuff now. What kind of porn do you like?'

'Anything,' I said. 'Interracial's always good. Sometimes bondage. Hentai.'

'You watch *hentai*?'

'I watch all of them. Gay is awesome. I can see why guys like it. There's a funny Scooby Doo one where he's bumming Shaggy. Although, technically, that's bestiality, which I don't endorse at all.'

'You ever watch lesbian?'

'Not really. Women don't do much for me, sexually speaking,' I said. *Unless I'm stabbing them at the time*, I thought.

'You ever been with another woman?'

'No.'

'How about anal? You ever try that?'

I stopped rocking on him for a moment and looked down at his face. For a second he morphed into Craig. 'I'm not into pain unless I'm the one inflicting it.' And I tweaked both his nipples, hard.

'Ahh! OK, OK.' He laughed. 'No worries.'

I rocked back on forth on his pole for ages until I came – I had to trawl up some dark, dark memories to get that one out of my system and finally, with my eyes closed and thinking about lying underneath Julia as her blood ran down the sides of my neck, I came all down his cock.

'God, you look hot when you come,' he breathed, holding my tits as I caught my breath and flumped down so we were chest to chest, stuck onto each other like two slugs.

'Mmm,' I said, not opening my eyes.

'Keep going, baby. Don't stop. Help me come again.'

I climbed off and sucked him to fruition. He was quite the growler.

Spooning in bed naked with his flaccid wet cock pressed in between my buttocks and his right hand kneading my boob, he said, 'I know we haven't known each other long but... I think I'm falling in love with you, Rhiannon. Rhee? Did you hear what I said?'

I pretended to be asleep.

Sunday, 19 May

Me and Craig went over to his mum and dad's house for lunch – roast pork, crunchy crackling and all the trimmings – though Elaine is on Weight Watchers and her portion was so tiny it belonged in my doll's house. She also refrained from having chocolate sponge and custard for pudding, preferring a bowl of cold strawberries and eulogising about how 'lovely and local' they were.

AJ has been texting me non-stop since our night of wild passion. Most of the time I can't be bothered to text much back except *Mmm, me too* and *Yeah, cum hard for me, baby, ooh I like that* while I'm doing the washing up or vacuuming the spare bedroom. It was quite hot when he started texting me at Jim and Elaine's though. Risky, see? Me likes the risky cos Me's a risky pixie.

During the afternoon snoozefest on the sofas, I was reading their local newspaper trying to spot errors in their editorial, when I came across a story – a former nursery nurse, jailed for six years ago for abusing children in her care, is due for parole this month – Sandra Huggins. Her mugshot was about as ugly as you could imagine – somewhere between Rose West and a lard drip on an oven door. Jim looked over my shoulder.

'Yeah, parents round here are up in arms about that. Elaine's friend Mandy, works at the Co-op, she knows her sister. Family want nothing to do with her. She'll be hard-pressed to find any friends round these parts.'

'I didn't know women could be paedophiles,' I said, closing the paper. 'What do they call them, feedophiles?'

'Monsters,' said Jim as Tink jumped up onto his lap and curled herself around like an Arctic fox. 'And that lad who disturbed the pony in that field out Hazelford way – Elaine couldn't sleep for weeks after that. Sick in the head some people.'

'What do you think should happen to her, Jim? When she comes out?'

'Shouldn't *be* let out, should she?' he replied. 'Should be left to rot there like Hindley and that other one. But no, they'll probably give her a false name and a job, all at taxpayers' expense. Elaine's sick with nerves that she'll try and join the WI.'

'What would you do if you met her in the street?'

He shook his head. 'I'd kill her. Most people round here would. She's a freak of nature in't she? Should be put down.'

Correct answer, *ding ding ding!* Give that man a speedboat!

See, I'm not so strange in wanting to kill the lusus naturae of our community, am I? I just do the things people only ever *talk* about doing. If only they knew, I'd be so popular, I really would. Everyone would love me, even the *Daily Mail*. They might start a petition to get me released or a Crowdfunding campaign to get some T-shirts printed or something.

I knew about Elaine's sundry neuroses, of course. I knew she had problems sleeping when the house down the street had been broken into. She couldn't even handle firework night – every Fifth of November, she was one Roman candle away from a nervous breakdown so nowadays when the locals had a firework party planned, she'd take a few Valium and go straight up to bed. Many a time I'd helped myself to a few from her medicine cabinet. You never know when extra-strong sleeping tablets might come in handy.

And I was happy to see she had just recently replenished her stocks when I went up to use the loo.

Monday, 20 May

Had the day off today. I didn't do anything really. I just wanted to do anything other than work. I googled Sandra Huggins to see what the status was of her parole application – nothing to see. I'd like to take my time with that one. I'd like to do a Julia on her. Maybe bring in a little electricity, like I'd seen Dad do once through a crack in the window of a dusty warehouse.

But where would I put her now I don't have access to Mum and Dad's? Hmm, that's a poser.

Talking of which, the FOR SALE sign has gone up on the front lawn. Jamie from Redman & Finch called me to say there had been two viewings already – one was by the Pembrokes – the couple with the four big dogs who'd looked at it when it was off the market – and that one was 'very promising'. So it looks like the biggest part of my childhood is going to leave me soon. I will miss it. Well, I'll miss the garden. And the peace. And Henry.

AJ came round to the flat for a quickie at lunchtime.

'Do you feel guilty?' he asked, lying on me, my legs wrapped around him, my foot soles rubbing along his thighs.

'No,' I said, as his full heaviness pressed down on me. 'I like it. It's hot, being an adulterer. Do you feel guilty? About your auntie?'

'No way. I've wanted to fuck you since I first got here. This has totally been worth it. God, I love you.'

'Kiss me,' I said. He kissed me. 'Fuck me again.'

And he did, using his middle finger to tease my clit as his cock did the hard work. I came pretty hard myself the second time. The kid might only be nineteen but give him his due, he knew his way around a vagina. He must have been watching some YouTube tutorials in the interim, I surmised. When we were done and he was limp but still on top of me, I said...

'Stay there for a moment.'

'Why?' He smiled, kissing my neck again.

'Just lie on me for a second. No, don't fidget. Stay right there. Still.'

'What do you mean?'

'Just lie on me, like you're dead.'

And he did. He completely relaxed himself so he lay dead on me. And I came again, gripping on to him, with him just lying there, doing nothing at all. I bit down on his shoulder. It was almost rhapsodic in its ecstasy.

'Woah!' he said. 'You had some more left in the tank then, did ya?'

I nodded and held him to me and silently, holding on to him, I began to cry into his warm neck. Ten thousand porn vids with hard-core in-and-out close-ups didn't come close to the intensity of that one single moment.

'Hey, you all right?'

I sobbed. Actually sobbed. 'Yeah. I just love it so much.'

'Aww, baby, I love you too. I really do.'

Thursday, 23 May

I've just realised, I haven't had the Dad dream in over a month. It has died with Derek Scudd. Maybe he was put on his earth for something useful after all.

Also, they're planning this year's Christmas party already in work.

It's May.

Joy wants to get the rugby club booked up 'nice and early because they were fully booked last year' so she's asked for the deposits by tomorrow. She's also talking about ordering a dress she's seen in the Simply Be catalogue. How small is a person's life that they get excited by shit like that over six months beforehand? I don't know whether to laugh, cry or punch her in the non-melty part of her face.

Wrote up my Marvel movie review – I gave it a 1* rating, and that was for the usherette who said he liked my shoes. Paul Spurdog said 'You do realise you're going to get emails from all the fan boys, don' you?' I said, 'Yeah. Bring it.'

AJ and I have found a new game to play – texting each other photos of our genitalia. At first I was hesitant because it's hard to take flattering angles of oneself without cropping, angling or filtering the shit out of them, but it got to be quite fun. He's very demanding – he doesn't realise how difficult it is to hold one dildo in your vagina, while fingering your ass *and* taking a photo at the same time while standing up in your office toilets but, by Jove, I think I've cracked it.

It was Paul's birthday today. Instead of cakes he brought in home-made granola bars cos they're healthier for you'. You could have cut the atmosphere with a knife, which is ironic because you needed a hacksaw to get through the granola bars. It was like chewing a log. Fucking clean eaters.

Oh, and we've had a firm offer through on Mum and Dad's house, less than one week after it went live on the estate agent's site. So it looks like we've sold.

Seren phoned me this afternoon, full of glee. She actually sounded like a sister, for once, rather than a bitter old shrew who ran a girls' orphanage who I always imagined I was talking to.

'I can't believe it's finally going to happen.'

'Yeah, well, it was bound to eventually, wasn't it?' I said. It was my turn to be the bitter old shrew.

'I'm sorry if you felt under pressure with it all, Rhiannon. We could just really use the money at the moment. It's going to be such a massive help. Cody's job is basically hanging by a thread. He might have to relocate to Vermont so we've been looking at houses there.'

'Vermont? Where Ben and Jerry's comes from?'

'I don't know. Look, did you contact that house clearance firm I emailed you about?'

'Yes,' I said. I was in no mood for her whiney bullshit today.

'How much are they offering?'

'They offered a grand.'

'A thousand pounds? For everything? *All* the contents?'

'Yes, Seren. A grand. And I didn't go with them anyway, I gave it all to the Hospice who looked after Mum. For free. For charity. The house is empty now. You left me to deal with it all so that's what I've done.'

'Rhiannon, some of that furniture could have been worth something.'

'I. Don't. Care.'

'Rhiannon, let's keep this civil, all right? I don't want to be talking to you any more than you want to be talking to me.'

'Damn right. Well, we're nearly there now aren't we? Final hurdle and then you can carry on pretending I don't exist, can't you?'

'It's not like that, Rhiannon.'

'Of course it is. It's been like that for years.'

'Can you blame me for not wanting anything to do with you?' she said, her voice lowering. 'After what you did?'

'What I did for *you*, you mean?'

Her voice was now little more than a fluttery whisper. 'Oh, so you do remember then?'

'You never forget your first time.'

'Ugh, you give me chills.'

'You wouldn't have a husband and kids and a sun-kissed existence in Yankee Doodleville if it wasn't for me.'

She was trying not to cry, I could hear it in her voice; her quivering breaths. 'I woke up… covered in my boyfriend's blood… and you were stood there smiling. Dad covered for you. He knew what you were. You're a psycho.'

'I'm not a psycho. Not completely. I checked.'

It all came spewing out then. How my violent rages had made Mum's life a misery. How my lying and stealing and arson period had brought her cancer on. How she still had scars from where I cut her with scissor blades. How I would fake tears to curry favour with Dad. How I got away with so much because Mum and Dad felt so guilty about making so much money from my fame as the Priory Gardens Survivor. How Nanny said I got the Devil in me after Priory Gardens.

'You're a cunting liar,' I said. 'I bet you dribble all this crap to your friends, don't you? How I was such a horrible sister, tormenting you, cutting your hair, serving up your favourite parakeet for dinner. What's the real story, Seren? *I* got the hammer to the skull so *I* got all the attention. *All* the sympathy. And what did you get? Fuck. All. They might have left you half that house but it was *my* celebrity that bought it in the first place. You should be licking my feet.'

Her breath was catching. 'That hammer... smashed all the love out of you.'

'Point being?'

There came a long pause. Then the click and the line went dead.

Ungrateful, worm-infested cunt jockey from Hell. I'm so DONE with sisters. I'm so done with *families*. I wish she'd gone under Wesley Parsons' tyres, not Joe Leech.

'*You're a psychopath.*'

My grandmother said a similar thing the day the undertakers brought Granddad back to the house. I'd been at horse riding. I remember walking into the living room and he was just lying there, in his coffin. Hands folded on his chest. Eyelids stitched shut. So much make-up on he looked like something out of a drag act. My grandmother stood behind me as I looked down, scanning his body from feet to face. I saw her face in the mirror above the fireplace.

You should see what you've done, she'd said.

That was the last summer I spent at Honey Cottage. The last time I saw Granny. The summer before Julia.

AJ wasn't in today – ill apparently, according to Claudia – so I had to make all the coffee, do all the filing *and* get Ron his lunch. I was so stressed at lunchtime I texted him. He was in bed watching *Star Wars* (eye roll). I missed him being around. I missed his little love messages in my cappuccino foam. I missed watching him walk past my desk. I missed making him laugh.

I texted him: *Come back to work and sort the cables out under my desk. Then accidentally on purpose stick your head between my legs.*

Oh, God, don't tempt me. Streaming cold though, babe. Miss you heaps!!! Come over and rub some Vicks on me xxx

Even through his snot he couldn't resist me. They never can.

*

BTW – Claudia's house is MASSIVE. It's one of the newbuilds on the hill on the way out of town. It looks like a show home. Open plan kitchen with grey granite work surfaces you can see your reflection in. Copper accessories. King size beds in all four bedrooms. Huge cinema-style TV in the lounge. Everything coordinated. Everything clean. Everything top of the range.

Next door to AJ's room was a little box room, completely bare but for a lemon yellow border all around the centre. The border depicted little bees and flowers.

'Is this a nursery?'

'Yeah,' he said, 'for the baby she's not going to get. Sad, innit?'

'She's a mum with no baby,' I said.

We went to the cinema after work. I can't remember anything about the film we saw – some crap about mermaids – but the theatre was empty and we were in the back row the whole time, testing the squeak in the chairs.

Friday, 24 May

1. *Creepy Ed Sheeran – hanging around outside my office again today, this time with a black eye. Good*
2. *Edmund – the 'Golly gosh' and 'Crumbs, I had better get a wriggle on if we're going to make that deadline' and 'Me and some chums met up for a chinwag' is getting on my last tit*
3. *People who leave their dogs in cars on hot days – would you leave your child inside your lit oven wearing a fur coat while you went and 'just grabbed a coffee'?*

My nightmares have stopped. I thought it might be a fluke at first but I haven't had a single bad dream since I offed Derek Scudd. How cool is that?! Better than Nytol. I should bottle it and sell it... *Peedol: Kill a Paedophile now and have night's sleep every night of the week. While stocks last. Not available in pharmacies.*

Had lunch with Daisy Chan again. The Reaper still dominates most of our conversations and, for the rest of them, she's quizzing me about my family. I'm beginning to tire of it. I gave her the bare facts over an avocado salad at The Roast House.

'You said your parents packed you off to stay with your grandparents in Wales?'

'Yeah, at Honey Cottage. It's my favourite place in the world. My granny had bright red hair and walked around the place barefoot in ethnic clothes. She said you have to walk barefoot in the summer "to get connected to the soil and the earth".'

'How lovely,' said Daisy. 'I love Wales. We used to go there on trips to Monmouthshire with the children's home. What did you do there?'

'Make cakes for the tourists. Horse-riding. Pick the vegetables for the box scheme. Swimming. They had a river running right past their cottage. One summer my sister Seren came up with me and we stayed out lying on the hay bales in the fields until it got dark. In the days we used to get on.'

'Sounds idyllic.'

'It was. Until Granddad died. Then Granny wouldn't let me visit. She blamed me for his death.'

'Oh, gosh. Why, what happened?'

'He had a heart attack while he was swimming. He liked wild swimming. Said it always woke him up, ready for the day. I'd gone out with him just to watch. And that's what I did. I stayed on the bank and watched. I watched him drown.'

'Oh, my gosh.'

'He had a heart attack. There was nothing I could do. '

'How old were you?'

'Eleven.'

'That's awful.' I nodded. 'Why don't you and your sister get on?'

My fork clattered loudly to my plate at the exact right time to cause a bit of a scene and have some of the other patrons looking my way. 'I think I'm done with the inquisition for today.'

Daisy's cheeks immediately suffused with red. 'Sorry. I was doing it again, wasn't I?'

'If you're so fascinated by my family, why don't you just look them up in the *Gazette* archives? They're all there: "Local Boxer

Hero's Father Dies in River Tragedy"; "Local Boxer Hero's Wife Loses Brave Fight with Cancer"; "Priory Gardens Survivor is Local Boxer Hero's Daughter". Pretty sure Ron only gave me the job as receptionist because I was a local sleb.'

'I'm so sorry, Rhiannon. I just like hearing people talk about their families. I like hearing you talk about *your* family. I can see how much you loved them.'

'Can you?'

'Yes, of course. You talk about your dad like he was some kind of god. I've never had that, you see. A dad to look up to. A big sister to play with. My parents and I moved here from Qingyuan City when I was just a baby. Four months later, they were both killed in a car accident. They'd just dropped me off at nursery. I had no one else.'

'Oh,' I said, not quite knowing what to say.

'I went into care. I was fostered out a few times – nothing really stuck. I was a bit odd. Had a bunch of insecurities – OCD, anxiety. I just couldn't seem to settle anywhere. Then in my early teens I developed an eating disorder. I was just too problematic.'

I nodded. That explained the thin. 'How did you... get better?'

She sighed. 'I guess in time, with a lot of love, a lot of patience from other people, you just do. I also had massive determination that my life would be better. That I would achieve something. It gives you a killer instinct I think, when you have a bad start. Sometimes anyway.'

'Mmm,' I said. The similarities between us were suddenly striking. We were going to be friends at this rate if I wasn't careful. After that, the ice between us broke and we had quite a pleasant lunch hour. I'm not used to this – just being friends with someone because they're friendly, not for what they could do for me.

Maybe this is where I've been going wrong.

Saturday, 25 May

1. *Women who go shopping with their husbands then moan about it – did you honestly expect them to be helpful?*
2. *Queue-jumpers*
3. *Stores who make their shop assistants ask about a thousand questions when you eventually reach the till. Did you find everything you were looking for today, madam? Would you be interested in 25 per cent off Katy Perry's new perfume, madam? Would you like a £1 Toblerone today with your Tampax, madam? Would you like any stamps or batteries with your clit vits, madam? SHUT UP AND LET ME PAY!*

So, first thing, Lucille and her sister Cleo came round and took me shopping for our prostitute outfits for the Weekend That Must Not Be Named. Never have I ever felt as out of place or awkward as I did when we were going around those shops, collecting up every scrap of shoddily made tight neon Lycra we could find and the cheapest gold jewellery our contactless cards could buy. The only thing that made it in the least bit enjoyable was that every now and again I got a WhatsApp nake from AJ.

Just woke up. Had a dream about you and woke up with this...

Lucille sent me into the changing rooms with every leopard-print, thigh-skimming, knicker-showing, breast-enhancing, camel-toe-inducing bit of material she could get her hands on. And the worst part was she and Cleo looked good in all of it – I looked like what I was – a miserable fat twat in cheap tarts' threads.

Baby, I need you again. I've got a permanent hard-on for you. I cum every time I think of us together.

'Yep, that's it, that's the one,' said Cleo, as I came out wearing my selected outfit – skin-tight leopard-print leggings, black miniskirt, patent leather wedges I could barely stand up in, a neon pink boob tube and large gold hoop earrings. I tried not to notice either of them staring at the areas of flab my clothes refused to hide. 'How will you have your hair?' asked Lucille, scraping it all up into a hooker topknot for me, then letting it all down again. 'Like that? Or maybe pigtails?'

'Shaved off against my will in front of several baying Dutch villagers perhaps? No, not pigtails, for God's sake.'

I turned back to look at them – Cleo smiled briefly. 'How about a high ponytail?'

'Well, I wouldn't want to cheapen the effect.'

'Fake tan!' cried Lucille.

'Shit, we forgot!' said Cleo and I was ushered back into the changing room tout de suite to fold everything up so we could pay for it (the entire outfit plus shoes came to less than £15 so we're talking real-assed quality merchandise here).

Rhee, can I see you tonight? I need to see you. Send me some pix to be going on with, would ya? Love u xxx

I sent him some up-the-skirt shots and several of my tits pressed together while I was changing. Within seconds, he'd fired back an image of a wet patch on his duvet.

Ur awesome. Love you – AJ xx Kissy face emoji followed by cat and chicken emojis for some reason. Then I realised it was a pussy and a cock. Yawn. Such a child, yet somehow I enjoyed the shopping expedition more because of him.

I heard Cleo and Lucille talking while I was in the changing room – bitching about Imelda and how she was micro-managing everything. How Lucille had 'just about had it up to here' and how Cleo was 'will be glad when this bloody wedding's over'. *Très intéressant, j'ai pensé.*

Then we hotfooted it to Superdrug for a shitload of tan towels.

Monday, 27 May

1. *Wesley Parsons*
2. *Makers of Sylvanian Families – they have discontinued the seaside restaurant I was going to ask Craig to buy me for Christmas. There's one on eBay but you don't know what idiot has crapped on that*
3. *Aerobics teachers – particularly Cleo Fullerton. And I thought I was a sadist*

It's getting impossible to avoid AJ. He was like a dog on heat all day today. His texts are becoming increasingly more cloying and suggestive and he says something to me every single time he passes my desk, even if it's just 'Your window could do with a wipe.' I didn't know if that was a euphemism or what. I have to have sex with him again soon as he's clearly gagging for it. Not exactly a hardship but some nights you just want to eat Crunchy Nut Cornflakes, watch *EastEnders* and shave your pits, you know?

Claudia and Ron had their joint birthdays today – and both had chosen to have the day off. I don't think there's anything sexual going on there. I just think they're both too tight to buy their own doughnuts. So selfish.

Imelda and Lucille texted to see if I wanted to come to Cleo's aerobics class after work – an *actual* aerobics class, rather than an excuse for sex-with-AJ or feeding-my-hostage. I think she was short on numbers. Therefore, my intended evening of hot bath, leg-shaving and chat-rooming with random dick slappers from around the world was shunted in place of ear-splitting Nicki Minaj, kicking the air in front of my face and sweating through my Juicy Couture. I had to sit out the jumping jacks marathon due to a dizzy spell but I do feel tighter. I do feel better about myself. I don't actually want to kill anyone tonight.

Maybe that's the answer to keeping the world safe from my tendencies – sheer fucking exhaustion.

Tuesday, 28 May

Took Tink to the new vet's surgery in town first thing for her annual injection. She was a brave girl but it cost me an arm and a leg, a springer spaniel attacked her in the waiting room, *and* the vet had rapey eyes so I think we'll be going back to her old vet.

Linus has been off work for six days now. Nobody's knows why. 'Mystery illness' seems to be the party line, which probably means he's tried to top himself, like Mike Heath. Quite a few people have tried to top themselves at the *Gazette*. It's always the quiet ones. Too many people bottle stuff up. Except Inept Plunket of course. She's always crowing about the time many moons ago when she jumped from the multi-storey. It was only the first level and she bounced off the roof of a Shogun so nothing to write home about.

AJ cornered me in the staffroom. He asked me if I've 'gone off him' cos I wasn't talking to him so much at work or texting back as quickly. And he called me on my bullshit 'just so busy' answer. So I told him:

'I get bored easily, AJ. That's all. It's just a bit of fun, you and me, isn't it?'

'No, it isn't. Not for me. I'm in love with you, I told you that.'

'Yeah, I think it's just a crush, dude.'

'No, it's not. I mean what I say. You said it too.'

Mmm, don't think I did, I thought, but continued stirring my coffee. 'I don't actually want this,' I said, pushing my mug away.

'OK, well, I still want to see you. No strings, if you like.'

'Just sex?'

'Just sex.' He smiled. 'Please. I'm begging you. I need to see you.'

I couldn't help but smile. It was nice to be wanted. He seemed desperate. It's very attractive, being *thought of* as attractive, isn't it? I liked that he wanted me so badly. I had the strongest urge to say No to him, to make him suffer in his longing, but there was something I wanted even more than that. I said, 'OK. On one condition.'

'Name it.'

'I want to try something different.'

'Anything. Name your price.'

I turned to him and said, 'I want us to do it outside some-where. And I want you to pretend... that you're dead.'

His face fell. 'Dead?'

'Yeah. Pretend you've died. And I'm fucking your corpse.'

He didn't say anything for a long time. He checked the door, like he'd heard someone come in, but no one was there. 'That's pretty sick stuff.' He laughed. It was a nervous laugh but there were ribbons around it.

'We all have our little kinks.'

'Do you, like, watch porn about dead things too?'

'No, of course not.'

'I won't be stiff though. Dead things are stiff, aren't they?'

'Not immediately. And not for long.'

'OK,' he said, not smiling. 'I can do that.'

After work, I drove us out to the country to the woods at the back of Mum and Dad's. The day was still hot and hotter inside the forest, stifled as we were by the closely grouped trees.

I found the spot where me and Dad buried Pete's body and we lay the picnic blanket down there on top the pine needles and soft brown earth. AJ did his best pretend-corpse impression but he was too alive; too heartbeat and warm. Thankfully, I didn't need much foreplay though – just the thought of what lay buried beneath us was enough to get me wet. I have dry leaves and pine needles in all the orifices right now, but I have to admit, it was good today.

'Tis turning out to be a fine romance.

*

Had another dizzy spell cooking tea tonight and I couldn't eat anything. Craig's worried about me, the nob. It's been very hot today and I haven't drunk anything but a half-bottle of water left in my car for the past three months. He said I should be taking better care of my body to prepare it for our little Criannon. I said he should check if gravity still works by jumping off the balcony.

I've eaten my way through the entire day, like The Very Hungry Caterpillar's Even Hungrier Larvae. I've had…

1. *A bowl of muesli with full fat milk and two pieces of buttery toast*
2. *1 x banana dipped in Nutella*
3. *A Rhubarb and Custard Naked bar and a full fat hot chocolate*
4. *Sausage baguette and a Twix*
5. *A doughnut (Krystle in Sales' birthday)*
6. *A Flake*
7. *A (giant) handful of peanuts*
8. *A(nother) banana, dipped in Nutella*
9. *2 x toast and jam when I got in from work*

10. *Spaghetti Bolognese (from scratch, with balcony oreg-*
    ano), cheesy garlic bread
11. *Banana and custard*

Preggo? Nah. I'm not falling for that one again. I'm just
greedy, that's all. The worst part about it is I'm STILL hungry.
Maybe I'm just thirsty. I'll have a Capri Sun and see if that does
the trick.

*

The Capri Sun didn't do the trick. Am still famished. Going to
order a pizza before my chrysalis starts to form.

Wednesday, 29 May

1. *Maths teachers – specifically all the maths teachers I've had*
2. *Sandra Huggins*
3. *Wesley Parsons*
4. *Vets – Tink's annual quickest injection ever has cost me over £50. The actual factual FUCK can you justify that?*
5. *Michael Jackson – OK was he or wasn't he because I've been wanting to listen to 'Thriller' for the past year now and I still don't feel like I can*

You would think I had backstage passes to meet Queen Bey herself today, the mood I've been in. Absolutely buzzing. We dropped off Tink with Jim and Elaine first thing – they had her bowls of water and food all ready and had made up a brand-new dog bed beside theirs in their room. They were talking about 'taking her to the park to feed the ducks' and the possibility of a day at the beach. They're so desperate for a decent grandchild, it's pathetic. The one they have, Mason, from Craig's errant sister Kirsty is, by Jim's admission, 'a shit' who plays on his phone at the dinner table, steals from Elaine's purse and most shocking of all, helps himself to Jim's digestives without being invited. Since Mason hit the teen years, they hardly see him at all.

Craig drove up to Birmingham, on the condition that I drive back. Stopped at Michaelwood services so I could empty my bursting bladder and we also crammed in a McDonald's. I was still ravenously hungry after, so I got a takeaway hot chocolate and a lemon-and-poppy-seed muffin in Starbucks while he 'went outside for a vape'. I followed him, pretending to stop and smell the bucket flowers outside Marks and Spencer. He was talking on the phone. To her. I saw him mouth the words 'I love you too'.

I can't exactly be jealous any more though, can I? Not when I've been re-enacting the *Kama Sutra* with AJ on the days of the week that have a Y in them.

We got to the hotel by lunchtime. Once we'd parked up, I was harangued for twenty-six minutes about the hotel I'd booked because we 'didn't need to be in the city centre'. According to Craig's map app, the Crowne Plaza was right by the venue and he suggested we 'cancelled our booking at the posh place and go there instead'.

No, I said. We *had* to stay in the city centre because I wanted to go shopping tomorrow morning 'for Mel and Jack's wedding present' and some 'nice chocolates for Jim and Elaine to thank them for having Tink'. He eventually relented, grumbling all the while.

Yay yay, I get my way.

We walked past The Glass Tree pub on the way to the train station, once we'd dumped our bags with the concierge. It was an all-day palace and there were mostly families in there eating pies with gravy drips down the sides. I only peeked inside but there was no sign of Parsons. He would be on the night shift, of course. Like me.

Kicked around town for a bit killing time and picked up a Subway and a colossal bag of pick 'n' mix from a Tesco Metro we passed as we headed to the train.

'Are you still in a mush?' I asked him, once we were seated and I'd begun on the strawberry bonbon layer of the pick 'n' mix.

'No,' he sulked, studying a pizza flyer he'd been handed at the station.

'You are,' I crooned in his ear, giving it a little bite. 'Come on, we've got a nice king-size bed, power shower, Gideon Bible in the drawer and everything.'

'Still don't see why we have to stay in one of the most expensive hotels in Birmingham, nowhere near the gig. Crowne Plaza's right next door.'

I got right up into his face, smelling my own sickly strawberry breath ricocheting back off his cheek. 'You're not taking me on holiday because of your stupid football fortnight, so I'm having one night in a posh hotel. All right?'

He shrugged and stared out the window.

'Anyway, look on the bright side, we could make our baby in that king-size bed tonight, couldn't we?'

'Woah,' he said, a smile slowly creeping back onto his face. 'You sure know how to put the wind back in a man's sails, don't you?'

'Yes,' I laughed.

He laughed too, fumbling in the pick 'n' mix bag for a shrimp. 'You're so horny lately. I read something online about women being easier to get in the mood when they're pregnant. Or trying to get pregnant.'

'Well there you go then.' He reached for a sour-apple MAOAM and unpeeled it, holding it out for me to take. I shook my head. 'No thanks. I've gone right off them.'

'I only got them for you.'

I rifled around in the bag for another bonbon.

'When did you last do a test?'

'Few weeks ago?' I reached into the bag for a gummy bear. 'I won't be pregnant, Craig, it's a waste of money.'

'You do seem... different lately.'

'In what way?'

'Well, you've whacked on a bit of weight, haven't you?'

'Stops me getting kidnapped.'

'You're off coffee, and now MAOAMs. They're your favourites.'

'Pull the other one,' I said.

He was right. I'd had two dizzy spells in the past week alone. Coffee and sour-apple MAOAMs *were* my two favourite things but I couldn't go near either of them any more without gagging. And then there was my food intake in general – I was troughing like Henry VIII. My stomach was noticeably rounder – like period bloat that hadn't shifted. Lucille and Cleo hadn't been able to take their eyes off it when I'd been trying on the prozzie outfits in town. Did they all know something I didn't?

No, no, no, it couldn't be. The Pill would see to that.

'If you are,' he said, 'do you want to get hitched? Maybe now's the right time.'

'Married? Seriously? Why now?' I asked.

'Dunno. Just seems right, if you are. You're always saying weddings are a waste of money and that your side of the church would be half empty so I've never forced it. But if we had a baby on the way, maybe we could.'

'Do you want to?'

'Yeah,' he said. 'It would force us to grow up, wouldn't it?' Force *him* to stop shagging Lana Rowntree, he meant. This proposal was guilt-edged. 'Let's do it anyway. Let's do it, fuck thinking about it. What do you reckon? Do you wanna?'

'Yeah,' I said. 'I do.' Bluff called.

He beamed widely. 'So are we engaged then?'

'I think we might be,' I giggled and he leaned in and kissed me softly, cupping the back of my head in his big rough palm. 'So where's my engagement ring then?'

'Oh, you want one of them as and all, do you? I don't know, so demanding...' He fiddled about in the pick 'n' mix bag and pulled out a red jelly ring with a yellow diamond on top.

'Gis your hand.'

I held it out. He rubbed the ring along my fourth finger.

'There. We'll go round the jewellery quarter tomorrow for a proper one, shall we? Mrs Wilkins?'

'Uh, I ain't Mrs Wilkins yet, pal. I don't remember Marilyn singing "Haribos are a Girl's Best Friend".' We kissed to seal the deal.

I wished so much, right then, that this was all real. That this wasn't a sticking plaster. That I hadn't heard him say he loved Lana on the phone. That this meant he was mine for ever.

I ate the Haribo ring while he was in the toilet.

At the arena, the lines were enormous. A lot of fans had camped out overnight to get to the front. I wasn't good with killing time – killing men, yes, killing women, no problem but killing time? Hideous. The gig itself – once Her Majesty had finally seen fit to show herself just after 8.30 p.m. – was pretty spectacular. She did all the hits, plus a few new ones, changed her outfit twelve times (Craig kept count), blinded us with glitter and pyrotechnics and got a bit of audience participation going. We were repeatedly asked:

'If you're proud of who you are and where you're from, say, "I slay!"'

I got some fiendish glee shouting that out to almost sixteen thousand people, none of whom meant it as literally as I did. It was a pretty glorious feeling. The woman is a goddess sent to earth to show us all what we could have been if we weren't so scared – one moment she's a soulful crooner with a voice that can hit any note a song throws at her, the next minute, a ferocious stick of dynamite tearing up the stage like a panther. I got quite emosh several times.

Do you cry to Beyoncé? was not a question that had appeared in the BuzzFeed psychopath quiz but, if it had, my result might not have been quite so perplexing.

We took an AGE to get back to the station – just shuffling for most of it and travelling for almost as long as the gig. We didn't get back into town until midnight. Craig always insists on leaving when the performer says 'This is the last song', but tonight I wanted to drink it all up and be full to the brim with it and her before we even thought about leaving.

In town, The Glass Tree pub was heaving. There were clusters of men and women out the front smoking under the street lights and a guy being sick in the gutter as his mate laughed and rubbed his back. I stopped outside.

'Go in for last orders, shall we?' I suggested. 'I'm pretty parched.'

'You had a Coke coming back.'

'Yeah, well, I'm still thirsty. Come on, just one, eh? Nice cool lager...'

'I'm pretty tired, babe. Come on. There's water in the room.'

'I want an alcoholic drink and I need the toilet.'

'Again?'

'Yes, again. Come on.' He did one of his extra-long sighs but I got my way and we went in.

In the centre of the bar was an enormous glass tree, made up of crystal leaves dipping down from a trunk and branches made entirely from clear wine bottles – it was quite a sight. All around were booths and little tables made from beer barrels. All walks of life chatted and laughed and the noise was tremendous in my already-ringing ears. The restaurant next door was just as packed and the maître d' had sweat patches the size of two pancakes under his arms. Ugh.

'We're never gonna get served,' said Craig, fumbling in his wallet for a note. 'Do you know what you want?'

And then I saw him. Wesley Parsons – walking through the throng of people as though his bollocks were too big for his underpants. He plonked some empty glasses, down on the end of the counter and took his place behind one of the pumps.

'Did you hear me?' said Craig. 'We're never gonna get served here. Let's go back and see what's in the minibar.'

'You go and find us a table. I'll go find the loo and get the drinks. What do you want?'

'Draft lager. Budweiser or Stella if they've got it,' he said.

It's remarkable how much something doesn't matter if you know there's something good at the end of it. Like those kids outside the venue tonight – some of those girls had been camped out for three days to get the best view of their queen. And they were happy and joking and playing games on their phones, not even bothered by the wait they had endured. They knew their moment would come – and when it did, it would be worth it.

And so did I.

I had waited a long time to talk to Wesley Parsons, my best friend's killer. And, yes, he had 'paid his dues' to society. And, yes, he was 'dreadfully sorry for the pain he had caused'. And, yes, I should leave him to get on with his life now. But we don't always do what we should, do we? We do what we want.

And I wanted to kill him. Tonight.

When I eventually got to the bar, after a ten-minute queue for the toilets, it was covered in spilled liquid and the lights reflected back at me in the puddles.

'Yes, love?'

I saw myself in the mirror behind him. Him and me. Together.

'Vodka and lemonade, please,' I said, marvelling at how close he was. 'And whatever lager you've got on draught.'

'Stella?'

'Yeah.' I rooted around in my purse.

He didn't chit-chat or flirt like I'd expected him to. He didn't even recognise me. He pulled Craig's pint and made my V&L. Asked if I wanted ice. That was it.

'Nine sixty, please, love.'

I saw us both in the mirror again – my face and the back of his head. Wesley Parsons' head. The one I'd been searching for. Waiting for. Building up to.

'Can I have a cocktail stirrer, please?' I asked him, prolonging the moment.

He handed me a stick and I handed him a tenner and our fingers grazed in the exchange. He didn't make eye contact, or say anything else. When I didn't take the drinks, he finally looked up at me.

I grabbed the drinks. A guy to my right was hollering at him and waving a £20 note in his face.

I took one last look at him and turned my back, negotiating my way through the throng to find Craig.

I couldn't do it. I couldn't fucking do it. All this time I'd been dreaming about it, planning it, gazing at his Facebook photos like some love-struck fan, on fire with desire for the moment I would shove my knife into his ribcage and twist it ninety degrees to the left. Then right. Then back again. But I'd froze.

Craig was doing tricks with beer mats at our barrel near the back of the pub, ensconced between a table full of students who looked like rejects from the Hitler Youth and a gaggle of girls covered in L-plates and feather boas.

'You all right?' he shouted over the din.

'Couldn't you have wiped this?' I said irritably at the puddles of liquid on our barrel top. 'It's all over the floor underneath as well. Ugh.'

'I waited ages for this one and had to grab it when it was free. Haven't had chance to get my mop and bucket out yet.'

We sipped our drinks as the conversations of the hens and the Hitler Youth infiltrated our consciousness.

'D'you get me any nuts?'

'You didn't ask for nuts,' I said.

'They're on the bar, free.'

'Oh.'

I'd already crumbled Elaine's sleeping pills up into Craig's pint by this point, thinking I had twenty minutes to coax Parsons outside to a back alley under the guise of my Facebook-couched pseudonym. But my heart had totally gone out of it. I couldn't do it. I'd allowed too many other thoughts to barge in and take over. That's why queuing and long train journeys are bad for me – I think too much. I had thought so much, I'd begun to unpick my reasoning.

I'd killed Dan Wells because he'd propositioned me.

I'd killed Gavin White because he'd attacked me.

I'd killed Julia because she'd attacked eleven-year-old me.

I'd killed Derek Scudd because he'd attacked those two girls.

There was a reason for all of them. But Joseph had run into a main road to retrieve his football and Parsons was running late. He'd served twelve full years for going thirty-six in a thirty zone and taking one too many decongestants. Pretty face like his, he'd probably been butt-fucked in his cell every night. And now he was working three jobs. It *was* an accident. Killing him wasn't like a credit note to get Joseph back – he was dead, mouldering in his coffin at St Mark's. That was fucking that. There was no reason to do this. And every likelihood that I'd get caught this time. We were in a city centre. There was more CCTV cameras than people.

And if I got caught, that meant I would have to stop.

Craig was already showing signs of sleepiness halfway into his pint.

'Come on, it's been a long day. Let's go to bed.'

*

By the time we got into the lifts, Craig was at the leaning-against-
the-nearest-wall-and-closing-his-eyes stage. I *can* resist when I
need to. I'm *not* a complete psychopath. Fuck you, BuzzFeed.
At least 8 per cent of my brain is good. Rational. Normal. I did
not see this coming.

*

Craig flopped down on the bed next to me, fully clothed and
completely comatose. I was nowhere near sleepy. I sat up watching Newsnight but I couldn't take any of it in. His phone pinged
in his pocket. I pulled it out, slowly as not to wake him, and read
the message. Lana. *Thinking of you. Missing you lots – L xxxxx.*
     I text her back: *Missing you too Baby. We'll be together soon,
I promise. I love you – C xxxxx*
     I went into the bathroom and splashed my face. 'I don't know
this city,' I muttered. 'I don't know where the quiet streets and
alleyways are. Someone will see. Someone will hear. He doesn't
deserve it. I don't care. I don't care. I DON'T CARE!'
     Even with my shouting, Craig was still sound.
     I needed it tonight. I needed someone, anyone else. Some
backstreet bastard waiting for a drunken woman alone stumbling back from the clubs. The odds are higher here. Bigger city.
More bastards. I had to find one.
     So I went out. A woman alone. In a little black dress. Black
boots. Full red lipstick. Long hair. A woman like this would be
vulnerable on the streets of Birmingham tonight. That's what
I've always been told. Don't dress provocatively. Don't ask for
trouble.
     Maybe trouble shouldn't ask for me.
     I walked past the pub. And I kept on walking. Through piles
of litter, past clumps of moving sleeping bags in shop doorways.
Past the shopping centre and away from the main clutch of shops

where the streets opened up and more alleyways presented themselves. Side streets with no lighting. Industrial estates. Blocks of lock-up garages. Men out alone. A few called out – I didn't hear what, there was water in my ears. I had to lure them. Away from others. Away from the main streets. *Come with me. Come with me. Follow me. Try to grab me. Please try to grab me.*

I passed a brightly lit kebab shop, an all-night chemist and a pub who's last orders bell was being rung.

And I kept on walking. I didn't know where I was going and I became lost and panic started to set in, tempered only slightly by the earlier vodka at the pub. My knife was in my pocket and my hand was on the black handle the whole time. I was safe as long as I had it. I was safe and I was calm. But I was growing desperate. Simmering. Any attempt made to jump me now, any shadowy lurker out for an easy lay would get it both barrels. I'd tear him limb from fucking him.

The streets were all but empty but for the odd car or van. The odd man walking alone. The odd prostitute, tapping her stilettos. The odd dog bark in the distance; the odd car speeding, packed with groups of young men. Too many to handle at once. Too many to take. Someone called out from a passing car. I heard it.

How much for a jump, love?

Gissa suck, prozzie.

Maybe I was in the red-light district.

But nobody approached me. Nobody crept up behind and put his big rough hands over my mouth, or forced them up my dress and yanked my knickers past my knees. Nothing.

A group of Asian men smoking on a corner outside a pub called The Bull called out to me. I didn't hear them; I just saw the ends of their cigarettes blazing in the darkness of the street. One of them crossed the road. I couldn't even make out what shapes his lips were making until he was right up close. Too many witnesses.

'Are you all right, love?' he said. 'Are you lost?'

'Yes,' I said and carried on walking. None of them followed, or tried to touch me. They were just laughing. I heard the word 'wasted'.

I passed a garage and a private car park with overflowing skips. Everything looked the same. Streets were bathed in shadow and the only sounds were the distant hum of motorway traffic and cats or rats dislodging empty bottles from low-lying walls. Smashing noises – ringing out across the night sky as clear as church bells. I walked away from them. Somehow I ended up at the coach station. A line of taxis queued up outside.

'Where to, darling?' said a forty-something guy with brown shaggy hair behind the wheel of the first cab. He folded his paper and placed it on the passenger seat.

'Town centre, please. Glass Pub. Glass Tree Pub.'

'Yeah I know the one,' he said as I clambered in the back.

His voice wasn't Brummie – he sounded Mancunian. The route he took me on wasn't the route I had taken but a more residential one. He tried to make small talk. Asked where I'd been. If anyone was looking after me.

'I don't need looking after,' I told him.

'Shouldn't be out at this time, love. Bad streets at night for a woman alone.'

'I don't care.'

'You been to Beyoncé?' he said, noting my I SLAY T-shirt that Craig had bought me at the arena merch stall. 'Done quite a few runs from there tonight.'

'Yes,' I said.

'The wife likes her. She tried to teach the kids that song of hers. What's it called? The ring one.'

'"Single Ladies",' I said.

'That's it,' he said, patting the picture on his dashboard. It was a small mounted picture frame – three young boys sitting in a pit on a beach, dabs of suncream on their noses. Surrounded by little castles. 'She does it to wind me up. The littl'un, Anthony, he tries to outdo his brothers, doing all the actions, you know—

'Pull over, I'm going to be sick.'

'Oh, Christ,' said the guy, 'hang on then.' He swerved into the nearest car park, pulling the handbrake on beside a large bunch of weeds and a vandalised phone box.

I opened the back door as quick as I could and pretended to throw up in the shadows behind the phone box. The engine was still running. He leant out the window as I started coughing.

'I think the last place you need to go to is a pub, darlin', don't you think? Why don't I take you home, eh? What's your address?'

'I don't want to go home,' I said. 'Take me back to yours and fuck me.'

He laughed. 'Uh, I don't think that's a good idea, darlin', do you?'

'I want you to. I'm ready for you. I'll go down on you. Make me get down on all fours like a dog. Fuck me here, in the car park.'

He laughed again; the way Craig laughs. The way Gavin White would laugh.

The way a bad man laughs.

'Sorry, love, I'm spoken for.'

'So?'

'Come on, get back in and I'll take you home. Now we're not going to have any trouble, are we? I don't want to leave you out here.'

I took the knife out and walked over to the driver's window and, before he could see it coming, I stabbed him once in the throat. In, then out. And again. And out. And in and in and in and in and in – a breathless, starving frenzy. When he'd stopped wriggling, I reached over him and switched off the engine. I opened his driver's door and unclicked his belt and pulled him onto the ground and stabbed him harder and again as he lay there, gasping, a pulpy red mass where a man used to be.

I stood over him and watched his last breaths. Gazing into his eyes. It was just him and me, in the moment. At once, I felt my knickers moisten and my balance restore. I bunned up my hair. I wiped my face and my knife on the hoody and washed my hands over his head with the bottle of water wedged into his footwell pocket. I could see the Odeon lights on the horizon and I knew the hotel was near that.

'Oi! Oi, you! Come back here!'

I posted the wipes and the water bottle and Craig's hoody into various bins along the way. Then me and Beyoncé, fresh from our slaying, walked home, unaided, sucking the blood from our fingertips.

I didn't hear the sirens until I was back outside the hotel. It only dawned on me then that someone, the man who'd called out, had seen me.

Thursday, 30 May

1. *The inventor of headphones packaging*
2. *Sandra Huggins*
3. *Smokers – having a crippling addiction to nicotine not only permits them ten minutes away from work every hour, but also an aroma of old man's pocket.*
4. Daily Mail *articles on side boob, underboob, overboob*
5. *People who bang on and on about carbs being evil – normally sanctimonious gym bunnies like Cleo, and Paul in the office. Because body shaming isn't body shaming when you're trying to save someone's life. Apparently*

Craig didn't move all night – he slept in his clothes diagonally across the bed and I took the sofa bed. After my shower, I had slept soundly too. But I didn't have time to enjoy the moment or feel balanced or happy about it because as soon as my feet hit the bedside carpet, my head began to swim. Another dizzy spell. I sat on the edge of the bed. God, I wanted to die. I could still taste the taxi driver's blood in my mouth. Then the rivers of spit began to flow into my cheeks. Iron in my spit. I ran to the bathroom and threw up everything I'd eaten in the past week.

It was as I was sitting beside the toilet bowl on the freezing white tiles, resting from my fourth major upchuck, that it occurred to me why I could be vomitous.

Womb invader.

I went out as soon as the shops were open and bought another pregnancy test from Boots. All quiet on the Western Front. No police around the front entrance, no police on the main street. No 'Have you seen this woman?' posters up yet.

I did the test. Two lines in the little window.

I immediately went back out to Boots and bought two more tests, one of which was based on pink spots. One spot = not preggo; two spots = preggo.

I did the test. I got two pink spots.

I gulped down another bottle of water from the minibar and tried the third test, which denoted clearly whether you were Pregnant or Not Pregnant – designed for the more promiscuous moron.

Mine. Said. Pregnant. 3–4 weeks.

It might as well have added, *What are you, blind or something? You're pregnant, bitch, DEAL WITH IT.*

'Holy mothering bollocky shitting hell,' I gasped, sitting down hard on the toilet seat. 'But I haven't missed a Pill…'

I couldn't finish the sentence because I *had* missed one. The morning after I slept with AJ for the first time. It just totally went out of my head so I took it later in the day. I didn't think it would matter. Oh my God, I thought. I'm pregnant with AJ's baby. And I only slept with him to keep his mouth shut about the major boo-boo. Now we were having an even majorer boo-boo. He's only a baby himself. He rides a skateboard to work for fuck's sake!

Now, I'm not stupid. It may look as though I've been a silly girl, going around having sex with all (Craig) and sundry (AJ) and not thinking twice about STDs or accidental womb invaders, but I had given it *some* thought. I knew that if this unfortunate little by-product *did* occur, I would be able to deal with it the same way I dealt with *all* uninvited guests. I'd kill it.

Jesus Christ, I've killed five men and two women, haven't I? I can certainly deal with a mass of cells in my abdomen. I put a reminder to 'Call Dr McGreasy' on my phone.

I ordered breakfast to the room and ate it in silence, thinking about my mass of cells. Bloody hell. AJ had got me pregnant. I'd only slept with him so he wouldn't tell anyone about me pulling the knife on him.

The local news came on while Craig was in the shower:

Police have launched an appeal after a taxi driver was stabbed to death last night near the centre of town.

Officers were called to Lombard Street, just before 1 a.m. this morning where emergency services found a man in his early forties and pronounced him dead at the scene. A cordon was placed around the area and forensic officers are carrying out tests. The man has not yet been named.

One local resident, who wished to remain anonymous, said the attack has shook her to the core.

'I looked out the window at about two and saw an ambulance and lots of police cars. All the police had guns. There must have been about thirty police vehicles there.'

[Another local pipes up, a toothless man called Brian.] 'We don't know what's happening. The first thing you think is terrorism. I think that's why all the armed police have come.'

Detective Superintendent David Fry popped up. 'I'd urge anyone in the area last night to get in touch. If anyone has any information at all about what took place here, please call 101 and ask for me.'

'What's this?' said Craig, coming out of the bathroom towel-drying his hair.

'Terrorist attack, City Centre,' I said, then looked down at his hand. He wasn't talking about the stabbing – he was talking about the small white stick he was holding. I'd disposed of the others carefully underneath rolls of tissue in the bin but I'd forgotten the first one and left it on the side of the bath.

I turned the telly off. 'Uh – yeah. Shit. I bought a pregnancy test.'

'You've already done it?'

'Yeah.'

'What do two lines mean?' His eyebrows rose. His jaw went slack. He looked up at me. His eyes filled with tears. 'What do two lines mean, Rhiannon?'

'They mean… that you're going to be a daddy.'

Saturday, 1 June

Since Thursday, Craig's talked about nothing else. He hasn't picked up his PlayStation controller once, nor has he seen Lana. He's also cried at a Huggies commercial and panic-bought a baby monitor he saw on special offer in Sainsbury's. Every single sentence he's uttered has been baby-related in some way.

> *'We'll have to clear out that spare room. What do you fancy in there – paint or wallpaper?'*
> *'My mum'll want to start knitting straight away. Dad'll make us set up an ISA for it.'*
> *'What size is it now?'*
> *'Are you gonna have drugs when you're in labour? Can I have some?'*
> *'I'll take some money out of my savings – pay myself some paternity leave. I wanna be around. My dad wasn't. He was always working. He regrets it now.'*

'*Ooh,* Look Who's Talking Too *is on Sky in a minute.'*
Alternatively, he'll sit there beside me on the sofa, stroking my stomach, which irritates the Golden Shred out of me. Last night he *talked* to it.

'You do realise you're talking to a lamb pasanda and half a naan bread,' I informed him.

'No, I'm not, I'm talking to my little boy. Or girl.'

'It's not even a baby yet.'

'What is it then?'

'A blob.'

'No it ain't. By this stage, its sex has already been decided.'

'Could be gender fluid. Might not *have* a sex.'

'. . . and all his organs are starting to grow. Can we work out your due date?'

'Craig, why are you being such a woman?'

'I'm excited, aren't I?' he said, reaching for his phone. He'd downloaded a pregnancy app. Aren't you excited?'

'Yeah, of course. I'm just a bit freaked out by it all, you know?'

When he went to the loo, I saw twenty-eight missed calls from Lana on his phone over the past four days. He hadn't responded to any of them.

Monday, 3 June

Two more agent rejections in the post, though one of them – a company called Hampton & Peverill said they *'thought it showed promise but needed work on characterisation'*. Assholes. I've Unfollowed them on Instagram.

Booked my doc's appointment – Wednesday 3 p.m. Time to get the little sucker out before Craig starts booking Lamaze classes and whittling a cot.

Linus Sixgill has been diagnosed with intraocular cancer – eye cancer, caught during a routine sight test. Must be why he's been so quiet lately. He's been signed off work pending further tests. I have to organise the Thinking of You card and present, of course. Christ, if he dies, he's going to be a martyr. And *my* Riot Lovers picture will go on his damn epitaph:

Here Lieth Linus Sixgill – Journalist, Riot Photographer Extraordinaire, Husband to an Editor's Daughter, Father to a Something Else, and Colleague to the finest Serial Killing Editorial Assistant the World Has Ever Known.

AJ and I went to our usual spot in the dark woods at lunchtime. He plays dead very well. I wonder how he would look if I whited him out a bit, perhaps blue-tinged his lips with Linus's joke lip balm. AJ would make a truly stunning corpse.

'I'm going to miss you,' I said, holding him against me when we were both sticky and satisfied and awash with languor on the forest floor.

He lifted his head up from my breast. 'Come with me.'

'What?'

'Come with me when I go travelling. We don't have to stay in the UK, we can go anywhere. My visa doesn't run out till December. You could get one too.' He licked down the centre of my breasts, right down to my belly button.

'Um... no.'

'Why not?'

'Because Craig?'

He hitched up my knees and put his head between my thighs. 'Leave him. You're always moaning about him anyway.'

I squeezed his head with my thighs like he was a little walnut. 'Because job?'

He prised his head out and laughed. 'You hate your job. You say it bores the tits off you.' He came back up to my chest. 'Which would be an awful shame if it were true.' He started suckling on my left one. 'God, how does your skin taste so good?'

I laughed. 'You're in fairyland, boy. I can't just bugger off on a whim. I have priorities. Can't you just be satisfied with fucking me?'

'Well, yeah, of course, but what happens when I leave?'

I drew a blank. 'The fucking has to stop, I suppose.'

'But won't you miss me?'

Thankfully, I didn't have to answer because at that second both of us stopped and looked into each other's eyes. We'd heard it at the same time – the snap of a twig, somewhere in the forest around us.

'Come on,' I said and we grabbed our clothes out of the knot in the tree and started getting dressed, hurrying back to the car. We were both unnerved by it, or them, whatever thing had made the twig snap, and, due to the echo, we couldn't be sure of the direction it had come.

On the way back, AJ pulled a leaf out of the back of my hair. He said, 'Do you think someone was watching us?'

'I don't know,' I said. 'I hope so.'

Wednesday, 5 June

1. *Newsreaders who stutter – put your goddamn teeth in and start again*
2. *Old people in doctors' waiting rooms – I don't know what that woman with the leg thing was in for but, my God, did she take an age. And she was about ninety. What's the point?*
3. *Children in doctors' waiting rooms – OK, you have a cough, I get that, stay home, eat Calpol and apply for a new set of lungs. Stop snotting over the* Hello! *magazines so I can't read them*

Police in Birmingham haven't got anyone for the Dean Bishopston murder. Last I heard they were interviewing two prostitutes and a witness has come forward to say they saw 'a blonde woman in the area – black hoody, black boots, running away from the scene'. The wife has made a tearful public appeal. She looked awful. Obligatory cardigan, Primark hair scrunchie, unnamed relative clutching her tissue-less hand. Way too washed out a complexion for black hair and eyebrows.

I'm going to dye *my* hair, I've decided. Back to my roots, I think, but I'm not going back to the Cumberbitch. I'm going to do it myself at home. As the saying goes, blondes might have more fun but brunettes know how to hide the bodies better.

My doctor's appointment was, well, enlightening. He said I'd need something called a medical abortion. No tubes or vaginal rinses – it was 'nice and early' so I'd just take two sets of pills. For some reason, I started to panic.

'What happens then?' I asked.

'Well, after the two visits, the pregnancy will pass.'

I got all short of breath, like I was panicking. 'Pass?'

'You won't be pregnant any more.'

'And that'll be it? So I'll have, like, a period and then no more baby?'

'Indeed,' said the doctor, checking his computer. 'One of the tablets will cause the detachment of the pregnancy from the womb lining and the second tablet will expel it, as it would during menstruation.'

I realised by this point that I *was* panicking. 'It's very tiny right now, isn't it? So it's not like an *actual* baby?'

'It's about the size of a poppy seed.'

Oh, why did he have to say that? Why did he have to use those words?

'Sorry, could I have a glass of water, please?' I asked. He went over to his sink and tore through a plastic tube of paper cups, filled one with water. He handed it to me. My hand was shaking.

'Perhaps you need some more time to process this, Rhiannon. Think about if it's really something you want.'

'No, no, I don't want it, I don't want it,' I said, sipping. 'This wasn't planned. Well, *I* didn't plan it.'

'But Craig *did* plan it?'

'Yeah, he wanted it. I didn't.'

He swallowed and looked down at his notes. 'Rhiannon,

there are people you can talk to about this, professionals who can guide you through the procedures. If this child is a product of forced sexual contact...'

'You mean *rape*?'

He nodded once, not breaking eye contact.

'No, no, it's not like that. I just wasn't all that fussed about having a baby, that was all. Will it hurt, when I take the pills?'

'You might experience some cramping but you can take painkillers.'

'Right,' I said, draining the cup but my mouth was still giving it the full Sahara. 'Poppy seed. Yeah. OK. Sorry, could I have another drink, please?'

'Do you want me to go ahead and book your appointment?' he asked, filling the cup again before getting his calendar up on his computer screen.

'No,' I said. I hadn't planned to say no. I just couldn't bring myself to say yes.

'No?' he said.

'No,' I said. 'I don't want the abortion. I don't know what I want really but I know I really don't want to do that. No, no, no.'

'All right, it's OK, take it easy.'

And I immediately started to calm down. My butterflies began to fly away and I could finally taste the bleachy water I'd been glugging and the relief that washed over me was tremendous. 'I'm sorry for wasting your time.'

It was the cold way he'd said it – *Detachment will occur. It will be expelled.* I couldn't do that. I couldn't see myself with a kid either but I definitely couldn't see myself killing one, however amorphous or poppy-seed-sized it was right now.

My poppy seed.

Jesus, what was wrong with me?! I'd bottled out of killing Wesley Parsons and now I'd bottled out of this. It was when he'd said 'poppy seed'. I just knew. I was awash with it. I walked out of there into the sunlight. Shock. Fear. Feelings; so many feeeeeelings! A 'mass of cells', he'd said. No, it wasn't just a mass of cells. It was *my* mass of cells. *My* poppy seed.

My family.

I cried like a little bitch, the whole way down the street. I had no tissues so I had to put up with snot trails up and down my sleeve until I got to my car and found my Kleenex.

I am the dumbest creature to have ever walked the earth. I'm like a T-Rex. Great bite on it but what the fuck is going on with the stupid tiny hands? How could I have thought the Pill was infallible? How could I think it would be so easy to get rid of a human growing *inside* me? I had taken sundry lives with a cold detachment but I could no more expel this baby than I could cut off my own head. He or she has bested me. He or she has moved in and clung on and said, 'I'm here now, Mum, and there's nothing you can do about it.'

Mummy – why did you cut off that man's penis?

Mummy – why do you take that big knife when you and Tink go walkies??

Mummy – what's that lady's head doing in our freezer?

Oh, God, how can this be happening??? How can someone like me be responsible for a baby? What if I hate it? What if I find myself leaving the window cord dangling too low, or keeping all the plug sockets unprotected or feeding it whole grapes in Pizza Hut just to see it choking? I'll be like Faye Dunaway in *Mommie Dearest*. All 'Scrub, Christina, scrub!!' and 'NO WIRE HANGERS!!!!' Or worse, my kid will turn out to be a maniac and I'll turn into my mum and just check out completely.

For Christ's sake, what am I saying? It's not even a child yet – it's just a full stop stuck to my womb lining.

No, I wouldn't do that. I wouldn't do anything to hurt Sam

or Imelda's twins or Lucille's two youngest, whose names I can never remember.

I don't know what this feeling is but if it's love, I can see why I've kept it at bay for so long. It hurts like a motherfucking dog.

Thursday, 6 June

We're in a heatwave, the weather-woman-who-can't-pro-nounce-isobars says. The Spanish Plume has moved from its Iberian plateau leading to sudden high temperatures. All the fans are on in the office and people have taken to sweating on cue, coming back from lunch with ice creams and having no pride in their own personal appearance whatsoever. Vests and flip-flops are now required attire. Atrocities.

I fell asleep at my desk this morning. First time ever. And my God have I been tempted to before. AJ nudged me, thankfully, before anyone else saw. He also pointed towards the puddle of dribble I'd left on my mouse mat.

I made a conscious decision to try to be happy today, for the sake of the Poppy Seed. I could have done a Kill List but I chose *not* to. I mean, there was the woman who stepped on my foot at the bus stop but she didn't realise so I let her off. Then there was Creepy Ed Sheeran, hanging around the bench opposite the HSBC, where I was getting my cash out. He was probably trying to shag it, like I'd seen him doing before, but each to their own, I thought. If he gets his kicks from benches and jumping out of bushes at lone women shopping in Lidl, well, *Vive la France*.

Me and Craig have a joint week off together next week, before he follows the England team around Holland for the championships and I go on the Weekend That Must Not Be Named. That's why I had to get cash out. And why I walked into town at lunch and raided Superdrug's mini toiletries aisle. I'm excited. I'm happy.

It's all very odd.

Even work was enjoyable (when I was conscious enough to enjoy it). Claudia is away – an all-girls holiday in Croatia with two friends – so me and AJ went back to hers at lunch and he cooked me scrambled eggs and asked if we could try out this position he'd seen in a porn film. It basically involved me doing a headstand and him coming at me and in me from above. I toppled over countless times and my neck had a crick in it all afternoon.

I didn't tell him about the Poppy Seed, though I did throw up in his bathroom. I blamed it on his scrambled eggs.

Craig's desperate to tell everyone about the Poppy Seed but I've said we mustn't until twelve weeks when it's more likely to go full term. Even *I* have downloaded that bloody pregnancy app now. Even *I* am speaking to my own stomach and giving it little nudges and taps and asking if I'm doing the right thing buying McAfee virus scan instead of Norton. I've also not felt any of my usual urges lately. I haven't been in the chat rooms and I haven't walked Tink at night either – Craig has been doing it, without me even asking. Poppy Seed will save the world at this rate.

Lana was puffy-eyed and quiet all day and so obviously avoiding walking past my desk. I heard Craig talking to her on his phone on the balcony after dinner – the dyeing part of my hair didn't take as long as I'd thought. I didn't catch the whole conversation – just a few 'I'm so sorry's and 'We both knew it was coming' and 'I have to do what's best for my family'.

I stood in the doorway as he ended the call.

'What do you think?' I said, swishing my brown hair like Lana does.

'Oh, my God,' he said. 'You look... amazing. What did you do that for?'

I shrugged. 'Just fancied a change.' His face was somewhere else. If I didn't know better, I'd have said he looked worried. It was the same face he made when his mum rang up that time and said she was going to jump off the roof of Morrison's 'cos she couldn't find Jim and the top wouldn't come off the Branston. 'Do you like it?'

'Yeah, I do, I *do* like it. Come here.' He pulled me into a hug and smelled the top of my head, then stood me away from him at arm's length to look at me.

'You're shaking,' I said.

'It's getting chilly out here, shall we go in?'

'You're sweating too. Who was on the phone?'

'Work,' he said. 'That guest bathroom I put in that woman's house has sprung a leak. I said I'd go over and fix it. Shouldn't take long.'

Hmmm, I thought. Maybe a booty call. Maybe a cry for help. I couldn't be sure and my inner jury was on a tea break.

'Are you worried about it?'

'What? Well I don't want to get sued if they flood, do I?' He was all breathless. His top lip was sweating.

'You won't get sued. You'll sort it out, you always do.'

'Yeah, I'll go now.' He grabbed his keys from the coffee table.

'Craig?' I said, his hand on the front door. He turned to me. 'It's only a tap.'

He nodded. 'Yeah, I know. See you in a bit.' He smiled, jogged back towards me and kissed my forehead. 'Love you. Both of you.'

I smiled. But a little bird was going round and round and round my head saying, *Why fuck Lana, why fuck Lana, if you love me so much then why fuck Lana?*

Friday, 14 June

Tonight I said goodbye to Craig for two weeks. I've been looking forward to having the flat to myself for a long time, but after spending the last week together, I think I'm going to miss him. I'm fairly certain that it's over with Lana. It's just a guess but he's been different lately. More attentive, fewer disappearing acts. So I've decided to bury it. Scrub the whole thing from my mind. Him and Lana didn't happen. He only belongs to me. End of. Brand-new baby, brand-new us.

We've done proper coupley things this week; things we haven't done for ages, and I know I haven't updated you once, Dear Diary, but I guess I only need you when I'm sad. When Happy comes along, I've got to hold on to it with both hands.

On Monday, we met Jim and Elaine and drove out to a country pub they both like, then trotted round a National Trust castle that smelled of damp and had about one stick of furniture and some sort of douche canoe that may have once been worn by Mary of Teck. History's never really interested me, beyond the Egyptians and their whole pull-the-brains-out-through-the-nostrils-thing but Craig held my hand throughout our tour. Tink had a run around the gardens with Jim as she wasn't allowed inside the house. Also, I saw an old man fall over and I rushed – yes rushed – to help him up. I didn't even laugh.

Had one text from Daisy – she said Linus is back with an eyepatch, Mike Heath has adopted a kitten, Claudia's back with a tan, AJ is pining for me and getting all the coffee orders wrong and Lana Rowntree from Sales has been in hospital but 'nobody knows why'. I kind of hope it's terminal.

On Tuesday, me and Craig had an outdoor lunch at Cote de Sirène on the harbour side. Went for a boat trip afterwards and took Tink for a run on the beach. The man in the boat gave her a tiny dog life jacket and I started crying – I just thought it was cute. We walked hand in hand again, talking about how things are going to change once Poppy Seed arrives; how he's going to manage work, what names he likes – Jackson for a boy, Jodie for a girl. Jesus, we're starting to look like a building society commercial.

On Wednesday, we drove to the retail park and chose paint for the spare room – B&Q had a sale on and Nigel's already reserved our spare bed for his teenage step-son. Or stepdaughter is it? Can't remember now – someone his ex-wife wants rid of anyway. We even went to IKEA to look at changing tables but Craig came away thinking he would build one from 'proper wood' (as opposed to the imaginary wood you get in IKEA).

On Thursday, we drove over to Wales. I'd told Craig about Honey Cottage and the garden 'big enough for a swing set' and the stables and the nearby primary school and needle after needle had finally pricked the surface of his interest. He didn't say yes but he didn't say no either. So we went and had a look at it, 'out of curiosity's sake'. I think he was a bit surprised to see the estate agent, Bronwen, on the doorstep when we arrived but once he'd got past that, we went in and had a look round. I started crying the moment I stepped over the threshold.

'Oh, are you OK? Did you catch your head on the beam?' came her light Welsh burr.

'No, no.' I smiled. 'I'm just happy to be here,' I said, wiping my cheek as Craig inspected the lintel over the doorway leading into the utility. 'I grew up here.'

'Oh, really?' She smiled, adjusting her glasses. 'How wonderful!'

The paint was peeling badly on all the doors.

'Yeah, my grandparents lived here. It's got the same smell.'

'It's quiet round here, innit?' Craig called out.

'Yes,' she said. 'There's a bit of noise from the stables along the lane sometimes but that's about it.'

We moved into the lounge. The inglenook hearth was exactly as I remembered it, except it was cold and empty and there were no logs piled up.

Craig ducked under the low beam. 'Does that river ever flood?'

'No,' said Bronwen. 'Well, there's nothing on the sheet about flooding.'

'Never flooded in my day,' I said, stroking the windowsill where I used to sit and watch the horses trot down the lane. The wood was cracked in one corner.

'When's your baby due?' she asked, her face pinballing from me to Craig.

'Not until next February,' I said.

Craig looked agog. 'We're not supposed to be telling anyone yet, it's too early.'

'Yeah, well, I'm excited, aren't I?' That seemed to shut him up and he walked to me and enveloped me in a bear hug.

'That's all right then, I suppose.' He smiled, wandering off to check beams and knock on walls.

'It's a proper family home, as you'll already know,' said Bronwen. 'The nearest primary school is in walking distance, just down the lane. You said you're a writer too?'

'From time to time,' I said.

'There's a bedroom upstairs that has been recently converted into a study. Good electrical points. They've finally got superfast broadband round here as well so that'll be a boon. The previous occupant was a writer as well and it's about the only room that doesn't need too much work on it.'

'That's great,' I said. 'Yes, I can see myself writing here. I can imagine having nice Christmases here.'

'Oh, yes, you could have gorgeous Christmases here. Roaring log fire, crisp walks in the countryside.'

'Bliss,' I said.

For a second, I saw Granddad's coffin in front of the fireplace. End to end. Hands crossed. Black suit. Make-up smudge on the lapel. Stitched-up eyes. But when I blinked, the coffin had gone. It was just the cold empty fireplace again.

A blank canvas, waiting for us to start painting our future on it.

Craig smiled, a broad all-encapsulating smile, looking down at my stomach. 'Can we have a minute to talk through a few things, do you mind?'

'Oh, sure, sure,' said the agent. 'I'll just be outside.'

When she had left, he said, 'Are you out of your mind?'

'Yes, can I help you?'

'What are you doing?'

'I want us to live here, Craig. The asking price was dropped again recently. We could *so* afford it. With my share of Mum and Dad's and the sale of your flat, we could buy it outright. We wouldn't need a mortgage or anything.'

'We haven't even talked about moving, let alone to somewhere like this.'

'What's wrong with this?'

He shook his head. 'Well, for a start it's right out in the sticks.

For another thing it's in another *country*. And while we're at it, it's a wreck.'

'It's not a wreck. Just think of the possibilities. There's a freshwater river, riding stables, a beach just down the road. Look at the size of the garden. We could grow our own veg! Keep chickens. Maybe a goat. Have flower beds all round the edge. I know the inside needs doing up but we could do that, together. It could be our project.'

He shook his head again. 'This is *crazy*.'

'It's my dream,' I told him. 'I don't want to bring the baby up in a smoky old town where he's breathing in all the fumes from the road and goes to school with kids who've got hypodermics sticking out of every arm.'

'It's a county town in the West Country, Rhee. Hardly the Bronx.'

'You know what I mean,' I said, pressing myself against him and rubbing the backs of his ears – always a winner. 'Yes, it's crazy, no we haven't talked about moving, and yes leaving everyone we know will be hard at first but we'll make new friends.'

'Oh, I get it. This is hormones talking, isn't it? I read about this on that app. Rational goes out the window when you're expecting.'

'Screw rational, Craig. We've been rational for four years and we're still treading water. You're bored, I'm bored. Let's do it. Let's just throw caution to the wind and move here. Raise our family *here*. I'll write books and grow veg and you'll pick up loads of local building work…'

He pulled back. 'This is the happiest I've seen you in months.'

'I think we could both be happy here. That's all.'

There was a pub within walking distance called The Heron so we went there for a heart-to-heart over scampi and chips. We didn't manage to iron anything out and he said when he comes back from Holland we'll *really* look into it properly. Bronwen says she'll keep us informed if she gets any other interest in the meantime but I've got a squiggly feeling in my chest that it's ours for the taking!

On Friday, we took Tink into town to get her nails clipped and Craig bought me a proper engagement ring – an 18-carat white-gold solitaire with 'Forever' engraved into it on the inside. It sparkles. We bought Tink a little diamond collar in a pet shop too so she wouldn't feel left out.

And on Saturday we FINALLY did a car boot sale! Made nearly £140 from junk we had stuffed in the spare room wardrobe. Had a Nando's to celebrate.

I checked his phone when he was taking the rubbish out – three texts from Lana Rowntree:

I'm going to do it again if you don't call me.

Baby, please talk to me. I can't stop thinking about you.

Don't think I won't do it. I've got more pills left you know, I will, I mean it. It's not fair to leave me like this.

He didn't respond to any of them. The next time I checked, they had all gone and so had her number.

He left hella early in his van as they had to catch the 9 a.m. ferry from Dover. He kissed me and lifted my T-shirt to kiss my belly before he went. He had to pick up Eddie and Gary on the way and they were meeting seven lads at Dover and for the games they *haven't* got tickets for, they are just going to 'sit outside and watch it on the big screens, drinking beer and having a laugh'. This comment normally would have annoyed the phelanges off me but not today. Everything seems brighter today. Like a wall has come down and I can finally see the sunrise beyond.

Sunday, 16 June

This past week alone I have found myself crying to...

1. *a commercial for Dogs Trust;*
2. *the idiot savant who won* Countdown;
3. *a CBeebies Book at Bedtime, read by David Tennant*
4. *a new strawberry appearing on my pot plant*
   and
5. *Tink doing 'Shake a Paw' for the First. Time. Ever*

The flat feels lonely without Craig. Tink's taken to sleeping with one of his socks. I keep talking to the Poppy Seed. I asked it this morning if it wanted Crunchy Nut or Shreddies for breakfast. Neither, it said. It wanted toast, four slices of, with peanut butter and a sliced banana.

Just like my daddy has.

Oh, fuck. Think I'm really starting to lose my mind.

Monday, 17 June

I'm not six weeks preggo yet and the sleepiness has well and truly kicked in. Today and yesterday I woke up, took Tink out around the complex, then went back to bed for an hour. I just want to sleep all the time.

I'm also forgetting EVERYTHING. Coffee orders – out of my head. Mid-sentence, I forget what I'm saying. And piss! I'm pissing for England! I can't even survive the drive into work without stopping off at the Drive-Thru McDonald's on the retail park to empty my blad. I'm sure every woman gets this when they're knocked up but I've never really taken much notice of what they've said before because it hasn't interested me. Now I'm trawling Mumsnet for advice: *Is it normal for morning sickness to kick in at lunchtime? Why do I need to piss every twenty minutes? Why do I wake up more tired than when I went to bed? How can I have just eaten half a loaf of bread and still be hungry?*

Can't trawl on there for too long though – it's like PICSO HQ.

And everything is making me cry. Everything. Daisy brought me back a lemon and poppy seed muffin from lunch and I burst into tears. I couldn't even tell her the real reason so I made up some shit about an old relative dying of a stroke after eating a muffin. She bought it anyway and Claudia gave me the afternoon off.

Lana wasn't in today. Nobody knows why.

Also – tit ache. MAJOR tit ache. They KILL! I can't lie on my front any more in bed and God help the next man who touches them – he may have to go the way of the Sabatier.

No, no, I've given all that up now. I'm being a responsible mother. I'm nesting and looking after myself and looking on the positive side. No watching of unsavoury Channel 5 programmes. No chat-rooming. No fishing. Do I miss it? I don't know. I'm too tired to miss anything right now.

It's precisely 6.26 p.m. There's been an earthquake some-where. Loads dead. Tink has just pissed on my strawberry plant. I'm going to bed for an hour.

Tuesday, 18 June

That hour turned into all night – missed dinner and everything! Woke up ravenous and ate two smoked salmon bagels and two and a half bowls of Crunchy Nut Cornflakes.

Phoned Craig at lunch. He's having a good time.

'That's so awesome,' I said. 'I can't wait to see you.'

'Me either. How's it going over there? Are you enjoying yourself?' Listen to me being all considerate. Told you I'd turned a page *brushes lapel*.

'Yeah, it's great,' he said. 'But for a few assholes.'

'Oh, really?'

'Didn't you see it on the news? There was some trouble at last's night's game. It's all over the papers here, not that I can read Dutch.'

'I didn't catch the news last night. I went to bed early.'

'Oh, well, a load of English lads went a bit nuts in the town square. A combination of too much beer and too much sun, I think. They've arrested dozens. I'm keeping my nose clean, don't worry.'

'Good,' I said. 'We miss you, Daddy.'

Unfortunately, late this afternoon, another boo-boo – AJ guessed about the baby. It was his last day today as well. I so *nearly* got away with it. I was in the staffroom, grabbing a bottle of water and I was trying hard not to vomit as he plated up his last ever doughnuts and stirred his last ever batch of coffees for the editors.

'Can I tempt you to a hot milky beverage?' he hammed, biting the top of my ear.

'Ooh, no thanks,' I said, as though he'd just offered to sacrifice a baby goat in front of me.

'You OK?'

'Yeah, fine, why?'

'You love my coffee. You said my lattes are better than Starbucks.'

'I feel a bit sick today, that's all. Bad curry last night.'

'Thank God for that. Had a horrible feeling you were preggo or something.'

He must have heard my tiny gasp because he almost dropped his doughnuts. 'You're not...'

'No.'

He dropped a teaspoon and it clattered to the floor. 'You are, aren't you?'

'Uh... well, a bit.'

'Oh, fuck!' he cried, closing the staffroom door. 'Is it...? Did I do that? Oh, shit. Oh, shit shit shit. Claudia's gonna kill me! My mum's gonna kill me!'

'It's very early so I haven't told anyone yet. Please don't tell, AJ, I mean it.'

'How far gone are you?'

'A month. Or so. Nearly six weeks.'

'And... it's mine? Like, deffo?'

'Afraid so. The dates work out. But you're the only one who knows that.'

'Oh, my God.' I pulled a chair out for him to sit down. 'I'm supposed to be leaving on Friday. My trains are all booked.'

'Oh, shit, yeah,' I said. 'I'm supposed to buy your present and card. Completely forgot about that.'

'You were on the Pill?'

'I was,' I said. 'It didn't work. Anyway, Craig thinks it's *his* baby and that's the way things are going to stay, all right?'

'No, it's not all right. Crikey, this is huge, Rhee. I need to be involved.'

'No, you don't. It wouldn't work anyway. We have fun, sure, but you're hardly father material.'

'I'm nineteen.'

'Exactly. Why don't I just buy you a Kylo Ren doll or something instead, yeah?'

'That's not funny. Don't patronise me.'

'Craig's nearly thirty with his own business. He's solid, dependable. Trustworthy. You work for Minimum Wage, live with your auntie, and you ride a skateboard. I don't even know what your real name is. We've got this, seriously. Step off.'

'It's not his baby, it's *mine*.' It was the first time I'd seen AJ actually say something without smiling. He was all strong and determined, all of a sudden, like he'd aged a decade in the last two minutes. And then I remembered all his 'My-dad-left-my-mum-when-I-was-a-kid' crap and my heart sank. Of *course* he'd want to stick around for it. Major boo-boo, Rhee. *Major* boo-boo, rising to Lieutenant General boo-boo of the Rhiannon Light Infantry. I should have kept my big fat trap shut and drank his coffee and then ran to throw up in the Ladies' like a good psychopath.

'This is all wrong. I have to be here for you.'

'I don't need you. Forget I said anything. Happy island-hopping. Happy... whatever else it is you're doing for the next six months.'

'Why are you being like this? Hey, we need to talk.'

'No, we don't,' I said. 'This is happening to me, not you.'

He shook his head. 'I know I'm not in any fit state to be a dad but... I want to try. This is too huge.'

'This conversation never happened. And if you tell anyone about this, I...'

He looked up at me. I could see it in his eyes, remembering the night I told him about killing the man in the park. Remembering the look on his face – the look that said I was a monster and he needed to get away from me. The Poppy Seed was my bargaining chip here and I needed to buy his silence.

'I'm giving you a Fire Exit here. You don't have to do anything. You're young, free and single. Fly. Be free. I'll never contact you, I promise.'

'It's Austin. That's my real name. Austin James.' It was only when he started crying that I left.

Bloody wuss.

Still no Lana at work today either. Bollocky Bill said she's 'away' and Carol thinks she's 'ill'. God knows what's going on there. Wonder if she's gone to Holland to track down Craig?

Wednesday, 19 June

1. *ISIS* – MasterChef's *been cancelled AGAIN, thanks to a bloody uprising in Kenya. British people were killed so, of course, it mattered enough for a Panorama special*
2. *Newsreaders who emote too much – just tell me about the school shooting, don't tell me how to feel about it*
3. *Shouty market stall holders – there was a French foods market on in the centre of town today (I have to do the write-up on it, of course). Excellent crepes but ferme la fucking bouche, Monsieur, there's a good chap.*

We officially exchanged contracts on Mum and Dad's house this morning – the money should be in my account within the next week, once the solicitor has done his bit of soliciting. I don't know how much but it's in the region of £300,000. Found out from Claudia that Lana Rowntree's gone off on sick leave. She hasn't left the country, apparently, and they didn't say exactly what had brought it on but Claudia tapped the side of her head as she told me.

Wandered around the French market that's popped up in the High Street. Ate a crepe. Threw up said crepe in the toilets when I got back to the office.

Tried to call Craig but it went to voicemail. He hasn't called all day. I would start to worry but I'm so tired I don't think I've got it in me. I wonder if anyone will notice if I just shut one eye for ten minutes.

*

I woke up to my phone buzzing on my desk. It was Craig, phoning from a police station in Amsterdam. He's been arrested.

'*What? What for?*' I shrieked.

'Violent conduct.'

'What violent conduct?'

'There was a skirmish in the town last night [England lost 3–0] and I was a bit pissed and I threw a bottle – only a plastic one mind – and it bounced off a riot shield. They slung me into a van and brought me here.'

'Is it just you who got arrested?'

'No, Nigel's in here as well but they won't let us talk to one another. Listen – I'll be all right but just in case they come round to the flat, can you flush the rest of my pot? It's in a box under the electric blanket in the wardrobe. Just a precaution.'

'They're not going to come here, that's silly,' I said.

'Please, Rhee, I daren't take the risk. I don't want a criminal record. It'll affect our chance of a mortgage for the cottage if we need one. Please, baby?'

'You're not going to get a record just for throwing a bottle at a riot shield.'

'Well, it didn't exactly hit a riot shield. It sort of ricocheted and hit a kid.'

'A kid?'

'Yeah. And it wasn't plastic. I lied. It was glass. He needed stitches.'

'God's sake, how could you be so stupid?'

'I know, I know. I haven't slept a wink. Bloody stinks in here.'

'Serves you right.'

'I know. The guy from the British Embassy says me and Nige could be banned from the Netherlands for life.'

'Bang goes the holiday home in Amsterdam then, doesn't it?'

'I have to go. I'll call you back tomorrow, all right? And don't tell my parents – not yet, they'll only worry. It'd finish my mum off at the moment, you know what she's like. Kiss the Poppy Seed for me. I love you.'

'Love you too, dickhead.'

Ugh, men! Can't live with them, can't hog-tie 'em and throw them into a ditch off the M5.

Friday, 21 June

Jim and Elaine collected Tink first thing – Elaine had been up since four, packing for their day at the beach. They didn't stay long – they never do – and they certainly won't drink my coffee or tea because I don't have 'their milk' and Elaine can't drink out of mugs. Neither does she do well in close-quarters accommodation. Craig hadn't called either of them to tell them about his little sojourn at His Majesty's Pleasure in Tulip Land yet. He said it would finish his mother off. I have to say, I was quite intrigued to find out what that would look like.

They were barely in the lift with Tink on her lead when AJ appeared at the end of the corridor, large rucksack on his back.

'The fuck are you doing here?' I asked him just as the lift doors pinged closed. 'Who let you in?'

'I dunno, some bloke. One of your neighbours.'

'That was my soon-to-be parents-in-law, you dickhead.'

'I know. I waited for them to go. Can I come in? I've got something to ask you.'

And boy did he ask me.

He held my face in his hands. He kissed my lips, fully but softly, then pulled back. 'I want us to be a family. Now you've sold your parents' place we'll have money to just bum around.

We can be free *together*. See some of the UK, see Europe and Russia, then in six months' time, I'll go back to Oz and apply to live here permanently.'

I turned round and walked back into the flat. He followed, closing the door. 'I don't want to "bum around". And I don't want to live with you. I want to put down roots. I want a family and a cottage with a river running past it.'

'You could have that with me.'

'No, I couldn't. You want to travel. *I* don't. I want Craig.'

'Well, that's another thing – he's been seeing someone. Lana from work.'

'Yeah, I know. So?' I said.

'Lana and Craig,' he said again, like I hadn't heard the first time. They're having an affair. He's been two-timing you. Having an affair. Shagging around.'

'I said, *I know*. Now can I please go and have my shower? I stink like last night's chicken carcass.'

He dropped his rucksack to the floor. 'What do you mean, you *know*?'

'I've known about it since Christmas. How did you find out?'

'Doesn't matter… you've known about this for six months?'

'Yeah.'

He laughed. 'And you still want him?'

I shrugged.

'Why?'

'I don't know what you mean.'

He shook his head. 'Rhiannon, I've loved you since the first moment I met you. You're *all* I think about. When I'm talking to other women, I'm comparing them to you.'

'I see you talking to Lana and Daisy all the time at work. You flirt with both of them.'

'It's only talking, that's all. Daisy's just a mate. And Lana's… well, she's batshit.'

'How do you know *I'm* not batshit?'

'Maybe I don't care. Maybe I'm crazy about you. I've thought about nothing else since you told me about the baby. I want to be a dad.'

'You want to travel, AJ. You told me once you never want to put down roots. The last thing you want is a ball and chain around your ankle.'

'I've changed my mind.'

'So what are you going to do then? Move permanently here and get a full-time office job? No more surfing, no more travelling. Gonna exchange your skateboard for a nice hatchback?'

'I wish you loved me half as much as I love you. I wish you'd give me a chance.'

'It's a crush, that's all. You don't love me. I'm fundamentally unloveable. I'm happy with Craig. He lets me be me. '

And then he got angry. I'd never seen AJ angry before. He kicked his rucksack across the wooden floor, sending it crashing against the occasional table and making the lamp wobble. 'You won't say it, will you? You never say it back.'

'It's just not the same for me.'

'Where is he? Where's Craig now?'

'Holland. He's watching all the England matches. Things run to their usual form, he'll be home this time tomorrow.'

'Right, well I'm gonna tell him I know. And make him tell you too.'

'What will *that* achieve?'

'It'll get this out in the open. It'll force him to make a choice.'

'He *has* made a choice – me. He's deleted her number from his phone. I checked. All this is pointless.'

'I'll tell him about the baby then. I'll tell him it's mine.'

My chest tightened. I fixed my eyes on him. 'No, you bloody won't.'

'I will. I swear I will.'

'Have you told Claudia? About the baby?'

'No, not yet. I wanted to wait for you. I wanted us to tell her together.'

'Well that's not happening.'

'She's got a good lawyer.'

'Is that a threat?'

'No, of course not. I just know he'll be able to tell me my rights, that's all. I want to be involved.'

'What if I don't want you involved?'

'You can't just decide that. That baby is half mine.'

'No, it's all *mine*. It's *my* poppy seed.'

'What?'

'Just fuck off, AJ. And take your blackmail with you. I need a coffee.'

'I'm not going anywhere. We have to talk this through. Wait – I thought you were off coffee?' He lingered by the breakfast bar. 'Look at me, Rhee.' I looked at him. 'We could be your family, me and Auntie Claude. She'd love it, you know how desperate she is to have a baby about the place. The nursery's there, waiting. It'll be perfect! It could work, I know it could.'

I grabbed the kettle and filled it from the tap. 'Yeah? How?'

'When we're done travelling, we can live with her.'

'Live with the Gulp Monster? Christ, no.' I unhooked a mug from the mug tree.

'I love you, Rhiannon. I want you with me. I don't know how many more times I can say it.'

'Why do you love me?'

'Huh? I don't know, I just do. I can't help it.'

'Just go, just leave me be.'

The kettle began to reach temperature. I could feel everything slipping away from me. My hands on the rope sliding. My feet kicking around for footholds but finding nothing but air. Craig meant Happiness. Craig meant Honey Cottage. Craig meant a future. And now there was this lanky Australian standing in front of it all, refusing to get out of the way, telling me I could come and live with him and The Gulp Monster, who'll call me Sweetpea and be all micro-managing and 'Oh, the baby looked like he needed a bath so I gave it one, hope that's all right,' and 'Oh, the baby was crying so I thought I'd give it a breastfeed, hope that's all right,' and 'Oh, I've enrolled the foetus at private school and measured her up for a uniform, hope that was all right.'

UGH! No. No. No. No. No.

It was like a fog clearing in my mind. Once I'd decided, that was that.

'You know I only shagged you to keep your mouth shut, don't you, AJ?'

'What?'

'So you wouldn't blab what I told you about Gavin White.'

The smile began to disappear from his face. 'Don't say that. I told you I wouldn't tell anyone.'

'And how long will *that* secret last? Till the next time I piss you off?' I opened the drawer and grabbed a teaspoon.

'No, of course not.'

'Do it. Tell the world, I don't care. You can tell them about Dan Wells, too, if you like.' I opened the fridge to get the milk. I put it down beside the knife block.

'Who? The guy in the canal?'

'Yeah. And Julia Kidner. And Derek Scudd. And the two men in the blue van. And my sister's boyfriend...'

'What?

The kettle clicked. The water boiled. The steam rose. My hand on the handle.

'It was me,' I said, lifting the kettle. 'I killed them all.'

And then I pulled off the lid and threw the water in his face.

*

There's never an Ebola outbreak going round when you want one, is there? It's just turned 2.48 p.m. and they've opened the vodka and are singing 'I Will Survive' at a volume somewhere between church bell and AK-47. I'm pretending to join in and laugh along but mostly I'm checking 'important emails for work' as the ancient minibus Lucille has hired rattles along the motorway.

Anni pulled out at the last minute, the bitch – Sam's got a rash – so that's my chance of intelligent conversation up the Swannee. I'm sitting beside a girl I've never met before called Gemma (or Jenna, I didn't actually hear) and she is apparently Pidge's best friend from Guides or Brownies or somewhere, again, I didn't hear because the bus is old and clanky and there's a deep-rooted smell of Chewits making me gag. Pidge is sat next to her. All the 'bad girls' are at the back flashing their tits at passing cars – Lucille's sister Cleo, normally a clean-eating fitness freak but today on vodka lollies and shots, plus Mel's work friends Bev and Sharon, two short, fat fifty-somethings with Imelda's Gary Barlow fetish. Bev has her children's names tattooed around her neck like a mayoral chain of office; Sharon has some West Ham symbol on her calf. Or it could be a swastika.

Not one of them has mentioned my new hair colour, even though I have pointedly remarked on all their various straightenings and Kardashi-extensions. Blister-filled pus-warthogs from Hell.

Cannot find the Happy in this situation. Not one bit of it.

Imelda and Pidge's Auntie Steph – who I surmise is in her early fifties but could easily pass for sixty – completes our throng. She's thin, short and tanned to a crisp, owing to a lifelong obsession with sunbeds. Asleep, she looks like a corpse painted with wood stain. Her opening gambit when the bus picked her up from her house on Magdalene Street was 'I had sex with twins last night. Brothers. It were magical.' I despised her on sight.

*

The minibus has stopped at the services for petrol (and a piss for me). Thanks to the Poppy Seed, I can't even drink my troubles away so I'm swigging from a decoy bottle of Smirnoff filled with water. I'm just hoping nobody asks for some because then they'll find out and I don't want that conversation yet. I'm still not fully on board with this whole One-of-the-Gang thing. At least, not with *this* gang. I do not want not be here. I want to be home. The vodka lollies are out of the cool box now.

God, I wish I could drink. Damn you, Poppy Seed! No, I didn't mean that.

*

We're on the road again. Just had to stop again at another services so I could have a piss and Cleo could violently expel six vodka ice lollies into a hedgerow.

*

A raucous Take That medley has started up at the back of the bus. And the smell of old Chewits and vodka barf is strong. And I can't even open a bloody window because they've all had their hair done. I actually hope we crash.

*

Finally made it to Toppan's Holiday Camp an hour later than scheduled, which meant that, tragically, we'd missed today's

Bucking Bronco (cue boos and hisses). Luckily, it's on again tomorrow (cue cheers and applause).

As I stepped down off the bus, one thing became clear – this was a wilderness and we were the fresh meat. All around us were snaking gravel paths with signposts that read TO THE FOOD or TO THE ARCADES or TO THE CLUB and along these paths walked large groups of men in England shirts, long shorts and flip-flops, wearing wrap-around shades, holding bottles and yelling romantic bon mots, such as 'All right, gorgeous, get your tits out while the sun's shining!' and 'Oi oi, the Bukkake Party's here, lads!'.

And to my never-ending cringe, most of my party obliged. Auntie Steph had copped off with an eighteen-year-old who was leering in the back window before we'd even disembarked. I haven't seen her since. They're all worried. I hope she's dead.

*

I'm in the toilet. I've just checked into Chalet 10, which I'm sharing with Pidge and Gemma/Jenna (note they've put the three quietest together.) It's small, stinks of chlorine and the beds were clearly leftovers from a refurb at Wormwood Scrubs – hard, metal-framed, squeaky. I daren't look at my mattress.

You can't move around here without some comment or a hand around your shoulder or your arse. And the worst part about it is the PICSOs are bloody loving it, which has properly highlighted how little I have in common with them – this place just isn't me. It's *all* them. I don't do socialising, I don't do drunken feel-ups and I don't do noise and this place is a honeypot for all of that. Why do I keep up The Act again? Someone remind me? Oh, yeah, that's right, I HAVE NO ONE.

Imelda (who is now in her weekend outfit of short white dress, feather boa, cowboy hat with veil, thigh-high boots, L-plates and a Bride-to-Be sash) has snogged three blokes already (her first dare is to kiss as many as she can in two days) and the Ronseal Corpse Auntie Steph has emerged again, clamped to the lips of a nineteen-year-old plumber from Warrington, who is so short he looks like her little boy.

If I were to do a Kill List here, it would be infinite. I would start with my friends.

*

Well, that was nice – afternoon cocktails in the bar accompanied by an impromptu Full Monty from a pack of 'saucy butlers' and a penis helicoptering four inches from my face. If only he knew what happened to the last guy who did that.

Talking of windmills, there's still no news from Craig.

The one good/bad thing about being out with the PICSOs is that they don't take much notice of anything I do so when they were ordering the drinks, I could go back to the barman and say, 'Make my Bend Over Shirley Temple a virgin please, kind sir' and they didn't twig. So far, so sober.

Bridezilla and the others had the most crude-sounding drinks on the menu – two Red-Headed Sluts for Bev and Sharon, Sex in a Glass for Lucille, a Leg Spreader for Cleo, Pidge and Gemma/Jenna had Golden Showers (they are loosening up by the minute) and Imelda went for a Tight Snatch and a Bang Me Senseless on the rocks. They've all gone over to the Laser Quest. I've said I feel sick from all the 'vodka' and I'm sitting on my squeaky bed wondering how easy it would be to fake my own death. How the hell does someone like me have fun in a place like this? Ugh.

*

CJ SKUSE

I'm sitting beside the pool. All the others are in it and everyone's got their tits out. It's like a tit soup. I'm so done with these people. I'd walk out now if I wasn't so bloody far from home. I have enough money for a cab. If I leave now, I could be home in time for... fuck, I'm being roped into a limbo competition. Pray for me.

*

It's 7.27 p.m. and we're all in our chalets getting ready for a night of drinking, dancing and Pass the Gonorrhoea. (I said I was on so I couldn't go swimming.) We've presented Imelda with her surprise scrapbook and done some predictable Ann Summers-sponsored games – Who Can Eat the Chocolate Penis First (won by Lucille), Who Can Lick All the Whipped Cream Off the Random Bloke First (won by Mel) and Strip Twister – don't know who won that. Don't really care if my heart stops beating right fucking now actually.

Apart from the odd 'spoilsport' comment from Imelda for not joining in much (I did limbo what more does she want?), I think The Act is intact but, to be honest, who cares? I'm now off out to do karaoke dressed up to gunnels in static fabrics which electrocute me every time I brush past someone woolly.

Still haven't heard from Craig. He'd have texted if he was out, wouldn't he? Maybe they've charged him.

*

It's 2.03 a.m. Pidge is lying with her face in a plate of chips. I haven't noticed it before but she's ugly. It's not even as though the nice person she is can make up for that either – she's deeply fucking ugly. There's nothing redeeming at all. Her nose is big, her eyes are piggy, her face is long. And her farts smell of roast pork.

Gemma/Jenna is snoring her head off, her skin blue from getting off with a body-painted Smurf. I vanished midway through the Sing-a-Longa-Abba-Thon to sit by the pool, splashing my toes in the water and talking to the Poppy Seed. All I could hear was people shagging in the surrounding foliage. The slurp of a tongue, the odd rhythmic moan, the rapid slippery fingering of a sixty-year-old woman's bucket fanny. It's like being in a Renaissance painting here, it really is.

*

Oh, God, this is like a bloody nightmare. Only nightmares end and this just won't. My so-called friends are loving it. I am not. I'm going to leave. Fuck The Act. I'd like to officially scrape off the People I Can't Scrape Off this weekend. We're moving to Wales soon anyway and then I'll never see them again with any luck.

Or maybe I'll kill them all in their beds, one by one. Stab, stab, stab, stab, stab, stab, stab stab stab. And an extra one for Auntie Steph, just she deserves it.

Saturday, 22 June

I chickened out of leaving. I've hardly slept due to bed squeak, strange smell in the bathroom and Gemma/Jenna vomiting in the sink most of the night. I tried doing my 'It's all right shh shh' bit and rubbing her back but I was really phoning it in to be honest. Craig's mobile is still switched off and I've had no messages in the night. Where the bloody hell is he? He knows I'm stressed out with this. So inconsiderate.

Also, the Poppy Seed is six weeks old today, but, to my sadness, I can't call him/her Poppy Seed any more because it's not the size of a poppy seed any more – according to the app, it's now as big as a grain of rice. So Happy Sixth Week of Growth Day, Grain of Rice.

I've rung Jim and Elaine – they're taking Tink to the beach today. Jim texted me a picture of the ball they've bought her which is about three times her size. They haven't heard anything from Craig either. They don't even know he was arrested.

Everyone's outside on the benches, muted in hangover, drinking Lambrini from paper cups and eating variety pack cereal from the boxes. We've brought half an off-licence with us but nobody remembered milk.

*

We've hit the beach. It's crowded and full of screaming children who keep knocking over my sandcastles and peeing in my moat (OK, one of them peed in my moat) so I've resigned to sitting back and taking in the scenery under a parasol while making a few notes. God, I'm turning into Samuel What's-his-face. Him who hid the cheese.

*

It's mid-afternoon and I'm watching five grown women spring about on a bouncy castle on a soundtrack of Shania Twain.

Auntie Steph has been back to the group, briefly, to say she's on her 'ninth shag and counting'. She nicked a couple of Lucille's fags, asked Bev for some change for the condom machine and buggered off again.

Still getting some serious side eye from Imelda and I've heard a me-related muttering about 'wet blankets', so I'm pretty sure I'm going to have to tell them all about Grain of Rice before too long. Dammit.

*

I've told them all about Grain of Rice. The reaction was as I expected:

IMELDA: I knew it, didn't I say she'd be preggers by my wedding day!
LUCILLE: Oh, congratulations, babe! That's amazing! You must be thrilled!
CLEO: Don't have a boy, for God's sake. Girls are so much easier.

BEV: It's gonna change your life, love. Most important job a woman can do. Forget careers and money – family is everything. My Carl tore me from earhole to arsehole though, so, for Christ's sake, have have any drugs on offer.
SHARON: No, don't have any drugs when you're in labour, trust me, it's so worth it. You don't ever bond properly with your baby if you have pain relief. I had a Caesarean with my Kimberley. We've never bonded.
GEMMA/JENNA: Aww, that's so great! Congratulations! When's it due?
PIDGE: You'll be an amazing mummy, Rhiannon. I'm so happy for you.

It took a lot for Pidge to say that, so soon after losing hers. She put her arms around me and gave me a proper squeezing hug. Then she whispered in my ear…

'You don't have to feel bad about me. I'm so pleased for you, matey.'

'Thank you,' I said.

Now this seems like a touching scene – a recently bereaved mother passing on her congratulations to a recently announced mum-to-be. But it's not. Because Pidge has now taken it upon herself to follow me around like a frigging shadow, making sure I'm never on my own lest I fall over, run into any perverts or, God forbid, the camp mascot Toppy the Toucan, who I've repeatedly announced I'm going to stab in the face if he does his 'Toptastic Tango' near me again.

*

The bouncy castle's been cordoned off until further notice – someone's puked on it. Bev says it wasn't her but I could smell it on her breath at lunch when she was reaching for a menu.

And it's been decided that I don't have to wear my prostitute outfit this evening. Apparently it's 'not right for an expectant mummy' so I'm wearing my red summer vest, white pedal pushers and black wedges instead. Everybody else looks like extras from *Chicago* and I look like I'm going to a barbecue at my gran's house. I feel even more excluded than ever. Pidge has gone to the loo so I'm going for a walk along the seafront while the bitch is occupied.

*

There was a fortune-teller on the seafront, past all the arcades and ice-cream parlours, in a little shopfront on her own. The shop was festooned with the usual crap – purple gypsy-chic shawls, incense sticks and scarves with marijuana leaves on them. The place wreaked of joss sticks, BO and, let's face it, desperation. A middle-aged red-haired woman with chronic emphysema, smoker's mouth creases and the most alarmingly drawn-on eyebrows sat in the back of the shop at a small round table. In the middle was the obligatory crystal ball on a claw-footed stand.

'Good afternoon,' she said, clearly putting on a Grand High Witch accent as she put out her fag on a foil ashtray. 'I'm Madame Gwendoline. How are you today?'

'I'm all right, thanks,' I replied. 'How much is it?'

'For Tarot reading? Or do you wish to have your aura read or your palm?' The accent was slipping – now she sounded like Manuel from *Fawlty Towers*.

'Uh, just Tarot, please.'

'Fifteen pounds.' She held out her hand. 'Cross my palm with ssssilver.'

'Yeah yeah.'

I gave her my last £20 and she presented me with my fiver

change and gestured for me to sit down opposite as she collected up the stack of large, dog-eared cards and handed them to me. 'You must shuffle these.'

'Why do I have to do it?'

'Because it's your life we're dealing with.'

'Fair enough.' I shuffled them the way my dad always used to when we played rummy, cutting them in the middle, then flicking up the edges so the two stacks sliced into each another. She watched me throughout.

'I want you to select five cards and hand them to me but don't look at them.'

I did as she said and she fanned out the five cards in a rainbow. I made a mental note not to give away any tells at all, then accidentally pulled my top free of my stomach. She smiled at me and turned over the first.

'Ah, yes, this card comes up a lot.'

'A hanged man,' I said. 'What does that mean?'

'It means you are at a crossroads. You don't know which way to turn. Lots of people who come to vissssssit me are at a crossroads; in their work or their relationships. You are bored at work, I thiiiiiiink.'

'Well, yeah. But most people are, aren't they?'

'You are looking for change, actively seeking out excitement.'

'Yeah, but most people are,' I repeated.

'Maybe you are looking for excitement in the wrong places.' Her head tilted slowly up at me and she stared into my eyes for the longest time. 'This card is telling me it's at home as well. You are looking for something different there. You are trying to mooooove on. Making plans, yes?'

'Okaaaay,' I said. A black cat sauntered in and started meowing at my feet. I reached down and it licked my fingers with its rough little tongue. I missed Tink.

'Love is tricky for you. You are in a long-term relationship, yesssss?'

'Yesssss.'

'And there is another?'

She meant AJ. 'Um, well, there was.'

'No, not a lover. Another person in this relationship. Part of you.'

'Oh.' Shit, I thought. How could she possibly know about that? My tummy's not *that* big yet.

She looked at my stomach. 'A child, yes?'

Now she had my full attention. 'Yes.'

'He is happy about this now. But he will come to be unhappy.'

'Probably 'cos it's not his kid,' I blurted. Fuck, dead giveaway. God, she was good.

She turned over the next card. It was a man with curly hair blowing a horn.

'Judgement,' she announced. 'You are sometimes quick to judge people. Some want to like you, even love you, but you won't let them. It's impossible for you. This could be a chance for an awakening. Allow people in. Open yourself up more.'

'Yeah, right,' I said. If opening myself up to the PICSOs meant getting my tits out or licking squirty cream off some hairy 23-stone welder called Keith then I'll remain stiff and uptight, thanks.

She stared at me again before turning over card three.

'Ahh... The Devil,' she announced.

'Fuck!'

'Now don't be frightened of this one. This might look scary but actually the Devil card can promote positivity. This card tells me you are somehow in bondage but you are not as rrrrrestrained as you believe.'

'Okaaaaay.' The black cat jumped up onto the table and Gwen shooed it away.

'You are the mistress of your own freedom. You don't have to be kept down as you are being kept down rrrright now.'

'So this could relate to the job? Or the relationship?'

'It coooould, yeeeees,' she said. 'If you despise your working environment, or your partner, this card is telling you that you do not have to stay for financial security. There is another way.'

'Mum and Dad's house,' I said, speaking *again* before my brain silenced me.

She frowned, looking down at the three cards together. 'There is something going on here, I can't see what it is, but something is toxic. Something troubling in this card. It's an unhealthiness. Some vice that is not doing you the good you think it's doing. Sugar? Drugs? Drink?'

'I used to like MAOAMs, before I got sperminated.'

'Whatever it is, you are bound to it,' she said. 'Addicted. I'm not judging you on this, my dear, this is just what ze card is telling me, but something you are doing is definitely not going to lead to ze happiness you think it will. It is torturing you, and it will torture others too. Do you know what else it could be?'

'Erm… nope.' I shrugged, jutting out my bottom lip to make even more of an *Honest, Gwen, I'm as pure as the driven snow* face. She turned over Card Four. It was a picture of a stern-faced angel with a huge sword in one hand and a severed head dangling in the other. 'Aha, ze Ace of Swords.'

'Nasty.'

'Again, not necessarily,' she replied, 'but all ze cards you've selected so far do seem to indicate new beginnings. Big changes on ze horizon. You are ready for new ventures, new jobs, new loves. Your truths will come out soon.'

'Will they?'

'Most certainly. I think you want to be free of something. There is a burden and the Ace of Swords is telling you zat you will soon not have that burden any more.'

I'd have put good money on the final card being the Death card. Any money at all in fact.

But when she turned it over, it was not the skeletal Grim Reaper I'd been expecting. It was a picture of an old wizard dude.

'Is that Dumbledore?' I asked her.

'No, it's Ze Hermit card,' she said, a little note of surprise in her voice.

'Oh. What does he mean?'

'Well actually, ze Hermit card doesn't come up often for me so it's unusual. It says you may benefit from time on your own.'

'So it's telling me to live like a hermit?'

'I think it means zat you don't work well with others. You need to have… no one.' Her eyes drifted across the table to the crystal ball and she rubbed it lightly with her right hand, then pulled her hand away as though the ball had become hot.

She became slightly breathless and reached for the stack of cards and began tidying them all away.

'My apologies. I get a little breath short. It is… ze cat hair.' She pulled a blue inhaler from her cardigan pocket and took two puffs on it.

'Sorry, go back to what you were saying about the Hermit card. I won't be on my own. Will I? I'll have the baby.'

'No,' she said, then remained tight-lipped.

'No what? No, I *won't* be on my own? Or no I won't have the baby?'

'It's not for me to say.'

'Well, it *is* for you to say because I've paid you to say it. You said I'll be on my own. And then you saw something in that ball. Was it the Grain of… the baby?'

She took another hit of her inhaler.

'Does my baby die?'

'I did see the baby. But I do not know…'

'What was wrong with it? What did you see?'

'I'm afraid we are out of time,' she said, putting her cards back in their paisley-patterned wooden box and moving them aside.

'No, what are you saying? Is my baby safe? What happens to it? You said I was going to be on my own. Please, I need to know.'

'I'm sure all will be fine.' The black cat appeared and started meowing at her feet and curling round her legs. She had got up from her seat shooed it away, guiding me back through the hanging shawls and tassels and out onto the pavement.

'I'll pay more,' I said. 'Give me another reading. Show me what's in the ball.'

'I can't. The cards and the ball have given you the information you need, my dear,' she said. 'Now I have an appointment I must get to. Good day.'

The sign outside said she was open till 9 p.m. in summer but she virtually pushed me out of the shop over an hour early and closed the door, flipping over the CLOSED sign and turning the key.

Fucking. Lying. Bitch.

*

It's just gone 8.45 p.m. I've stepped outside. All I can hear are the shagging moans of promiscuous Toppan's residents and the thumping music coming from the Club Hub. I'm in a bad mood, thanks to Madame Gwen.

I've been grinded, squeezed, stroked, manhandled and rubbed by everything from men dressed as Ghostbusters to Severus Snape to some barman called Richard whose front teeth had been knocked out in a rugby tournament. He asked me outright for full sex, in my chalet, 'with my mates watching'. I just asked him for ice.

Alfie – a cute, twenty-something student from Manchester – polite, tractable and thick as pig shit, had taken it upon himself to shag as many women as possible in one night. Apparently, I'm going to be Lucky Number 13. Lucky old me. I made a quick exit while he was buying me a vodka and lime that I had no intention of drinking.

I keep looking down at the tiny mound where Grain of Rice is growing. I don't want it to die. I don't know if I'll be a good mum but I know I don't want it to die. I don't know what to do. My phone's ringing...

*

I've just got off the phone with Craig. He had some pretty major news for me.

I was outside the Club Hub, music pulsing.

'It's about time, where the hell have you been? I've been checking my phone all the time.'

'Yeah.'

'Where are you? Have they let you out?'

'No. I'm still in prison. Rhiannon, listen – I wanted you to hear this from me, not them. Something's happened.'

Midges kept flying into my mouth. 'What?'

'Dutch police took my DNA when they arrested me and it's shown up on some database in England. And, I don't know how or why or anything but... my brief says English police are on their way over to interview me. About the murders.'

'What? That's ridiculous. You only threw a bottle, for God's sake.'

'No. It's nothing to do with the bottle. I don't understand it myself. They think I've done all this stuff and I haven't, I swear...'

Oh, shit.

'What stuff?'

'Those people in the paper. The bloke in the canal with no dick. The bloke in the park and that woman in the quarry...

they think I'm The Reaper. Fuck knows how but they've got evidence, Rhee. DNA. They've got my fucking DNA.'

'Is this a joke? Are you back at your hotel and doing a prank with Nigel or something?'

'I'm not joking, Rhiannon.' His voice had dropped to a whisper. He was crying. 'I'm not fucking joking.'

'I don't understand what you're saying.'

He sniffed and took a deep, raggedy breath. 'My DNA has shown up at two murder scenes. The guy who went in the canal...' He started rambling and I could barely understand him. 'I don't even— Rhee, I did not do this. I don't know how my stuff got there, I don't know how that bloke's cock ended up in my van...'

'Craig, I missed that, please tell me you've eaten coq au vin?'

He had to go and get his damn DNA taken, didn't he? He had to end up on that sodding police database. He had to go and RUIN EVERYTHING. I had to roll with it now. Roll all the way back to Plan A – making him pay.

'They found that canal bloke's penis in my van. In a bag. In my fucking toolbox. The one I don't even use any more since I inherited your dad's. I'm being framed. You do believe me, don't you? I. Did. Not. Do. This. I couldn't.'

'That's disgusting,' I said, trying to catch my breath. 'Why would someone sever a... penis? What DNA are you talking about? Hairs? Skin?'

'Semen.'

'Semen?' I said. 'That woman in the quarry... was raped.'

'I've never met the woman! I never touched her. Rhiannon, don't do this to me, baby, you're all I've got. You have to believe me, please please please...'

He sounded like a child. I'd never heard him cry so much.

'OK,' I said. 'OK. Say someone *is* fitting you up for all this. Say someone did put that thing in your van and... who? *Why?*'

I could hear him breathing. 'This is gonna sound proper bad okay but it's… a few months ago, I downloaded this app. I used it to chat. To people.'

'Women?'

'Yeah. All over the age of consent, I swear. I checked. And I know it's gonna make me look like a perv but loads of lads do it. Nigel does it. So does Steve. We just get… pictures and stuff. It's just a bit of fun. But somehow it's been hacked into and they've got chat logs of conversations I'm supposed to have had with all these blokes. Arranging hook-ups at hotels… exchanging photos…'

'Oh, Jesus.'

'Photos I sent to women but it's been made to look like I've got this secret gay life where I'd go out and… kill blokes and… wank over their corpses. I swear to you. I swear on my parents' lives. On our baby's life, I'm not, Rhee, I'm not gay. And I absolutely swear, I did not… '

'All right, all right, calm down. So you've been meeting these guys and one of them set you up?'

'No, I didn't meet anyone! I never met anyone from online. And I'm not gay. I only ever chatted to women. But someone's made it look like I have. Someone who had access to my… stuff.'

'I hope you're not accusing me of anything here.'

'No, of course not.' Silence. And then he just admitted it. 'Lana.'

'Lana Rowntree? From my office?'

'I was seeing her, for a while after Christmas. I dumped her as soon as I found out about the baby, honest. I wanted to tell you but I was afraid. She got nasty when I cooled things off. She started threatening to kill herself or worse. Hurting you.'

'I see.'

'The other week, when I said I had to go and see to that woman's leaky tap, it was Lana, threatening to slash her wrists.

She's done it before – she's got these scars. She's fucking flipped, man, she's crazy.'

'Yeah, women tend to do that if someone chews their heart up and shits it out.'

'She didn't love me. It was a fling, that was all.'

'Did you cum inside her?'

The line went silent.

'Did you cum inside her?' I repeated.

'Yes,' he said.

'How many times?'

'A few.'

'So you're telling me that a vulnerable woman who you were having an affair with cut off some random bloke's penis and hid it in your van, then scraped *your* semen out of *her* vagina, stored it, killed a woman and *another* man and left *your* semen at the crime scenes? Just to stop you from dumping her?'

'I know it sounds far-fetched but…'

'Just a tad.'

'It's the only way this could have happened. She hates me. *Really* hates me. I think she killed those people and she's framing me. Baby, I know I've hurt you but I swear I didn't kill anyone. You have to talk to her, Rhee. Get her to tell the police what she's done. Clear my name. I can't imagine how far this is gonna go but I don't wanna be in here. I can't do time. I need your help.'

'I know Lana, Craig. She wouldn't do this. It's your DNA at those crime scenes, not hers. Isn't it?'

'NO! Rhiannon, no! Don't be thinking that.' His voice had gone all squeaky. 'I'm not a murderer. I know I've been an asshole and a shit boyfriend but I ain't no murderer, darling.'

'Are they going to charge you?'

'I dunno. I called my dad. He said if they do, he's gonna get me a really good lawyer, one at that firm in town where he got his compensation for his back. I've thought it through – I'll sell the flat to pay for any costs and we'll move in with Mum and Dad till it's sorted. Dad said it'll be fine. They're planning to bring me back next week for a hearing. He hasn't told Mum yet. She won't be able to handle this, no way.'

That was the moment what was left of my world came crashing down around my feet. 'Hang on, what do you mean sell the flat? What about moving to Wales? What about Honey Cottage?'

'Oh, babe, that's a fucking pipe dream after this. This changes everything. I'm gonna need to sell the flat to pay for fucking lawyers at this rate.'

'No. You can't. We have to go. We were almost there, Craig. You were thinking about it. We were going to talk about it when you got back.'

'That was before all this, wasn't it? Babe, get a sense of perspective, that's not important now.'

And, just like that, my dream sailed down the river into the sunset, like it was always supposed to.

He could have got away with this. I'd warmed to him over the last few weeks. I thought things were going to change now. I'd had the epiphany about Wesley Parsons, then we found out about the Grain of Rice and we talked about making an offer on Honey Cottage and I thought we'd turned a corner to a bright new future.

Now we'd turned back again. And a terrible realisation came over me like a cold sweat.

'They're going to search the flat, aren't they?' I said.

'Yeah. But...'

'*When* will they search it?'

'Don't worry about the pot now. That's doesn't matter.'

I wasn't worried about the pot. I was worried about AJ.

'I have to go.'

'No, Rhiannon, don't hang up. Rhiannon, please, *please*!'

I could still hear him screaming pleases as I clicked End Call and turned it off.

It only dawned on me at that moment – maybe I *had* loved Craig. Why else would I have gone to such lengths to hurt him? To ruin him? You don't do that if you're just putting up with someone, do you? Maybe that's what love is. The thing that drives a killer to kill. To kill extraordinarily.

I heard that goddamn fortune-teller in my head again.

You don't work well with others. You'll be on your own. You will have no one.

I walked towards our chalet to grab my coat. There was a nip in the air.

Back on the seafront, it was windy and a few people were dotted about swigging beer bottles and smoking. The wind blew grit into my mouth and salt in my eyes. A child's bib had been dropped on the sea wall.

Madame Gwen was just folding up her board outside her shop and dragging it indoors. I watched her for a little while from the shadows of the multicoloured beach huts. The child's bib flapped in the wind and flipped over. There was a little brown dog on it, saying, 'Woof!'

I crossed the road.

'Hello, again,' I said. 'Can I come in for a minute? It won't take long, I promise.'

'No, no, you go. Leave…'

*

The beauty of a glass murder weapon is that if you throw it into the sea, it won't be found. They'll know what did it, of course they will – the claw-footed stand will be there with no crystal ball – but they won't know where it went and they won't know who bashed her skull in with it. Because who would suspect a smiley, happy young pregnant woman in a loose red summer vest and white pedal pushers, strolling along the pier on a summer's evening, on the way to meet her friends?

A woman wouldn't be capable of such savage acts of brutality. A woman wouldn't cut off a man's cock and hide it in the back of her boyfriend's van. I had meant to remove it when we learned about the baby.

I forgot.

A day ago, everything looked rosy. A day ago, I finally knew what I wanted. A day ago, it was just me, Craig, Tink and the Grain of Rice and I could see my life mapped out in front of me as though none of the rest of it – Priory Gardens, Canal Man, Park Man, Julia and the others – had happened. Yes, I had wanted to fit him up for those deaths in the early days but only cos I was angry. When the mists of anger had cleared a little and we knew the Grain of Rice was coming, I could feel things changing for us. He wanted me. He wanted *us*. I wanted to be better. I could envisage the life we would have – me and him and Tink and the Grain of Rice – at Honey Cottage. I could almost see the chickens clucking about in their pen. Almost smell my proud yellow roses in the flower beds. I was Happy. And Happy was my undoing. I told you. Happy's not meant for me.

I saw a baby... covered in blood.

Did she mean the blood I'd already spilled or the blood I *would* spill? She wouldn't say which baby. She wouldn't say if it had been one of the children at Priory Gardens or Anni's baby Sam or *my* baby, The Grain of Rice. She just would not say. So I'd stoved in her skull. I stoved in her skull as she lay cowering.

It can't be that. It *won't* be that; I *know* it's not that. Even on my reddest, angriest days I know I'm not capable of killing a baby. I'm a good 'mother' to Tink. I've never hurt her and she's my baby.

Except Tink's a dog. And the baby is a human. And I've killed more than my fair share of them.

'There you are,' said a voice. I was in the swimming pool, fully clothed, washing the last of Madame Gwen's blood from my hands.

'Just fancied a swim,' I said, shivering all over. 'You coming in?'

'You what?' He laughed, swigging from his can. 'You're a right nutter, you are.'

'So they all say.'

He smirked, pulling off his top and bombing into the water like a child.

And soon we were kissing and he had lifted me against him.

And then we were back in the chalet, soaking wet and he was penetrating me deeply on my squeaky mattress. I had missed out on my thirteenth spot – I was now number nineteen – funnily enough the exact age I was when I made my first kill.

It was fun. It was fast. I'm probably diseased now. But wasn't I always?

We dressed, then dried our hair and led each other back into the Club Hub to grind against each other to some ear-blistering Euro-techno/Arctic-Monkeys mash-up while the constellation of twinkling lights blinded us. I laughed as he kissed me. And we both sang along. And the rest of the PICSOs danced over to us and pushed him out of the way. Pidge handed me my handbag that she'd kept with her since I went to answer the phone.

'There you are, we've been worried about you. Everything OK?'

I nodded and gave her a hug. 'Yeah, I'm fine. Felt a bit off but my head's clear now.'

'Why are you all wet?'

'Me and Alfie went for a swim.'

Cue raucous cheering and tit-grabbing. Lucille rubbed my

tummy and kissed my cheek. Imelda gave me a sweaty PVC hug and wrapped her almost-featherless boa around my neck and told me she loved me. And we all linked arms for an impromptu cancan. And the lights bounced off our glittered cleavages and shining faces.

The lights all went red to white to red to white. Flashing and blinding. And the air grew hotter till my skin sweated. And my friends were all dancing beside me, hot and glittery and happy. We all looked good on the dance floor. And the music grew louder until my ears rang. As long as we were dancing, no one would see the blood under my nails. As long as the music played, we would be fine.

I dreaded to think what would happen when it stopped.

Sunday, 23 June

I'm back at the flat, finally. There'd been no cabs available last night thanks to a big football match and a gala event on at the winter gardens in town so I had to pay for an extortionate early morning one, nearly twice the fare. Hang the expense. I had to get back. I called Jim before I left. He'd said they could hang onto Tink for a bit longer if I wanted, but I said I needed her home with me. I'd missed her so much.

Little did I know, something of a personality transplant had occurred in the tiny Judas while she'd been away.

She spent about five seconds in my arms, licking my face all over until she got a whiff of something beyond the bedroom door and then it was all she was focused on. She became skittish and barky. Scratching at the floor outside, sniffing underneath it. Shaking with anticipation.

'Aww, bless. She thinks Craig's in there,' I said to Jim.

'I haven't told Elaine yet, about all this,' he said, sitting down at the dining table. I tried to get Tink to leave her post outside the bedroom but she wouldn't come to me. Snapped at me and refused her little bones and everything. 'This'll kill her, it will. What can we do, Rhiannon?'

'It'll sort itself out, it has to,' I said, sitting down opposite him and covering his hands with mine. 'They haven't charged him yet, have they? And Craig wouldn't do this. He just wouldn't.'

'Haven't slept a wink since he phoned. I mean, who would do this to him? Who's this Lana he mentioned?'

'A woman he's been having an affair with. From my office. She's a little... nuts, to say the least. Everyone at work says so. She's tried to take her own life before.'

He sighed, long and deep. 'Stupid sod. This is going to be all over the papers this week and there's nothing we can do about it. What's all this going to do to Elaine, eh? Doctor's already upped her medication twice this year.'

'Maybe this'll all blow over before we have to tell her?'

'I don't know about that,' he said with a grave stroke of his stubbly chin.

Tink was bum-shuffling outside my bedroom door and yapping like crazy. 'Tink? Are you all right, baby? Have you missed your Mum?'

'I don't know how to keep his mum safe from this,' Jim went on. 'How do I tell her he's been arrested, let alone arrested for murder?' I thought he was about to split wide open at the seams, but somehow he stitched himself back together. 'How are you doing anyway?'

'Fine,' I said, then back-pedalling. 'I mean I haven't slept a wink either but, well, it's all rubbish... isn't it? There's obviously been some massive mistake.'

'Damn right. Oh, excuse my language.' He handed me the business card of the solicitor Craig wanted to represent him. 'I've got a meeting at ten o'clock with her, see where we stand if he *is* charged, God help us. You'll stand by him, won't you? I know he strayed, Love, but... he really needs you now. He needs all of us.'

'Don't worry. I'm not going anywhere,' I said, clutching his forearm for reassurance and posting the solicitor's card in my jeans pocket. 'Listen, I would offer you a coffee but I've only just got back and I've got no milk in or anything...'

'Oh, don't worry, love. I just came to drop the little one off.' He looked sadly across at Tink. 'Seems like she's settled back in. Excited to be back with your mummy, aren't you, petal?'

Tink yapped at Jim and scampered over to start climbing up his leg.

'Oh, you want Granddad, do you?' He picked her up and she licked his cheek and pressed on his moobs like she had something urgent to tell him. 'I'm gonna miss this one. She's been a good distraction.'

I watched Tink, pressing on Jim's mood with her front paws. She was telling him. The little rat was selling me out. The moment I got up, she leapt down from his lap and scurried across the room, barking frantically and sniffing under the door frame. She knew, all right. She knew what was in there and she wasn't going to leave it alone. I put my hand down to her but she barked at me. She was dog-shouting at me: *I. KNOW. WHAT. YOU. DID. I. KNOW. WHAT'S. IN. THERE.*

Jim cleared his throat, like he was forcing something down. 'Listen love, if you want to, you could come back with us for a few days. I know Elaine is going to need the support when I tell her. You and Tink being there, it might, I don't know...'

'I've got work. I can't.'

'They'll give you some compassionate leave, surely to goodness.'

I shrugged. 'I doubt it.' Tink furiously scratched and scraped at the floor outside the bedroom like she was digging a tunnel from a gas chamber. She was not going to leave it alone. With a clench in my chest, I knew what I had to do.

'Jim, why don't you hang on to Tink for a while? Sounds like Elaine might need her more than me.'

'Eh? I can't do that, love. She's your dog.'

'Yeah, but she's very unsettled with Craig not being here. And she'll be on her own more now with Craig... I know how much Elaine dotes on her.'

Jim nodded. 'She cried when I said I was taking her back this morning. So did I in the car, just between you and me. Just temporary, like?' he said, the colour returning to his face. 'That would be wonderful.'

'Yeah. Just temporary. It would help both of us out, wouldn't it? I'll be over to see you guys soon. Let me get you some more food and her toys.'

'Alright, well that offer still stands, love. You need a break from this place, you come to us. Bed's all made up, you know that. Anytime you like. You don't even have to phone.'

'Thanks, Jim.'

As Jim dragged Tink away from the bedroom and put on her lead, she was still barking at me and sniffing the air in front of the door. My best friend – the one who'd been with me all this time, by my side, watching my back, there for me when no one else was, had finally had enough of my murderous shit. Shivering and growling, her little needle teeth all bared and gleaming. I didn't recognise her any more. I didn't want her around.

When they'd gone, I threw open the patio doors, allowing the already pulsing heat of the day to stream into the flat, along with the smells of the balcony. The basil had run rampant, as had the oregano. I ran the lemon thyme through my fingers, covering my skin with the delicious scent.

I went into the bedroom and peeled back the duvet.

'That was close,' I said, crawling across the bed towards AJ and kissing his cheek and cuddling into his neck. 'Aren't you going to ask me why I'm back early? Had a massive argument with the PICSOs. Got a cab back. I called Imelda a controlling witch and she smacked my face. I told Lucille she was spineless and she ran out crying. I told that Gemma/Jenna person she was a simpering idiot. Can't remember what I said to the others. One of them threw her Lambrini over me, I remember that.' I kissed him on his lips. 'We've got some uninvited guests coming. They'll want to talk to me. They'll take you away. I don't want them to. Everyone leaves me. I want you to stay.'

I kissed his lips, then pulled away to sit astride him, looking down on his closed eyelids and long eyelashes; his perfect naked form as my warm thighs straddled his freezing torso. And for the first time ever, I said it and I truly meant it.

'I love you.' I peeled off my shirt and lay down against him completely – our baby between us; my warmth becoming colder by the second. 'I wish I could stay here forever.' I closed my eyes. 'Maybe I will. This could be how it all ends.'

What the fuck are you doing?

'What?' I looked around. The atmosphere in the room had changed, as though Tink had walked in. But no one was there. I heard the voice again.

I said, What the fuck are you doing? The police are going to be here any second.

I looked at AJ's lifeless face on the pillow. It wasn't him.

No, I said it. You came back early to get rid of the body. So get rid of it.

I looked along the side of the bed. I looked towards the door. Then I looked down at my own stomach.

Yeah, me, down here. I'm all you've got left now. You better start listening to me if you want to get out of this.

'No. This is NOT you, Grain of Rice. This is NOT you.'

Of course it's me. Do you actually want the police to come here and find you like this? Do you want to go to prison?

'I don't care any more.'

Well, I care and you have to care to because I'm not being born in jail. You need to get him out of here. Pronto.

'How? It's broad daylight, for one, and, for two, I can't lift him. How do you suggest I get him down the stairs, across the car park, into my boot…?'

You know what to do.

'Do I?'

Yes. Cut him up.

'What?'

Get a power saw and cut him up. You can do it in the bath tub. Then wrap the pieces up, put them in suitcases and throw them in the sea…

'I can't do that!'

Or bury them in the woods behind Grandad's house, even better. You can buy a shovel when you buy the saw.

'It's in my head. It's all in my stupid, broken head. Stop talking to me.'

It's not in your head. Wake the fuck up and smell the decomposition. I'm telling you, you have to cut him up then he'll be easier to move. It's your only way out.

'I am not cutting him up. That's disgusting.'

Says the woman lying naked on top of a corpse.

'You're just a blob. What do you know?'

And through the silence of the freezing apartment came the loudest of knocking sounds on the front door.

I know you're in deep shit now, Mummy.

HQ
One Place. Many Stories

The home of bold, innovative
and empowering publishing.

Follow us online

 @HQStories

 @HQStories

 HQStories

 HQ Stories

 HQMusic